Follow me follow you

Follow me follow you

Laura E. James

Published 2014 by Choc Lit Limited
Penrose House, Crawley Drive, Camberley, Surrey GU15 2AB, UK
www.choc-lit.com

A CIP catalogue record for this book is available
from the British Library

ISBN 978-1-78189-187-2

Printed and bound by CPI Group (UK) Ltd, Croydon, CR0 4YY

To Alexander, Eleanor and Garry.
This book is most definitely for you.
No matter how many characters reside in my head,
you inhabit my heart.
Follow your dreams.
Always.
Love you.
xxx

Acknowledgements

To the wonderful band of sisters, The Romaniacs, who walked every step of this journey with me – thank you. www.theromaniacs.co.uk

To Sue G, Debbie and Hayley, who listened so patiently to my incessant chatter about this book and gave such solid feedback – thank you. Have I told you about the next novel, ladies?

With much thanks to my lovely friends, the experts: Alison Daniell, Alison Griffiths, Effie Merryl and Katherine Price for generously sharing their specialist knowledge and experience. Any errors are mine.

To the members of the Romantic Novelists' Association, and Off The Cuff – thank you for the friendships, guidance and opportunities you provide. It makes a world of difference.

Readers, reviewers and bloggers – thank you for buying the books, thank you for the outstanding work you do in spreading the word about books, and thank you for sharing your endless enthusiasm for books. You are priceless.

And love and thanks to my family and friends, in real life and online, for encouraging me, supporting me and keeping me strong during difficult times.

Bro – thanks for always being a protector. And to Mum, who shared her joy of books with me. Miss you.

To the team at Choc Lit and the lovely Tasting panel members – Rebecca, Jaimee, Melanie, Lynda, Mary, Betty, Sarah, Lisa and Vanessa. Thank you!

Chapter One

'I hate you.'

It wasn't the first time Victoria Noble recoiled at her son's hostility, but on each occasion she hoped, sometimes even prayed, it would be the last. Mondays triggered the worst attacks.

She looked at Seth across the breakfast bar, his arms folded and his scrawny legs swinging, left right, left right. His face and colouring was totally his father's, but his wild mop of irrepressible curls was hers. She sucked in his words. 'Well, I love you. And you're stuck with me.'

Was that the right thing to say to a four-year-old? Apart from a few well-intentioned, but unsolicited pointers from her sister, what Victoria knew of childcare came from the Internet. In hindsight, she realised she should have sought a more personal approach for raising a challenging boy, but requesting assistance wasn't a strength of hers. She was the Director of EweSpeak, Britain's most successful social networking site, and as such, was expected to have all the answers. It had been the same at school; her old science teacher was shocked when Victoria failed to demonstrate what happened when molecules weren't attracted to one another.

The image played out in her mind and she tilted her head. This was her and Seth. With the ease of oil repelling water, he resisted her attempts to steer him. Did it all come down to chemistry?

If he was one of her EweSpeak operatives, she'd have sacked him by now – or he'd have sacked her – but Victoria was intelligent enough to understand working with a child was nothing like working with employees. Not even young employees. They did as they were asked and weren't prone to throwing a paddy by the water cooler. She had taken time to choose her colleagues. They'd completed application forms, taken part in isometric tests and attended three interviews.

Seth arrived under less stringent controls.

Was it too late to ask for help?

The nanny was a godsend with day-to-day issues, but offered no insight into how she managed Seth, and today she'd called in sick with flu – news neither Victoria nor Seth were happy to receive, and the catalyst for the bullets of resentment Victoria was currently dodging. Both mother and child relied on the nanny to get them through the day. This particular one, Cerys, was the first to survive longer than three months, the first to find a way to relate with Seth, and, by some miracle, the first to whom Seth had become attached. All reasons why Victoria had said no to a temporary replacement and yes to waiting until Cerys was better.

The upheaval of introducing another nanny to Seth was more than he or Victoria could bear. Seth and Cerys had formed a bond; a friendly, mutually respectful, genuine bond, and he would do anything for her.

And nothing for me.

The thought wrestled its way down to Victoria's stomach and slammed it into submission. She used the excuse of collecting Seth's trainers from under the counter to bend double, hoping to ease the cramping.

She was thankful her son had someone he could love, who loved him back, and she was grateful for the care Cerys took of him, but it hurt. It hurt Victoria that as his mother, she'd fallen short of his expectations. And it crippled her not knowing how to set things right.

The next couple of weeks were going to be tough.

As she breathed away the last of the spasms, she straightened up. What did her sister say in times of trouble? It will pass? She was fond of Juliette, but she knew nothing about demanding children. She had four angels. Not to mention she was a natural-born mother. Victoria raised a brow. Juliette was a natural-born everything; communicator, socialiser, wife. The fact the two women were related was a constant source of amazement to Victoria who, by her own admission, was the complete antithesis of her sister.

Victoria groaned. Give her computers any day. She understood those. There was a logic to them she never found in people, not even in her own child. Algorithms she could handle; especially rigorously defined algorithms, but the thought of dealing with people on a daily, face-to-face basis was enough to keep her locked away in a sterile white office hour after hour, with only Juliette for company. Victoria never engaged with her EweSpeak flock. She baulked at the notion. The irony of her situation had not escaped her.

She regarded her son, who was still sitting at the breakfast bar, his arms still secured across his chest, and his legs still kicking back and forth. 'Shoes on!' she demanded, hoping the change in tone would spur him into action.

Seth crossed his ankles and the swinging came to a gradual halt. 'No.'

The coolness with which he responded sent a chill through Victoria and she was at a complete loss as to how to exert her authority. She traipsed the length of the tiled floor to the balcony doors and gazed out into the grey London sky. If there was a God, which she had fair reason to disbelieve, why had he sent her a difficult child?

She raised her hand to the glass and spread her naked fingers across the reflection of her face. There were days, like today, when she wondered if she was being taught a lesson for putting her career above having children.

When Seth was born, her husband … her shoulders sagged … her *ex-husband*, agreed to be the primary carer. He'd vehemently objected at first on the basis changing nappies was a woman's job, and in case Victoria had forgotten – because they'd not had sex since the birth of the child – *he* was a man. Victoria pointed out she was the main breadwinner and with EweSpeak to run, it made sense for her to go back to work. At the time, she was happy to do so. Nurturing was not in her nature.

After two months of bitter complaints, declarations of emasculation, and continued assertions of 'This is women's work', Ben Noble walked away, leaving Victoria shocked, and Seth fatherless. His parting shot was a scribbled note that read: *It's your turn to deal with the crap.*

Studying her image, Victoria noticed her brow had furrowed into deep ridges, and she backed away from the door. It was insane analysing Ben's motives; his conduct was as she had come to expect from his gender. The male sex first let her down when she was eighteen and had continued to do so ever since. That was almost half her life. The one man to stand by her was her father. That wasn't to say he never got it wrong, but when he did, at least he displayed remorse and that made his flaws forgivable.

Perhaps that was all it was with Seth. A flaw. A glitch. If she accepted it was his way, they might get along. With a sense of defeat, she turned, faced her son and forced a weak smile. 'Okay,' she said. 'I get it. You don't want to come to the office.'

His round face remained expressionless and his dark eyes still. His feet unhooked, he reached for an apple from the crystal bowl before him, and he jumped off the tall stool. 'No,' he said, clenching the fruit in his fist. Before Victoria had time to react, he drew back his arm and propelled the firm, green missile at her. It smashed into her chest. She took a moment to regain her breath, experience telling her it would take infinitely longer to recover from her despair.

This was not the first time her son had launched an attack.

She stooped to retrieve Seth's ammunition and breathed away the response to cry.

As she dropped the makeshift projectile in the bin, she kept her son under surveillance. He made no attempt to apologise; neither did he flee. His unrepentant eyes narrowed, and his knuckles whitened with the exertion of clutching another apple.

'Put it in your rucksack,' Victoria said. 'And be warned, if you're not dressed in five minutes, you'll come to work in your pyjamas.'

She trudged into the hall, where she gathered several large files and dumped them into her briefcase. She hoped it wouldn't come to it, but if she had to drag Seth into work kicking and screaming, then she would. As to who would be protesting the most, she was uncertain.

As Victoria slipped her feet into her shoes, Seth charged past and gave a forceful shove to her hip, knocking her off balance as he ran up the stairs of their split-level apartment. Victoria crashed into the wall and the side of her skull whacked the corner of the chrome coat hooks she'd had mounted a week ago. She steadied herself, fingered her temple and tested for blood. Dry. She left her hand resting on her aching forehead and concentrated on absorbing the pain threatening to swamp her. Enough was enough. She wanted to scream. She wanted to yell at the top of her voice and rant and rave, but the culprit was four years old.

And he was her son. The fact he provoked such intense feelings within her was proof she loved him. Wasn't it? The question banged around her sore head. She wanted love to flow through her veins. She wanted it to flood her heart and be her life force, but it was hard with a child who communicated with words of hatred.

Victoria studied her ringless finger. Love was hard. Full stop. Especially with a trampled heart. Twice she'd laid it in the open and twice it had been ridden roughshod over. Both men had said they loved her. Both men had lied. At least Seth was honest. Not once had those three little words passed his lips.

He struggled with Mummy.

As the adrenalin ebbed, so did Victoria's energy and desire to fight. Four years she'd lived like this. In bedlam. It was a miracle she hadn't been sectioned.

She yearned for the sanctuary of her office where she knew what to expect. In her virtual world, she was the one who pushed all the buttons and every response was as she'd programmed.

She checked her watch, walked to the bottom step and rested there, with her back, tense and hunched, to her son. She had to get to work. 'Seth. Please get dressed.'

A second after Seth's footfall halted, the apple clunked and thumped its way down each stair, coming to settle by the front door.

Victoria closed her eyes to it. Next week, she'd buy grapes.

'That's a nasty bruise.' Juliette leaned closer to Victoria and inspected her forehead. 'What happened?'

'I walked straight into the new coat hooks. Stupid of me.' Victoria focused on the sofa, where Seth was playing with his Nintendo DS, earphones in, oblivious to the world.

Juliette stepped away. 'You weren't thinking of Chris Frampton, were you? He has a lot to answer for.' She wiggled the white mouse on her desk and the small sheep cursor sparked the monitor into life. 'Seventeen years and he still plagues you.'

Victoria snorted. 'I was thinking about Ben, actually.' She directed her attention to her sister.

'That low-life. I wouldn't waste another minute on him.' Juliette pulled out her leather chair and settled into it, smoothing down her navy suit. 'He hasn't concerned himself with you or Seth. I'm surprised you even talk about him, let alone show Seth photographs.'

'Don't you think a boy needs his father?' It had crossed Victoria's mind several times that having Ben in Seth's life might moderate his behaviour. Seth's. Not Ben's. Although Ben would benefit from a shot of responsibility. She mirrored her sister, and assumed her position at her desk.

'I'd rather raise a child alone than subject him to an uncaring parent,' Juliette said.

'That's easy for you to say. You found the one decent man and married him.' Victoria studied her amazing, bright and disciplined baby sister, whose ebony-black hair stayed where it should, whose clothes never creased and whose life overflowed with pleasure and wonderful moments of tenderness. Thank goodness she hadn't suffered the humiliation and trauma of divorce. The tortured sister was Victoria's role. 'I'm glad you and Dan have each other,' she said.

'We may have been young, but Dan knew when he was onto a good thing.' Juliette cocked an eyebrow. 'Anyway, he signed a scrap of paper that said we're stuck with each other until death us do part. Unlike Ben-No-Balls, Dan believes that means something.'

Victoria placed her hands on the desk and forced out

a breath. Juliette saw only black or white, and made no disguise of the fact she was disgusted with Ben.

'I know Seth was a shock to you,' Juliette continued, 'but Ben agreed to look after him.' She jumped up from her chair. 'And I'll tell you what angers me the most. He watched you go through a traumatic birth, demanded you breastfed even though the very thought made you sick, and said you should have tried harder to be a mother. Do you remember? Then the pathetic excuse for a man walked out on you.' Juliette puffed out her cheeks and released a gust of air. 'Don't ever wonder if Seth would be better off with him *in* his life. It's a godsend he never came back.'

Clearly satisfied her point had hit home, Juliette resumed her seat and turned to her computer screen. 'So. Is that why you were late today? The blow to the head?'

'Yes.' Reeling from the conversation and sudden change of topic, Victoria was in no condition to elaborate; it was neither the time nor the place. She allowed herself a moment to settle before switching to work mode. 'How are our star clients doing?'

As efficient as Victoria, Juliette tapped on the keyboard and, after a fleeting silence, gave a nod of appreciation.

'What is it?'

'Your obsession, Chris Frampton. His flock's grown substantially in the last twenty-four hours. There's speculation he's returned to the UK.' She keyed in further information, and nodded again. 'The board will be ecstatic.'

Victoria rose from her chair and crossed to the coffee machine. 'Money grabbers. I should never have agreed to one.'

Juliette sighed. 'Not this again. It was sound business practice.'

'EweSpeak's a private company.'

'So?'

'So it doesn't legally require a board.' Victoria poured

two fresh coffees, returned to the desks and planted a hot mug in Juliette's hand. 'We could've developed the company ourselves.'

'No, we couldn't. It was turning in to Frankenstein's monster.' Juliette set aside her drink and clasped Victoria's hands. 'We needed an objective input. We needed legal and financial experts to advise. We *needed* an independent board to resolve our disputes.'

Reluctantly, Victoria nodded. As close as she and Juliette were, their opinions were invariably at opposite ends of the spectrum, and the board had brought an end to EweSpeak family feuding.

'Do you know why I finally agreed?' Victoria reclaimed her hands and reversed the hold. 'Because you told me I was like Mum.'

Juliette laughed. 'Well, you are. You're as stubborn as she was. And you believe your way is the only way. Which, by the way, it's not.'

Victoria grumbled as she released Juliette from her grasp. 'I don't force my religious views on others.'

'Granted, Mum was a bit zealous, but she was doing what she thought best. The same as you. And really, if going to church and reading the Bible was the worst thing that happened to us, I'd say we've nothing to complain about, especially when you think of people whose worlds have shattered.' Juliette pointed at her monitor. 'Here's a case in point. Your obsession.'

An image of Chris Frampton planted itself in the fertile garden of Victoria's mind. It was impossible to uproot. 'I am not obsessed with Chris bloody Frampton.' *Preoccupied maybe.* She dreamed of him often. Intimate, sad, confusing dreams. 'I'm not even sure which country he's in.'

She was, though, well aware of the buzz created by the recent sale of his Los Angeles ranch, and of the whisper he was looking to come home. The news was everywhere, and the worst of it was the voracious media wolves were digging up harrowing images from two years back, when Chris was grieving for his wife and son. Thank goodness they were keeping the other twin out of the spotlight. Victoria had no desire to revisit the scenes.

'Anyway, I'm interested in the future, not the past.' She looked in her son's direction. 'Seth? Milk?' No reaction. She raised her voice. 'Seth? Would you like a glass of milk?'

'No.'

It became apparent Victoria's despondency was more obvious than she'd intended, as Juliette scraped back her chair, kicked off her shoes and padded her way over to Seth. She removed his earphones.

'Please and thank you can get you a long way, you know.' She sat down, curled her legs up and pulled Seth to her.

Victoria noted the lack of resistance on her son's part. It wasn't jealousy that passed through her. As with Cerys, she was thankful that Seth had means of finding comfort. No. She knew what it was; she'd experienced it before. It was rejection.

'What's making you grumpy, young man?' Juliette's gilded voice glided into Victoria's thoughts. 'Is there something else you'd rather be doing?'

Seth snuggled into Juliette and sneered at Victoria. 'No,' he said. 'I like this.'

Was it possible for a four-year-old to understand manipulation? Seth used it with such devastating effect, it was difficult to think he didn't. He was the one person Victoria should make sense of, but although they shared blood, their circuitry was very different.

'I like it too, but both your mum and I have work to do. Shall I see what Uncle Dan is up to? I expect he'd like some help.'

Seth nodded. 'I like Uncle Dan. He doesn't shout.'

Once more, Seth glared at Victoria. She understood his implication.

Juliette moved away from him. 'Who dares yell at my nephew? I'll tell them off.' She stood and pushed her sleeves up. 'It's not those naughty nannies, is it?'

Seth copied his aunt and raised himself off the sofa. Pointing a skinny finger at Victoria, he said, 'She does.'

Both the allegation and her bruise stung. With her eyes fixed on Seth, Victoria watched him wind his way behind Juliette and peer from her side. In a small, but steady voice, he said, 'She shouts at me and I hate her.'

Juliette coaxed him to stand before her. She knelt to his level and took his hands. 'Now, young man, listen to me. Hate is a very strong feeling and saying that about your mummy is very unkind. It makes us both sad when you speak like that.' She glanced over her shoulder at Victoria before returning to Seth. 'All mummies shout from time to time. We can get just as grumpy as you, but we never stop loving you. I think you should say sorry and give your mum a big hug.' She released him and stood tall. 'Go on.'

As Victoria expected, Seth remained silent and still. She held out her hands, but Seth was too young to see it for what it was – a mother reaching out for her son. As he backed away from the gesture, Victoria wilted. 'Leave it, Joo. Call Dan and see if he can have him for the day.'

Victoria retreated behind her desk and tapped her monitor. The virtual world was beckoning; the world that didn't throw apples, and where hurtful words were deleted. If life had an undo button, she'd hit it right now. Start again. Never fall in love, never fall for a man's lies, and never fall pregnant. She flinched. She didn't mean that. She wanted Seth in her life, but she didn't know how to make it – them – work. 'There must be a way,' she said, quietly. Maybe the

Internet had more up-to-date information than when she last looked.

As she viewed the screen, Chris Frampton's face loomed large, his dark, floppy fringe sheltering the top of his doleful, brown eyes. Next to him was his stunning American wife, Lacey. It was a clever move including her in his publicity shots; he was such a private man, any glimpse into his personal life created a whirlwind of interest.

Nowadays, it was his manager, Tommy Stone, who was forever by his side.

Victoria rested her elbow on her desk and her cheek on her fist. The picture of Chris was taken shortly before the death of his wife and son. Following that, he became a recluse. He stopped filming, removed himself from the public eye, and was rumoured to be separated from his surviving son. If that was true, it was tragic.

But what a life Chris had led. A Portland boy born and bred making it big as a Hollywood action hero.

It suited Victoria that he'd hooked up with Lacey all those years ago. It allowed her to forget her past. Their past.

And it was forgotten until she developed EweSpeak and her youthful team of go-getters acquired Chris as one of their first clients. From that point, Victoria struggled to avoid hearing about him. A number of years ago, she received some sensitive information she'd been compelled to buy in order to bury it. The secrets she held had the potential to finish his career. Now, they would infect open wounds. Thank God she would never need to see him in the flesh again.

His bronzed, toned flesh.

She outlined his lips with her cursor. Chris had always been handsome. He was beautiful. And daring. He was the one man who'd shown Victoria what it was to let go and live.

And the first to betray her.

Chapter Two

Victoria was attempting to create the impression she was engrossed in her work. From the moment Dan collected Seth, she'd buried her head in buff-coloured files, raising it once to study her monitor. At that moment, she realised Juliette was watching her.

'I'm all right, Joo, honestly.' That was a lie. She was preoccupied with thoughts of Chris Frampton returning home, considering ways to stop EweSpeak's Board of Directors from travelling a destructive path, and despairing over her non-existent relationship with her son. She grimaced. 'Apart from the blinding headache.'

She thrust herself away from the desk and rubbed the back of her neck. Her life was too cluttered for her to make informed decisions, and too many demands were being made of her, emotionally and physically. Something had to give. 'I could do without this stupid business with the board.'

'Do you think they'll go ahead?'

Victoria huffed. 'Of course they will. They're motivated by money. They'll do whatever it takes to keep their bank accounts full and their fat backsides comfortable.'

'But they have a duty of loyalty, and their report states the move will secure the future of EweSpeak—'

'It only secures their position, Juliette. Let's face facts. We made bad choices, electing certain members to the board.

We were blinded by their past successes. They're cut-throat businessmen with reputations to uphold.' Victoria swung her chair round and gaped at her sister. 'I'll bet a year's salary there'll be redundancies.'

'But if charging clients to join will increase profits—'

Victoria cut her off again. 'Did you miss the bit where they proposed paying celebrities for exclusive bleats? It's ridiculous. It won't work. People will opt out. Our followers enjoy the personal contact, the chance to hold a discussion with like-minded souls, maybe even exchange a bleat with their idol. If it's sensationalism they want, they'll buy a glossy magazine, or worse, they'll flock to our competitors. They won't subscribe to our network.' She shook her head. 'It has disaster written all over it.'

'I don't see it. The board's acting in the company's best interest. We have to make money. And it's not just their pockets they're lining, is it?' Juliette waved a hand in the direction of the window. 'I don't hear you complaining about the flashy, two-seater sports car you've parked in our private garage.'

Victoria reached for the remote on her desk, and switched on the TV. 'I need a break.' She stood, gave her arms a stretch, and walked across to the sofa, collapsing into it, irascible and frustrated. Surely Juliette wasn't voting with the board? Victoria cast her eyes to the large screen, scoured through the programme guide, and settled on a news channel.

It was a mistake.

Wherever her eyes fell – the TV, online, mobile applications – Chris's then thirty-five-year-old haunted face appeared, vacant, pale and broken. There was no escape from the dated footage of him being jostled out of the way of bloodthirsty, aggressive photographers or being hustled into his ranch house by burly security men. Victoria had seen the images thirty, maybe forty times in the last couple of years. Every piece of technology in her office was broadcasting his grief all over again, and each time his name was typed, bleated, or beamed across the Internet, and for every second his tormented features were on public display, Victoria was on trial. Her technology, the company, the brand she had developed and grown was helping prolong his terror. To see this beautiful man reduced to a floorshow for the cheap seats made her sick to the stomach.

She jumped at a touch to her arm.

'Are you okay?' Juliette took the remote from Victoria, switched off the TV, and sat down. 'I'm sorry I called him your obsession. This must be hard for you.'

Victoria shrugged. Although she understood Juliette's concern, she didn't appreciate intrusion, and *sharing*, as her sister called it, was not Victoria's way. There'd been far too much of that already. A small shudder ran through her. 'It's complicated,' she said, hoping a few words, regardless of content, would appease Juliette.

'Well, his whereabouts has caused quite a stir. He's the number one name in everyone's bleats. He's all over EweSpeak.'

'He's trending?' It was what Victoria expected, but not what she wanted to hear. Pulling her knees up, she fastened them with her arms, laid her head on them, and closed her eyes.

'In all honesty, I'd be asking questions if it didn't trend,' Juliette said. 'It was a devastating story of epic proportions. Anything Chris does now will be measured against how he's survived his loss. EweSpeak is doing exactly what we've asked of it.'

Victoria's eyes burst open, and she threw up her head, as she felt raging heat radiate her cheeks. 'No. It's not. I didn't set out to wreck people's lives.'

The atmosphere in the third floor office was so thick and hot, even Victoria's slim frame struggled to draw a clean breath. She kicked out her legs, pushed herself up from the sofa, and opened a nearby window, taking the cold November air deep into her lungs. 'I can't do this to him. Not again. I'm not heartless.'

'I've been telling you that for years.' Juliette returned to her computer and tapped the keyboard. 'But you must remember, Chris willingly took centre stage. He was renowned for his ambition. We offered him a media platform, and he grabbed it with both hands.'

'That's not fair, Juliette.' Victoria reeled round as her sister resumed her seat. 'He was pursuing his dream.'

'Yes. He was. He was an unknown, jobbing English actor scraping a living together in America. Now look at him.' Juliette switched the monitor round. 'He's won two Taurus World Stunt Awards, goes drinking with Jason Statham, and has a star on the Hollywood Walk of Fame.' She picked up her mobile, wielding it in the air. 'The world first learned of Chris Frampton, actor, right here, on EweSpeak. Have you seen how many are in his flock?'

Victoria prepared to speak, but Juliette held up her hand, indicating quiet. Victoria obliged.

'And how did he gain support when he was lobbying the Academy to introduce a Best Stunt Oscar? By bleating to over three million fans, on *our* social network. *Three million.*'

'It's not all been one way. EweSpeak's benefited from his celebrity.'

'I agree. He's an excellent investment. Financially, I mean.'

Victoria snorted. 'But not emotionally? Thanks.' She turned, yanked the window shut, and then leaned her back against the cold glass. 'I'd just turned eighteen when he and

I got together. What did I know about relationships?' That excuse would hold no water with Juliette – she was eighteen when she met Dan. Nineteen when she had her first baby. Victoria changed tack before her sister objected. 'I'd not met anyone like him. He was exciting. Impulsive. Willing to try anything. So different from me. I was …' She thought for a moment, wanting to use the word with the most impact. 'I was *inspired* by him.'

'You loved him, Victoria. Say it.'

Victoria sealed her lips shut, shifted her weight from one foot to the other, and glowered at the floor.

'You're not incapable of it. Two minutes ago, you declared you have a heart.'

'This isn't helping, Joo.' Victoria rubbed her eyes, watering from staring so intently at the carpet. She blinked them into action, and looked across the room. Juliette's outward-turned monitor was in slumber mode, displaying a full-sized image of her four children, with Dan, splashing about in the sea. As Victoria's vision improved, she was drawn to two figures in the background paddling through the shallow waves. One was tall and portly, the other short and slim, with a mass of curly hair. Victoria approached the monitor. 'Who's this?' She pointed to the smaller figure.

Juliette joined her, looked and smiled. 'Seth. And that's Dad. We went to Weymouth for a few days last summer. Remember? You couldn't make it, so we took Seth. Bit of a squeeze in Dad's bungalow, but it was so warm, the boys camped in the garden.'

'Seth camped?' This was news to Victoria.

'Oh, yes. Didn't I say at the time? The girls and I stayed in the bungalow, but Seth slept in the tent with my Alex and Dan. Dad cooked tea for everyone on that single gas stove he used when we were children. Goodness knows how old that is.' Juliette swivelled the screen to its normal position and stepped behind her desk. 'It's such a shame you weren't there. Seth was very cute all wrapped up like a caterpillar. I'm surprised I haven't shown you the photographs.' She took her seat again and grasped the mouse. 'I'll find them now.'

Victoria responded with a distracted nod, revisited the window and studied the pedestrians below. The fact Juliette was reminiscing about Seth grated on her, but it was Victoria's fault. If she applied the same energy to motherhood as she did for work, she'd have earned that memory for herself.

She closed her eyes, endeavouring to corral her thoughts, shepherd the good memories to the fore, to prove she too had happy times. She wanted to promote those moments she'd shared with Ben – their first kiss, his marriage proposal, Christmas at Klosters. Not one of them came.

Rejecting the image of Chris barging its way to the front, she attempted to recall Seth's milestones. She scrunched her eyes tighter, putting the squeeze on her recollections, forcing them through the narrow tunnels of her mind, but she saw cavernous, black holes. She couldn't unearth her son's baby gurgles, first tooth, or his toddler steps, no matter how deep she explored. There was no trace. They did not exist.

With her composure threatening to split at the seams, she put her hands on the window, and leaned into them. As if choking on chalk, she swallowed down the sensations and they plummeted like lead bullets to the pit of her stomach.

Once she recovered her poise, she opened her eyes and squinted through the haze her breath had left on the glass. The world below was abstract with blurred shapes and blended colours, but as Victoria stepped back and the cloud shrunk, her view became clear and well defined. It was all about perspective.

'Juliette?' Her voice was soft and small. 'Juliette?'

Stronger now. She twisted to meet her sister. 'How do you rate me as a mother?'

There was a long silence before Juliette answered. 'I understand work is important for you. In many ways, it defines you, but I also know being a working mum is hard. We're not in a position to drop everything and run home to our children, however strong the desire. I suffer from ten types of guilt starting with leaving home before the children wake, to forgetting to ask what they ate for tea.' Another lengthy pause. 'Considering your situation, you do well.'

For Victoria, the reply was too calculated. 'I don't want diplomacy, Juliette. I want honesty. I'm not a good mother, am I?' She noted Juliette was spinning her wedding ring around her finger. It was a sure sign she was uncomfortable with the moment. That was all the reply Victoria required. She held up her hand. 'It's okay. You don't have to say anything.' It was a horrible realisation that others perceived her as a poor excuse for a mother. She clutched at her stomach.

'Victoria? You're very pale.'

With her insides reacting to the maelstrom in her head, Victoria felt faint and nauseous and presented no resistance as Juliette guided her back to the sofa. With a gentle push on her shoulders, she sat, assumed the hunched recovery position and waited for the dizziness to settle.

Two distinct and unpleasant insights emerged from the darkness: *Seth hated her* and *it was her fault.* Instead of living life to the max as she once had, she'd invested her time in developing EweSpeak, and in the process, lost her husband and gained a son full of resentment. At some point, she'd made the decision to escape into the virtual world.

As she searched her memories for answers, one stood out: the night she and Chris Frampton made love on Chesil Beach. Was that her conscience suggesting betrayal was responsible for how she lived her life? She'd have to review that later. Right now, she had her son to think about. 'I need to fix things with Seth, before it's too late.'

'What do you mean *fix things*?' Juliette's nose wrinkled. 'What things?'

'Everything. You heard him. He hates me.'

Juliette knelt at Victoria's feet. 'All children say stuff like that when they don't get their own way. You've had a difficult day, that's all.'

Victoria shook her head. 'No. Every day is difficult.' She blew hard air through her lips. 'I need to distance myself from the business, and concentrate on my son. I don't want to wake up one morning to find mine or Seth's world destroyed by my short-sightedness.'

'Victoria, you're a visionary.' Juliette jumped up, grabbed a sheet of paper from the desk, ripped it in four and scribbled money signs on each quarter. She let them fall like confetti onto the couch. 'You took this scrap of an idea and turned it into a multi-million dollar business. How is that short-sighted?'

'I'm not talking about EweSpeak. I'm talking about my son. I've been blind to his needs. Selfish.' Admitting it didn't appease Victoria's guilt. *So much for a problem shared …* 'This is important, Juliette. Put yourself in my shoes. What would you do?'

Juliette retreated to the coffee machine, paused, seemingly caught in thought, and then pressed the power button. 'I have it easy, don't I? Of course it's important. You must go. How long do you think you'll need?' Not waiting for the drips of water to finish splashing into the drink, she withdrew the mug. 'A week? A month?'

Victoria shrugged. It was pointless guessing. 'Tell me how long it will take for me to get to know my son and I'll give you a date.'

'You don't know?'

'Nope.'

'You always know.' Juliette sipped her coffee. 'You plan your life to the nth degree. You don't do spontaneity.'

Victoria raised her eyebrows. 'It's caught me on the hop too, but it feels right.' She shrugged again. This was all new to her. Winging it was Juliette's speciality. 'I'm the only parent Seth has. It's time I behaved as one. I was given this most precious gift, and I let it slip through my fingers. Gone.' She stared at the ragged strips of paper Juliette had written upon. 'I love the protection EweSpeak provides, it's my sanctuary, but I love Seth more, despite everything.'

'I'm not sure I understand.' Juliette's face was crumpled; folded in on itself.

Victoria collected the four paper examples of empire building, scrunched them into rough balls and aimed them at the metal bin beside her desk. 'No. Nor do I, but I can't go on like this.' She pointed to her bruised forehead and waited for Juliette's reaction.

'That wasn't an accident?' Calmer than Victoria expected. 'Not exactly.'

'Well, what?' A definite rise in Juliette's tone.

'Seth was angry, he pushed me, and I fell onto the hooks.'

Juliette approached the Chesterfield. 'Seth pushed you?' She perched on the back. 'He was angry, and he *pushed* you? But he's four. It must have been an accident.'

'The push was no accident. The whack to the head was a bonus.'

'How can you say that about your own child?'

'Because it's true. It's happened before. Kicks to the shin, thumps to my back. Missiles. And sometimes, it bloody hurts.'

'But he's only four.'

'I know. You've said that already.' Victoria was losing

patience. Juliette disbelieved her. This was the very reason she'd not mentioned it before. If her own sister thought she was lying, what chance did she stand telling others? 'Forget it, Juliette. Forget I said anything. I thought I could talk to you. I thought you of all people would listen. More fool me.'

Victoria rose from the sofa, moved over to her desk, and sank on to the chair. Blindly, she rooted through her desk drawer, gathered a few items together, and dropped them into her bag. She stood, ready to leave. 'I'll be back for the board meeting, otherwise, consider me on sabbatical.' She covered the distance from her desk to the door with determined speed, and snatched at the handle. 'I'd prefer you didn't discuss this with anyone.' As she waited for confirmation to her request, she saw Juliette's eyes glisten and her mouth tremble.

'I'm sorry, Victoria. I had no idea. I realise Seth can be a handful, but to lash out so violently? I can't imagine it. He's never done it to me.'

'That's because he doesn't hate you. Or wish you dead.'

'He's said that?'

Victoria nodded. 'Even though he's only four.' She released her grip on the handle, and bowed her head. 'I don't know how to put things right, but I'm hoping time away will provide a bit of perspective.'

'Where will you go?'

'Dad's. He always has an answer.' Victoria gave a half-hearted laugh. 'Not necessarily the right one, but he's a good starting point.'

'And Seth adores him,' Juliette added.

'Apparently.' Visiting her father was another of Victoria's shortcomings. She couldn't recall the last time she'd driven to Weymouth. She must have taken Seth for a visit as a baby. 'He'll be surprised to see me. Us.'

'He'll be over the moon. And you'll be the first to meet his new lady friend.'

The women stared at each other, before Victoria gave a tiny shake of her head. 'That'll be fun. I hope Seth behaves.'

Juliette stepped forward and embraced Victoria. 'I'm so sorry it's come to this. I should have helped you more.'

'None of this is your doing, Joo. And you did try. You drove me round the bend with your helpful hints and subtle suggestions. Have you forgotten the arguments?'

The hug was abandoned and Juliette shook her head. 'I should have stood my ground. Insisted I helped.'

'It wouldn't have made any difference. I wasn't listening. I was too busy proving I was capable.' Victoria released a low, drawn out sigh. 'Nothing new there.'

'Still, I wish you'd told me sooner.'

'I wasn't ready until today. Just thinking about it makes me feel sick. Talking about it … Well, you know me. I like to work things out for myself.' Victoria drew her sister to her and kissed the top of her head. 'Right. I'll be back to stick a rocket up the board's fat backside, so don't do anything daft.' She pulled away and searched Juliette's eyes. 'It's your vote, but use it wisely. Think about what I said. There'll be members round that table who'll see this as an opportunity to reduce costs and stamp on our authority. What's left of it.' *The conniving bastards.*

Chapter Three

Chris Frampton pushed open the square framed door to Hope Cove Castle and peered in. 'Don't know about you, Tommy,' he said, without looking behind, 'but my hope is the heating's on.'

His friend's heavy footsteps crunching along the gravel drive were accompanied by the word, 'Wuss.'

'You're calling *me* a wuss? You're the one who's whinged all the way here about the British weather.' Chris clapped his hands to keep his blood moving. 'Right. I'm going in. It's arctic out here, and I'm about to lose a finger to frostbite.' He shivered, made his way into the building and dumped his rucksack on the marbled floor.

Inside wasn't much warmer.

'It's England. It's winter. Told you we should've stayed in LA.' Tommy's voice echoed round the hall.

Chris grimaced and rubbed his neck. The journey had sucked the last of his energy and now he wanted to be cosy, comfortable and alone. 'I've never been in here. Not in the actual property.' He breathed in the atmosphere. It smelled old. Musty. He liked it. It gave him an immediate sense of history. He knew of the castle's origins; he'd heard of the death of the old man who'd lived here when Chris was a boy, read reports pertaining to its brief spell as a hotel, and he was aware it had stood empty for many years. The rumour it was haunted had little impact on Chris.

24

He didn't believe in ghosts.

Not anymore.

'This is some reception area.' Tommy whistled. 'Are you coming in, Rick?'

The long-haired, lanky youth, standing in silence on the sand-coloured stones, gawked at the first floor windows. 'Yeah. All right.' He shuffled past Tommy, acknowledged Chris, and headed for the stairs, taking them two at a time. Within seconds, he'd gone.

'The English girls are going to love his American accent,' Tommy said.

'If he ever meets any.'

'I'll make sure he does.' Tommy's eyes narrowed. 'I'll add it to my list of godfather duties.'

'I'm not sure your taste in girls would suit my son,' Chris said, a gentle smile putting to work lapsed muscles.

'There's nothing wrong with my taste in women.' Tommy, his nostrils flared and his jaw clenched, stared at Chris.

'Hey! Easy.' Surprised at how quickly the mood had blackened, Chris remained silent and scanned the room. Dramatic was the word that came to mind. His eyes were drawn to the large, brick fireplace at the end of the hall. Its surround and mantle were simple in design, and carved from grey-white Portland stone. A basket of logs nestled in an alcove to the right, and in the left recess, was a burgundy, leather porter's chair. A gold gilt mirror hung above the fire.

'Let's get this monster blazing. I don't suppose you've got a lighter?'

'No, *because neither of us smoke*. And I wouldn't use one to light this anyway.'

Tommy's ugly tone matched his dense scowl. Chris put it down to the long flight, the different time zone, and the grey, damp miserableness of the English weather. He attempted to lift his friend's spirits. 'I was a cub scout. Got any sticks?

I could rub them together.' Going by Tommy's unchanged expression, humour wasn't the key. Perhaps sincerity was. 'Seriously, mate, I don't know what I'd do without you. You're my right-hand man.'

'Dogsbody, more like.' Tommy freed himself of his luggage, lumbered across the length of the hallway and bent down. 'Well, at least there's kindling, but we still need a match.' He groaned as he straightened up and rubbed his knees.

The men had known each other too long for Chris to take offence. Tommy was prone to the occasional bout of self-pity, and under normal circumstances Chris would talk him round, but these weren't normal circumstances – such an idealistic view no longer existed.

'Go and get some rest, mate, I'll sort it later.' Chris patted Tommy's back and waved in the direction of the stairs.

'No. You're all right.' Tommy pointed to the basket. 'There's a box of matches on the logs.'

Chris stayed for a few seconds more before leaving the hall through a door on the right. It led to a light and airy conservatory that overlooked the castle terrace, and beyond that, the sea. The menacing, ashen clouds had shifted, revealing an arctic-blue sky, and the winter sun was streaming down, glinting off the glass of the building, but warming the conservatory. Chris removed his coat and laid it over his arm. His fatigue-laden limbs gained a renewed buoyancy and he strode across to the double doors. Surprised to find a key in the lock, he tested it and jiggled the handle. The door opened. He was used to heat and dust and sounds of motorbikes and horses, but here he was exposed to the chill of the English Channel, the roar of the sea and the taste of its salt upon his lips. He ran his tongue around his gums. It was there too. And so instant. Gulls swooped ahead, cawing and calling, following a small fishing vessel, and the men aboard shouted obscenities, chasing them off. Trees creaked in the breeze, and the grass whooshed in time with their elder statesmen.

Stepping onto the patio, Chris filled his lungs. 'Why did I never bring you here, Lacey?'

The wind picked up, licking the skin on Chris's arms into tiny peaks and bumps, so he shook out his coat and put it back on. The mobile phone in the pocket buzzed. He hooked it out, switched it off, and shoved it in his trouser pocket. It would be another EweSpeak update.

The wave of interest the sale of the ranch had caused, shocked him. His name appeared on multiple online forums several times a day, but the main hub of activity was EweSpeak, with its constant bleats. Mostly, people were discussing Chris's career, voting on their favourite Frampton film, describing in great detail the stunts he'd performed, and lamenting the loss of a great action hero. It was all a bit surreal, as if it was he who had died, not Lacey and Todd. He bolted his hands behind his neck. In many ways, he had.

He turned and regarded the roofline. Somewhere up there, all on his own, was Rick.

He'd been alone for two years.

Chris lifted his hands to the top of his head and let out a breath weighted with guilt and fear. Rick was unreachable. Not Chris, not Tommy, not even the highly-qualified, highly-priced doctors in the States found a way through. They spouted terms like 'survivor's guilt' and 'survivor's syndrome', asked about sleep patterns and nightmares, and told Chris to keep notes on any physical difficulties Rick suffered. They tried grief therapy, counselling, and sitting him in a room with other children who'd lost a parent or a sibling. They even prescribed medication. Rick didn't take it.

Letting down his arms, Chris turned to face the sea. The fishing boat was out of sight now, but the gulls were still swirling in its wake; a metaphor for his life without Lacey and Todd.

A hand landed on his shoulder.

'Fire's lit.'

Chris shrugged away from Tommy's hold. 'Now the inquest's over, I honestly thought coming home was the answer. I thought reconnecting with my past would help give me back a sense of who I am, and then I could share that with Rick. Build a new relationship with him. Show him we can make it work.'

'It might, given time.'

'I don't know.' Chris watched the birds disappear over the horizon. 'I waited almost two years for that inquest. I was left drifting, and I'm scared I won't find my way back.'

'You found your way here.' Tommy loosened the muscles in his neck and stretched out his arms.

'Yeah. And I've torn Rick away from his friends, and put an ocean in the way of his memories.' Chris edged onto the grass and noticed the depth and darkness of the wooded area. Bleak. 'I didn't think it through. I acted on impulse. Didn't calculate the risks. Rick has nothing here.'

'He has us.'

'I can't be his mother, Tommy. And I've never been anyone's brother.'

'You're his father. If you tell him this is home, he'll have to accept it.'

Tommy's attitude was bordering on indifference. Another moment to put down to jet lag.

'It's not his home, though, is it?' Chris said.

'Wherever we are is home.'

Tommy had a point.

Chris dragged his palm over his face, and scratched his chin. 'I guess a drastic problem requires a drastic solution. I hope this is it. I can't lose him, too.' He waved a see-you-later salute in Tommy's direction and walked through the ornamental garden into the summoning copse.

As a youth, he'd spent many summers wandering through the woodlands of the Hope Cove estate. He mapped the area, identifying places to ride his BMX, and built courses to test his skill. Like the trees around him, Chris's dreams were planted and nurtured there. He was trespassing then, but the old man who owned the castle never ventured beyond the lawn, and Chris was never caught. The memory triggered a smile. And a glimmer of hope. This was the stuff he wanted to share with Rick.

He turned on his heels and set off to find him.

Chris scanned the landing. Out of the six rooms on the floor, one door was shut. He knocked on its oak panel and waited. Silence. Too much, in fact. 'Rick? Can I come in?' Indistinct mumbling and scuffling footsteps confirmed his son was inside. 'Rick?'

'Yeah. All right.'

It wasn't all right. That was obvious. In those few words, Rick expressed his intense irritation at being discovered. It wasn't the new dawn Chris wanted, but at least he wasn't sent away. He entered the room and joined his son at the window. 'Great view.'

'Yeah.'

Turning to assess the space, Chris nodded his approval. 'Good choice. Have you checked out the other rooms?'

'Yeah.'

'And?' He addressed his son with a half-turn of his head.

'They're okay.' Rick smoothed his hand along the stone sill.

'But you prefer this one?'

'Yeah.'

Chris crouched against the wall and threaded his fingers

29

together. He was accustomed to this style of conversation – no eye contact, lack of interest, closed answers – it was how Rick communicated these days. 'So what's this room got that the others haven't?'

'A bed.'

'Ah.' Chris smiled. 'Excellent choice then.'

'Yeah.' Rick slouched his way across the floor to the deal breaker. 'It's all right.' He lay down, put his hands behind his head, and closed his eyes. 'For a British bed.'

Was that humour or a disparaging remark? It was difficult to know, but regardless of its intention, the comment was volunteered, and coming from Rick, that was a rare and remarkable thing. Chris wanted to capitalise on the moment – break the cycle of stilted, one-way dialogue. 'Tommy tells me the containers are at the port already. Lorries should be here in the morning. Can you survive in the British bed until your American bunk arrives?'

'Yeah.'

Back to the monosyllabic replies. Disappointed, Chris eased himself onto the carpet, scratched his index finger through the thick, blue pile, and decided on the next topic to not talk about. 'Glad the agents managed to sort out some furnishings. Gets us through the night.' No response. 'It's a big, old place to fill. Fancy helping me? We can buy online.' Still nothing. 'I took a gander around the gardens, earlier. It brought back some memories. Do you remember I told you about this place? I used to sneak into the woods when I was a lad. There was a way through from the beach. I wonder if it's still there. Fancy a recce later?'

Although he wasn't directly looking at his son, Chris was aware Rick was now propped up and staring at him. He wasn't sure how to react. He wanted to engage, but his instinct told him to remain focused on the floor. God, he so wanted to look at his son.

'Gander?'

The gruff, two-tone voice, finding its way to manhood, surprised Chris, and he laughed. He couldn't help it. Hearing what he considered an English word spoken with a LA accent was funny. He brought himself up sharp though, when Rick slid back down the bed. 'I'm sorry, son. You caught me off guard. It's not a word I expect you to use.'

Rick grabbed the end of the duvet, and pulled it over his head. 'Ditto,' he said. Then after a slight pause, 'We'll look tomorrow. Yeah?'

Amazed, Chris gaped at the quilt-covered mass on the British bed. Rick had poked fun at him. As Chris replayed the words, a smile took command of his mouth. 'Yeah. All right,' he said, certain Rick would detect the pleasure in his voice. 'Tomorrow.'

Chapter Four

Juliette Higham @EweTwo
Keen to read your thoughts on diversification within
the business world. How far is too far?

The silence in the car between Victoria and Seth was
familiar and comforting. It was a marker they had reached a
truce, following a sixty-minute battle of wills, with Victoria
requiring immediate action and Seth refusing to respond.

In between clothes packing, disposing of the kitchen
perishables, and securing the apartment, Victoria had
encouraged, bribed, cajoled and shouted at her son to get
a move on. In return, Seth expressed his wish Victoria
was dead, called her every animal within his range of
knowledge, and shut himself in his room. Employing her
shoulder as a battering ram, Victoria's body took several
hard knocks against the door before she gained access,
where she discovered Seth had built a barricade of books.

She pulled up to a red light and checked on her son. He
was safe in his child-seat, busy huffing his hot breath on the
window, and fingering sketches in the mist. Victoria activated
the climate control and switched on the sidelights. She hoped
to reach Weymouth before dusk, but with the November
rain greasing the roads, conditions were slow. She tapped the
steering wheel. 'Pops will be surprised to see you.'

In her rush to leave London, she'd not had time to call
her father, and her mobile was languishing where she'd left
it on the kitchen counter. Her ruckus with Seth had seen to
that. 'It's funny not having my phone,' she said. 'But I quite
like it. It's liberating. It's like the time my car broke down

and the rescue mechanic put me on a hard tow. The only control I had was over the brake pedal. Of course, I had to trust he knew what he was doing, but once I got used to it ...' She heard herself and stopped. Her choice of topic was never going to entice a four-year-old into conversation. 'What do you think Pops will say when he sees us?'

Seth didn't answer. The mist had cleared from his window and his attention was now on the contents of the glove box. Victoria clamped her mouth shut. Seth knew the rules. He shouldn't have opened the compartment and he shouldn't be raking through her personal items, but Victoria was tired of fighting. If she was serious about breaking the cycle, it had to come from her. *Learn when to pick a battle.*

As they continued to wait, a motorbike roared across their path, making both occupants jump.

'Shit!' Victoria covered her mouth and glanced at her son. Had he heard her swear? It was difficult to tell with his professional poker face. 'Naughty motorcyclist, scaring me.'

The car behind blasted out three impatient beeps, shocking Victoria into action. With no concern for the lights, she rammed the gear stick into *Drive* and pulled away. It wasn't until she'd crossed the junction, that she acknowledged her carelessness. If she'd run a red, both her and Seth would have been in pieces, scattered over the tarmac. That was the speed of change. Life turned on a penny. It brought home to Victoria how little respect for it she had shown.

'You said shit.'

Victoria kept her eyes on the road. 'Yes. I did.'

'That's a bad word.'

'Yes.'

Victoria waited for the challenge, and it came as Seth shuffled to face her.

'I get told off when I say bad words.'

Victoria nodded. 'So do I.' If eyes had lasers, Seth's would be burning a hole in her ear right now. She brushed over it with the flat of her hand and smoothed down her curls; a fruitless act, as immediately, they reverted to their natural position. She wrapped her fingers around the wheel and locked out her arms in anticipation of a major eruption from Seth.

As the seconds passed and nothing came, she chanced a peek. He appeared to be studying her. Or assessing – she wasn't sure, but it unnerved her to the point where she inspected his hands for missiles. Empty. It was his eyes causing the damage today.

'Does Pops tell you off?'

The question was so unexpected and engaging, Victoria laughed. 'Yes. And so does your Aunty Joo.' She relaxed and her elbows dipped, as she looked forward to a rare exchange with her son.

Seth settled back in his seat. 'You said shit.'

Victoria slumped, and her expectations went with her. No conversation. She was naïve to think Seth would act out of character.

'I'm going to tell Pops you said shit.'

'That's enough.' Desperate not to raise her voice, the words were hissed out, sounding more aggressive than assertive. She tried again. 'No more swearing. It's rude and I don't like it.'

Seth kicked out at the glove box and threw himself further into his seat. 'I don't care.' He folded his arms and turned away from Victoria. 'I hate you.'

The brief insight into normality, the few seconds of how wonderful their life together could be, was wiped out by his three little words.

'Well, you know what?' Victoria said. 'There are times

when I don't much like you.' It was an unforgivable disclosure, but enough was enough. Nothing he said now would make her feel worse.

'I know.'

Except that.

Victoria's stomach whipped over, and the bullets of sorrow and regret she'd swallowed earlier, exploded. The pain machine-gunned through her gut, and she swerved off the road. She hit the engine's stop button, slapped her hands on the steering wheel, and buried her face in her arms.

Her floodgates had opened, and a river of remorse, and a stream of sadness poured from her. An adulthood of repressed emotions screamed with relief at their sudden freedom, their piercing wails ricocheting around the car. Victoria's ears throbbed, her eyes stung, and her ribs ached, but it was what she wanted. To reconnect with real life, she had to suffer, experience agony, and accept that she had made terrible mistakes.

Exhausted by the outpour, she fell silent and raised her head, expecting to find Seth glaring at her. He had his eyes closed, his hands folded in his lap, and his lips sealed. He was humming. Victoria picked out the tune of *Old MacDonald*.

The song came to an abrupt halt when Seth opened his eyes. 'I wish you were dead,' he said.

Defeated by his detached air and direct words, and no longer capable of speech, Victoria stared at him. As with EweSpeak, the opportunity to create a most wonderful thing was hers, but with no capacity to nurture, her relationship with Seth had been destroyed.

The company she could deal with, but her son …

A bitter taste of rising bile coated the back of her tongue, the muscles in her jaws tensed, and her breathing quickened. Losing control frightened her, but with her barriers down and reserves spent, she offered no resistance. Before today, she would have denied herself this ultimate form of release.

Racing to exit the car, she flung open the door, scrambled onto the grass and willingly went with the moment. Within seconds, the poison was expelled from her body.

She wished her conscience had the facility to do the same.

Once her muscles stopped trembling, she returned to the car, took a bottle of water from the side pocket and refreshed her mouth.

Seth scowled at her. 'I want Pops.'

'So do I.' Crushed and spent, Victoria climbed into her seat and shut the door. 'I'm sorry. I was angry and upset. I didn't mean what I said.' She risked a light touch to the back of Seth's neck, but he pulled away.

'I did,' he said.

Victoria started the engine, planted both hands on the steering wheel, and concentrated on the road. If she thought about Seth for too long, she would cry again, and this time, she might not stop.

Chapter Five

Victoria stopped the car outside a small bungalow raised
a few feet from road level. The digital dashboard read six
o'clock, but it seemed much later. Shattered and drained,
she was relieved they had reached Weymouth; the emotional
strain had taken its toll and she was ready for sleep. Seth
had already succumbed. She took a moment to study him.
He was curled on his side with his knees drawn up to his
stomach, and he was using his hands for a pillow. He was
untroubled and peaceful. That expression didn't exist in
daylight hours.

Although Victoria was reluctant to rouse him, she
released his seat belt. 'Seth,' she called softly. 'We're at
Pops' house. It's time to wake up.'

Under the orange streetlight, he yawned and stretched,
his skinny body quivering with tension. Hostility blazed
from his eyes.

'I don't want you here,' he said, his voice steady, his
intent clear. 'This is mine and Pops'. You don't come here.'

'Of course I do, you've forgotten, that's all.' As Victoria
spoke, her hair bobbed forward and concealed her face.
For once she was grateful for her wayward whorls, as they
veiled the heat of guilt burning her cheeks. 'Come on,' she
said. 'Let's surprise your granddad.'

At full stretch and on tiptoes, Seth held down the button

to the bell and Victoria retreated from the front door. They'd arrived unannounced and she had no idea how her father would react. The small pane of obscured glass at the top of the door went from black to yellow, as an interior light illuminated the building. 'He's home,' she said. 'You can take your finger off the bell.'

'It's not yours,' said Seth, swapping hands.

'Hold your horses. I'm coming.'

Hearing her father's familiar tones settled Victoria's nerves, and when the door opened, Frank's huge grin expressed his delight at seeing his daughter and grandson.

'Well, goodness me. Who's this, then?' He saluted Victoria, and then extended his arms to Seth. 'Come and give your Pops your tightest hug.'

Seth threw himself at Frank as Victoria looked on. The chemistry between them was palpable, and their acceptance of one another enviable. Victoria didn't want it any other way; she just wanted some of it for herself.

'Are you coming in, love?' Frank held out his hand and gestured for Victoria to take it. He pulled her in. 'Your timing's impeccable. There's a pot of tea on the table.'

Victoria closed the door, and followed her dad and son into the kitchen. She surveyed the room and frowned. She didn't recall granite worktops. Or white walls. 'Have you redecorated?'

Frank laughed. 'Two years ago.'

'Has it been that long since my last visit?' She squirmed, and avoided eye contact with Seth, who was standing by Frank's side. 'Sorry.'

'Don't be sorry. Of course I'd love to see more of you, but I know you're busy.' He ruffled Seth's hair. 'I've seen lots of this little fella, though. And his cousins.'

Seth skipped across the brick-red Marley tiles, and stopped in front of the fridge.

'May I see what's inside please, Pops?'

'Yes, you may. But first you must go to the toilet and wash your hands. Okay?' He smiled at Seth.

Victoria grimaced as she waited for the tantrum.

'Okay.' Seth trotted into the hallway and out of sight.

The shift in his behaviour was astonishing.

'Are you all right, love? You look stunned.'

Victoria blinked. 'I am. Does Seth always do as you ask?'

Frank opened a cupboard, retrieved a cup and saucer, and put them next to a set already on the table. 'Mostly. Do you still take milk?'

Victoria nodded. 'He knows his way around here.'

'It's important he feels at home.' Frank chuckled. 'He's very like you.' He poured the tea and passed Victoria hers.

'He is?'

'Oh, yes. He doesn't take kindly to change.'

'How is that like me?' Victoria was adaptable – she had to be with technology developing at a breakneck speed.

'There's an inflexibility about you. Your last school report said so.' Frank winked.

'Dad! That was seventeen years ago.'

He sipped his tea. 'You objected to your mother dusting your room because she moved your books. And you sulked if you missed a meal. As for the bathroom timetable—'

Victoria held up her hand and smiled. 'I get the point. I prefer order to chaos.'

'And Seth's the same.'

Based on the evidence she'd already witnessed, despite its brevity, Victoria had to agree with her father's evaluation.

'It's not rocket science,' he said. 'Children like to know where they stand. Now, you both must be hungry.'

After something to eat, and once Seth was in bed, the two adults settled in the living room.

'I'm sorry to pitch up unannounced, Dad.'

'No apologies needed. The spare bedroom was already made up, and I can dig out the blow-up mattress for you. It's still got a bit of life in it.' Frank reached a hand across the divide of his armchair and the sofa in which Victoria was sitting. 'You and Seth are always welcome. This is your home.'

She smiled at her father. 'I appreciate the sentiment, but that's not true. This is your place. I've never lived here.'

'You know what I mean. I'd have the rooms packed with the lot of you if I could. Do you think we might do Christmas here this year?'

A little squashed, but it was a distinct possibility. 'I guess so,' Victoria said. 'I haven't any immediate plans to leave.' She saw the surprise hop onto her father's face. 'Hasn't Juliette called?'

'No. Has something happened?'

Lots of things had happened to Victoria – the business was sucking the life out of her, life was sucking the life out of her, and her son had declared war on her. Not wanting to spoil the evening, she shrugged. 'Fancied a change.'

'What about Seth's playgroup?'

'It's not compulsory. A few weeks out of the system won't hurt him.'

Her father looked doubtful. 'He won't be happy if you upset his routine. Perhaps you could take him to one here.'

'Maybe.' Victoria sunk into the sofa and closed her eyes. She was beyond tired. 'I haven't given it much thought.'

'No plan, Victoria. You always have a plan.'

She heard the surprise in her father's voice. He was right. Her whole life was spent making lists, drawing systems diagrams, and sketching out her next five years. Always the planner, always a plan. Right up until that morning, she'd had a plan. Then, she'd gone freestyle. She opened her eyes. 'I'm trying something new. Juliette gets by on winging it.'

'You know what your mother would have said to that?'

Victoria tutted. '*You are not Juliette.*'

Her father nodded. 'Well, that's right, love. Juliette relies on her instinct. You use logic.'

Victoria propped herself up. 'We're talking about Seth missing a few weeks of the Christmas term.'

'You'll miss his nativity.'

'I'm an atheist, Dad.'

'Mum brought you up to believe in God.'

'No. She brought me up to believe that *she* believed in God. I never did.'

'Still,' he said, 'it's Seth's first one.' Her dad had a tiny smile playing on his lips. 'Can we at least upgrade you to agnostic? For Iris's sake?'

'Dad. That doesn't work on me. Mum's dead. End of. There's no afterlife, or spirits, or angels, thank God.' Victoria's speech came to an abrupt halt as she swallowed down her last words and reacted to her father's obvious amusement. 'It's a saying.'

She shuddered as a chill tingled along her spine. The idea that dead people watched over her provided no comfort whatsoever and she found it astounding that Juliette had faith in such nonsense and still enjoyed a healthy sex life.

No. Life after death was a ridiculous notion, with no supporting scientific evidence.

'How many weeks *are* you planning to stay?' Her father's voice jogged Victoria back to the earthly plane.

'Like I said, I don't have a plan. Is it a problem?'

'Of course not,' said Frank. 'I said you can stay as long as you like. This is your home.'

And there they were, back at square one; in someone else's home, spending an indeterminate number of nights sleeping on the living room floor on an old, camp air bed. *This is what happens when I don't make a plan.* A holiday cottage was an option; at least she'd have a proper bed.

'Dad. You're a genius.' Victoria leaped off the sofa and planted a noisy kiss on her father's cheek. 'Fancy a drive to Chiswell tomorrow?'

Victoria dashed out of her dad's Ford C-Max, dived into the letting agents and returned five minutes later with a set of house keys in her hand. She waved them at her father, who was occupying the passenger seat of his car. Victoria slipped into the driver's side, catching sight of Seth in the rear-view mirror. He was browsing through a catalogue. 'What's he doing?'

'Choosing his Christmas present. How did you get on?' Frank gazed in the direction of the estate agents.

'It was easier than I expected. They've failed to let it for three months. No one knows why. Saturday staff. I'll speak to the manager on Monday.' She passed the keys to her dad and rubbed her hands together. 'It's a bit nippy out there. I hope the cottage is warm.' She buckled up. 'Ready?'

Frank nodded and they continued on their journey. 'It'll be freezing,' he said, reaching into his coat pocket and withdrawing a silver hip flask. 'Just as well we have central heating.' He winked, unscrewed the cap and swigged down a mouthful. 'Victoria?'

She declined the offer. She'd only known him put whisky in his hip flask, and she didn't much care for that. 'I'm driving, Dad. *Your car*. But thanks anyway.'

'You'll be glad of it later.' He waved it under her nose.

'We'll see,' she said. 'Take it away.' She gave the flask a gentle push, and heard her dad chuckle, but he did as requested. 'What do you think it'll be like inside?'

'Apart from cold?' Frank chewed over the question.

'It will need cleaning.' He paused. 'Of course, it will be completely different to what you've become accustomed.'

'That's not an issue, Dad.' She'd already been shocked back to life that week; another jolt would settle the rhythm. 'I just hope Seth likes it.'

Frank nestled the hip flask back in his pocket, and patted Victoria's knee. 'As long as the little fellow is with you, he'll be happy.'

It was a wonderful sentiment, which remained uncontested. There was harmony in the car, which Victoria wished to maintain.

They crossed a small roundabout onto the causeway that linked Weymouth to Portland.

'Ferrybridge is swish.' Victoria executed a cursory examination of the area. 'Is that the sailing academy?'

'The National Sailing Academy, if you don't mind. Did you see it on TV during the Olympics? Princess Anne was here.'

Victoria smiled. The pride in her father's voice was unmistakable. Leaving for the mainland fifteen years ago made no difference; Portland was still his island. 'I caught glimpses of the Olympics,' she said. 'It looked fabulous.' She negotiated a second roundabout, which marked the entrance to the marina.

'That's Portland for you.'

'Have you considered moving back?'

Frank shuffled in his seat and ran a hand through his thatch of white hair. 'I've thought about it.' He flipped down the visor and peered into the mirror. 'Found anything, Seth?'

Victoria noted the brief answer and the immediate change of subject, and it intrigued her. In the back of her mind she had a vague recollection that her dad's new flame was a Portlander. She pushed him for information. 'How seriously have you thought about it?'

Frank released a forceful sigh and faced the windscreen. 'Seriously. But my home is with your mother.'

And there was the problem. Iris Paveley. The woman who, even in death, got her own way.

As much as she'd loved her mother, Victoria and Iris's relationship was strained. With God constantly held up as the example for Victoria to follow, living up to Iris's standards proved difficult, especially since Victoria's scientific, logical and practical brain insisted no such deity existed. But she'd wanted her mother to love her, so she'd submitted to her wishes. Sadly, saying grace before every meal, reading the Bible each night before bed, and reciting the Lord's Prayer at lights out, made Victoria resent religion with a passion.

Worse than that, she resented her mother for not encouraging independent thought.

And for not allowing her the space to grow.

Victoria reined in her anger before speaking. 'Dad, if you want to move, then move. You don't have to answer to anyone.'

'You'd be surprised.'

'I wouldn't,' Victoria said, under her breath. There was no doubt in her mind that her mother and father's marriage was intense – they'd loved and fought in equal measure – but Iris never compromised. It was always her way. She had personally adopted the old saying 'It's my way or the highway', and the highway was never offered as an alternative. To think she still exerted that control over her father upset Victoria.

'It's time you lived life your way, Dad.' She tried to gauge his response, but he'd adopted Seth's poker face. 'It's been eight years.'

'I know,' he said. 'That's what scares me. Your mother will have mastered omnipotence by now.'

It was typical of her father to provide light in a dark

situation, and his comment extracted a laugh from Victoria. 'I think she managed that long before she died. That's how she knew every painful detail of my life.'

Frank coughed. 'That wasn't omnipotence. That was nosiness. She read your diary.'

'So that's how she knew all my secrets.' Victoria shook her head in mock disbelief, then checked her rear-view mirror. Seth, leaning against his window, gawked back. There was an unnerving depth to his eyes.

A boy his age should be carefree and unburdened, she thought.

'Pull in.' Frank's gentle instruction drew Victoria back to the road.

She tapped the indicator stalk, crossed to the opposite side of the road, and parked outside a blue fronted building. Once she'd switched off the engine, she looked out of her window. 'Chiswell Crafts? When did the fish restaurant become an art shop?'

'About six months ago. And it's not an art shop. It's a craft centre.'

There was an edge to her father's voice that piqued Victoria's interest. 'Have you been in?' She watched him making a hash of undoing his seat belt.

'Once or twice,' he muttered, becoming flustered with the buckle.

Victoria reached across, and with a swift press of her thumb, set him free.

'Thank you.' His words were directed at his breast pocket. 'Did I tell you Juliette phoned?' He raised his voice. 'Last night. You'd already gone to bed.'

Well, that came out of nowhere. Either her father was attempting another change of subject, or he had a bone to pick with her. Regardless of which it was, the topic of Chiswell Crafts was closed.

'She's worried about you.' Frank checked on Seth. 'Said you had a run-in with the little feller.'

'Something like that.' Victoria lowered her voice. 'Can we talk about it later, Dad? Not here.'

'Can we get out please, Pops?' Seth's voice floated to the front of the car, so light and sweet. He was different with Frank. Gentle and compliant, responding well to his grandfather's natural manner.

Victoria didn't possess a natural manner. Her touch wasn't gentle and her love was not an object of beauty; it was a weapon of mass destruction, and she'd wielded it without care. No wonder Seth rejected it. No wonder he wished her dead.

She glanced out at the blue façade of the rustic craft shop, pushed open the car door, and breathed in the salty air. 'I'd forgotten this smell.' Closing her eyes, she lost herself to the moment, and the memories of her youth came skipping forward. Within one breath she was crunching along the pebbled beach, happy and carefree, hand in hand with her young lover, with the crush of the stones beneath her feet, and the sensation of prickled soles lingering once she'd returned to softer ground. By the second breath she was in his arms, strong and protective, his gentle kisses enticing her, inviting her to places she was desperate to explore.

'Are we getting out, then?'

Victoria was brought back to reality by her father's voice and a nudge to her arm. She looked over to the cottage that was once her nan's. One more area of her life she'd abandoned.

'Take the keys then.' Frank jangled them under Victoria's nose. 'You have first look and I'll get Seth.'

Victoria hid her reluctance with a forced smile, took the keys and climbed out of the car. She scanned her surroundings. She'd been away long enough for Chiswell to change. It was still a small village, but houses had been updated, a few new ones built with Portland stone had been squeezed in, and shops had changed hands. She noted the 'open' sign on the craft centre door.

Frank and Seth appeared next to her on the pavement. 'After you,' her father said.

Victoria took two steps, turned and evaluated the terraced cottage before her. Nailed to its wall was a piece of driftwood, and painted on it were the words, 'Crab Cottage'. She frowned. 'I don't remember a name plaque. In fact, I don't remember giving it a name.'

She walked up the three steps to the front door and picked at the flaking woodwork. 'Dad, it's awful. The frame's rotting away. The agents are meant to be keeping an eye on this place. That's what I'm paying them for.' Hit by the sudden fear the cottage was wrecked and stripped bare, she invited her father to take over. 'I don't want to go in first. You open it.' She handed Frank the key, stepped back and stood with Seth. Her father fiddled with the lock, pushed open the door and disappeared inside. After a few minutes, he resurfaced.

'Well?' Victoria said.

He motioned a so-so action with his hands and pulled the door wide open. 'Come and see for yourself.'

Seth marched in and vanished into the black.

Keeping her mouth shut, for fear of ingesting insects, Victoria squeezed past her father and waited for her eyes to adjust to the dark hallway. She sniffed the air. 'It smells a bit odd.'

Frank laughed. 'There are no dead bodies.'

'I meant it smells damp.' She hadn't considered the possibility someone or something had died in there. She cast a look of suspicion. 'You have checked everywhere?'

Frank nodded. 'Everywhere. Apart from a bag of rubbish

in the small bedroom, the rotting wood, and the fact there's no central heating, I'd say you could move in tonight.' He pulled his hip flask from his pocket and presented it to Victoria. 'Would you like some now?'

She didn't respond; she was gaping at the brown stain on the ceiling above. 'Oh, Dad, I'm so sorry.'

'What for?'

'This.' She waved her hands wildly over her head. 'I've let you and Nan down. You should never have agreed to sell this place to me. I can't take care of anything.'

'Now then, madam, your nan left this cottage to me to do with as I wished, and I wished for you to have it. Your need was great as I recall.' Frank unscrewed the metal cap of the silver flask. 'As was mine. You and your mum needed to live apart.' He sipped down the contents, shuddered and replaced the lid. 'You two got on much better from that point.'

'Maybe, but it caused arguments between you and Mum.' Victoria recalled the day the property changed hands. Her mum went ballistic. 'She thought I was too young to rent, and definitely too young to live alone.'

Frank smiled. 'We only argued once. When I reminded her what she got up to at nineteen, she quickly backed down.'

The comment surprised Victoria, but she chose not to dwell on her parents' youth. She had enough difficulty coming to terms with her own.

'Anyway,' Frank continued, 'you've bought and paid for it since then. I've had nothing to do with it for years.'

Victoria's gaze returned to the stained patch above, and she fired up with rage. 'My poor house!'

Now frantic to examine the rest of the cottage, she shoved open the door to the front room and instantly noticed a collection of small black holes in the carpet in front of the fireplace. There were too many to count. 'The rug's gone,' she said, dropping to her knees and fingering the damage. 'And they've had a coal fire without a guard. Look at these burns.'

'I know, but it's just a carpet and you can afford to replace it.'

Frank paused, which drew Victoria's attention to him. She saw his brow ruck.

'In fact, you can afford to buy a new home.' He put the flask in his pocket and stepped further into the room. 'Why do you want to live here when you can have any home you want?'

That was a good question. An excellent question. Victoria rolled off her knees and onto her bottom, and leaned against the grubby fabric sofa. 'I don't know.' Was this what it was like to be Juliette? Surviving by instinct. Winging it. It wasn't an entirely pleasant feeling. She looked up and saw her father smiling. 'What?'

'You really don't have a plan, do you?' He eased himself onto the floor next to Victoria and put his arm around her. 'You're EweSpeak's very own little lost lamb.'

'Something like that.'

'Are you going to tell me what's going on?'

Victoria propped her head on her father's shoulder and brooded over the question. With Seth in the house, she couldn't say much.

At that moment, as if summoned by the power of thought, her son appeared in the doorway.

'Can I go upstairs, please, Pops?'

'Is it safe, Dad?' Panic flitted through Victoria's stomach. Her instinct was to keep Seth within grabbing distance.

'It's a bit dirty, but sound enough.' Frank smiled at the boy. 'Go on. But don't touch anything.'

With a turn of heel, Seth was gone.

Victoria hauled herself up and walked to the window. There was very little to see outside. 'I'd forgotten how quiet it is here.'

'You're used to city life. I bet you can't sleep without the constant hum of traffic.'

'Maybe.' The truth was she was ready to enter the realms of unconsciousness for a hundred years. Perhaps that would solve her problems. Do the *Sleeping Beauty* thing – well, the Sleeping Geek thing – and wait to be rescued by a handsome prince.

'What are you thinking?' Frank asked.

'I've got my back to you, Dad. How do you know I'm thinking?' She wheeled round to face him.

He smiled. 'You're the cerebral one of the family. Your brain's permanently on the go.' He rose from the floor and joined her at the window, where they perched against the sill. 'My question stands. What are you thinking?'

The sound of footsteps crashing down the stairs alerted Victoria to her son's arrival, and once again, the chance for an open discussion was thwarted. 'All right?' she said. 'Anything up there I should know about?'

Her question was greeted with a shrug. Such a simple action that conveyed so much. Her genuine attempt to share the moment with Seth had been cast off like an old, unwanted coat. Since it was the fashion, Victoria shrugged too. She didn't do it for effect, but it won an inquisitive glance from Seth. His hazelnut eyes softened.

He'd discarded the outer shell.

The amazing lightness in Victoria's chest and her rapid pulse of excitement were making her high. Had she not anchored herself to the ledge, she would have floated away.

'Do you need to know about the spider?'

The gravity of Seth's tone grounded Victoria.

'What spider?'

A worried expression embedded itself behind Seth's eyes, and he looked at Frank. 'Should I talk about the spider, Pops?'

'To tell you the truth, lad, I'm not sure. Your mum's not keen on our eight-legged friends.'

It was obvious to Victoria her father was struggling to maintain a straight face. His cheeks were twitching, and his eyebrows had a Mexican wave all of their own. 'What's so funny?' she said, a swell of giggles building in her stomach. Whatever it was, it was contagious.

Frank cleared his throat. 'You asked Seth if there's anything upstairs you should know about. He doesn't know what things you should know about. Until you tell him, he can't answer. See? Easy.' His smile broke free. 'Let me soothe those wrinkles of confusion.' He brushed a finger across Victoria's forehead.

She gave his hand a gentle swipe. 'It's easy if you're under six and over sixty. You're clearly going through your second childhood.'

'And loving it,' Frank said, laughing. 'Now, remember, Seth's only four. Keep your question literal and ask him to show you the upstairs rooms.'

'Be exact. Got it.' It hadn't occurred to Victoria to apply the same logic to a child as she did with computers. *Feed in the correct information.* She was good at that. 'Will you show me the rooms upstairs, Seth?' Nervous of his reply, she checked his eyes. To her absolute joy, the worry had vanished, and they'd remained unguarded.

'Do you need to know about the spider?'

Victoria smiled. *Her son had made her smile.* It was a huge moment, and nothing else mattered – not the silly house name, not the million black halos on the carpet, and not the horrible stain on the ceiling. Nothing. She was ready to fly.

'What a great plan,' Frank said. 'You two go on. I'll take another scout down here.' He grinned at Seth and indicated for him to leave the room. 'You too, smiler.' He kissed Victoria and ushered her into the hall.

She glided towards the stairs. 'Let's take a look at the rooms, then.'

Seth ran ahead and Victoria followed.

'I lived here for five years,' she said. 'That's almost as long as you've been alive.'

Seth continued climbing.

'And then I moved to London. I was twenty-four. Seems so young these days.'

'It's old,' Seth said.

Victoria puckered her lips. 'It certainly feels like a lifetime ago.'

Once they'd reached the dark landing, Seth scurried in through the first of three doors, and Victoria aimed for the furthest one. She waited a moment before entering the bedroom, watching for Seth. He'd gone into the bathroom and she expected him to exit any second, but there were no signs of movement. Whatever he'd found, it was keeping him entertained. Victoria recoiled as an image of a large spider crawled across her mind. There were bound to be spiders in every room – the cottage had been neglected.

Her buoyant mood rapidly nosedived, and she hit the ground with a bump.

She was responsible for the cottage's state of disrepair.

Par for the course, she thought. *Everything in my life needs fixing.*

She couldn't bear to think what her neglect had done to her old bedroom. It was the place where many fantasies were imagined and many dreams were realised.

EweSpeak was one of them.

She opened the door with caution. To her utter relief, the room had been loved and well cared for. Given how badly mistreated downstairs was, she stood on the threshold and wondered why. Perhaps the view of the sea made it everyone's preferred room.

She'd spent many hours here herself in her younger days, learning computer basics and studying courses in programming. She was good at it. Her logical brain found it easy, and the isolation of the work suited her. With her desk against the window, she would observe the people on the beach, unnoticed.

Juliette would visit from time to time and try to entice her out, but socialising wasn't on Victoria's agenda. She was uncomfortable in crowds, saw no point in drinking herself into oblivion, and hated karaoke with a vengeance. It was all right for Juliette. She was gregarious and witty, and had a natural affinity for people, qualities Victoria didn't possess.

With a bold stride, she entered the room. The decoration and the furnishings were different to when she'd lived there. The walls were brightly coloured, when she preferred creams and whites, and net curtains that flounced with lace had replaced her Venetian blinds. Her double divan had gone too, and in its place was a ladder-less cabin bed, but the electric atmosphere remained, her copper coils conducting it and her brain, working like a battery, providing the voltage to power her system.

The skin on her skull contracted. She thrilled at the sensation. It was life-affirming. Juliette would say it was proof that although Victoria had been gone many years, her room had not forgotten her. Victoria didn't think like that. The house was made of stone, with walls thick enough to withstand a small explosion. It was nothing more and nothing less. It didn't hold memories. She did. And the ones she'd made here, she remembered.

That's what created the energy.

'This is all right.'

Her father's voice surprised her. She turned and flattened her hand to her front. 'Dad! Don't creep up on people. You'll give someone a heart attack.'

'Sorry. Unintentional.' He pushed the door to and inclined his head. 'Seth's pretending the bath's a go-kart, and he has a spider for his mechanic. But you don't need to know about that.'

Victoria took a deep breath. Her father often used gentle humour to ease her into difficult conversations.

'Would you like to talk while we have five minutes?' Frank patted his pocket. 'A shot of Dutch courage first, maybe?'

Safe in her favourite room, and touched by her father's concern, Victoria was moved to speak. 'What you saw downstairs with Seth and me, he and I talking and getting along, it's not how we are. Not normally. We have a very strained relationship. And it's my fault. I realised I've never been a mother to him, and he resents me for it. In fact, he hates me.' She faltered, and pressed her palms together, as the words clawed their way into her heart. 'And he's every right to. He's angry with me, violent. He strikes out. Verbally and physically. And I don't know what to do.' She turned back to the window and studied her father's reflection, shocked to see he was lost, like her. Like Seth. 'I'm frightened, Dad. What if I can't repair the damage?'

'Oh, Victoria.' Frank grabbed her sleeve and yanked her to him, encircling her with his arms. 'I had no idea.' Echoes of Juliette. 'I don't have an answer right now, my darling, but it'll be all right. I promise.'

His action triggered Victoria's tears, and she rubbed and pulled at her eyes to prevent their dispersal. 'I was too busy maintaining the business. I fooled myself into believing

I was providing Seth with everything he required. But it wasn't enough. I wasn't giving him what he really needed. And it's up to me to make it right.' She buried her face in her father's neck and allowed the emotion to carry her through. She wasn't frightened to let go anymore.

'I'll help you,' Frank whispered. 'You know I will. There's nothing here that can't be fixed.'

Victoria's gut fell away and years of pulling at the thread and tightening the knot, unravelled in an instant.

Chapter Six

Chris poked his head round Rick's bedroom door. The mass of duvet was more or less as he'd seen it last. It was possible his teenage son had spent the entire night in one position. Jet lag was a whole new experience for Rick. 'How was the British bed?' Chris asked.

'All right.'

'Tired?'

'Yeah.'

'Up for that scout about later? I discovered a self-contained apartment last night. It must have been something to do with when the castle was a hotel. It's got its own entrance and a connecting door to the kitchen. It'd make a cool bachelor's pad.' No response. 'Tommy's been out hunting. He speared a packet of bacon and rounded up some eggs. Fancy some brunch?'

'Yeah. All right.'

'See you in five.' Chris pushed the bedroom door fully open. Tommy was already cooking and the smoky smells had found their way upstairs. 'Or sooner,' Chris said, rubbing his growling stomach. It was good to feel hungry. Amazing, in fact. He'd lost too much weight over the last couple of years. Food was a chore rather than a pleasure, but the cheeky sea breeze had flirted with Chris's appetite and teased him back to the table.

He trotted downstairs and followed his nose to the

kitchen. When he arrived, Tommy was standing at the side, cursing.

'Smells fantastic.'

'Small miracle. Bloody handle's fallen off the pan. Thank God the lorries are coming today.' Tommy turned and waved a shaft of black plastic at Chris. 'I thought you told the agents to spare no expense.'

Chris wandered further into the room and examined the contents of a corner cupboard. 'Not quite. I requested new sheets and towels, and beds, if they were needed, otherwise, I told them not to replace anything. I guess the porter's chair was left over from the castle's hotel days.' He reached into the cupboard. 'There's a saucepan in here. Do you need it?' He pulled it out. 'We could have scrambled eggs.'

Tommy placed the broken handle to the side and pushed up his sleeves. 'Are you making them?'

Chris baulked at the condition of the pan. 'Nope. This is rank.'

'Fried it is, then.' Tommy returned to his work. 'You seem more settled today.'

Chris shoved the old pot away and hitched himself onto the counter. 'Hmm. Maybe. I'll feel happier when our stuff's arrived.' He hated being separated from his personal items – photo albums, marriage and birth certificates, medical records. He liked to have them under lock and key and under his jurisdiction at all times. Currently they were packed in a cardboard box marked 'Private. Office', doubtless stuck in the morning traffic on the A31. He'd sealed the box himself. There were things inside for his eyes alone. 'What time do we think the lorries will arrive?'

Tommy flipped an egg over. 'Not for another couple of hours. If they're not here by midday, I'll call the shipping company. Right, sit down.'

Chris obeyed, and waited at the kitchen table. 'Brown sauce. Cool.'

'Hmm. Not sure your son will approve.' As Tommy served Chris with a plate of bacon and eggs, Rick shambled past. 'Hungry?'

'Yeah.'

With brunch eaten and the formalities of clearing away sorted, Chris issued Tommy with instructions to call him as soon as the containers arrived. He grabbed his coat, threw Rick his, and invited him to join him in the garden. 'Come on. Let's find the entrance to the beach,' he said, heading into the shade of the trees.

Where to? Which direction? Chris dredged the bottom of his memory and fished up an image of a hedge, and a drop down to the pebbles. 'We can't go wrong if we head for the sea,' he said.

He urged Rick on, desperate to share something of his past with him. As they walked, fragments of memories linked together to form a picture; an old ruined section of wall, a tomb with a skull and crossbones engraved upon it, a grey stone archway – all clues he was going the right way.

'Look at that.' He pointed to a headstone. 'That's a grave of a smuggler.'

Rick stopped beside the yellow, fuzz-covered rock. 'Yeah. Right.'

Chris smiled. Teenagers were so cynical these days. When he was a youngster, the thought he was intruding on a pirate's resting place scared the living daylights out of him. He loved it. 'I used to ride my bike through here.' He saw Rick nod, and they continued on their trek. 'It was reckless. Look at the rough terrain.' As he spoke, his foot caught on a thick root of a tree and he crashed to the ground. 'See,' he mumbled, removing the barbed thorns of a bramble from his cheek.

Rick tutted, pulled a tissue from his jeans pocket, and crouched. 'Call yourself a stuntman.'

The words spoken, and the tenderness Rick applied to the wound, sent chills through Chris. His son was in there and he was beginning to fight for his freedom. 'Thank you,' Chris said, taking the tissue from him. 'I'm good.' He held out his hand. 'Help your old man up?'

There was a chance he'd refuse. There was a chance he would walk away. Chris watched for Rick's reaction and saw his chest fill with air, his eyes acquire their troubled expression and his mouth converge into a question mark. Then, within a blink, he stretched out his arm, hooked fingers with Chris, and hauled him to his feet.

'Stuntman,' Rick scoffed. 'Fall guy more like.' Then he stuffed his hands into his pocket and continued through the undergrowth.

'Wait up!' Chris's call had no effect. Rick continued walking. As long as he stayed within the grounds, he wouldn't get lost, Chris reasoned, although the stumble had knocked Chris from his path.

He searched the area, eager to regain his bearings. He'd got this far on instinct and luck. He'd seen two or three landmarks further back, but nothing for the last few minutes. He closed his eyes and listened, as he did when he was a boy. In those days, he was so familiar with the castle's grounds, he established which tree he was under by the pitch of its whistle as the wind travelled through its leaves. He never told anyone – they'd have thought him crazy. He held his finger to his lips to concentrate his mind. He heard squeaks and screeches, but nothing identifiable. It was a stupid idea. The trees were old men now, not youthful saplings as they were then. That explained the cacophony of creaks. 'Poor old buggers,' he said, as he opened his eyes.

Then he saw it. The most venerable gentleman of them all.

The great oak.

Chris knew precisely where he was. He crossed the spiny, moss crusted roots that had broken through the ground, placed a hand on the ragged trunk, and searched for the scar he'd inflicted when he'd lost control of his bike and crashed. 'Sorry, old guy. I was young. And a little careless.'

The words triggered visions of Todd disregarding his warnings to take it easy, scrambling his motorbike across the dry land of the ranch, and wheel spinning dust over the cars. He was fearless, like Chris.

Scrunching his eyes shut again, Chris held onto the oak. Its silent support gave him the strength to deter the advancing flashback. He pushed the images away, inhaled the fresh, earthy scent of the tree, and grounded himself. 'Thanks, old man,' he said, resting his head on the rough bark.

When he opened his eyes, he saw the evidence of his youthful collision – a lesion that had withstood the rigours of age. He scuffed at it with his shoe. The last time he'd seen it, he'd been with Vicky Paveley. Glad to have another picture in his mind, he carried on with the thought. 'Vicky Paveley. Do you remember her? I brought her to meet you. We lay on the ground and used you as a headboard.' *Innocent times.* 'Then we went to the beach …' He traced the outline of the laceration with his index finger. 'I hadn't meant to fall in love with her. It was a real wrench when I left for America.'

His journey from teenager to man was accelerated by the trill of his phone. Tommy's text tone. 'Containers here,' the message read.

'Our stuff's arrived,' Chris said to Rick, who had retraced his footsteps and was now examining the bark of the old oak. 'Coming?'

Rick stepped away from the tree and shook his head. 'Gonna find the beach.'

'On your own?'

'I guess.'

No. That wasn't the idea. They were meant to do it together. Chris berated himself. It was his suggestion to poke around the woods, and it must have taken all the courage and enthusiasm Rick could muster to agree to tag along. 'Ah, sod it. The unpacking can wait. Let's find that beach.' Chris trusted Tommy not to open the box marked *Private*.

Victoria spent five minutes wrapped in her father's arms. It was healing – a sensation she didn't expect. She couldn't recall when she was last held that long.

Calm, and with her emotions in check, she was able to speak again. 'Can we talk about something else for a while? Tell me about your lady friend.'

Frank loosened his hold, and cleared his throat. 'Her name's Olivia DeVere. She's an artist.' He paused. 'She runs Chiswell Crafts.'

Victoria pulled away and eyed her dad. 'Well, that explains your reticence to chat about the art shop.'

'Craft centre,' Frank corrected. 'It wasn't reticence. It wasn't the right time to engage in the subject. I'm not sure now is the right time, but since we're having a half hour of honesty, I'll indulge you.' He smiled. 'She's nothing like your mother.'

'Mum was a one-off.' Victoria scaled the ladder-less bed, leaned against the wall, and invited her father aboard. He declined.

'The same could be said for Olivia.'

'Do I get to meet her?'

'Would you like to?'

'Of course. She's the first woman in your life in eight years. I want to know what she's got that reeled you in.' Victoria pointed to the window. 'Apart from a great view.'

'That was top of my list.' Frank laughed. 'It's early days, but ...'

'Are you happy?' Victoria jumped down and landed beside him.

'Are you?' Frank's brow wrinkled.

'I asked first, Dad.'

His face lifted and exuded joy. 'The happiest I've been in a long time.'

Victoria threw her arms out and pulled him into a tight hug. 'If she makes you happy, then what more can you possibly want?'

He grinned and repaid the squeeze. 'I wasn't sure how you'd take it.'

'I appreciate you thinking of me, but this is your life. You didn't interfere when I married Ben.'

'I wish I had.'

They separated from the hug, but clung to each other's arms.

'Well, one day, I might learn from my mistakes,' Victoria said.

Her dad smiled. 'We're never too old to ask for help. Or listen to our elders.' He winked as they relinquished their hold of one another. 'I'm not sure Seth will understand about Olivia. Do we tell him?'

Victoria bit down on her bottom lip. 'Let's play it by ear.' It sounded like a sensible course of action.

With her father at the craft shop, and Seth still playing in the bathroom, Victoria stole five minutes for herself. She climbed back onto the bed and surveyed the autumnal seascape. No matter what the time of year, it was awe-inspiring. In the summer, it had the blue of lapis lazuli, and today it was the colour of green tourmaline crystal.

In her youth she'd spent hour upon hour walking the

coastline, exploring the coves and searching for smugglers' caves. Wherever she went, the sea stayed with her. She'd forgotten how much it meant to her. Where had that sense of wonder gone? At some point, she'd become clinical, cynical and sterile.

She propped herself against the woodchipped wall, and appreciated the vista. She'd spent a happy, carefree summer on Chesil Beach when she was eighteen. She'd passed her exams, arranged a place at college, and was in love with Chris Frampton. For six weeks they lived on that beach, skimming stones, jumping waves, and kissing. He was her first love, and she'd fallen in the way only a teenager could, expecting they'd be together forever.

On that beach, buried beneath the stones, was her soul.

She pinpointed the exact spot from her window.

A knock sounded on the front door and she hopped down from the bed, grabbed her coat, and ran down the stairs. She greeted her dad in the cold hallway.

'Victoria, this is Olivia DeVere.' Frank held open the front door. 'Olivia, meet my oldest daughter, Victoria Noble.'

The woman's smile alone was enough to warm Victoria. She shook Olivia's paint-splattered hand, and discreetly studied her. Her blonde hair was piled into a topknot, she wore very little make-up, and her clothes had a life of their own. Underneath an open green ranger's mac, she wore a thin, white cotton blouse partially covered by a heavy, paisley waistcoat in varying shades of brown, and a pair of red Dr Martens were framed by an ankle length fawn suede skirt. The elegant name did not match the jumble of clothes heaped around the rotund form.

'Lovely to meet you, Olivia. How's the craft business?'

Olivia smiled. 'Your dad was my sole customer, and not only did he not buy anything, he gave me a reason to shut up shop.'

They regarded one another. Olivia's Caribbean-blue eyes, although weathered at the corners, radiated the energy of a twenty-year-old.

Victoria blinked. 'I'll fetch my son.' As she turned to climb upstairs, Seth emerged and ran down, stopping in front of Olivia.

'Hello, young man. You must be Seth. Your granddad's told me all about you.'

Victoria looked from the woman, who was too well informed for comfort, to Seth, who was prone to act up at any moment.

'Right,' said Frank, stepping between them all and rubbing his hands. 'Let's go looking for pirates.' He pulled Seth's coat together, threaded the rugby-shaped buttons through their loops, and gave a gentle squeeze to the boy's cheek. 'Be good.'

Seth dashed from the house and ran up and down the pavement, thrusting an air sword at imaginary adversaries. The adults filtered outside one-by-one.

The sun was working hard, trying its level best to warm the air, but the sea breeze was still creating a nip. Victoria buttoned up her jacket and pushed her hands into her pockets. There was no point offering them to Seth. She'd tried that before and was given such a display of disdain that she'd stored the image away as a prompt to limit public demonstrations of affection.

'He's full of energy,' Olivia remarked. 'I love to see youngsters out in the fresh air. Too many of them are stuck indoors on those wretched computers.'

'Messing about on social media pages? Messaging their friends as opposed to ringing them? That sort of thing?' Victoria held her breath waiting for a reply.

'Exactly.' Olivia laughed, and threaded an arm through Victoria's. 'You're very serious. Your dad's told me all about

EweSpeak and how much of a whizz on the computers you are. I bleat.' She smiled. 'Tell me about yourself while we walk.'

Her voice was undemanding, but her hold was firm. Victoria tried, but failed to withdraw from the close contact. She used her free arm to indicate to Seth he should walk alongside, but he charged ahead. 'Next right,' she shouted, and he vanished around the corner.

The three adults walked a little way up the pavement, entered an alleyway and ambled towards the beach. Seth was already on the stones and skipping close to the water's edge.

'Step back from there. I don't have a change of clothes for you.' Again, Victoria was ignored by her son as he dared the sea to soak him. She shook her head, her attention drawn to the sea defences – gabion baskets – wire cages filled with pebbles. They were larger than she remembered. 'Have these houses flooded recently?'

'Not since I've been here,' Olivia said. 'There's been plenty of trouble in the past, but I'm led to believe that's been dealt with. Why?'

'My cottage is damp. It smells musty.' With a quick tug, she finally freed her arm from Olivia's and touched the cold, metallic structure. Her back tingled as a memory transferred from her fingertips to her core – Chris's weight pushing her against the wall, as he kissed her. 'These are sturdy enough,' she said, shaking the chill from her spine.

'Perhaps your bath's leaked.'

'Maybe.' Something else to patch up. The list went from broken pipes to family relationships. Talk about diverse. 'Got a lot to repair,' Victoria said, pushing her feet into the pebbles. She tried a smile, failed, and then continued on her way. 'So, how did you and Dad meet?'

'He's not told you?' Olivia fell into her stride. 'The poor

old soul was having a quiet drink at the Harbour Inn when I collared him. Such a handsome man, I was compelled to sketch him.'

Frank looked over his shoulder. 'I'm a model now.' He grinned.

Olivia turned her head towards Victoria. 'He won't agree to pose nude, though. I'd love to sculpt him.'

Victoria's eyes flashed from Olivia, to Frank, and then to Seth, who was too busy chasing waves to catch the conversation. Thank goodness for small mercies. 'I'm not sure how I should respond,' she said, keeping her eyes on her son.

'Say whatever springs to mind. Be spontaneous,' Olivia said.

Victoria cocked a brow at her neighbour. 'I tried spontaneity and this is where it's left me.' Her arm received a squeeze.

'I think you should try again. It's good for the soul.'

The soul I've buried back there. Victoria's muscles tensed. She was thinking too much to be spontaneous. She made a conscious effort to drop her shoulders and straighten her back. She'd spent so many years hunched over a computer, she'd lost all sense of poise. From the corner of her eye, she caught Olivia doing the same.

'Well, that helps your breathing,' the older lady said, sounding surprised. 'I should spend less time at my potter's wheel and more time walking. Right. You've had long enough to think of something spontaneous. What have you got?'

Victoria cringed. As much as she was warming to Olivia, she froze under the spotlight, and there was no escape. Olivia's eyes tracked her. Victoria loosened the top of her jacket, and the cold air rushed for her neck, its icy licks curling around. That was better, but she needed to bring the moment to a close. 'I have nothing.'

'Then I have a question. Does Seth always ignore you?'

Taken aback by the sudden change of topic, Victoria struggled to reply. She was duty-bound to take offence and use a 'How dare you?' tone, but the word 'Yes' was flashing behind her eyes like a jackpot winner alert. She didn't answer.

'I have another question, then,' Olivia continued. 'For no reason other than to settle my curiosity, tell me why you're considering living at the cottage.' She came to a standstill. 'You have the means to buy from new.'

Victoria gazed at the horizon. It was still, straight and defining. 'I like it,' she said. 'It's home.' She assumed her reply wasn't adequate enough to satisfy Olivia, but to her surprise, her neighbour didn't follow through.

'Seth's going to have wet feet.'

Victoria nodded.

'I love his hair. Curls on a boy are gorgeous. And what long lashes he has too. He'll have girls fighting over him.' Olivia puckered her lips. 'There may be trouble ahead.'

'Thanks for the warning.' Girlfriends? Good Lord, Victoria couldn't think beyond how to get tea down him, let alone contemplate his future love life.

'If he's anything like his Pops, he'll have women falling at his feet.'

Victoria caught her father and Olivia exchange a glance. 'How many women have you got on the go, Dad?' The words were out before Victoria had time to edit herself. She covered her mouth with her hand to stop the giggles from escaping. The look on her dad's face was priceless. It measured somewhere between shock and delight.

Olivia was the first to laugh out loud. 'Now, that's spontaneity,' she said. 'I told you it was good for you.'

The amiability of the moment enveloped Victoria and she too laughed. Was it possible her soul wasn't weighed down by seventeen years' worth of Chesil Beach pebbles? The idea that she could let her youth go was liberating. For too many years she'd towed it behind her like an old comforter – something familiar to cling to when times got rough. She was imagining burying it at sea when Olivia's voice drifted in.

'Have you eaten?'

Victoria's mind returned to dry land with a growl of her stomach. 'No, I haven't.'

'Harbour Inn it is,' said Frank, taking Seth by the hand. 'Inside or outside table?'

'I'd rather go in.' Victoria rubbed her hands together, before jamming them into her jacket pocket. 'I'm not used to all this fresh air.'

'You can't beat a decent sea breeze.' Olivia shuffled in the stones until she was facing the sea, held out her upturned palms, and closed her eyes. 'Try it, Victoria. Let the wind run through you. It's a wonderful feeling.'

This woman is as mad as a box of frogs. Victoria caught Olivia peeping at her. What the woman conveyed with one eye was astounding. Scary too. Victoria yanked her hands from her pockets and exposed her palms to the breeze.

'Close your eyes,' Olivia said. 'Your dad's got Seth, and apart from us, the beach is empty. Come on. It doesn't cost a thing.'

'Except my dignity,' Victoria grumbled.

'Apart from that.' Olivia lowered her arms and looked at Victoria. 'Trust me. It'll blow away those stuffy London blues. You'd pay a fortune in the City for this type of treatment.'

'Cruelty, you mean.'

Olivia laughed. 'I knew you had a sense of humour. See, it's working already. Now, close your eyes and give yourself to the breeze. Let go. And if nothing else, take joy in the knowledge it's free. Like all the best things in life.' With her smile gradually fading, Olivia followed her own instructions.

The woman is indomitable, Victoria thought, as she closed her eyes. That was a good trait. Perhaps some of it would blow across to her. She braced herself for the onslaught of the easterly, which, when it hit, took away her breath. It cut through her, but it was invigorating.

Then the sounds found a way in. The cacophony of gulls, the chinking of the pebbles, the waves ... The waves reminded her of something. Their rhythm, the gentle shush as they swayed along the shore ... A heartbeat. An unborn baby's heartbeat.

'What are you doing?'

Victoria opened her eyes to find Seth staring at her.

'You look silly,' he said.

'Your mum may look silly, young man, but I bet she feels fantastic.' Olivia, so visibly refreshed by the experience, manoeuvred Seth into position and told him to close his eyes.

Victoria watched on, astonished with his compliance.

'When I don't know how to tell people I'm frightened, or sad, or angry, I come down here and let the wind and the sea work their magic.'

Seth, his eyes pinging open, tilted back his head. 'How?'

'Sometimes I scream really loudly. Nobody hears because the wind carries it out to sea.'

'Do you say bad words? She said shit.'

He pointed to Victoria, who nodded. Denial was futile.

Olivia raised a hand to her mouth, but it didn't conceal her smile. 'We all say stuff we shouldn't, and yes, even I swear, but the wind is very forgiving.'

'And healing,' Frank chipped in.

'And free,' Olivia said, turning to Victoria.

'Like all the best things in life.' Victoria smiled. *Indomitable and persistent.* 'I bet lunch costs though.'

The Harbour Inn wasn't far, and at Olivia's insistence that fresh air was good for the soul, and despite Victoria's protestations, the women settled at a table fronting onto the pebbled beach. As Frank took Seth by the hand and led him into the building, Victoria was unnerved by Olivia's expectant look. Questions were about to be asked. Perhaps she should get in first. Use diversionary tactics. 'Have you always run your own business, Olivia?'

'Lord, no. This is my pay-off for years of working in schools.'

Now the display with Seth made sense. 'A teacher?' Victoria ventured.

'Yes. From when I left university until I retired three years ago.'

A woman with staying power. 'What did you teach?'

'Children.' Olivia chortled and then adopted a serious expression. 'Art and design, mostly. Sometimes music. Both together on occasion. They're great forms of self-expression, don't you think?'

'If that's your thing,' Victoria said, suppressing a pout. 'It's never worked for me.'

'And yet EweSpeak began as a fan site for Annabel Lamb.' Olivia stared out to sea.

Victoria twisted in her seat so she was facing her. 'You're very well-informed. Did Dad tell you about Annabel?'

'Look, he's very proud of both you and your sister, but he hasn't a clue about your business. I searched on the Internet and found an interview Juliette had given after Annabel won UK Starz.' She met Victoria's eyes. 'I couldn't find much about you. It's all Juliette.'

'That's how we like it,' Victoria said. 'Juliette's happy in the limelight. I'd rather stay out of it.' Perhaps Olivia would take the hint and cease the interrogation.

'Well, how you've managed that I'll never know, but I'm impressed with how you've built the company. A fun project to support a local girl in a national singing competition to global domination.'

Victoria tutted. 'It's hardly global, but yes, when Annabel won the competition she and EweSpeak did very well out of it. When the media wanted to see the face behind the success, we gave them Juliette's. She was expecting her first son at the time. For a while, it was complete madness.'

'EweSpeak or the pregnancy?'

Interesting question. 'I meant the business, but, yes, in my experience, pregnancy is madness too.'

'You weren't prepared?'

'I was *so* not ready for children.'

'I meant for the fame and fortune that EweSpeak brought, but now's a good time to speak about Seth. May I be direct?'

What could Victoria say? She'd raised the subject herself. Besides, she had the feeling *no* wouldn't work with Olivia. 'Go on.'

'Does he always battle for control?'

Victoria hadn't considered that the knocks, bangs and arguments were about seizing power. She assumed Seth was acting up or attention seeking. She swallowed. 'We fight. No. That's not right. He fights. I stand and take it.' The instant the words were out, the bruise on her temple throbbed. She massaged it. Thank goodness the wind was blowing in her face, otherwise Olivia might mistake her tears for those of sorrow. She leaned back, as the older lady zoomed in for a closer inspection.

'Did you want children?'

'No.' The guilt of answering the question honestly swirled in Victoria's gut. 'But not once did I say I wished Seth wasn't here.'

'Did you think it?'

Victoria resigned herself to what she deemed the inevitable and decided to continue speaking openly. It was possible the eccentric, wise old teacher would have a solution to her problem. 'Maybe. I don't recall. My emotions were all over the place. I was laughing one minute and crying the next. It was horrible. I didn't enjoy pregnancy, the birth was worse than I ever imagined, and I resented my body for having a mind of its own. I had no control. The baby cried, my breasts leaked, and everyone insisted I tried feeding him. I had midwives grabbing at me, manhandling me, attaching this child to me like I was a machine. When you're told it's best for the baby and the nurses look down their noses at you because you've asked for formula and a bottle, and when you never planned to be sitting, ripped, stitched and sore in the maternity wing of the local hospital, things get crazy. I was crazy. And then I bled for six weeks. It was sheer misery and I wanted my life back.'

Victoria came to an abrupt halt, astounded by her own outpour. 'I'm sorry. I had no idea I was going to say that.' She stopped pretending the wind was causing the tears, pulled a tissue from her pocket and dabbed her eyes. 'No one listened to me back then. It was so hard.'

Olivia smiled kindly. 'Expectations are high, Victoria. The world assumes you'll fall in love with your child the minute you lay eyes upon him. We're not all programmed that way. Love can take time. And it needs nurturing.' She patted her heart. 'Tell me more. Your dad says you returned to work immediately.'

Victoria drummed her fingers on the slatted surface of the table. 'I did. Ben, my then-husband, and I agreed I'd work and he'd be the baby's main carer, but being a father wasn't manly enough for him. He left when Seth was two months old.'

'Did you stop working?'

'No.' Victoria stilled her hands. 'I employed nannies. A day one to start with, but it wasn't enough. Seth cried twenty-four seven, and I was struggling. I don't need much sleep, but he had me up so many times I didn't know what day of the week it was. In the end, I employed a night nanny, too.'

'For how long?' Olivia, who was now sitting side-saddle, crossed her legs.

'Until he was out of nappies. The day nanny still comes. He gets on with the current lady.' Victoria released a great, long breath. 'It's taken five agencies to find the right match.'

'Did the others provide inadequate care?'

'Now, there's a question.' Victoria scooped back her wavy locks. 'Yes.'

'So you thought you could do a better job?' Olivia's eyebrows knitted together.

Victoria laughed. 'No. I never thought that. I thought they should.'

Olivia scanned the pub door. 'The boys will be out in a minute, and I want to get this straight in my head.' She uncrossed her legs, stretched them and rotated her ankles. 'You and Seth didn't bond, his main carer left early on in his life, and he's had an interruption of care every few months since he can remember. That's right, isn't it?'

Victoria assumed a head in hand pose; that way she avoided Olivia's stony expression, and took the weight off her neck, as its sinews and muscles strained under the stress of the inquisition. 'Yes,' she mumbled. 'That's right. Can we just agree I'm a terrible mother and move on?'

'We could, but it wouldn't help. Let me think for a moment.'

Victoria sat upright. What was there to think about? She was about to speak when her dad and son emerged from the pub.

'Want to see the specials board, ladies?' Frank called.

Both shook their heads. The topic of conversation had eaten away at Victoria's appetite. 'Just a lemonade please, Dad.'

'Cod and chips.' Olivia smiled as she looked up and waved the boys back into the pub. 'They'll only be a minute, so I'll be quick. When I was teaching I had a child not dissimilar to Seth. He was adopted, been through the care system, fostered. He was troubled. He attached to strangers far too easily, and was violent towards his parents.'

'But Seth's mine. I most definitely gave birth to him.' Victoria leaned back a little. 'How is this relevant?'

Olivia gestured for Victoria to keep silent. 'I'm no expert, but it's possible Seth has a condition known as child attachment disorder.'

'He has a disorder? It has a name?'

'Google it. Find some forums with people who have first-hand experience.'

The conversation ceased as the pub door swung open and Seth, followed by Frank balancing a tray of drinks in one hand, trotted to the table.

Victoria returned to her head in hands pose, trying to absorb the last few minutes. *Child attachment disorder?* As soon as she had a quiet half hour, she'd research it. If there was something in there that would help her connect with Seth, she'd give it a go. She looked up, and mouthed *thank you* to Olivia.

Frank directed Seth to Victoria. 'Sit next to your mum, then.'

Victoria saw her son push against her father's hand.

'Well, at the very least, pass her this drink, please?' Frank attempted to hand Seth the glass of lemonade.

'Dad. Don't.'

'See,' said Seth, with an air of triumph. 'She doesn't want me to.'

'That's not what I said. I'd love you to sit next to me.' Victoria opened her arms out in welcome.

'Fibber.' Seth knocked the glass from Frank's hand and shoved hard at the table. It didn't move. He slapped his tiny hands down and screamed. 'I don't want to be here. I don't want to sit next to her and I don't want to pass no sodding drink. It's all crap. She's crap and I hate her.' He dodged Frank's grip and ran a few yards down the beach, scattering shingle in all directions. 'I hate it here and it's her fault.' He pointed a quivering finger at Victoria. 'I wish she was dead.' He whirled round and ran.

Victoria left her seat like an ejected pilot, lost her footing on the loose pebbles, fell and cracked her knee on the bench. She winced with the pain, but had no time to attend to the injury. She scrabbled to her feet and hobbled after her son. 'Seth! Come back!' It was a pointless attempt to stop him in his tracks. She knew he would keep going. He wanted to be as far away from her as possible. He was fast, and the distance between them was growing, and nothing Victoria did seemed to close the gap.

That summed up their entire relationship.

With the beach coming to a natural end at the foot of a large cliff, and with darts of pain firing along the length of her leg, Victoria slowed down. Seth had nowhere to go, unless he took a swim, and that wasn't going to happen. It wasn't until he came to a halt at the foot of the imposing cliff that he bothered to see who was after him. Victoria bent over, rubbed her leg, and used the time to catch her breath. No need to run now. He wasn't going anywhere.

When she looked up, Seth was disappearing through a cluster of hedges to the left of the rocks. He shot off like a greased weasel.

'God damn it!' Victoria signalled to her father that she was going on, hoping he'd refrain from phoning the police.

She'd deal with this. Seth wasn't missing and he was not a runaway. He was just a boy with a problem. A problem Victoria didn't yet understand.

Running in the cold wind with tears in her eyes hurt more than the pocket explosions in her knee. She mopped her face with her sleeve.

As she reached the foot of the grassy slope, she recognised where the hedge backed onto. It was a way in to Hope Cove Castle. She had no idea if the property was occupied, but at least Seth would be safe within the grounds.

She clambered up the slippery incline and searched for the opening. It wasn't meant for public access. It was a breach in the hedgerow Chris had found in his youth. Victoria had been through it once.

'Where are you?' *Think*. Seth appeared to have gone through the middle, but with her vision distorted by wind and water, Victoria wasn't sure. 'Seth!' She shifted further along the hedgerow, pulling apart spiky sections of privet.

As she rammed her hands into another part of the hedge, she felt it give.

Chapter Seven

'Did you hear that?' Chris strained to see into the darkening forest, and then looked at Rick, who pulled a *what* face. 'I thought I heard someone call.' With Rick unperturbed by the shout, Chris carried on. 'I can't believe we got lost.'

'*You* got lost,' Rick mumbled.

'Okay. In my defence, it was a lifetime ago I was last here. Things have changed.' He brushed his hand against a fern. 'Plants have grown. A lot. I like it.'

'Yeah. It's all right.'

Chris smiled. He didn't mind that Rick had retreated to his word comfort zone; he'd had more from him on this trek than he'd heard in two years. His concerns from yesterday had vanished, and he was confident the move to England was what he and his son needed.

'It's funny to think I was your age when I first came here,' Chris said. 'I'd practise for hours on my bike. Jumps, turns, skidding stops. Then I'd go home and show my dad.' He pointed to his left and then headed in that direction. 'I'd spent years trying to make him proud of me, make him happy, and finally I'd found something that worked. I hadn't realised it wasn't me who'd made him sad. Of course, I understand now. He'd been lost in grief for my mum. Do you remember I told you she died when I was eight? Pneumonia. I can still hear her struggling to breathe.'

Chris looked at Rick, suddenly aware of the delicate turn the conversation had taken. 'Oh, man. I'm sorry. It's too much. Do you want me to stop?' Receiving a muted no, Chris took in a lungful of air, and moved the story on. 'My dad swore he'd never love again, and he didn't. He never got over losing her.'

A silence followed as pictures of Lacey flooded Chris's mind, so real he could smell her fresh, meadow scent, feel the silk of her dress against his arm, and hear her whispered words of devotion. It hurt.

That same pain had destroyed his father and left Chris fighting for his affection.

He couldn't let that happen with Rick. Wouldn't.

'Will you ever get over Mom and Todd?'

Never, Chris wanted to shout, but the uncertainty and pain in Rick's voice choked him. Instead, he grabbed Rick's arm and yanked him into a close bear hug. It had been a long time coming. His tall, lanky teenage son was so small in his arms. So fragile. Like Lacey. 'Never,' Chris finally said. 'And I don't want to. It's hard, but we'll be all right. As long as we're here for each other, we'll get through.'

After a few seconds, Rick pulled away and wiped his hand across his face. 'How did you end up in America?'

For the first time in two years, Chris had made a proper connection with his son. It didn't matter that within a blink of a teary eye it was gone, it was progress, and more than he could have ever wished for so soon after landing in England. He took a deep breath, the damp autumnal air once more returning him to his youth. 'It was your granddad's idea to try Hollywood. Have I not told you that before?'

The blank expression on Rick's wet face indicated not.

'Yeah. I was nineteen when he suggested I apply for summer work in the US. He said I could spend my spare time checking out film studios and acting courses, and maybe swap my university course for something in that field. Did I mention I was on a gap year?'

Rick shook his head.

'I was all set to go to Keele, that's in this country, but Dad was so insistent I make a career out of my bike skills, and America was the place to make it big, I got on board.' It was another time in Chris's life he recalled with twenty-twenty vision. 'He even said a good-looking lad like me should have no trouble lining up acting jobs.' Chris smiled. It wasn't often he received compliments from his father. 'Anyway, I looked into the holiday work, filled out some forms, had an interview with a very snooty woman, and attended something they called *orientation*.'

'Where were you going? Kennedy Space Center?'

Chris had Rick's full attention.

'Ha! Not quite. I'd applied to do some odd job work at a small film studio, and they accepted me, promising they'd help me with acting classes. They even said if things worked out, they'd sponsor my university course. It was unbelievable.'

Rick was nodding. 'You must have been, like, so excited.'

'Oh, yeah. It was a big deal.'

'And you went? Just like that? And met Mom and Tommy?'

Chris reflected for a moment. He hadn't told Rick the whole story, about how he'd fallen in love with Vicky Paveley weeks before he was due to head out, how the thought of leaving her crippled him, how he'd decided *not* to go to America. He stopped short of explaining how his father pushed ahead anyway, selling his car and his shares to finance the trip, how it was presented as a fait accompli, with no turning back.

And there was no way Chris was going to share private details with his son about his last night with Vicky, when they'd walked barefoot across the pebbles of Chesil, pressed up against the defences, and stolen kisses from one another. They'd made love, there and then. In the sea. It was their first and last time together.

That was not a story to share with Rick.

'Yeah. I went. Just like that.' Chris's heart pumped guilt through his veins. Why, at that moment, had his mind undressed Vicky and planted her on that beach? The beach he was about to show his son. 'I think we should head back,' he said. 'Tommy will have sorted something to eat. We'll find the trail tomorrow.' Desperate to move away from the area, he took several large strides in the direction from which they'd come. He assumed Rick was following, but when he checked over his shoulder, there was nothing but a wintry jungle. 'Rick?' he called. 'Are you coming?' He strained to hear the reply.

'Later.'

Much to the relief of his pride, Chris found his way home without trouble, memorising the route for the next attempt at finding the hidden entrance. As he left the cover of the wood, the cold wind bit into him, carrying the sound of men's voices on its icy tail.

Chris walked around the side of the castle onto the front drive, where two large container lorries were now stationed. A stream of workers clad in black boots and orange aprons, scurried back and forth, filling Chris's new home with his old things.

'Mr Frampton. What a pleasure to meet you. I'm a huge fan of your films. I'm one of your flock on EweSpeak.' The man, wearing brown overalls, a flat cap, and fingerless gloves, approached Chris, hand extended.

Chris gave it a firm shake. 'Thanks. You're the foreman?'

The man waved his clipboard. 'I am. And may I say how very sorry I am about the loss of your family. I can't imagine what you must have gone through. How is your son?'

'He's fine, thanks.' The foreman meant well, but Chris was in no mood for social chit-chat, and he certainly wasn't about to discuss Rick. 'Are you done here?'

The man sucked air through his teeth. 'We'll be another couple of hours yet, Mr Frampton. We've finished upstairs, and we've made a start on the kitchen. Oh, and your office is almost sorted. Mr Stone took care of it.'

Chris didn't wait to hear more. He ran towards the entrance, gravel exploding from under his feet, squeezed past the wall unit in the hallway, and headed for the office. If his box was already there, he needed to safeguard it.

He burst into the room. Tommy was hunched over the large leather-inset desk. There was no sign of the cardboard container.

'You all right, mate?' Chris edged closer to Tommy. Something was wrong. It was rare to find his friend still. 'Hard day?'

Tommy pushed himself upright. 'Unbelievable.'

Even with the distance of the room between them, Chris could see the tension in Tommy's jaw. Something was most definitely wrong. Chris's stomach lurched. Where was that box? He scanned the area once more.

'Looking for something?' Tommy bent below the level of the desk. A second later, his head appeared, followed by his hands, presenting the innocuous brown box. Its open flaps increased its height by another foot. He dropped it onto the green leather. 'This, perhaps?'

'There it is.' Chris forced a smile and kept his tone casual. 'You're unpacking?'

'Thought I'd make a start.'

'Well, I'll sort that one.' Chris moved closer to his target and reached out. Tommy shoved it towards him. Chris peered inside. The files were in disarray. Was that the result of the journey, or had Tommy nosed through them? He picked up the top sheet. It was Lacey's treatment record. That answered his question. As did the hate in Tommy's eyes. 'You read this?'

Tommy nodded. 'It took me a moment to make sense of it, but I've got it now.' He slammed his fist against the desk. 'You've kept this from me all this time. That letter goes back seventeen years.' He snatched the report from Chris's hands. 'HIV?'

'Keep your voice down.' Chris knocked the tabs on the box closed, and stabbed at the 'Private' sign. 'What the hell were you doing opening it?'

'Is that the best you can do?' Tommy shook his head and sniffed. 'Unbelievable. Fucking unbelievable. I loved Lacey.' He paused. 'She was my friend.'

'She was my wife!'

Silence.

Tommy sneered. 'I deserved to know.'

Chris raised a clenched fist, storing his ferocity within. 'Why? Scared you'd have caught something?'

Tommy laughed, threw the papers towards the box and stepped out from behind the desk. He made a beeline for the door. 'I can't believe you kept it from me.'

Chris raced across the room. 'It was private. Lacey didn't want anyone to know. We paid a lot of money to keep it that way. Can you imagine the fallout if it had been made public?' He saw Tommy's head dip.

'So, you didn't trust me. That's what it boils down to.' Tommy looked up. 'I'm the boys' godfather. When Lacey was laid up from her Caesarean, I took my turn at night feeds and nappy changes. To this day I remember how to make up formula. I used to think, *I'll be doing that for my boy, soon*. But it never happened, because I devoted myself to looking after you and your sodding career. I was so relieved when Lacey quit the porn scene. I worried about her. I knew there were unscrupulous directors out there. I knew there were careless actors. Is that how it happened? Was she infected by a careless actor?'

Everything Tommy said was true. Chris had no comeback. He gave a small nod and retreated behind his desk. 'I couldn't tell you. It wasn't my decision.' He clasped the cardboard box to him, finding comfort in the act. 'This will remain between us, won't it?'

'Don't count on it.'

Chris strained against every sinew in his body to resist unleashing his fury. 'This stuff is private. It has nothing to do with you.' He was close to lashing out, but the moment was diffused by the arrival of a removal man carrying a leather executive's chair.

'In here, Guv?'

'Yes. That's fine.' Chris tracked the man as he left. He turned to Tommy. 'You have no right.'

'Does Rick know?'

Chris snorted. 'Of course not. And for now that's how it's going to stay. He's got enough to deal with.'

Tommy's brow lifted. 'He deserves to know. You should tell him. Like you should have told me.'

With that he left, slamming shut the door.

It took a few minutes before Victoria's eyes adjusted to the gloom and density of Hope Cove grounds. She'd been here when she was eighteen. Chris had shown her, the day before he left for Hollywood.

'Snap out of it,' she said, aware her mind was travelling down a dead end.

Seth hadn't replied to her calls. It was his way of punishing her. For everything. 'Where are you?' There was little chance he was hiding in the undergrowth. He was a runner – his purpose was to get away from Victoria, as far as possible. It was an interesting thought when paired with her next; that she had been the one who put the distance between them.

She arrived at a small glade, and examined it for evidence of Seth's journey. There was nothing other than a sense of familiarity. If she was right, there was a great oak nearby. It would be enormous now. She continued on her course until the tree loomed into view. Its top was lost – out of sight, towering over everything else in the grounds.

'Which land is up there, today?' Victoria asked, a memory of her favourite childhood book flashing through her mind. 'Something far away.' She ran her hand along the greying bark. 'Well, you've withstood the test of time. I wish I'd aged as well.'

'What's your dad called?'

Victoria stepped out from behind the tree. There was no one there. She definitely heard a voice. It wasn't soprano Seth's. This was more like an adolescent's – a voice on its gravelly passage to manhood. And American. She was about to call when a familiar, high-pitched voice replied.

'I don't have a dad.'

'Huh. I don't have a mom. She died. Dad wants me to talk about it, but I wanna be left alone. Keep her in my head, you know?'

'I have Cerys. She's my nanny.'

'You mean, like, your mom's mom?'

There was a silence. 'I don't know.'

'Does she live with your grandpa?'

'No. My granddad is called Pops. He has Livia. She's very old.' Another pause. 'Cerys's face isn't creased like Livia's, and her hair isn't crunchy.'

'Cerys is younger. Cool.'

Prompted by the 'crunchy' remark, Victoria crushed her curls in her hand. When she released them, they bounced back into shape. 'I possess young hair.' At last, something in its favour. She continued to eavesdrop.

'Cerys takes me to school, or to the shops to buy shoes. Sometimes we play in the park. I like Cerys.'

'Yeah. She sounds nice. What about your mom?'

Whoever the young lad was, Seth was happy chatting with him, and undetected, Victoria could learn more in the next two minutes than she would in a lifetime. The risk was that she wouldn't like Seth's answer. The delay of indecision took the power from her.

'She doesn't like me.'

Victoria fell against the oak, as the air was sucked from her. She forced herself to inhale, and counted to three before letting it out. With her head spinning and her field of vision constricting, she slithered down the rough trunk until her bottom hit the ground. She brought her knees to her chest, and rested her forehead upon them.

'Man. That sucks.' The American.

'I'm bad. I get cross. She shouts at me and I throw things,' Seth said.

Not ready to stand, Victoria raised her head and opened her mouth, hoping words and not vomit would pour out. She wanted to yell, 'It's not your fault. I do love you', but her voice was that of nightmares – snatched by the wind, and sacrificed to the universe. She'd heard enough and was desperate to reveal herself, but unable to move or speak, she was forced to hear the conversation play out.

'You throw things at your mom?' The American's shock was evident by the rise of his vocal pitch.

'Sometimes. You talk funny.'

'So do you.'

With a throat dry from forced gasps of air, Victoria swallowed, wincing as her saliva, like acid, burned its way down.

'Your voice is squeaky,' Seth said. 'And you say "mom".'

The older boy laughed. 'You think my voice is squeaky? Heard yourself, lately? And you say "mum".'

'I don't.'

'Seriously? Well, what do you say? What do you call her?'

Victoria imagined the look of scorn on Seth's face.

'Her name is Victoria, but I don't call her anything.'

'Listen … what did you say your name is?'

'Seth.'

'Listen, Seth, you only get one mom. You need to look after her. I promise you'll miss her when she's gone.' The American's words were halted by the ringing of a mobile. 'I gotta go. Dad says lunch is ready. You should get home. Do you know your way?'

'Yes. Can I come tomorrow?'

'Yeah. All right.'

Nothing further was said.

Giving herself time to recover, Victoria continued resting against the tree. Seth wasn't that far away, and the likelihood was he would retrace his steps and walk right past her. Cerys had told her he had an uncanny knack for remembering routes.

As she hauled herself to her feet, he wandered into view. He stopped and appeared to analyse the situation. 'Are you lost?' he said.

What a question. Victoria was floundering in an ocean of unknowns. 'A little,' she said. 'What about you?'

Seth shook his head. 'Shall I show you the way?'

Please, God, yes. If He did exist, He wouldn't mind a non-believer asking for help, would He? She smiled. 'I'd appreciate that. Thank you.' She considered offering her hand, but Seth was already on the march home, clearly confident of the route. 'Who was the boy you were talking to?'

Without missing a beat, Seth said, 'Rick. He talks funny and he says his dad's famous, like those men on TV.'

Victoria stiffened. On the rare occasion when Seth had decided to converse with her, his words struck her dumb.

The man she thought she would never see again was back.

With her thoughts centred on Chris Frampton, and Seth running most of the way, the walk to the pub took less time than Victoria would have liked. She had plenty to occupy her mind.

Unless Rick was visiting his father's old stomping ground, his presence in the wood suggested the Framptons were living at Hope Cove Castle. As the crow flew, that was less than a mile away from Victoria's cottage. The probability of running into Chris was unnervingly high.

She was convinced she would unleash years of hurt and resentment the moment she saw him. What he did to her the night before he left for LA was unforgivable. He had ruined her, body and mind. Because of him, she'd thrown herself into her business. Because of him, she had a failed marriage, and a child she didn't know how to love. Chris's actions had stunted Victoria's emotional growth and stolen her innocence.

As she approached the inn, she emitted a faltering sigh. She was being unfair. It wasn't all Chris's fault. She shouldn't have allowed him to take advantage of her, but at eighteen, she was naïve, and in love. She thought they were destined to be together forever.

And what about Lacey's history? She couldn't let on that she knew. She had paid a lot of money to keep those details from surfacing. If the board had wind of Lacey's blue movie career and HIV, they'd have insisted EweSpeak broke the story. Victoria didn't want that. At the time, she'd kidded herself it was to avoid tarring EweSpeak with a bad name, but in reality, she did it to avoid causing Chris further pain and anguish.

That didn't mean she'd forgiven him for using her.

This was not the new beginning she had in mind.

She discharged a small, frustrated scream, and the wind whipped it out to sea. To her surprise, it was good, and what felt like a sheepshank knot in her stomach uncoiled. The second of the day. Maybe there was something to Olivia's method of letting go.

In that short journey from the wood to the pub, Victoria had covered a lot of ground.

The hugs Frank and Olivia bestowed upon Seth, which he accepted with little resistance, took the sting out of Victoria's eyes.

'Don't reprimand him,' Olivia whispered. 'Trust me on this.' She turned to Seth. 'We're so pleased you came back. We waited right here for you.' She crouched to his level, and took his hands. 'We will always be around for you, and you can talk to us anytime.' Her next few words were spoken directly into his ear, which made him giggle. Olivia unfurled. 'Right. I'm jolly well starving. Let's get that *very* late lunch, and afterwards, you can come and look round my shop and choose something to take home.'

As Victoria drove a sleeping Seth and her father home, she reflected on the day. There was nothing she could do about Chris Frampton, and as much as she wanted to avoid him, there was a small chance seeing him would bring closure. It was a scary thought, but if, or more likely, when they met, she'd have to wing it. Until then, it was pointless worrying. Juliette would be proud of her.

That brought Victoria to thinking about EweSpeak. She had promised her sister she would return and fight the new proposals, which she had every intention of doing, but the desire to be in charge had weakened. She didn't need the hassle, and she had more money than she knew what to do with, besides, following the visit to Chiswell Crafts, Olivia's declaration that the best things in life were free was firmly implanted in Victoria's brain.

The shop was jam-packed with exquisite works of art that Olivia had created from beach booty – driftwood, defunct fishing nets, shells, gulls' feathers. She sold the finished articles for very little profit, and yet lived a life full of riches.

The common perception was money made life easier. Hard, cold cash bought freedom, and yet it was a protector and a guardian, and an excellent cushion when things got too much. For Victoria, it bought silence, nannies, and the luxury of never saying no. It alleviated the burden of responsibility. Her problems were remedied by throwing coins at them. Overflowing treasure chests had been cast in Seth's direction.

Victoria pulled up at a red light, the houses to the side shielding the car from the sun. The inside temperature plummeted and the light dimmed. She rubbed her hands together. 'Stop hiding behind things,' she muttered, keen to move out of the gloom and return to the warmth.

'What was that?' Frank wriggled in his seat, settling in an upright position. 'You're hiding behind things? Like what?'

'Not me. The sun. It's disappeared behind those buildings.' But her father's question planted a seed in Victoria's mind. She considered the possibility she was using money to provide cover, when what she needed was exposure.

Her eyes registered the green aura of the traffic light, and she resumed the drive home. 'Olivia asked why I'm thinking of renovating the cottage when I can afford a new build,' she said. 'I couldn't answer at the time, other than to say it felt right. I thought it was something to do with it being Nan's old place, and my home for five years, but Olivia's made me think differently.'

Frank chuckled. 'She has the knack of doing that.'

'Money's crippled my personal growth. I've never had to resolve problems outside of the office. I've paid people to take care of my home life.' Victoria had her father's unswerving attention. 'Something else occurred to me. Do you remember Chris Frampton?'

Frank scratched his chin. 'Was he the one whose dad owned that huge yacht in the harbour?'

'Not him. The one after. I knew Chris from college. We got together after I left.' She glanced at her dad. 'You must remember him. He was mad about bikes.' She saw the grenade drop as Frank's blank expression exploded with recognition.

'Chris Frampton. The lad who made it big in Hollywood? I liked him. Well, I did until he upset you. You were heartbroken when he left. Stayed in your bedroom for months. And I thought he was such a gentleman.'

'Hmm. Not that much of a gentleman.' Victoria stared ahead, glad of a reason to avoid her father's glare. 'I believe he's moved into Hope Cove.' She pressed on, not giving her father time to react. 'Anyway, I was thinking about him and how my perception of relationships was set by a single moment in my youth. I let my guard down and gave in to love, and then was used and discarded, like an old, oily rag. Because of that, I've spent years avoiding emotional turmoil. I've used EweSpeak as an excuse to disengage from the real world.' Her grip on the steering wheel tightened. 'I need to change, Dad. I want to be a good mother, and I want to find love.'

'So money and Chris Frampton are to blame for the state you find yourself in?'

Victoria smiled. 'No. The way I dealt with them brought me to this point. There's no one to blame but myself. It's just taken a while for me to work it out.'

'So, what's next, or are you still riding the wave of spontaneity?'

'It's not my strength, is it?' Victoria laughed. 'I'll compromise. I'll work to a flexible plan. How's that?'

Frank patted her knee. 'Sounds like a decent proposal. What will you do first?'

Her father's use of the word *proposal* sent her mind scurrying in the direction of EweSpeak again. She needed to get back to London and sort out her case for voting against the board, but she had lost the sense of urgency, and the thrill of the fight. Her priority was Seth.

A surprised 'Huh!' left her mouth as she realised she was already changing. 'I'm going back to basics. I'm going to stop using money as my guardian, and discover for myself that the best things in life *are* free. And I'm going to look into this child attachment disorder Olivia mentioned. There must be things I can do to help Seth, and if I learn from it too, who knows? We might forge a decent relationship.' She drew up to the bungalow. 'And money can't buy that.'

'No. It can't.' Frank unclipped his seat belt. 'And what about EweSpeak and your sister?'

'I won't let the business or Juliette down, but Seth has to come first.' She'd not said that before. Her son was continually beaten into second place by technical difficulties, or rampaging board members. Another *huh* escaped, as Victoria's understanding took a huge stride. Her mother had always put her faith first and Victoria had resented that big time. No wonder Seth felt unloved. No wonder he reacted so violently against Victoria. The name he heard most often issued from his mother's lips was EweSpeak.

'Seth,' she said, thinking how like a sigh his name was.

She could say it a thousand times and still not make up the difference. Once more. 'Seth.' This time, it was a statement of intent. A promise.

As the container lorries rumbled into the distance, Chris returned to the study; the box had to be emptied and its contents secured. With Rick camped out in his bedroom, and no sight of Tommy, now was as good a time as any.

He gathered together Lacey's medical papers. They described her condition and treatment in explicit detail. Her death certificate and autopsy report were part of the bundle, too. He'd considered burning them before leaving America, but they offered such an insight into who Lacey was and the choices she had made, that his gut reaction was to keep them for a time when Rick was mature enough to understand. Explanations were for the future. Tommy had no right interfering now. No right calling the shots. Chris shoved the papers into the bottom drawer of the filing cabinet, and ensured it was locked.

Systematically, he emptied the box, keeping his mind occupied on menial tasks – sharpening pencils, testing each pen for ink, sorting and arranging, until with one final skim of its base, he found three sealed condoms. Shaken, he stepped back and crumpled into his chair. He'd always kept condoms in his desk. The last time he and Lacey made love was in his office. It was a memory so sharp and vivid, it brought both intense pleasure and pain.

He'd watched her, from behind the blinds of his converted barn. He'd savoured her glorious figure, as she'd exited their homestead, danced across the dusty ground, and halted outside his office. He was familiar enough with her behaviour to know what was about to happen. Thirteen years of marriage, two boys and an unrelenting work schedule for Chris, fuelled his and Lacey's love-life rather than killed it.

His attention was drawn to his boys horsing around in the dry Los Angeles dirt. At eleven years old, Todd and Rick were cheeky, mischievous and as full of life as their mother. It brought a smile to Chris's face.

'Where are you off to, boys?' Lacey's voice.

'Riding.' The boys' standard reply.

'Behave yourselves.' Lacey's warning. Almost a reprimand.

Chris eased the vertical slats of the blind further apart, pressed his cheek close to the warm glass and strained to see his wife. There was nothing but a tantalising ripple of her white hem. He pulled away from the window as the door opened and a bare foot appeared across the threshold.

'Rick. Get Tommy to go with you. He's in the homestead. And Todd. Be careful.' Lacey stepped into the room, placed her hands behind her back and lent against the door. It closed with a satisfying click. She regained her breath, smoothed down her hair and touched her lips. As she lifted her eyes, she took a small pace forward.

Her cheeks were red.

Enjoying the spectacle before him, Chris waited a few seconds before closing the blinds; he was reluctant to banish the LA sun from his office. The light produced a golden aura around the stunning woman gazing at him.

Lacey withdrew from the sunlight, brushed her arm against his, and coaxed his hand away from the cord. 'The boys,' she said, adding a shrug to her sideways nod. 'They don't need to see everything.' She pulled the blinds shut.

'They're definitely off to the stables, aren't they? Only the arena's all set up. The bike, the ramp. And there's no one there. I've sent the team home for the day. I've nipped back to confirm my calculations.' Chris's sudden anxiety threatened to destroy the highly charged moment, but he had good reason to worry. His lads were fearless. They'd grown up on a huge ranch, with a Hollywood stuntman for a father. And Todd had the Frampton reckless gene. 'Lacey, they're not going near the arena, are they? They're safe, right?' He flipped his fringe from his eyes. 'The stunt's been a real bugger to master.'

Lacey weaved her fingers through his, and nodded. 'Relax. They're going riding. Tommy won't let any harm come to them.' She raised her hands, bringing Chris's with them, and rested them against her collarbone. 'I think your director's expecting too much. If I asked you not to go through with this stunt, would you stop?'

He bent to look into her eyes, cloudy blue like an English summer, so mismatched with her heavy American brogue. 'It's who I am, Lacey. It's what I do, what we do, and it's given us this incredible life.' He paused to reflect on the last fifteen years in the USA. As a Brit in a foreign land, he'd worked hard in a tough and potentially lethal industry to fulfil his schoolboy dreams. Would he give it up because his wife asked him? Without a moment's hesitation. He kissed her forehead and straightened up. 'I'll call my agent and tell him it's off.' He unthreaded his fingers, walked across to his large, leather-inset desk, and reached for the phone.

Lacey padded after him, stole the handset and bedded it in its cradle. 'You have an obligation, a contract to honour. Are you absolutely certain you can conquer this stunt?' She searched his eyes.

'Yes,' he replied, with confidence. There was no pretence with Lacey. She detected a lie based on how he breathed the words, and his acting skills counted for nothing in her presence. 'I just want to double-check my figures before I go for the practice run.' He removed a pile of paper from the desk, and hitched a leg over its corner, kicking off his unzipped boots in the process. 'You know me. I'm a belt and braces kind of chap.'

Lacey edged towards him, straddled his lap, and looped her arms around his neck. 'I love it when you get all British.'

He pulled her to him until their lips met, and he melted in the warming welcome of her mouth, its familiar softness a pleasure to explore. As they broke apart, he gathered her long, blonde hair in one hand, lifted her chin with his other, and kissed his way to the hollow of her neck. Her response was immediate, and her tiny hums of delight permitted him to continue. Releasing her hair, he reclined a little and ran his hands over her shoulders, curling his fingers until their backs rested an inch above her breasts.

'Don't stop,' she whispered. 'It's what I came here for.'

He let his fingers drop beneath the top line of her virginal white dress. Today she had no bra. 'How do you do that?'

'What?'

He noted the gentle arching and he slid his hands further, his touch causing her to catch her breath. 'How do you manage to surprise me every time?'

All those years together and she still caught him off guard, still thrilled him. She'd hunted him down this afternoon with the intention of making love; he'd seen it in her eyes the minute she'd left the ranch house. It was a look that never failed to arouse him.

He removed his hands from her breasts, and aware of her groan of dissatisfaction, altered his posture and traced her collarbone with his tongue. To know the woman's body so intimately that he could locate every perfect imperfection blind, to be granted license to roam over every curve with his mouth or his hand, and to shiver with anticipation each and every time he touched her, was proof of their love.

Her hot hands clasped his head as she pulled him up and tasted his lips. He never knew what she was going to do. There was nothing staid about their love-life; nothing predictable. No complacency. Some days they would simmer for hours, on others they would boil over in minutes.

He seized her hand as she reached for him. 'Not yet,' he whispered, following her line with his free fingers until they found her hips. He shuffled off the desk, taking Lacey with him, easily lifting her slender frame, and locked her to him with a powerful kiss. His grunt exploded in her mouth as she swung her legs around him and gripped tightly. He carried her across the office, and laid her on the cool couch, shaking his padded, leather jacket off and discarding it on the floor. Rearing above her, he took her in with fresh eyes. As a couple, they constantly evolved. It was a complex relationship, built on the most basic foundation of trust.

Chris knelt at Lacey's side and released her from the thin straps of her flimsy dress. She dipped her shoulders and pulled her elbows through the loops, maintaining constant eye contact. She raised her hips, and he slipped the dress from under her legs, setting it on top of his jacket. She lay, exposed, womanly, and forever his. He wanted for nothing, except …

'What's the matter?' Lacey gently massaged the scarred skin above his brow. 'Is it the stunt?'

He smiled. 'No. I'll have it sorted by tomorrow.' He flicked his hair down, and then trailed his index finger along her thigh. 'I wouldn't die for a stunt, Lacey, you know that. I'd be trapped in Purgatory, forced to watch you love another man.'

'I couldn't love another man. Not the way I love you.'

Her sincerity ruptured Chris's heart. 'You're still young, Lacey, and if I died tomorrow, I wouldn't want you living the rest of your life unloved.'

Lacey propped herself up, her hair tumbling over the arm of the sofa, the blonde contrasting with the dark leather. 'What you've given me will last both lifetimes, this one and the next. But it will be me watching you from the other side. You'll follow me over.' She produced a weak smile, concern invading her eyes. 'And there is a life after this, Chris. You know I believe that.' She shook her hair free from the couch, laid down, and took a deep breath. 'Why are we talking about this? You said you were confident you can make the stunt work.'

'I am.' He flattened his palm, worked it along her leg, and onto her abdomen, pausing to toy with the smiling white line that ran across it; her badge of honour and the boys' entrance to the world. 'A scar for a scar,' he muttered, before kissing a trail along it.

When he and Lacey first got together, it was clear they both wanted to raise a family. They agonised long and hard over the risks of her becoming pregnant, with the awful possibility of the virus passing to the baby foremost in their minds. Adoption seemed the way forward, until Lacey read a real-life story in a magazine; an HIV positive woman, receiving IVF and the correct prenatal treatment, had given birth to a healthy girl. It was all Lacey needed to push ahead. That, and a discreet, but expensive clinic that guaranteed the Framptons' anonymity.

'Do you remember how tiny the boys were when they were born? Wouldn't believe it to see them now.' Chris smiled, almost able to feel their baby weight in his arms.

'I remember they didn't like the taste of the medicine the clinic prescribed,' Lacey said. '*And* I remember how we celebrated when we received their final negative result.'

A warmth spread through Chris as he recalled the moment. 'It was a good day.'

His hand continued its journey north along Lacey's front and came to rest in the valley of her chest. 'I'll leave the bike till tomorrow.' He saw the questioning look on Lacey's face. 'I wouldn't risk what we have. I love you too much.'

'Can you love me too much now?'

That was his cue to help Lacey move beyond the emotion of their conversation and find a place to set her senses free. The heated passion of a few moments ago had cooled into a deep-rooted desire to connect, and the earlier glint of fire in Lacey's eyes had fanned to a smoulder. A smoky, sexy smoulder. Instinctively, Chris's body reacted. He kneeled tall, pulled off his black Genesis T-shirt, and added it to the growing pile of clothes.

When he glanced at Lacey, she was grinning. 'What?' he asked, leaning over her, blowing his balmy breath onto her body. 'Are you laughing at my vintage shirt?' He moved closer.

With her eyes closed, she nodded her reply, Chris stealing her voice by tending her breasts, his hands caressing each in turn, his mouth hovering above their centre. He quietly hummed, knowing the vibrations would heighten Lacey's arousal, but stopped as her fingers reached below the level of the sofa. She freed him from the tight restraints of his leathers. He pushed them down to his knees, stood up and pulled each trouser leg off, his socks going with them. He took a moment to appreciate the peace that had settled within.

His tranquillity was broken by Lacey clearing her throat. He looked at her and instantly knew what she required of him. He nodded, sauntered back to his desk, and rummaged through the drawer. He didn't love her any less for it, but to go with the flow, take her naturally and make love without conditions was something he longed for; something they both longed for, but Lacey had written the rider way before Chris came along. Or rather, the unscrupulous agent and the diseased actor had. Chris and Lacey's complicated life together was about trust and compromise, and hiding the truth of her HIV from the world, which included their twin boys and their best friend, Tommy Stone.

Chris pulled a square pack from his desk and returned to his wife. He sat on the edge of the sofa and studied Lacey's face. 'It's all right,' he said. 'And I understand. We've both taken risks in our line of work.' Lacey more so. He kissed her furrowed forehead. 'This is an important piece of safety equipment.' He waved the packet in front of her. 'It's like my bike leathers. I wish they rolled on and off as easily.' There, he'd made her smile. Almost.

She sat up, took the packet from him and tore at the corner. 'I wish I'd met you before all of this.' She discarded the foil wrapper and inspected the condom. She nodded, Chris understanding the tiny gesture as an indication she was satisfied with its integrity, and he, in turn, offered himself up. Proficient in her handling of it, she slipped the rubber over him. She sighed. 'I want to give you all of me. I always have.'

Chris rose to his feet and tenderly brought Lacey with him so they stood toe to toe. She hooked her fingers behind his neck, and the static arced between them. 'You give me everything,' he said, drawing one of her legs on to his hip. 'And I love you for that.' He spread his weight between his feet, and with one hand clutching her bottom, he pulled Lacey's other leg up. 'You've given me two incredible boys,' he said, as he walked towards a section of wall by the door, encouraging her to rest her back upon it. He watched her intently, giving her time to adjust to the chilled surface and then with a kiss to her neck and a bite to her ear, he hitched her higher, before easing her down upon him.

He searched her face for signs of discomfort, but she had already closed her eyes and was beginning to moan in time with his movements. She was glass in his hands; fragile, delicate. Transparent. Today, she carried the guilt of her past, punishing herself with thoughts of her misguided youth, fighting for liberation from them. Yesterday, she was wild with destructive energy. Tomorrow ... Tomorrow, she might be as free as a bird.

He altered his position and increased the pace, Lacey staying with him. He kissed her neck again, attracted to the silken skin, and she responded with a tighter squeeze inside. He whispered words of love and messages of reassurance, taking her gently, understanding her needs and reading the signs she displayed for him. Today she needed to know it was okay to let go. That's why she had come to him. 'Nothing's going to happen to me,' he whispered. 'I'm safe.' With those words, he felt her contract. They climaxed seconds apart, Chris following Lacey, and they collapsed against the wall, their bodies pressed together.

Chris set her down, and wiped a trickle of sweat from her lip. 'I love you, Mrs Frampton.'

He was about to kiss her when he was caught by the sound of gravel footsteps crunching at speed in their direction. He held his finger to his mouth. He wasn't ready to become Dad or Chris Frampton, actor. He was still the lover, the husband. The alpha male. He jumped when someone thumped the door.

'Dad! Dad! You gotta come!'

'It's Rick.' Chris pointed to his naked form. 'Okay, bud, give me a minute.' He scrambled across to the sofa, and searched for his leathers.

'Dad? Mom? Is Mom there? Mom?' Rick's voice raised a tone as he continued calling. 'You've gotta come to the arena.'

'I'll go.' Lacey ran over to her dress, picked it up and slipped it on. 'See you outside.'

By the time Chris thrust himself into his trousers and stumbled outside, all that was left of Lacey and Rick was two pairs of footprints and the kick-dust swirling above the ground.

Bootless, Chris followed Lacey's steps, running over stones and dirt without flinching. He was desperate to reach the arena. A second before he caught up with Rick, who was standing at the entrance, he was stunned by an ear-bleeding roar of an explosion. And then darkness.

'Did you hear me?'

Chris snapped back to the present and jumped to his feet. His head was swimming and the room was swirling; an eddy of condoms and pencils. He moored himself to the desk before looking up. Tommy, with an overstuffed rucksack, filled the space between the doorjambs.

'I said I can't face Rick and I don't want to lie to him. I need to work out what I'm going to do, and I can't do that here.'

With Tommy's words registering, Chris tried one last time to ram his point home. 'This is Lacey's secret, Tommy. If you loved her, you wouldn't betray her.'

With a final shake of his head, Tommy turned and walked away. 'Don't hold your breath,' he said.

Chapter Eight

With all the will in the world, Victoria knew her relationship with Seth would only grow if it was what they both desired. Regardless of the recent success, Seth made it clear he wanted little to do with Victoria. He'd spent the early part of the evening with Frank, playing with his old, wooden train track on the floor of the living room in the bungalow, then after tea, when Victoria suggested she took Seth for his bath, he'd run screaming along the hallway, and shut himself in the spare room.

Victoria stood by the children's bedroom and fingered the five nameplates fixed to the door. Her dad said he'd made them during an over-sixties woodworking course he'd attended last year. The quality was as good as any Victoria had seen at craft fairs. Not that she'd been to many. Juliette had dragged her round one, suggesting it was an excellent afternoon out for the children. It wasn't. Still, Victoria admired and appreciated her father's skill.

The room itself was cosy enough. The bottom bunk had a *Thomas The Tank Engine* duvet cover, there was a green toy box full of jigsaws and bears at the foot of the bed, and adjacent, was a set of five blue drawers, one assigned to each grandchild.

Yesterday, Seth had gone to bed without fuss, but that was with his Pops tucking him in. Tonight it was a different story. With Frank going out, it was down to Victoria to get Seth to bed, and he was not happy with the situation.

Victoria moved away from Seth's room and knocked on her father's door.

'I'm not doing it.'

'I haven't asked yet.' She swore under her breath.

The door opened and her father, dressed in a pink shirt and pale blue trousers, entered the hallway. 'If I put Seth to bed it will become his routine, and I'll be stuck doing it until you move out.'

Astonished at her father's choice of words, Victoria gawked at him. '*Stuck* doing it?'

'It's one of the privileges of being a grandparent. All the fun and none of the responsibility.' Frank smiled.

'Tonight, Dad. Once. That's all. Please.' She tugged on his shirtsleeve, reminiscent of when she was a child. It was the one way she knew of getting round him. The prospect of facing a stroppy boy, bathing him and tucking him into bed panicked her; Seth didn't want her near him. 'Was *I* that difficult?'

Frank grinned. 'I learned to call it by a different name. You were independent.'

Victoria digested the comment. 'So I was difficult?' She tutted and shook her head. 'And at what age did I become easy?'

Frank failed to stifle a laugh. 'Victoria, my lovely, logical daughter, you have never been easy, in any sense of the word.' He tapped his nose and pirouetted along the corridor. 'I'm off out. Olivia and I are hitting the arcades. Don't wait up.'

Victoria huffed and then narrowed her eyes. Seth had to go to bed and she had to put him there. Unsure as to how she was to achieve the impossible, she entered her father's room and sat on the end of his bed.

Her hardest ordeal to date was being pregnant. How was getting a four-year-old to co-operate worse?

She cringed at the sound of the front door closing. It was her and Seth now. It was time to sink or swim. Perhaps she'd tread water until her child liked her.

Rising up, she straightened the duvet and, feeling like a condemned woman, walked the Green Mile to Seth's bedroom.

'It's a bath, followed by a bedtime story,' she muttered, pushing open his door. She geared herself up for one more battle, and then saw Seth. He was fast asleep, with the duvet tucked lightly around him. His clothes were in a pile on the toy box, and his pyjama top was all skew-whiff, twisted around his chest.

It should have been a moment of wonder for Victoria, but all she could think was that her son was so against her putting him to bed, he'd struggled to do it himself.

She tidied his clothes, switched off the lamp, and left the bedroom. She'd bathe him in the morning.

Swallowing the cocktail of sadness and relief, Victoria made her way to the kitchen. Like the rest of the property it was compact, but it had every convenience her father required; a fridge-freezer, an electric oven, and a kettle. Victoria rooted through the eye-level cupboards in search of a jar of decent coffee – she tolerated instant, so long as it was granules. She found a new jar of Kenco, which received a nod of approval.

Usually at this point on a weekend, with a mug of strong coffee for company, she would dismiss the nanny and settle at the computer, catching up on a lost day's work. Every minute of her waking hours was utilised to the maximum. Inactivity was abnormal.

She perused the kitchen wondering how to fill a few seconds while waiting for the kettle to boil. There was a disorderly pile of cookbooks shoved against the side of the fridge-freezer, with extracts of recipes escaping over the top of an ancient

Hamlyn's All Colour Cookbook. A vegetarian version of the same stood open on the iron bookstand. That explained tonight's nut roast, which, alarmingly, Seth ate with gusto.

Life in Weymouth had certainly changed since her last visit.

The kettle clicked off and Victoria made the coffee. It was an archaic way to produce a hot drink. Her coffee machine was sleek, efficient and fast.

Frank did not have to live like this. Victoria would have given her parents whatever they wanted. She'd offered to buy them a house overlooking the sea at Bowleaze: she'd asked her father to choose a four by four, but he'd refused, preferring his faithful five door hatchback, and she'd suggested paying for a cleaner to visit the bungalow twice a week to free up her mother's time, but Iris was appalled at the idea. They were happy with their little home, fronting onto Lodmoor marsh. If they went into the loft, they had a sea view. If there had been a window.

Grabbing her mug from the side, Victoria wandered into the living room and sat down. The peculiarity of idleness was waning. Five minutes, and then she'd carry out her research. Her father's computer was old, but workable. She sipped her coffee. When was the last time she spent an entire evening watching television? It must have been in her teens. That shocked her. She tried to recall where she was and what she had been watching.

It was shortly after she'd moved into her cottage and Juliette was staying with her. They were celebrating their first weekend of independence, with crumpets for tea, and the *Antiques Roadshow* on TV. Juliette joked about hidden treasures in the cottage and how they shouldn't throw paraphernalia away without running it past Mum.

They never did find a secret stash.

What a strange race we are, Victoria thought. We're surrounded by technology, with incredible advances being made by the day and yet we want to know the value of our old pieces of tat. How on earth do we manage to advance when we cling so desperately to the past?

Her logic unsettled her. She was as guilty as the next person when it came to examining the past for clues to the present. Even when she was married to Ben, she fantasised about Chris. It was adulterous, but she couldn't stop herself. The dreams evolved from her analysing why Chris chose Hollywood over her. She hadn't learned from them. All she knew was it hurt.

She clasped the mug to her breast. If she'd understood that life was precious, why had she pulled the plug on reality?

'Where's Pops?'

Victoria spun round as Seth's question broke the silence. He was so small.

'I want Pops.' He remained in the doorway. 'There's a dragon in my room.'

Victoria raised her brow. 'A dragon? I don't think so.'

Seth's eyes widened into saucers, and his hands balled into white-knuckled fists. 'There is.' He stood rooted to the spot.

Victoria hoisted herself up and approached him. She saw the dark stains of tear tracks running from the corner of his eyes to his chin. 'We need to wash your face and get you back into bed.' She put her hands on the tops of his arms and rotated him to face the bathroom. 'March.' His resistance pushed into her palms. 'Seth. Bathroom. Now.' She applied a gentle pressure as encouragement, but he refused to move.

'There's a dragon in my bedroom.'

'Seth. Dragons aren't real and if they were, they wouldn't fit in this tiny bungalow.' She peered over his head. His pyjama top was still skew-whiff, his trousers helter skeltered around his legs, and his big, hazel eyes were gathering swell. She relaxed her hands and felt him take a deep, shuddering breath.

It wasn't unreasonable to assume Seth had a virtual world – Victoria had one, and until recently, it had been her escape, but maybe Seth's was a universe where dragons were the fiercest creatures ever. She released her hold, stepped in front of him and crouched. 'Would you like to stay up for a while?' As she was discovering, it was good to take time out from the virtual world.

He nodded.

'Okay. Shall I see if Pops has any hot chocolate?' That worked for Victoria when she was a child.

'Yes. Please.'

She didn't show it, but Victoria's heart performed a somersault.

With their mugs on the coffee table, Victoria and Seth occupied opposite ends of the same sofa, and settled down to watch a cartoon about a talking bear. It made little sense to Victoria, but it was gentle, and there was nothing in it resembling a dragon. Five minutes after finishing his drink, Seth was asleep.

Victoria watched him and a sense of peace washed over her. 'Definitely can't buy that,' she said, pulling her duvet from the air bed. She laid it over Seth, stepped away, and smiled. She had put her son to bed.

The old Victoria would argue the sofa was not a bed, but the old Victoria wouldn't have spent thirty minutes with her son, trying to understand *Little Bear*.

However, the old Victoria would collect as much information as possible on a condition about which she knew nothing and which Seth might or might not have.

She headed for the computer. 'Right, child attachment disorder. Let's get acquainted.'

Chapter Nine

At some point during the night, having carried Seth to his bed, Victoria removed herself from the spongy air mattress, and settled on the sofa.

She was disturbed by a rush of cool air hitting her face as the living room door opened and Frank strolled in.

'Morning, sleepy head,' he said. 'Tea and toast?'

He proffered a mug and plate to Victoria, who pushed herself up and scrunched her hand through her disobedient curls.

'Given up with the mattress?'

'I had the fidgets. Couldn't settle. Thanks, Dad.' She took the breakfast items from him. 'How was your wanton gambling?'

'I came back with an empty wallet.' He grinned and sat next to Victoria. 'I did have a win on the two pence shove machine, but in a moment of recklessness, I ploughed it straight back in and lost the lot.'

Victoria grimaced. 'You must quit when you're ahead. I've told you that.'

Frank delivered a perfect expression of remorse. 'If I'd listened to you, I'd have come home a whole three pound in profit.' He grinned. 'One day, Victoria, I'll be rich beyond my wildest dreams. A millionaire. All in two pence pieces.'

'If I sell my shares in EweSpeak, I can make you a millionaire now.' Victoria saw sternness tighten her father's face.

'Oh, no.' Frank shook his head. 'I said I'd help, not be your get-out clause. If you think having money is a problem, you need to find a solution. I'm not it. What would I want with a million pounds? Besides, that cottage of yours is going to need a cash injection to get it up to standard. Surely it's an acceptable investment.' He tapped the duvet. 'But I appreciate the offer. I know who to come to if I find myself in financial straits.' His grin returned. 'Last night's loss does not constitute a financial strait.' He rose from the sofa and left the room.

Victoria smiled. A good dad was worth his weight in gold.

He was right. It was going to take money and effort to refurbish the cottage. It needed a complete overhaul; re-plastering, re-wiring, re-plumbing, new windows and doors, new flooring – the list was endless – but her father's suggestion of simply throwing cash at it grated on her. That was precisely what she was trying to avoid. She chewed on her toast while digesting the problem.

Perhaps compromise was the answer; after all, it was difficult to ignore the pound signs on her bank statements. She could get estimates for the essential repairs, such as electrics and heating, and set a budget to complete the rest of the work herself. There was no need to go on a spending spree. She could project manage, her dad was handy with a paintbrush, and Olivia had an eye for design. Surely between them, they could make the place habitable. They could tackle it one room at a time.

She kicked off the duvet, stood and rubbed her back, stiff from a restless night. Would the purchase of a new bed be considered frivolous?

As she left the living room, she heard voices drifting from the kitchen. Her father and Seth were seated at the table, enjoying breakfast. Seth's broad smile, aimed at his granddad, broke as he bit into a slice of toast.

'There you are. I thought you must still be in bed,' Victoria said. 'Good sleep?'

Seth nodded as he picked up his beaker of milk.

An acknowledgement. Don't overreact. 'I guess I should take a shower and get dressed. I can't remember the last time I was in my pyjamas this late in the morning.' She ambled towards the bathroom. 'I'm thinking of making it a habit.'

After a luxurious half an hour of pampering, Victoria borrowed Seth's room in which to dress. Her morning showers were the place her working day commenced. Many problems were solved under hot running water, and plans were often hatched as she dried herself down, but today she had made the unprecedented move of permitting herself thirty minutes of not thinking. It hadn't been easy. In fact, it had been impossible with pages of facts and figures about child attachment disorder fighting for recognition.

Last night's research had been an eye opener. So much of it made sense. So much of it explained Seth's behaviour. And so much of it was down to Victoria.

She threw back the lid of her suitcase. How was this not thinking? What she required was a power-off switch, like her computers.

She took a long blink, pretending to reset her system. 'Focus on something else.'

Rifling through her clothes, she pulled out a fresh pair of Stella McCartney jeans, and her most expensive Milly cardigan; it was rusty-red, embellished with black beads around the neckline, and it fitted her beautifully. She gave the clothes a gentle shake and proceeded to dress.

The door pushed against her and Seth walked in.

'What are you doing?' He sat on the lower bunk and swung his legs.

Victoria covered her top half with her cardigan. She wasn't used to an audience. She was even less used to Seth asking questions. 'Dressing,' she said. 'Then I'm heading off to the cottage. Would you like to come?'

'Would I see Livia?'

'I don't know. The shop might be closed today.'

Seth's expression darkened. 'I want to see Livia.'

Seeing the rapid degeneration of his mood, Victoria sat next to Seth, and accessed her mental notes, gleaned from the Internet. *Your child is fighting for control. Never belittle or dismiss his feelings. Don't take the abuse personally.* Clear, well-defined instructions. All Victoria had to do was apply them.

She relaxed her jaw. 'You'd like to see Olivia. That's nice.' She cringed at her choice of words and waited for the backlash. When nothing came, she cautioned the tiny moth of excitement fluttering inside to avoid the extinguishing light. 'What would you like to do if Olivia's not in?'

'Go home.'

'To the cottage?'

'No.' Seth's foot kicked out. 'Home. With Aunty Joo.'

That wasn't Seth's home. Did he mean London? *Rein it in,* Victoria told herself. *Apply the rules. Don't take the abuse personally. See it from his point of view.* 'Change is scary, isn't it?' She honed in on her buttons, and waited for a reply. From the corner of her eye she saw Seth freeze, his small body rigid, his mouth the only moving part.

'I want my house and I want my friends.'

Victoria's moth buzzed and plunged to the ground. 'Moving down here is called a new start,' she explained, as she slipped the bottom button through its slit. 'You'll see lots more of Pops, and we can get to know Olivia properly. And you can see your friend, Rick, again,' she said, clutching at one weedy, dry straw. She wanted to add that she and

Seth would have more time together, but doubted he'd see that as a positive. 'How about we give it a try? For a short while. If we don't like it once we've made the cottage nice, we'll chat and decide what to do.'

Getting through to a four-year-old was a major stretch for Victoria, and her head was pounding. She'd managed one breakthrough in the last twelve hours, resolving the dragon problem, but that was a doddle compared to explaining why Seth had left his friends behind. And no matter how often she mentally reiterated the new advice, she took everything Seth said personally. It was ingrained. He said and did things to hurt her.

Her resolve was fading. Her son was unhappy, and she could settle this now. Assuming Cerys had recovered from the flu, all Victoria had to do was take Seth back to London, hand him over, and stay out of his way.

Victoria clamped her hands around her head, hoping the pressure would stop the incessant throbbing. It was pulsating with the power of a sub-woofer.

'Okay.'

Seth's voice startled Victoria and she looked at him. 'Okay, we'll stay for a while? Is that what you mean?'

'Yes. I like Pops and Livia.' Seth shuffled to the end of the bed, lifted the lid off the toy box, and busied himself raking through the contents.

His silence closed the conversation, and Victoria eased herself up from the bunk. 'I'll call you when I'm ready to go.' She turned and crossed into the hall, surprised at the outcome, but relieved to be out of the room.

'I don't like the new house.' Seth's voice followed her into the passageway. 'I don't like the new house, and I don't like you.' He got up and pushed the door shut.

In quiet disbelief, Victoria gave a gentle nod. Apart from the banging headache, it had gone well.

Hate had been downgraded to *don't like*.

The terraced cottage was grimmer than when Victoria had viewed it last. It was dark, dank, and dreary. As Seth darted upstairs, she breathed warm air onto her hands, and gave the ceiling a cursory glance. She wasn't positive, but the stained section above the foot of the stairs appeared to be bulging. Did that mean water was still leaking? From the bath? Or from the immersion heater or the water tank, one located in a small cupboard on the landing, the other in the loft? It was hopeless speculating – she hadn't a clue about these things.

What she did know was the place was going to cost thousands to make it anywhere near fit for human purpose.

'Back to basics, Vicky,' she muttered, reminding herself of her new outlook on life. 'But where to start?'

When the EweSpeak office was refurbished, the first item she saw on site was a huge skip. She nodded in approval. 'A skip it is. They can't be that expensive.' Searching for her mobile, she groped in her jacket pocket for a few seconds, then tutted as she recalled leaving it in London. She crouched on the bottom step. 'Use your brains, girl.' She sat still and silent for a moment, before smiling. 'Olivia's bound to know who can help.'

As far as Chris was concerned, the conservatory, with its natural light and panoramic view of the gardens and sea, was the best room in the entire castle. It was even more magnificent during dark, with the moon and stars for a ceiling.

He'd dragged the porter's chair through from the entrance hall into the conservatory, and positioned it to the right of the terrace doors, where he'd spent a fair chunk of the night, trying to second-guess Tommy. He'd even formed strategies to deal with the fallout, should the news of Lacey's HIV enter the public domain.

Tommy wasn't known for being a drama queen, so the fact he'd taken the news so personally troubled Chris. When he married it to the way Tommy had declared his love for Lacey during the row in the office, an unpleasant taste bubbled up from his gut and smothered his tongue. It was bitter. Nasty. There was something in Tommy's presentation that made Chris uncomfortable. 'I loved Lacey,' Tommy had said. Stated, in fact. And then he'd hesitated, as if he was considering qualifying his statement.

On many occasions, Lacey had expressed her fondness for Tommy, and openly admired his knack for getting things done. She concerned herself with his emotional well-being, too, asking Chris if Tommy ever spoke about a special woman in his life. The question even cropped up once during their lovemaking.

Chris had thought nothing of it at the time, but if there was something more than friendship between Lacey and Tommy, that could explain Tommy's reaction to her HIV.

Snapping shut his eyes, Chris denied the notion further access.

His main concern right now was for Rick, and he'd given serious consideration to telling him the truth. If it came from Chris, he had some control over what his son learned – or at least, he had control over the way in which the news was conveyed, and that meant there was room for damage limitation. But if Tommy blurted it out …

Aware of approaching footsteps, Chris opened his eyes and made out he'd just woken. He stretched his legs, flexed his arms, and yawned.

'Are we eating?' Rick strolled into the room. 'It's almost twelve. Has Tommy gone to the store?'

'No, he's hasn't, but we can eat.' Chris jumped out of the chair. 'What do you fancy? Fish and chips?'

'Fish and chips?' Rick's face narrowed with confusion. 'The British have some weird food combos.'

Chris laughed. 'Chips are what you know as fries, and what you call chips are called crisps. And while we're on the subject, jelly is jam, and jello is jelly.' He checked Rick's expression once more, then waved a hand in the air. 'You'll get the hang of it. Anyway, there's a fish restaurant not far from here. By the time we're sorted, it should be open.' He avoided mentioning Tommy. 'We'll take the beach route. I think I know how to find that entrance.' Chris smiled. 'All right?'

'Yeah. All right.'

They left the conservatory, returning moments later wrapped in their jackets and hats.

'How's the jet lag?' Chris asked.

Rick pulled on his gloves. 'Okay. It's my stomach that's complaining. Is Tommy coming?'

Should Chris enshroud one lie with another to conceal the first? After two years of little conversation, Rick was talking, and Chris had no desire to cut across those fragile lines of communication.

As hard as it was to shake betrayal from his mind, Chris looked at his son, managed a glimmer of a smile, and shook his head. 'He's gone away for a few days. Something about catching up with old friends. Not sure when he'll be back.'

So. There was his answer. He wouldn't tell Rick the truth. Instead, he'd cast the second mould to his set of Russian doll lies.

They ventured onto the patio, locked the conservatory doors, and headed for the woodland, Chris concentrating on the path, to avoid facing further thoughts of Tommy and Lacey. He found the entrance to the beach with ease this time, and he ran down the bank onto the pebbles. The biting wind nipped at his cheeks and howled in his ears. He tugged his hat down. He'd forgotten how cold it was along the front. Rick followed.

'Not far,' Chris mouthed.

As they passed the Harbour Inn, they turned off the beach, walked through an alleyway, and came to a standstill outside the first of a terrace of three cottages.

'Are we lost again?' Rick asked.

Chris faced the road, and gave the area a quick once-over. 'I could have sworn there was a restaurant here. I took—' The cold air caught the back of his throat, and he coughed. The moment was long enough for him to change his story. There was no point bringing Vicky Paveley into the present. She needed to stay in his head, especially now he was reliving the last few moments he'd spent with her, naked, making no-holds-barred love in the sea. 'I used to go there,' he said, walking further along the pavement.

As he passed the end cottage, he heard a woman's voice. It stopped him in his tracks. The tone, the inflection, and the rhythm of the words could have been spoken by Vicky. A shiver spiralled down his spine as he recalled who the building belonged to – old Mrs Paveley, Vicky's nan.

The memory was a powerful thing.

'I'm sorry, Seth. I promised you half an hour ago we'd see Olivia, didn't I? I got caught up with sorting the kitchen. Come downstairs and we'll go now.'

Chris reeled on the spot. The voice wasn't in his head. It was behind the door of Vicky's nan's cottage. This was too weird. It was a coincidence, pure and simple. Old Mrs Paveley would have passed away years ago. Vicky was on his mind, that was all.

'You okay, Dad?' Rick proceeded in the direction of the craft shop. 'You look spaced out.'

'Yeah. I'm fine. I was wondering what happened to the restaurant.' He knew his actions betrayed his words, as his eyes were fixed on the cottage door.

The door that was opening.

'Seth! Are you coming?'

The familiar voice, matched with the unruly, copper hair, sent a chill through Chris. The woman sounded like Vicky, and bore a remarkable resemblance too. He had to be hallucinating; imprinting Vicky's image on this poor, unsuspecting lady. He nodded in agreement with himself. Jet lag. He was suffering from jet lag.

When the woman stepped onto the pavement, two feet away from Chris, the rotation of the earth increased tenfold. Unsteady, and with his head spinning, he collapsed against the wall of the cottage. When she turned to him, and recognition raced across her face, it was all Chris could do to stay upright.

The shock appeared to be all his.

'Hello,' the woman said. 'It's been a while.'

Chapter Ten

With Rick now at his side, Chris pushed away from the cold bricks, and straightened his clothes. Vicky Paveley was still not a part of his history he was willing to divulge. Whatever happened next, he had to provide his son with a rational explanation, and one that didn't create too many questions. 'Rick, this is an old friend of mine. We knew each other many years ago, before I moved to America.' He removed his hat and shoved it in his pocket.

'Like, an old girlfriend?'

'Well …'

'I'm Victoria Noble.' Victoria extended a hand to Rick, who, to Chris's surprise, returned the gesture. 'We dated. Nothing serious.' Victoria smiled. 'You must be Rick. My son, Seth, is inside. I believe you've already met. Curly hair, asks a lot of questions.'

Rick nodded.

'You know Vicky's … Victoria's son?'

Again, Rick nodded. Chris appeared to be the only one overwhelmed by the situation. Victoria was very much in control. She took up the story.

'Seth found his way into the grounds of Hope Cove and the boys got chatting. Your son was very kind to him.' She turned to Rick. 'Seth's not always the easiest of boys to get on with. Thank you.'

Chris raised his hands. 'You knew we were here, then?'

That made sense of Vicky's ... Victoria's cool reception. 'Question. When did you become Victoria?'

'When I grew up. The Noble bit happened when I married.'

Victoria Noble. There was a familiarity to the name Chris couldn't put his finger on. Victoria Noble. Nope. Whatever it was, it had gone. Perhaps Rick had mentioned it in passing.

'So, married with children.' Chris cursed himself for producing such a pathetic statement, but what else could he say? *I've been thinking about our last night together. I remember what it was like to hold you. Kiss you. Love you.*

It was irrelevant now. Their lives had moved on. They'd both found love with other people. Good, honest love. Well, until Tommy's outburst, Chris *believed* his marriage to Lacey to have been good and honest.

He pressed a palm to his forehead. There wasn't enough room in there for simultaneous thoughts of Vicky and Lacey.

'Divorced, with a son,' Victoria said. 'My husband left when Seth was a baby.'

Chris noted the clipped words, and the bitterness with which they were spoken. He formed the distinct impression he was expected to apologise, but for what, he didn't know. 'How are your mum and dad? And sister?' *Really? Small talk?* He ran his hands over his head, and clasped his fingers together. 'Sorry.' There. He'd apologised. It wasn't for the right reason, but it loosened the air around him. He glanced at Rick, who was watching the scene intently. 'Perhaps the four of us could meet at the Harbour Inn for lunch tomorrow? The boys could play baseball on the beach, and we could ... talk.'

What was he doing? Seeing Victoria had turned him into a teenager. He felt clumsy and awkward; a little shy, even.

How did this woman still have the power to do that to him? *Get a grip, Frampton.*

'Seth's not five yet. I think baseball's a little ambitious. And Dad and Juliette are fine, thanks.' She paused. 'I lost my mother a few years ago. Stroke.' She looked back into the cottage, before continuing. 'And to save you asking, my nan died when I was nineteen.' She produced a lame smile and cast her eyes to the pavement. 'Lunch and a chat would be ... interesting, but I can't do tomorrow.'

Ah. The brush-off. Well, he had just stamped his size eleven boots all over Victoria's memories. Maybe it was best if they avoided one another. Neither Chris nor Vicky were the people of their teens, despite the ease with which he could recall their time together. 'I'm sorry about your mum. And your nan. I expect there's plenty I don't know. Lunch another time?' He watched as Victoria pushed a stray curl behind her ear, and then heard her huff as it bobbed out again. He smiled. That hair had once danced the entire length of his body.

'I have to go to London for a meeting, but if it goes well, I'll be back the next day. We could arrange something after that.'

Victoria's response nudged the glorious image from Chris's head. 'If you're sure? That would be great.' Not such a bad idea, after all. 'You should drop in at the castle.'

'Dad? Can we go now?'

Rick's question and an accompanying shove brought Chris sharply back to the necessities of everyday life. 'You hungry?'

'Er. Yeah.'

'Is that Rick?' Seth's voice floated onto the street from within the dim cottage. 'I want to see Rick.'

His tumbling footsteps ended in an almighty crash that sent debris and dust blasting through the open door.

'Stay here!' In an instant Chris was in the building,

surrounded by fallen plaster and thin strips of wood, with freezing water biting at his ankles. As he stumbled and staggered his way through the rubble, his mind blinded his eyes to the bleak interior of the house.

Deceived by the devastation, and confused by the chaos, he was searching for his son and wife. He set his hands on his crown and consciously slowed his breathing, drawing air deep into his lungs. He choked and gagged as the smell of burning flesh hit the back of his throat. He recognised the stench immediately. Instinctively, he fingered the scar above his brow. 'One blast too many,' Lacey had said to him, the night he'd earned that particular badge. Tommy's touch to his arm startled him and returned him to the harsh reality strewn all around. Chris scanned the area. 'Where's Rick?' he said. 'He was standing right there.' Chris pointed to the entrance of the arena, and waved away the paramedic fussing around him. 'Where is he?' He struggled to his feet and leaned on Tommy.

'He's all right,' Tommy said, his voice cracking. 'A few splinters, cuts and grazes, but he'll be okay. He's on his way to hospital.' Tommy glared at the paramedic, who took the hint and backed off.

'Where's Todd?' Chris said. 'Where's Lacey?'

In one swift movement, Tommy threw his arms around Chris and clutched him to his body, his mouth pressing on his ear. 'She's in the arena,' he said. 'Lacey and Todd. They're both in there. Todd was riding your bike. And something really bad happened.'

The words fell on Chris like coins from a fruit machine, and suddenly he understood. The explosion, the rancid stink of singed skin, the acrid taste of smoky fuel on his tongue. Todd had crashed, and somehow both he and Lacey were caught up in the deafening chaos. 'I have to get them out, Tommy. I have to save them.'

At the entrance to the mechanic's pit, Tommy braced himself and rammed the door to the stunt arena. It flew open, releasing a ball of heat, which forced the men to retreat. 'You all right?' Tommy asked.

Chris gave no reply. He was concentrating on not retching. The smell was stronger here; nasty, suffocating. He held his hand over his nose and took shallow breaths. The sound of Tommy gagging almost sent him over. 'I can't see anything,' Chris said, his eyes straining through the dirty orange haze, but as they adjusted to the peculiar light, he edged forward, able to identify the wraithlike outlines of people working on the scene. The further he ventured, the easier it became to zone in on the pockets of activity.

Neither man spoke; Chris was shocked into silence by the wreckage at his feet and by the extent of the carnage sprawled across the arena floor. There were a handful of small fires left unattended while the crew fought to gain control of a larger blaze in the centre, a bewildering number of police were shouting orders to one another, sealing off the main entrance with tape, and the blinding flashes of cameras were cutting through the fetid fog.

Chris kept his eyes level, drawn to the two men in all-in-ones making their way to the fractured and smouldering test ramp. They stopped next to a smoking crater guarded by a firefighter. Chris crept closer, unnoticed and unchallenged. From his peripheral vision, he saw the scorched ground. Was it his imagination, or could he feel the earth's heat on the soles of his bare feet? He jumped as Tommy's grasp tightened and pulled him back. Undeterred, he shrugged him off and advanced another foot. He needed to know what the two men in coveralls found so fascinating. They were examining the area beyond the crater. With stinging eyes, Chris tried to make sense of the blur of red and white. 'What is it?' he shouted to Tommy. 'Can you see?'

His mistake punched him in the gut, as he realised his question should have asked who, and not what. 'Lacey? Todd?' His foot knocked against something soft. Something wet. He refused to look down, scared of what he would see. He'd dealt with explosions as a stuntman, riding through fragments of skin and bone, and kicking away burning limbs, but this was not a film set, and the remains underfoot were not prosthetics.

'Seth!' A woman's voice sliced through the mist, providing Chris with a view to the real world. He wiped his sticky palms down the length of his thighs, and concentrated on clearing his mind. Flashbacks weren't memories. Flashbacks were man-eating monsters that swallowed him whole and regurgitated him at the entrance of his practice arena, and, over and over again, forced him to relive the moment when he discovered the lifeless, shattered bodies of Lacey and Todd. It was as traumatic as the day it happened, only now he'd learned to manage the aftermath. Except the blinding headaches. He endured those.

He loosened his coat, hitched his sleeves to his elbows, and shook the tension from his arms. 'Focus, Frampton. Remember why you're here.'

Another yell from outside prompted him to move. Vicky's boy was in there, and he needed to get him out. 'Seth! Where are you? Shit.' Find the boy. Save the boy. Chris coughed as the dust attacked his throat. The choking would be a hundred times worse for his boy; a thousand for Lacey.

'You said shit.'

Seth's voice wrenched Chris away from the brink of another hallucination, and lifted him to the no-man's-land between fantasy and reality. Purgatory.

Play it cool, Chris told himself. *Swallow the tears, gag the scream. Hold back the vomit. This is now.*

With his conscious sight returning to the hall, he spotted the tiny black silhouette of a boy standing on the stairs. With a cry of relief, he splashed across to him, gathered him in his arms, and carried him to safety, seconds before another horrendous crash shook the building.

And the people outside.

'Everyone okay?' Chris hugged Seth's small body close to him. 'Are you all right, buddy?' A muffled yes prompted Chris to relax his hold. The boy's cheeks were flushed, and his hair was grey, but apart from that he appeared unscathed. Chris set him on the ground and fluffed the dust from his mane. 'I thought the fright had turned your hair white.'

He looked at Victoria, who was standing silent and still, her arm around Rick's shoulder. The blood had drained from both people; Rick with a fevered complexion, and Victoria, the colour of pearl.

Chris crouched down and took Seth's hands. 'I think your mum could use a hug.' He directed him towards Victoria, but the boy clung to his fingers. 'It's okay. You're safe.' For a small lad, he had a vice-like grip. Chris turned his head to speak with Victoria. 'I don't think anything fell on him, but you should check him over.'

'Chris needs to see to his own son, Seth.' Victoria stepped away from Rick. 'And I need to know you're all right.' She invited her son to stand with her, but it took further words of encouragement from Chris before the reluctant child relinquished his hold, and went to his mother.

As Chris pulled Rick to him, he saw the tears welling in his eyes. 'Oh, man. It's okay. I'm okay.'

'All I could think about … Mom … Todd. You … ' With his words strangled by emotion, Rick leaned into Chris, and buried his face in his chest.

'I'm sorry. I didn't mean to scare you.' Chris wrapped

his arms around his son, and kissed the top of his head. 'I couldn't leave Seth in there. You understand, don't you?' Saving one boy's life in no way made up for losing Lacey and Todd, and it did nothing to ease the guilt Chris lived with, blaming himself for their deaths, but he couldn't stand by and watch another person lose someone they love. 'I wasn't in danger. I promise.'

Rick lifted his head. 'You're all I've got, Dad.'

Victoria, placing a hesitant hand on Seth, took a deep, trembling breath. What the Framptons had lost was beyond anything she'd experienced. She was saddened by the death of her nan and mother, but hard work had seen her through the difficult first few months. It was apparent time had healed very little for Rick.

'I'm sorry about your house,' said Chris, Rick still clinging to him. 'The ceiling's down. You can't live there. It's a bomb site.'

Victoria released a half laugh. 'Thanks for breaking it to me gently.' She tipped her head in Rick's direction. 'Is there anything I can do?'

'Give your son an extra big hug, and tell him you'll be there for him.'

If Seth allowed it, she'd do it in an instant. A hug, a kiss, and words of reassurance seemed the perfect things to give right now.

Sod permission. She was going to do it.

She leaned over the top of Seth, and embraced him right around his tiny frame. 'You poor boy. You must have been terrified. I'm so glad you're safe, and I'm so glad I have you.' She waited for him to resist, expecting him to scream, or punch his way out. What she didn't expect was his quivering body retreating into hers. And she hadn't anticipated the overwhelming sorrow his vulnerability elicited from her.

He was probably in shock, and his move to safety instinctive, but for the second time in his life, he'd turned to Victoria for comfort and protection. 'I want to be here for you, Seth. Be the person you need me to be. A mum you can love.' She spoke quietly, ensuring their conversation was private. Time alone would tell if he understood.

'Goodness me! What on earth has happened here? Is everyone all right?' Olivia darted from the doorway of the craft centre, bent down in front of Seth, and brushed her fingers along his cheek. 'Well, there are no tears, but your clothes are filthy.' She looked to Victoria. 'Everything okay?'

'We're a little shaken.' Victoria pointed to the cottage. 'The ceiling collapsed. I was out here, but Seth was on the stairs.' As the enormity of the situation hit home, her words and emotions tumbled out. 'He could have been killed. I could have lost him, and all because I have this stupid bee in my bonnet about going back to basics. This place needs to be demolished. Knocked down. Every trace wiped out. It's a death trap.'

She stood upright, and guided Seth into Olivia's arms. 'I'm irresponsible and selfish. I'm not fit to be a mother.' As soon as the words hit the air, she wished she could suck them back. They weren't what Seth needed to hear. She covered her eyes with her palms, and rubbed away her tears. As she removed her hands, she caught sight of Chris, his eyes wide with concern, and Rick, whose face, previously dappled, was now blanket white. 'I'm sorry,' Victoria said.

Rick took one pace forward. 'Ma'am? May I say something?'

Victoria frowned, and then indicated for Rick to continue.

'I'm thirteen, right, and I don't understand what's going down between you and Seth, but how can you say you're a no-good mom? When I was scared because Dad was in that building, and you were out here, scared for your son, you stayed strong and took care of me. Made me feel safe. That's not easy. I don't do safe, do I, Dad?'

Chris supported his son's statement with a slow shake of his head.

'Your arms told me Dad would be all right,' Rick continued. 'So, for what it's worth, Mrs Noble, I'd say you're a pretty good mom.' With his face now glowing with colour, he grabbed Chris's sleeve, and pulled him in the direction of the castle. 'See you soon, Seth,' he shouted.

Victoria marvelled at her arms: they'd protected Rick.

Olivia looked on. 'Who was that? The man looked familiar.' She marched Seth towards her shop, and opened the door. 'I've got it! He's Chris Frampton, that stunt actor chap. What's he doing on Portland?'

'He's come home,' Victoria said.

'Do you know him?'

Victoria's gaze lifted from her arms, and she stared into the distance. 'I thought I did.'

'People change, Victoria. Don't be too disappointed in him.'

She'd spent half her life feeling let down by him, thinking his actions were those of a coward, loving her, then leaving her, and she had plenty of unmanageable, inexplicable sensations flitting around her body, gratitude being one of the more logical ones, but she detected no disappointment. She gasped. 'I didn't say thank you. For getting Seth out.' She twisted round and studied her son. 'What would we have done if he'd not been there, Seth?' It didn't bear thinking about. 'We must make sure we thank him next time we see him.'

'Is it bad inside?' Olivia ushered Seth into the craft centre.

'I've not seen it,' Victoria said. 'But Chris says it's uninhabitable.'

'Then I suggest you close the door, and worry about it tomorrow.' Olivia invited her in.

'That would be nice, but I'm fighting the board tomorrow. Besides, I should call the insurance company. They might send an assessor out today.' She sighed. 'May I borrow your phone, Olivia?'

Chapter Eleven

There had been little value in going to bed. With Seth crying
in his sleep, and Victoria's mind running over the events of
the past day, she'd have fared better staying up. She would
have watched over Seth, and avoided the all-too-familiar
dreams featuring her and Chris Frampton.

She yawned and pressed the button on her car door.
The window descended into its groove, and the cold air,
taking no prisoners, murdered Victoria's hair. 'Bloody hell,'
she muttered, flipping the switch to thwart the onslaught.
She'd have to carry out major repairs before she entered the
boardroom.

Major repairs. Huh. That's what the assessor from the
insurance company had said about the cottage. Talk about
stating the obvious. Still, he was organising three approved
builders to provide quotes, and a firm to install dehumidifiers.

'The trouble with water damage,' he'd said, 'is the time
it takes to dry out. Don't expect to be in here before six
months.'

Bloody burst pipes.

'So this is what it's like going back to basics.' Victoria
pulled into her parking space at the EweSpeak office, as the
radio announcer brought the seven-thirty news to a close.
She'd been on the road a little short of three hours. There
were a number of cars on site, including Juliette's, and a

natty Audi Victoria didn't recognise, but none that belonged to the bigwigs. Good. That gave Victoria and her sister time to prepare their case.

As she locked her car, and caught sight of the empty passenger seat, Victoria's thoughts turned to Seth. It had been a wrench leaving him with his granddad. The shock waves from yesterday's disaster were still rippling around her system. Along with dreams of Chris Frampton, the *what ifs* of the collapse plagued her throughout the night. Beyond the occasions Seth was crying, Victoria rose three times, concerned for him, but he was tucked up, safe and sound in his bunk. Her behaviour was irrational, but it was a need to know she hadn't lost her son, and it was a response over which she had no control. Two weeks ago that would have frightened her.

'Morning, Mrs Noble.'

Victoria returned the greeting to the front desk clerk, congratulated her on her neat appearance, and proceeded to the lift. As she waited for it to reach the ground floor, the main doors to the building swished open, and footsteps click-clacked across the tiles.

'It's all right, I know my way thanks.'

Victoria smiled. She knew that voice. She looked back to the entrance in time to see Annabel Lamb produce her most practised smile and breeze past the receptionist, who was staring, open-mouthed. It was a common reaction to Annabel; winning UK Starz had made her an international singing sensation.

Annabel waved cheerily at Victoria, and skipped into the lift. 'Are you coming?' She grabbed at Victoria's briefcase, yanked her in, and gawped at her hair. 'Do you want me to get the hedge that did that to you?' She grinned, then threw her arms around Victoria. 'Oh my God! It's been ages. How are you?'

'You mean apart from looking like I've been hauled through a bush?' Victoria laughed. 'I'll be fine as soon as I've tidied myself up and had a decent cup of coffee. How come you're so bright and breezy this time of the morning?' She regarded the perfectly made-up Annabel, in awe of her energy. 'In fact, how come you're *here* this early?'

'It's a bird and worm thing. Your office?'

Victoria nodded and watched as Annabel stabbed at the number three button. Not even the starting jolt of a lift unbalanced her from her six inch heels.

Annabel viewed her reflection in the mirrored doors, flirted with the CCTV camera in the top corner, and winked. 'That should cheer the old bugger up.'

The lift halted, the doors pinged open, and Annabel blew a kiss at the lens as she exited.

Victoria followed, shaking her head. 'Sid's retired. That's our new, young security officer you've just ruined.'

'Nonsense. A rush of blood to the head never harmed anyone. I bet you'll get the best day's work out of him, ever. I may go and inspect his productivity later.' Annabel's eyes twinkled with mischievousness, before she adopted a serious expression. 'First, I have some business to discuss.'

'Well, both Juliette and I are in today. We have a board meeting.' Victoria reached to open the office door.

'No. Let me surprise Joo.' Annabel rapped her knuckles against the wooden frame. 'You wait there.' She pointed for Victoria to stand to the side.

'Annabel! What a lovely surprise. How are you?' Juliette peeped through the slim opening.

'I'm well, thanks. Are you going to let me in?'

Juliette opened the door enough for Annabel's skinny frame to slip through.

Victoria quickly followed.

Annabel scanned the office, then cocked a brow. 'Still

sticking with the neutral shades? You need some colour in your lives.' She turned her attention to Juliette, stood straight and tall, and spread her arms wide. 'This is called "I'm waiting for a hug".' She grinned. 'It's been a long time.' She enveloped Juliette in a warm embrace. 'And look who I found lurking by the lift.'

Victoria placed her case on her desk, and smiled. 'How's it going?'

Juliette shook her head. 'I'm struggling to see a way through. The three hours' sleep I managed last night hasn't helped. The details are up on my PC if you want to take a look.' She approached Victoria and kissed her cheek. 'How are you?'

'Tired, too. It's not looking hopeful, is it?'

'No. I think coffee will help, though.' Juliette brushed her fingers through Victoria's hair, and smoothed it down. 'Tell me about Seth and your cottage, later,' she whispered.

Annabel clapped her hands. 'You girls have the best coffee. Still taking yours black, Joo?' She danced across to the machine and before receiving a reply, made three drinks. She handed them out and then sipped at her own. 'I don't understand your choice in décor, but I forgive you. This coffee makes everything right.'

She wheeled Juliette's chair to Victoria's desk, and perched upon it, her back at ninety degrees to the seat. She placed her cup on the inset leather of the desk. 'I have a problem, and I need your help.'

Victoria, now seated, leaned on her elbows and clasped her hands together. 'Go on.'

'I have a stalker. Well, I have several, but this one's becoming a problem.'

'What are the police doing about it?' Juliette asked.

'I haven't told them. I can't afford for this to go viral. The saying that any publicity is good publicity is rubbish. You and Victoria know that, and that is why so many celebrities bleat on EweSpeak. You understand integrity, and most of all, privacy.'

'Yes. We do.' Victoria glanced at Juliette. 'Shame the board doesn't.'

Annabel pushed on. 'Anyway, I don't think the police would take it seriously at this stage, but I've seen it happen before. This needs to be nipped in the bud now.' She picked up her coffee and drained the cup. 'You emailed me a while ago about a new add-on. Something to do with rounding up wolves in sheep's clothing.'

Juliette nodded. 'SheepDog. Don't you have that already?' She retrieved Annabel's' mug, refilled it, and returned to the desk.

Annabel shook her head. 'Never followed up the email.'

'Don't you have people to do that sort of thing? Shouldn't your manager be looking out for you?' Juliette was frowning.

'I fired her.'

'It's not a problem, Anna. I'll sort it.' Victoria logged onto her PC, and made a note to fast-track Annabel's request. 'You should still tell the police. We can provide documentary evidence of him pestering, and we can track him and block him, but we can't protect you.'

Annabel waved her hand. 'I will if it gets worse. Now, what's this about the board disrespecting our privacy?'

Victoria rolled back her chair, and crossed her legs. 'They have big plans.'

'Like making two departments redundant,' Juliette added, grabbing her mug and stomping over to the washroom door. 'Victoria and I built this company together, and they sit on their fat backsides, scheming, and rubbing their hands together, watching their wallets expand with their waistlines.'

The outburst surprised Victoria. Up until that moment, she had no idea which way Juliette was going to vote. The last time they had spoken, she was offering reasons as to why the board's ideas were worth considering. 'Good to hear you've come to your senses. I thought I was going to have to twist your arm.'

'I never said I was on the board's side. I was considering all the facts. That's solid business practice. You taught me that.' Juliette clicked down the handle to the washroom, and disappeared inside. 'Well, I've looked at the facts and I don't like them. This is our company, Victoria, and one fact I hate is that we don't have control anymore. It gets on my—' Juliette stopped.

'Tits?' Annabel supplied. 'Go on. Say it. I know you want to.' She looked at Victoria, and grinned.

'To be fair, certain members of the board are chauvinistic, misogynistic men of restricted growth,' Victoria said.

Laughing, Annabel craned her neck in the direction of the washroom. 'So tell me why the sexist dwarves are culling departments.'

'To bump up their pensions.' Juliette marched back into the office and stood before Annabel, her hands planted firmly upon her hips. 'How can they be so heartless?'

'But I love EweSpeak. I feel responsible for it. And the people who work here.' Annabel looked at Victoria. 'If I'd not asked you to set up the Annabel Lamb support page, none of this would exist. I don't want people losing their jobs!'

Juliette rested a hand on Annabel's shoulder. 'That's not the half of it. They've told us we need to change direction and actively pursue bleats from the rich and famous, goad them into action. Provoke them to respond. Sensationalise everything.'

Annabel reached for Juliette's hand, pulled it down, and

contained it in hers. 'We don't want to be sensationalised. That's why EweSpeak works.' She breathed a long sigh. 'Do the board have the power to enforce these changes?'

Juliette nodded. 'It's democracy at its finest.' Her head dropped.

'Victoria?'

Victoria threaded her fingers together. 'I know it's not what our clients want, but we need to convince the fence-sitters to come down on our side. As it stands, we will be defeated. We simply don't have enough guaranteed votes.'

'I've talked a couple of the reasonable members round,' Juliette said, 'and two more are erring on our side, but it's not enough. You were right, Victoria. Money talks.'

'It speaks bloody volumes,' said Victoria. 'It's talked me into many places I no longer wish to be.' Both ladies looked at her. 'I'll explain later.'

Annabel released Juliette's hand, and rose to her feet. 'Can I help? Can we use my celebrity status somehow to sway the undecided? Talk to the board and tell them what a shit idea it is?'

Victoria circled her thumbs around themselves. Annabel *could* act as a spokeswoman for the celebrity clients. She *could* implore the board to reconsider. Convince them the A-listers would quit EweSpeak the instant the changes were implemented. Distract them with her golden hair and glorious figure long enough for them to enter the cross in the wrong box. It would be one hell of a show.

'Thanks, Anna, but we don't have the time. The meeting will be done and dusted by ten o'clock. Votes will have been cast and counted, and EweSpeak will be rocketing its way to planet Obscurity.'

Juliette slumped into her freshly vacated chair. 'The frustrating thing is, I'm confident my two waverers would vote with us if they saw the tide turning. They usually go with the majority. They don't like to stand out. You know the sort.'

'What would it take to turn them?' Annabel paced the floor.

'Someone to stand up and be counted. Someone to show them the error of their ways.'

'Damn it! I should have accepted the thirty per cent share you offered me years ago. I'd have kicked ass in that boardroom.'

'Don't lose any sleep over that. Proportion of share doesn't give us proportional vote. It's one vote per person. That was how we set it up. We thought it fair, didn't we, Victoria?'

Victoria gave an absent-minded hum. A memory was battling its way through the facts and figures occupying important space. 'You would kick ass, Anna. You kicked mine when you knocked back my generous offer, but I forgive you. Do you know why?' She locked eyes with Annabel.

'Because I'm adorable?'

'Yes, that, and because I also recall, vividly now, you saying ... and I quote ... "If it stops you getting all tight-arsed and anal, I'll take one per cent".'

Chapter Twelve

A grin swept across Annabel's face. 'I did say that, didn't I?'

'Yes. And my tight arse is ready to forgive.' Victoria gave in to a smile. Annabel's growing enthusiasm was contagious.

'I can't believe I forgot about my share.'

'That's international stardom for you.'

'What's your excuse, Vicky? How could you forget?' Annabel's tone was playful. 'I guess that's what world domination of the social network scene does for you.'

Juliette joined in with the banter. 'Having four children is my excuse.' She chuckled. 'This is amazing. The answer was under our nose all the time.'

'So, to clarify, I'm entitled to vote?' Annabel tilted her head.

'Yes.' Victoria and Juliette answered in unison.

'Look at you all smiley.' Annabel marched towards them. 'Right, I've thirty minutes to bone up, and ten to lead the hesitant two from the dark into the light.' She ushered Juliette from the chair, trundled it behind her desk, and settled down. She wiggled the mouse. 'Let's kick some butt.'

Victoria followed suit and called up Annabel's client notes. She whistled. 'Your file's not been accessed in years. No wonder we forgot about your share.' She clicked on a thumbnail of a document, and an image of the certificate appeared on the screen. 'Thankfully, we have details of your one per cent. The board are bound to ask for evidence.' She hit the print button, and reclined. 'I bet they knew about this.'

'But decided not to mention it?' Juliette scooted behind Victoria, and examined the information on the monitor. 'So this won't be a surprise, after all?'

'Surprise isn't my word of choice,' said Annabel. 'The sneaky buggers.'

'Oh, we'll still suck the wind from their sails. No Caribbean cruise for the fat cats this year.' Victoria collected the sheet from the printer and tucked it away in her briefcase. She peered at Annabel. 'What are you doing?'

'Looking at all the facts before I decide on my vote. It's solid business practice.' She kept her eyes on the screen.

Victoria closed hers. Annabel's arrival was so well-timed there had to be more to it than coincidence. Her presence could ultimately prevent the demise of EweSpeak. It was almost enough for Victoria to believe in a greater power.

Ironic it came in the form of Annabel's lunatic follower.

After a moment of quiet reflection, Victoria eased herself back into work mode, and said, 'While you do that, I'll sort out your stalker.'

'Well,' said Victoria, as she exited the boardroom, 'I didn't expect three resignations.'

'Are they worth mourning?' Annabel asked.

'The Tiresome Trio? No. The first two who declared their intention were the troublemakers, and the third had no power without them. There was little point him staying, and he knew it.'

Juliette caught up and chipped in. 'It will be good for the company. Think of the money we'll save.'

'And no departments face the chop.' Annabel smiled. 'An excellent morning's work.'

Victoria stopped and touched Annabel's arm. 'We couldn't have done it without you. Thank you.'

'It was a total buzz. Is it wrong that I enjoyed myself?'

Juliette laughed. 'I love the cut and thrust of the business world. It's not all pinstripes and bowler hats.'

Victoria withdrew her hand, and continued walking down the corridor. 'You impressed me, Annabel. You were reeling out facts and figures like you were reciting the names of your family. How did you remember them all?'

'I'm a quick learner. It helped me through the early rounds of UK Starz. My mentor would change the song choice the day before the live show. It drove me nuts, but I trusted his judgement. It caused the downfall of one or two of the other contestants, though.'

'How's the singing going? You've been quiet lately.' Classical was more Victoria's idea of music, but she kept an ear on the local radio, particularly at breakfast. 'When's your next tour?'

'I'm due to go to Japan in three months.' Annabel stopped outside Victoria and Juliette's door. 'I don't think I can do it. I've had enough. I need something new. Something challenging. The only challenge I face is making sure I'm in the right city on the right night. It's hardly algebra.'

The women stepped through into the privacy of the office, Juliette excusing herself from the conversation. 'I'm going to get on with the paperwork,' she said. 'While the meeting's still fresh in my mind.'

Victoria and Annabel repaired to the sofas.

'So you're bored?' said Victoria.

'Yes. And disillusioned. I feel there's more to life than prancing around a stage, singing relics of songs that should have been consigned to the bargain bin years ago.'

'Oh dear.' It was an understated reaction, Victoria realised, but she said it more by way of letting Annabel know she was listening.

'Performing doesn't give me a natural high anymore. Maybe it's my age. I don't know.' Annabel pouted. 'I appreciate everything this lifestyle has given me, but enough's enough, don't you think?'

Victoria understood perfectly. She'd felt the same recently. Perhaps they were both going through a mid-life crisis.

'Anyway,' said Annabel, 'tell me what you've been up to.'

It was past ten by the time Victoria was back in her father's bungalow. Seth was asleep in his bunk, and, in the living room, Frank was dozing on the settee. The TV was happily chatting away to itself. Victoria wished she could climb straight into bed, but since her father was already occupying her room, she wandered into the kitchen, dumped her briefcase on the table, and made a hot chocolate.

While she loved her dad to the moon and back, she couldn't stay with him for six months. There simply wasn't the room. And it crossed her mind that she was cramping his style, as well as his living space. His relationship with Olivia was still fresh and new, and once he resolved the issue of Iris's memory, he would want Olivia to stay over.

There were four options available. Victoria could rent somewhere, buy a new property, or stay in a hotel – all of which were out of the question, as she refused to be a slave to money – or return to London.

She shuddered. Even though today's meeting exceeded expectation, and the future of EweSpeak was bright, Victoria was no longer a moth drawn to the light of the company. Nearly losing Seth had rammed home how much she loved him, and now more than ever, she was determined to set things right.

Juliette and Annabel, once they'd squeezed blood from the 'proverbial stone that is Victoria', listened to her plans to step back from EweSpeak. When she told them about Seth's possible disorder, and her need to put him first, they were supportive and encouraging.

Victoria clicked open her case and pulled out a thick wodge of paper – research Juliette had downloaded and printed out that afternoon, to back up what Victoria had already learned. She smiled. 'You truly are an earthbound angel, Juliette.'

She sat at the table, pulled her mug closer, and read the title of the top sheet. *Child Attachment Disorder: Symptoms and Behaviour.*

By midnight, Victoria had read enough. Words like *anxiety* and *psychopathology*, and phrases such as *insecure mother-child attachment*, and *behavioural inhibition*, bit at her conscience. Not all of it applied, and some papers were extracted from medical reports even Victoria struggled to understand, but there was plenty to which she related. And there were enough pointers to indicate Olivia's suggestion was not far off the mark.

The next thing, once Victoria's guilt subsided, was to decide on a course of action. An official diagnosis was the accepted procedure, but she knew, through Juliette's experience with paediatricians and hospitals, it was not necessarily the fastest. Still, she'd register with a local GP, and go from there. In the meantime, she'd continue to read and absorb as much information about the condition as possible.

Or maybe, she'd go to bed. 'I should be a pumpkin by now,' she muttered, gathering her papers, and placing her empty mug in the sink.

She looked in on her father. He was settled on the sofa, his face relaxed, and his mouth ejecting gusts of air, as he released the deeply inhaled breaths. Victoria silenced the TV, grabbed the duvet from the corner of the room, and laid it over him. 'Night, Dad.'

The decision not to wake him was two-fold: she didn't want to disturb such a peaceful sleeper, and the promise of a night in a decent bed, namely his, was too great to resist.

She crept into Seth's room to retrieve her night things. He too was sound asleep.

'Night, my boy,' she said, pushing his tousled mop from his forehead. 'Sweet dreams.' She hoped his brush with disaster gave him no more nightmares. She hoped her dreams of Chris would be a little more conventional. 'Oh, sod it,' she said, after a moment's rethink. 'Bring them on.'

She left Seth, entered her father's room, and changed into her nightclothes.

The last sensation she remembered was her body sinking into the mattress.

Chapter Thirteen

The Harbour Inn, situated so close to Chesil beach it was almost afloat, overlooked the steel-grey sea. The wind was whipping the water into a frenzy, and strands of the white horses' manes broke free and lashed onto the pub's windows.

Having retreated inside, Victoria edged away from the glass, and attempted to smooth down her curls. The hour she'd spent that morning making her hair presentable had been blown away in less than a minute.

She sighed. It didn't matter what she looked like. This was nothing more than lunch. She'd said as much in her note to Hope Cove Castle, suggesting a date on which she and Chris could meet. *Bloody dreams.* In the two weeks since she'd first bumped into him, her dreams had become less and less inhibited. Several mornings running she'd woken convinced she was beneath, above or beside Chris, in the throes of making love, and after the last unbridled fantasy, she wasn't sure she could look him in the eye.

It's just lunch, she reminded herself.

She shook the visions from her mind, and glanced at Seth. His nose was pressed against the pane. The spectacular weather was holding his interest. *His* hair was great.

A waitress, wearing regulation black, and sporting a Santa's elf hat, placed one hot chocolate and one lemonade on the table. Victoria smiled her thanks, and reclined. The bench, though dressed with cushions, was uncomfortable, but its style was in keeping with the rest of the interior; dark mahogany beams across the ceiling, white wooden sash windows, and porthole lights. Christmas decorations hanging overhead like jungle vines brought colour, but it was the heat and glow from the central log burner that gave the room its warmth. The place had character. More than Victoria remembered. Not that she'd paid much notice to it in her youth, her eyes and mind being all about Chris.

She checked her watch. Quarter to one. She and Seth had been there fifteen minutes. Granted, she'd not specified a time for lunch, but half-twelve was the standard.

A sigh of disappointment seeped out. He wasn't coming. 'Will I ever learn?'

She gave Seth's elbow a gentle nudge. 'Hey. Your drink's here.'

He turned from the window, and reached for his lemonade. 'Are they called white horses because they're white?'

Victoria smiled. 'Yes. And because they look as if they're galloping towards us. Like horses.' She cast an eye to the outside world, and jumped back as two blurred figures, clad in black, ran past the window. More staff, she thought, directing her gaze to the flickering fireplace.

The flames, like tree sprites revelling in ritual, jigged with wild abandon – something Juliette suggested Victoria did once in a while. 'Dance as if no one's watching,' she'd said. 'Let go. Lose yourself to the moment.' But Victoria couldn't. The first time she'd done that, she'd given away more than just her pride. And in exchange she'd gained a broken heart.

For now, it was safer to lose herself to the flames, where the risk of getting burned was obvious.

She stared at the centre. It was white hot, like molten glass ready for shaping, and surrounding it was a blazing cloak of gold, hemmed with pink, and tipped with red. Threads of purple weaved their way across the bottom, like an African sunset. It was dazzling. It was hypnotic.

As she was drawn in deeper, childhood memories surged forward – images of her and Juliette on Guy Fawkes Night, holding sparklers in their mittened hands, waiting for the bonfire to be lit; their dad huddling them together, and covering their ears from the rockets and bangers exploding in the sky – the magical, shimmering waterfalls and palm trees, appearing from nowhere and blossoming above them. Catherine wheels, tacked onto the back fence, whirling and whizzing, spitting sparks, and singeing the larchlap panels. Fireworks illuminating their garden—

The cracking and popping of the log burner snapped Victoria from the spell. She blinked, looked at Seth, and then lowered her head. If she dropped dead right here, right now, she wouldn't feature in his memories.

'Been waiting long?'

She raised her head, relieved to hear Chris's voice, glad to be diverted from the path her thoughts were taking.

'You looked miles away.' He claimed a chair, took off his wet, black jacket, and threw it over the back. 'Sorry. I couldn't remember what time we said.'

Victoria straightened her neck. 'We didn't.' She risked a look at his face. No rush or flush was forthcoming from her stomach, so she relaxed a little. 'I want to thank you for what you did the other week. I know I put it in the letter, but I need to say it. What you did was very brave. You saved my son. Thank you.'

Chris puffed out his cheeks. 'Glad I was there.'

'So am I.'

For a fleeting moment their eyes met. His were darker

than she remembered, and in no way repentant as she'd assumed. More soulful. His whole life was there, open to her, if she could interpret. It had been many years since she last delved that deep into a man.

She looked away, pretending to be distracted by the boys wandering across to the pool table. 'Rick's very good with Seth.'

'He likes him. He told me about their meeting at Hope Cove.'

Victoria rubbed at a non-existent mark on the table, nervous of what Chris knew. 'Well, they seem to get along,' she said, desperate to move the subject on. 'Shall we order?'

Chris shifted to the front of his chair, and perched on the edge. 'Before we do, I want to apologise for putting my foot in it the other week about your mum. I didn't know she … I didn't know you'd lost her.' He bowed his head and drew his finger down the length of Seth's glass, prompting the condensation to flow into a delta of tiny rivers. 'I remember she was tough on you, but I also remember you loved each other.' He issued a sympathetic smile as he looked at Victoria. 'It doesn't matter what age you are when you lose a parent, it's hard.' He paused, giving another thoughtful wipe of the glass. 'It's when you lose both, you realise you're an adult. You're the end of the line. Every decision you make is yours, and yours alone. You have to deal with everything.' He fell silent.

Victoria gave a brief nod, suddenly in a quandary as to how to respond. Chris had lost far more than she could ever imagine, and here he was offering her words of comfort. It wasn't right. He was the one in need of heartfelt sympathies. Cautious of infecting raw wounds, she said, 'I'm sorry about your dad. I read your notice on social media.'

'Thank you. I guess he's finally happy now he's reunited with Mum.'

'And I'm sorry about—'

'It's okay. You don't have to say anything.' Chris picked up the menu and held it in front of his face.

It seemed to Victoria he was using it as a buffer.

'Now. Lunch,' he said. 'What do you recommend?'

If Chris hadn't been so definite in his action, Victoria would have pushed her point home, and passed him her condolences. Instead she too focused on the menu. 'Dad says the carvery's good, but that could be him craving meat. I think he's turned vegetarian, or ... what's the word for fish eaters? Pescetarian? Still, I'm game.' She smiled.

'Carvery it is, then. You've not eaten here?'

'Not since ... ' She paused, and reviewed her answer, deciding to stick to a simple and less controversial, 'No.'

'But your cottage is so close.'

'I live in London.' Victoria thought she saw Chris's expression drop. It was a tiny movement of the brow – it lowered by a millimetre. He must have noticed her staring, because he brushed his fringe down. Still, she was sure that was disappointment on his face.

'I moved years ago, for work, but I'm thinking of coming back,' she said, testing the water. 'Seth and I need time together. A new life. I'd like to strip everything down and go back to basics. Find out who we really are. We're staying with my dad at the moment. It's a bit of a squeeze. An air bed in the living room wasn't quite the level of basic I was looking for.' She waited for Chris to respond, but his eyes were glazed, as if no one was at home. He clearly wasn't interested in her plans.

Cross with herself for being stupid, she stood, squeezed out from behind the table, and headed for the bar. 'Three adult and one child's carvery please. And a jug of water. Table nine. Thanks.'

She spent a moment leaning against the dark wood,

wondering if this meeting was such a good idea. She was yet to establish what she hoped to gain from it. Closure? Friendship? Love? She picked up a beer mat and folded it in two. She wasn't looking for love. Not from Chris Frampton. That was far too complicated, and best left tucked between the sheets of a diary, than a bed. Even her fantasy bed. She closed her eyes. 'Don't go there, Victoria,' she muttered.

'Everything okay?' Chris slipped in beside her. 'Trouble with the order? I can choose something else.'

'No. No trouble.' Not with the food. Not with the order. Where the warmth of his body seeped through her clothes – there was trouble. 'I'm waiting for the water.' The cold water that would cool her and shock some sense into her.

Chris gestured towards the table. 'You sit down. I'll bring it over.'

Glad to be released from the tension, Victoria withdrew and settled back at the bench. The boys were within her view. Rick was showing Seth how to hold a cue. Three times he showed him, and three times Seth got it wrong. Rick grinned, and tried again. For a lad of thirteen, he had immense patience.

A tray of glasses and a jug filled to the brim with water, ice and lemon slices was placed under her nose.

'There you go,' said Chris, pouring out a drink and handing it to Victoria. 'You know how to live.' He winked.

'I'm not really a fan of alcohol,' she replied.

'You never were.'

And there it was. The first reference to their past.

'Annabel Lamb was though.' Chris laughed. 'Do you remember? Always the one with the bottle of vodka at the college discos. She had that old guy at the off-licence wrapped around her little finger.' He paused to sip from his glass. 'She really hit the big time. I had no idea she could sing. Great voice. Are you two still in touch?'

'I saw her a couple of weeks ago when I went to London for that meeting I mentioned. She came to the office.'

'Ah, yes. Your meeting. How'd it go?'

'Like a dream, once Anna showed up. She's quite a business woman.'

'Doesn't surprise me.' Chris refilled his half-pint, tutting as three ice cubes and a lemon slice sloshed in. He scooped them out and dropped them into Seth's empty lemonade glass. 'So, what is it you do?'

Victoria stiffened. She wasn't prepared to find out his reaction to the news she was the head of EweSpeak. Or that she'd followed his every move from the moment he signed up to the network, and been responsible for creating publicity surrounding the death of Lacey and Todd.

'I run my own business,' she said, directing her attention to the bar. 'Oh, look. We can go up to the carvery. I'll get the boys.' Relieved to have been called by the chef, she left the table and approached the two young pool players. 'You look like you're having fun.' She smiled and offered Seth her hand. He thrust his cue in it and walked off.

'Yes, thank you, Mrs Noble.' Rick took the cue and returned it to its rack. 'He's a bright kid. You know, for a four-year-old. He loves his technology.'

'He does?' It was news to her, but hearing the surprise in her voice, Victoria altered her intonation. 'He does.'

'He says you're pretty good with computers. That you're the boss in a big building in London and he isn't sure, but he thinks you might work with sheep. His words.' Rick's smile was partnered with one of his shrugs. 'Dad's rubbish at all that stuff. We're still not online. We need Tommy to come home and sort it.'

Victoria was quickly processing Rick's stream of information: Seth had spoken about her. He understood her role at work, and EweSpeak was lodged in his memory banks. Thank goodness it had stayed there. Mental images of her dressed as Bo Peep were welcome, if it meant her role in her company was kept from Chris. At least until she'd worked out how to tell him without making herself sound like Annabel's crazed stalker.

'Tommy's away?' That surprised Victoria. She'd formed the impression the Framptons' manager never left Chris's side – his bleats suggested as much, and it was rare to catch footage without the two men standing cheek by jowl. He was certainly visible during the aftermath of the motorbike tragedy.

Victoria put her hand on Rick's shoulder, and guided him to the food bar.

'Yeah. He's seeing friends,' Rick said. 'It's a bummer. Dad can't cook.'

'No? I'm not much of one either.'

The conversation paused as they joined the queue for the carvery.

'Looks like Dad's getting along with Seth.' Rick smiled and pointed to the front of the line.

Victoria raised her head and saw Chris settling Seth on to his hip. He nestled her son's back in the crook of his arm, and pulled him in. Seth responded by resting his fingers on the back of Chris's tanned neck.

They were pointing at the meats on the pass.

It looked so natural. Two pieces of Victoria's puzzle she would never have put together, fitting so perfectly. It was a beautiful sight.

Not knowing if she was about to laugh or cry, Victoria covered her mouth.

'Are you all right, Mrs Noble?'

'Hiccups,' she said, faking one for good measure. 'Empty stomach.'

She collected two plates and passed one to Rick. 'Seth

will have the turkey,' she whispered. 'With carrots and potatoes, and he'll drown it in gravy.'

'Dad will go for the beef. With everything. Apart from broccoli.' Rick shuffled along the line.

'What's wrong with broccoli?'

'We hate it. Mom used to make us eat it. When she wasn't looking, Todd would scrape his onto Dad's plate. He got away with it every time.'

'What did your dad do?'

'He ate it.' Rick laughed, causing Chris to turn round and raise a questioning eyebrow.

Victoria smiled and waved for him to concentrate on collecting his food. 'That was sweet of him. And what about you? Did you pass yours to your dad, too?'

'No. I couldn't do that to him. Anyway, it pleased Mom to see us eat well. It made her happy.'

On the occasions Victoria was in charge of mealtimes, there was always a battle; always a refusal from Seth to eat what was put in front of him. She'd be happy too, if he ate well. He devoured everything Cerys dished up. Victoria sighed. 'Can you pass on your good habits to Seth?'

'I'll try, Ma'am.'

The wild wind of earlier had settled into a brisk breeze, and the sea presented nothing more than a few trotting ponies, rather than herds of charging white horses. Despite her initial reluctance, Victoria allowed Chris to talk her into a walk along the beach. The boys, being boys, ran ahead. They were seen disappearing through the hedge into the Hope Cove grounds.

'Who'd have thought?' said Chris, pulling his jacket tight. 'There's a what? Eight … nine year age gap between them? They've totally hit it off. Mind you, Seth's a cracking little lad. He says the funniest things. I can see why Rick likes him.'

'I think that's more to do with Rick being a kind and thoughtful young man,' Victoria said. 'He's considerate of other's feelings.' Did that sound bitter? She hadn't meant it to. Chris wasn't acting offended, but she wasn't sure she could tell if he was. Their past was a long time ago, and they were different people now.

What she knew about Chris Frampton, actor, was either made up by the press, or presented by Chris's PR team. She knew what he wanted her and three million others to know, like all the celebrities on EweSpeak's books.

He used to be spontaneous, vibrant, exciting – everything Victoria wasn't. He injected energy and enthusiasm into life. 'If it's not worth doing properly, it's not worth doing at all,' he used to say, adding, 'and if you do a good job, expect appreciation and success to follow.' He was so sure of himself. So certain he'd achieve. He allowed nothing to get in the way of what he wanted. Including Victoria.

Yes. Her comment was bitter. Chris had used her and then dumped her for a life of fame and fortune in LA. Before he hit thirty, he was seen as a perfect husband, a wonderful father, and one of the most influential stunt actors in Hollywood. At eighteen, Victoria had been discarded like litter, thrown on the pebbles, and washed underneath. Shortly after she hit thirty, she was a deserted island.

'Vicky? Victoria? I was saying, I worry about Rick. He stores stuff up, you know. He rarely mentions Lacey or Todd. I've done everything in my power to get him to come to terms with the accident, but I can't get through. I thought I was making some headway when we first arrived here, but it was a one-off. He doesn't talk. He doesn't cry. I'd forgotten what his laugh sounds like until today. Can you imagine that? He must be hurting. I'm his father, and I should be able to help. I feel so inadequate.'

Inadequate was Victoria's area of expertise, first as a

lover, then as a wife, and now as a mother; a state to which she had grown accustomed. But Chris, inadequate? She hadn't expected to hear that.

'These last two years have been so hard on him. He withdrew from his friends, he stopped going to school, and he shut himself away in his room. He wasn't living. I decided to move back once the inquest was through. I had to do something. Anything to break the cycle, you know? It's early days, but this needs to work. Has to work. Otherwise ...' Chris froze, casting his eyes and his words out to sea.

Victoria stood beside him not knowing what to say. His body language indicated *inadequate* didn't cover all he was experiencing. His hunched shoulders and bowed head suggested *useless, helpless, and worthless* were nearer the mark, but Victoria kept the thought to herself; saying it out loud would convince Chris he was right, and he was anything but.

In that moment who he used to be became irrelevant. Who he was now was all that mattered, and Victoria discovered he was alone and lost. Desperate. He was a grieving widower who'd outlived one son, and was searching for ways to fix his surviving boy, no matter what the personal cost. He was a man to whom failure was not an option, and Victoria understood that. It made Chris a hundred times the hero portrayed by the media. It made Chris a man she wanted to help. If she was to succeed, she had to let the past go. All of it.

She swallowed the bitter pill of betrayal, accepting that given time it would work its way out of her system, and she could flush it away with all the other rubbish she'd fermented over the years.

She had consumed, rather than continue to be consumed.

She edged closer to Chris, and with her heart pounding in her head, wrapped a conciliatory arm around him.

Chapter Fourteen

With a violent jerk, Chris freed himself and stepped aside.
'What are you doing?' He glared at Victoria, clenched a
hand where hers had been, and gritted his teeth, blocking
the surge of anger from overflowing. He should yell at her,
ask her who the hell she thought she was; demand to know
what right she had to touch him, but the look of sheer
horror plastered across her face was preventing him. As was
his prickling conscience.

He had overreacted and scared her, and for that he was
sorry, but the last woman to lay hands on him was Lacey.
He'd carried that feeling for two years, cherishing it,
sustaining it, remembering the warmth of her embrace and
the depth of her kiss. It was a perfect memory of a perfect
moment; the final time he'd set her free. The final time she'd
loved him.

And now it was gone.

But there were other reasons for his anger: Lacey would
never forgive him if she knew he'd welcomed Victoria's
hold, and he was cross with himself for wanting to be
cared for, because that meant he was betraying his wife. He
couldn't explain that to Victoria.

He removed his hand and studied his palm. 'I'm sorry,' he
said. 'I didn't come back for this. For you.' He shoved both
hands in his pockets. 'And I don't want anything from you.

Not for me.' He chanced a look at Victoria. Her horror had been replaced with wide-eyed astonishment. So extreme was her expression, Chris faltered. 'I'm sorry,' he repeated. 'I should have kept my thoughts to myself. I wasn't asking for comfort. No one can give me that.'

He lowered his head, turned into the wind, and headed up the beach, praying Victoria wouldn't follow. He released a forceful breath when he heard the hollow scuffling of pebbles. 'I'll get Rick to bring Seth home later,' he said, hoping to cut Victoria off at the pass.

'I prefer to collect him now.'

Her concise words and terse tone informed Chris there was no point arguing. He motioned for her to go ahead, but she pulled alongside and maintained his pace. He braced himself for what was bound to be a bollocking.

'Is this what Hollywood does to a man? Turns him into an arrogant, narcissistic prat? I was offering you support. Showing you you're not alone. Nothing else.'

An elderly couple walking towards them, watched with fascination as they passed by.

Chris scraped his fingers through his hair. 'Vicky, seriously, I can't deal with this now.' Her hug had set in motion a huge ball of confusion; memories of their past, how good it was to be loved by her; thoughts of Lacey and how much he loved her. Shame. Duplicity. It was one enormous mass, rolling around his head.

Victoria steamed on. 'Ten minutes ago I was prepared to forgive because I saw a different man to the one who deceived me seventeen years ago. I saw a loving father whose sole purpose in life was to help his son live again. I believed that was who you'd grown into. But you've not changed one bit. It's all about you, isn't it? And once again, you tricked me. Well, congratulations. You are truly a great actor.'

Chris snorted. Tricked her? Deceived her? He drew breath to ask what the hell she was on about, and then decided against it. He needed to be away from her, not engage with her. Life was complicated enough. 'Get your boy and go home.'

'My boy? My *cracking little lad* who was happier in your arms than mine? You think he'll come willingly? He doesn't listen to a word I say. He kicks and spits at me, he swears and throws apples in my face, and he can't even call me mum. And do you know why? Because you damaged me. You battered my emotions, and screwed them into the ground. And I couldn't bear it. I took refuge in my work, and disconnected from the real world. I threw everything into making my business a success, and because of that, I have a failed marriage and a son who hates me.'

She came to a sudden standstill, bent double and threw up. It splashed off the shingle and onto Chris's trousers. As she straightened up, Victoria cuffed her mouth, and closed her eyes. 'You know what? If I could go home, I would, but in case you'd forgotten, the bloody ceiling's collapsed.' She looked at Chris. 'I'm going to the craft shop. Ask Rick to bring Seth there before it's dark.' She kicked some loose stones over her sick, apologised for catching Chris's legs, and took off.

He watched her leave the beach, the mad, passionate, turning-his-world-upside-down-woman, who had more issues than *The Beano*. He'd heard everything she'd said, but it knocked about inside his head like an iron clapper. 'This is going to take some sorting,' he muttered.

Now back at the castle, the boys were camped out in Rick's room, and Chris was sitting in his uncomfortable porter's chair in the conservatory, seeking answers from the trees. They weren't held accountable for anything. Except for when a gale knocked them over and they crashed through someone's roof.

That's how he was feeling – as if he'd been tossed around in a tornado and spat into a whole new world. Dorothy, he wasn't. Tin man, maybe. At least he understood the value of a heart. As for the Wicked Witch of the West ... He couldn't tell if Vicky held him responsible for her failings, or if she was knee-jerking at his rebuff. Telling him he was a selfish father hurt, but he realised that was the point. She was biting back, with the jaws of a lion.

He fidgeted, first by pushing his spine into the chair and then by crossing and uncrossing his legs. Everything was uncomfortable; his position, his situation, and his conscience. Among a whole list of misdemeanours, Vicky ... Victoria accused him of deception and self-absorption. And somewhere in her tangled web of words, she'd declared he was responsible for everything bad in her life. That wasn't possible. He'd lived in America for the past seventeen years, and he'd left Vicky in a good place. And anyway, it had been her decision to cut off all communication. His dad was very clear on that.

'She said she's not interested in a long-distance relationship,' his dad had said during Chris's first phone call home. 'And staying in touch would be pointless, especially since you two have run your course.'

Chris had been shocked by Vicky's response, convinced she'd spoken the words in bitterness, but his father said not. 'Hurt women are never that blasé about love. And to think she was the reason you almost gave up your dream. Lucky I sent your forms off.'

'Yeah. Would seem so.' Love had changed everything for Chris. He'd set aside his application for summer work in the US. He'd set aside his dream to study acting in an American university. He'd set aside his future. All to stay with Vicky Paveley.

'You're destined for great things, my son,' his dad added. 'And you'll find true love, like your mum and I did. And it'll be with someone worthy of you.'

Chris thought Vicky was that woman, so to be disposed of with a verbal wave of the hand was heartbreaking.

Vicky … *Victoria* accusing him of deception and self-absorption didn't make sense. The only deception he was guilty of was pretending to forget her.

'Hey, Dad. I'm going to take Seth home.'

Chris rose from the chair, stretched his back, and smiled at the boys, who were lingering in the doorway. 'You ready?'

'Yes,' said Seth. 'I'm going to Livia's.'

'Should I come too?' Chris directed the question at Rick.

'You're okay, Dad. I can manage. I'll wait until Seth's gone in before I head back.'

'Go on then. Get a move on. Your mum will be waiting.'

'Yes, but I'm going to see Livia. Livia's nice,' said Seth. 'She likes me.'

Choosing to ignore the implication that Victoria didn't, Chris said, 'That's good. I like you too. If your mum says you can come and visit again, that's fine by me. You're very welcome here.'

He crouched down and offered his hand, expecting Seth to shake it. Instead, he was almost knocked off his feet as the four-year-old launched himself at him. 'Wow. Good hug,' Chris said, squeezing Seth to him. 'You are the man.' As they broke apart, Chris raised a palm for a high five. Seth stared at him.

Rick stepped forward. 'Like this.' He indicated for Chris to stand. Both men put their arms in the air and smacked their hands together, ending the ritual with a firm grip of each other's fingers. 'It's called a high five.'

Seth glanced from Chris to Rick, and back to Chris, put his hands in his pockets, and smiled. 'You're funny.'

'Oh, yeah? Well, you're funnier.' Chris pulled a face and ruffled Seth's hair. 'Go on. Off you go. See you later, buddy.'

He nodded at Rick, who guided Seth from the room.

There was constant chatter between the boys from leaving the conservatory, to the front door slamming shut, and it lightened Chris's heart. The change in Rick was astounding. His four-year-old friend possessed a quality the highly-paid, highly-qualified professionals lacked. Chris couldn't identify what it was, but he wanted Seth to visit, if Victoria allowed. Chances were slim.

But it wasn't only Seth that Rick got along with; Chris had seen his son deep in conversation with Victoria too, and they'd shared a joke. A joke! It remained to be seen if it was a one-off, or if Rick related to her in some way.

Chris leaned against the door frame and drummed his fingers on the jamb. What would he have to do to get Victoria on board? That was the question he was leading to before he was forced to take cover from her verbal Gatling gun. He doubted Victoria would respond to the waving of a white flag right now. The mood she was·in, she'd shoot holes in it until it resembled a second-hand paper doily.

Perhaps it was just as well. Rick had made a friend – the first one in a long time, and although it wasn't an association Chris would have encouraged, it worked. For both boys. Adding Victoria into the equation could upset the balance.

She'd messed with his equilibrium.

He peeled his hand off the door frame, and made his way to the kitchen. With Tommy on walkabout, cooking duties were down to him. They could order out, but they'd done that a lot over the last couple of weeks, and anyway, Chris wanted to do something for his son. A thank you for making progress.

Lacey used to say preparing meals for family and friends

was a privilege, never a chore. She often asked Chris to help, but when he wasn't filming, he was planning and perfecting his next stunt. He could count on one hand the number of times he was her commis chef, but he was surprised by how intimate the experience was – the two of them, working together, achieving the same end. Providing for their boys.

Tommy was always keen to assist, and he'd picked up Lacey's culinary skills. He was a natural. How intimate had he found the experience?

'Don't think about it.' Chris sifted through the shelves that lined the pantry, pulled out a can of beans, a tin of tomatoes, and a box of eggs. It wasn't haute cuisine, but with a few rashers of crispy bacon to go on top, and a slice of crusty bread, it covered the major food groups, something Lacey and Tommy were keen to enforce.

'Lacey and Tommy?' Chris would have known if they'd had an affair, wouldn't he? Lacey had a high sex drive, but Chris matched her, and he loved her with such an intensity she had no need to turn to another man. And she loved him. She told him so every day.

He bashed two pans onto the hob, shoved the can of beans under the electric opener, and watched it rotate. The rhythmical whir of its motor settled him, and his mind eased.

Tommy was messing with his head. That was all. Revenge for being kept in the dark about Lacey's condition. It was pathetic. Childish. Seth behaved better.

The lid popped on the first can, and Chris poured the contents into a saucepan.

It was hard to imagine Seth losing his temper and attacking Victoria. He was such a little thing, scrawny, and defenceless against someone as ferocious as her. But that's what she claimed. *He kicks and spits at me*, she'd said. Well, if she dealt with Seth the way she'd handled Chris, it wasn't any wonder the boy didn't like her. Chris didn't much like that side of her himself. She wasn't the girl he left behind.

He slapped six slices of streaky bacon into the frying pan and pushed them around with a fish slice. Then he sloshed the tomatoes in with the beans, giving the pan a shake to mix the contents together.

His mind was as active as his hands.

The girl he'd left behind. *You damaged me.* The girl he'd made love to, and then left behind. *You battered my emotions, and screwed them into the ground* ... An unpleasant sensation gathered at the back of Chris's throat. Whatever he felt about their night on the beach, it was dawning on him that Victoria believed she was a one-night-stand.

And that was the reason she'd wanted nothing more to do with him.

He had to set her straight. Explain what happened and why it happened. He needed her to know what she'd meant to him. Not for his sake. For hers. And Seth's.

However he chose to do it, Chris had to prove he was not an ogre.

'All right?' Rick, closing the front door, strolled into the kitchen, bringing the outside freshness with him. 'Seth's home.' He waved at the variety of pans on the cooker. 'Smells great. You're getting good at this.'

Chris delivered the plates to the table, leaned on the back of his chair, and looked at Rick. 'Listen. I've something to ask you.'

Chapter Fifteen

'I love the smell of your shop.' Victoria inhaled. She was relaxed, with Seth sitting quietly in the back room engrossed in creating a masterpiece 'like Livia'. 'Fresh sharpenings and strawberry erasers. Takes me back to my schooldays. My pencil case smelled exactly the same,' Victoria said.

'Saturday's the day I make a point of my blunt pencils.' Olivia laughed at the pun and nodded to the waste-paper basket. 'I spent an hour on them this morning.'

'Really?' Victoria hovered over the bin, the bottom of which was covered in pinked wooden shavings. 'How very different our lives are. I spent an hour at the harbour hooking bait onto a crab line. Fish and raw bacon.' She waggled her fingers under her nose. 'And like your shavings, the scent's lasted well.'

Olivia laughed. 'Your dad said you were taking Seth crabbing. What a lovely idea.'

'Hmm. Lovely idea, not such a lovely activity.'

'It didn't go well?'

'My fault. I set my expectations too high. I spent half the time hauling Seth back from the edge of the wall, and the other half telling him we couldn't bring the crabs home. At one point, I had to ask him to stop naming them.'

'Sounds like a highly successful morning to me.' Olivia was clearly appreciating the humour of the situation. Her eyes were giving her away. 'Did Seth enjoy it?'

'Hard to tell. He wasn't happy when I told him we had to put the crabs back. Nor when I stopped him putting the raw meat in his mouth.' Victoria rubbed her hands together hoping to eliminate the smell. 'As bonding experiences go, it was testing. I don't remember it being stressful when Dad took Juliette and me.'

Olivia dug around at the back of her counter and pulled out a packet of antiseptic wipes. She took one and passed the rest to Victoria. 'Well, fair play to you. I'm proud of you for trying. You'll look back on this day as a good one.' Olivia cleaned around the till.

Victoria helped herself to a cloth, put the pack on the counter and gave her fingers a vigorous clean. 'I hate to think how Seth will remember it.'

Olivia stopped what she was doing, put both hands on top of the till and looked at Victoria. 'He will remember he went crabbing with his mum.'

Olivia's words slowly percolated, and Victoria nodded. Together, she and Seth had created a memory. With a bit more practise, they might even manage some good ones. 'He named the biggest crab Stuart.'

'I used to date a Stuart. Took him ages to come out of his shell. Wish he hadn't bothered. He was ever so snippy.'

Victoria raised her brow and gave Olivia a reproachful look. 'I think it's time I sidestepped this conversation, before your jokes make me crabby.' She smiled and used the natural break to move on. 'What are these?' She pointed to the round web-like items hanging from the ceiling.

'Dreamcatchers.'

'They look a little like spiders' webs.'

'That's what they represent. The Sioux say they catch the bad dreams the way a spider's web catches and holds whatever touches it. You hang it over the bed, and then the good dreams slide down the feathers to the sleeping person.'

Victoria gave the brown feathers a gentle ruffle. 'So, they filter out nightmares?'

'Yes, but I don't expect you to believe that.' Olivia ventured out from behind her desk, stood on tiptoe, and unhooked the lowest dreamcatcher. She blew the dust off, and passed the item to Victoria. 'Do you have nightmares?'

'Not nightmares, but I've had some very strange dreams.' The confession slipped out before Victoria had time to think.

'Oh?' Olivia pulled out a long-handled, rainbow-dyed duster from behind her desk. 'You can tickle this over the other dreamcatchers while you fill me in.'

Victoria laughed and swapped her Sioux gift for the colourful cleaning tool. 'I can't tell you. You're my father's partner.'

'And that proves how open-minded I am.' Olivia directed Victoria to dust. 'I take it that actor's been on your mind?'

On her mind. On her bed. On her kitchen floor … He'd been everywhere in her dreams. She waited for the embarrassment to warm her cheeks. There it was. 'No, really. I can't tell you. I hadn't meant to say anything.' She returned the duster and smiled. 'You have to stop spiking my coffee with truth serum.'

'Spoilsport.' Olivia placed a cool hand on Victoria's face, and it instantly removed the heat. 'Do you ever dream of your mother?'

The question was asked at such a tender moment, it pained Victoria. She wanted to say yes, she'd often dreamed of her providing a consoling touch, as Olivia had, but she hadn't. 'No dreams. No nightmares,' she said, taking Olivia's fingers in hers. 'Does that disappoint you?' She didn't want it to.

'Nothing you do disappoints me, Victoria. And I believe your mother felt that way, too.'

The ladies dropped hands, and Victoria wandered across to the stool. 'If that's true, then she only ever shared her thoughts with God. He never disappointed her. It was a lot to live up to.'

Olivia hummed as if agreeing. 'Frank said she was a committed Christian. I didn't have her down as a zealot, though.'

'That's exactly what she was.' Victoria slipped onto the stool. 'But it wasn't just with her beliefs. She was uncompromising with everything. I must have been twelve, thirteen when I realised I was going through the motions just to keep the peace. I didn't believe in God. I mean I *really* didn't believe. If I challenged Mum for proof, she'd point to the Bible.'

'To be fair, it's quite well documented in there.' Olivia picked up a pencil from the floor and delivered it to its rightful container. 'But I understand what you're saying. You're a woman of logic. Someone who likes concrete evidence.'

Victoria nodded. 'And I never found it in The Bible. All I saw were stories. I understood the messages behind them, and I appreciated the comfort Mum gained from them, but that was all. I was sick of being preached to and I hated pretending to be someone I wasn't. I'd had enough.'

'You fought back?'

'In a way. I took charge of my emotions and didn't allow Mum to stomp all over them. She fervently insisted I believed, I explained coolly why I didn't.' She stopped, halted by the mental image of Seth in his skewed pyjamas, insisting dragons were real. He'd fought to make her listen, and he'd refused to let her trash his feelings. It was Victoria and her mother all over again. That was bad enough, but worse was the realisation Victoria was more like Iris than she knew. That thought scared her. Thank God she was already trying to change. 'Passion versus reason,' she said, continuing her thread. 'I loved Mum, but we had some almighty fall outs.'

'Almighty? What an interesting choice of word.' Olivia busied herself reorganising a row of shell sculptures.

In the short time she'd known her, Victoria had learned this was Olivia's way of giving her the stage without the glare of the spotlight. 'It's ingrained,' Victoria replied. 'Anyway, my head became proficient at ruling my heart, and it worked. Life was less painful. Until I fell in love.'

'Ah. That old chestnut. I'd like to tell you it gets easier as you get older, but it doesn't. Glucosamine helps, though. And HRT.'

'Olivia!' A laugh exploded from Victoria, and she rocked backwards on the stool. On the verge of tipping over, she threw her weight forward and clung to the desk. With her heart in her mouth, she waited for the stool to regain its stability. She whistled with relief as it clunked into position. 'Glucosamine aside,' she said, 'I was talking about love, not sex.'

'How did that go down with your mother?'

'Oh, we didn't talk about love. Not real love. And sex was avoided like the plague.'

Olivia stopped tidying the shelves and looked sternly at Victoria. 'God's love was real to your mum. And perhaps she wasn't comfortable discussing sex with her daughters.'

'She wasn't comfortable discussing anything. That was the problem. Unlike you.' If only Iris had been more like Olivia. 'I'm not much of a talker and I put it down to nurture rather than nature, having never been encouraged to express myself, but I've told you more in the last few weeks than I care to recall. How do you do it?'

Olivia winked and tapped the side of her nose. 'I think you know the answer to that.'

'Truth serum?'

'It works every time. Coffee?'

While Olivia sorted the drinks, Victoria looked in on Seth. 'How's your picture coming along?' She crouched next to him, resting her arm along the back of his chair. The small camping table Olivia had set up was struggling to contain the paper, pencils and pastels she'd supplied. Victoria gathered a few rogue chalks together and pushed them into the middle.

'I'm drawing the castle,' Seth said, lifting his head from his work. He twirled his paper round for Victoria to see. 'This is Rick, and this big one is Chris, and that's me.' He pointed to the smallest figure. 'I'm doing a five with Chris.'

The three stick figures, surrounded by trees, donned large smiles and huge mitten-shaped hands. Seth's was in the air.

'It's fantastic,' Victoria said. 'I love the trees, and that looks just like you.' The crayon scribbles on top of his head was the giveaway. 'What's a five?'

Seth gave an impatient sigh, grabbed Victoria's arm and spread her fingers out. He patted it with his hand. 'See. A five. Rick showed me.'

And now, Seth was showing Victoria. She glanced at his hair, searching for fairy dust, a preposterous idea, but the only one she could entertain. Magic had been cast. 'That was the best high five ever,' she said, staring at her child in wonder. 'The best.'

Retrieving his picture, Seth chose his next colour and with slow, deliberate strokes, started to create a beautiful summer's day sky. 'Thank you,' he said.

The spell was broken by the call of, 'Coffee!' but Victoria didn't care. The sense that something amazing had happened between her and Seth survived.

'So, lunch with your actor chappie,' Olivia said as Victoria entered the front of the shop. 'I didn't push you on it the other day, as you were clearly in no mood to talk, but was it that bad?'

'Lunch was great. It was the walk afterwards when it went to pot.' Victoria collected her mug from Olivia and nodded her thanks. 'The man drives me mad.'

'In my experience, when a man has driven me mad it has meant one thing,' Olivia said, sitting Victoria on the stool.

'He's arrogant?' Acerbity was worth a shot. With Seth merely yards away in the stock room, Victoria wasn't convinced this was the time or the place to be discussing affairs of the heart. Not hers, anyway. She tried another diversionary tactic. 'Does Dad drive you mad?'

A wide grin took possession of Olivia's mouth. 'Do you want me to tell you?'

Without hesitating, Victoria raised a hand. 'No. Never.' She smiled. 'I was trying to take the heat off me.'

'You don't have to tell me anything.' Olivia stepped across to the stock room, said something to Seth, and then pulled the door to. She returned to the counter. 'But if you did, I would never repeat it.'

Victoria didn't doubt it for one second. There was something about Olivia that oozed trust. And so far, she'd provided nothing but good advice and positive guidance. Victoria set aside her mug, lifted her feet on to the foot bar, and rested her hands in her lap. 'Chris and I go back a long way. He was my first … ' She paused, embarrassed by the advancing confession.

'Lover?' Olivia tendered, as she hitched herself onto the sales desk.

'Not the word I'd use now, but at the time, yes.' Victoria pushed the sleeves of her jumper to above her elbow. Uncomfortable conversations made her hot. And itchy. She scratched her neck. 'He was the first and Ben was the last. With no one in between. A fact I put down to Chris's treatment of me when I was eighteen.'

With no interruption from Olivia, she kept going. 'I was so in love with him. Whenever I saw him, even from a distance, my stomach looped-the-loop. He was confident, funny, and gentle. I was studious, quiet. Got these wretched things.' She scrunched her hair. 'He's so good-looking.'

Victoria's eyes flicked to Olivia's, as she realised her last statement was spoken in the present. As usual, Olivia was straight-faced. Victoria continued. 'I couldn't believe a man like that would want to be with me. Turned out I was right. He got what he wanted and then took off to LA without a second thought.'

It was a moment she'd relived a thousand times, if not more. She resented him for it, but couldn't shake the feeling they had unfinished business.

'So what went wrong yesterday?'

'According to Chris, I'm convinced he's come back for me.' Victoria jumped off the stool and offered it to Olivia. 'Talk about self-centred.'

Olivia stayed put. 'What's given him that impression?'

'I put my arm around him when he was upset. It was a gut reaction.' Victoria threw her hands in the air. 'I'm trying so hard to go with the flow, act first, think later, but it's bloody hard work. I thought he and I could at least be friends. I'd like that. And his son is lovely. He's a little lost, but he and Seth get along so well. They're a real tonic for one another. It could have been easy.'

'With you still hanging on to the past?' Olivia gave a look of disapproval.

'But I wasn't! I'd let it go. I saw his pain, and I understood his sense of uselessness. For a split second, he and I were the same. Then I comforted him, and it all kicked off. I told him he'd ruined my life.'

'And?'

'And what?'

'Had he? Or was he being a bloke?' Olivia swung her legs back and forth, her heels clonking against the counter.

Victoria gaped at her. Leg swinging was Seth's tell when he was boiling up a head of steam. 'Why would you say that? He built me up just so I'd feel good enough about myself to sleep with him. Then he smashed every tiny trace of self-confidence I had.'

'How old were you both?'

'I was eighteen and he was nearly twenty.'

Olivia stilled her legs and looked at Victoria. 'A lad that age either fancies a girl or he doesn't. He has no time for psychological games, believe me.'

'So why did he leave the day after we had sex?'

Olivia shrugged. 'I don't know. Maybe you should ask him.'

Victoria flopped down onto the stool, sighed, and shook her head. 'I'm so rubbish at this.'

'What? Life?' Olivia smiled. 'I bet you'd pass with flying colours if there was an exam at the end.' She slid down from the desk, pulled the creases out of her skirt, and headed for the back room. 'I'm going to check on Seth.'

She stopped on her way past Victoria and placed a hand on her arm. 'Talk to Chris. Explain how you feel, but remember, he's suffered a huge loss. He won't be thinking straight, not even now. The death of a partner is crippling. The death of your child is paralysing.' She lifted her hand away. 'Talk. It's the only way to sort this out. And now seems like the perfect time.' She nodded toward the main door, and made a quick exit through to the stock room, closing her and Seth inside.

In anticipation of the shop door opening, Victoria shepherded her rebellious curls behind her ears, wiped her sticky palms over her hips, and squared her shoulders.

The tension increased at the ting of the brass bell.

Chris hovered over the threshold, a scolded dog waiting to be called by his forgiving master. Victoria nodded for him to proceed.

'We need to talk.' He pushed the door shut.

His voice was dry – vapourless – but it was soon apparent the moisture had travelled to his eyes, and it was threatening to escape.

'I don't think talking will cover it.' As Victoria spoke, a cloud of overwhelming sadness loomed above her, darkening her thoughts. She stood and retreated behind the counter. Proximity to this man interfered with her thinking and right now clarity was imperative. She waved her hand in the air, as if to disperse the fog. 'You overreacted.'

'I did. But with good reason.'

That wasn't an apology. 'Go on,' Victoria said, determined to stay on track.

Chris's eyes searched the space in front. 'Until you, the last woman to touch me was Lacey.'

The words ripped through Victoria's conscience, shredding her preconceived ideas into bloody fragments of guilt. In her misguided effort to comfort Chris, she'd bled over the one remaining trace of his wife.

She slumped against the wall and looked at her hands. Before she had time to respond, Chris appeared at the counter, his fingers raised to his lips.

'Is there somewhere we can talk?' he said.

'The pub would have been my choice.' Chris peered from the kitchen of Victoria's cottage, through to the hallway. 'It's not safe in here.'

As far as Victoria was concerned, nowhere was safe when Chris was near. She closed the back door. 'This room's fine.' The drone of the dehumidifiers reminded her how far away she was from moving in.

'Still, I don't think we should stay long. What did you want to look at?'

Victoria didn't want to look at anything, especially not Chris's face across the table in the cosy, snug Harbour Inn – the place he'd suggested. It was too familiar. Too easy to slip back in time. By coming to the cottage, their conversation would be limited. Neither person would want to stay in the dark, damp excuse of a home for any longer than necessary.

'I wanted to remind myself what a disaster my life is. I leave a trail of devastation.' She swept an arm through the air. 'This is a living example.' It was part truth. She saw Chris's torso rise and fall as he took a deep breath. His leather jacket creaked with the movement. 'Rick okay?'

'Yeah. Well, for him. You know.' Chris shivered, rubbed his hands together, and turned up his collar. 'Are you sure we can't go somewhere warmer? It's not healthy here. Text Olivia, tell her we're going to my place.'

'No!' Victoria blocked the doorway. 'No,' she said, with less insistence. 'This is neutral ground.'

'It's not. It's your cottage.'

'It doesn't feel like mine. There's nothing of me here, is there? If there was, it's lying dead among all that rubble.' *Like the piece of me buried on Chesil Beach.* 'I think we should say what we need to, bid our goodbyes, and go our separate ways.'

'You what?' Chris took a pace towards her. 'Is that what you want?'

Victoria inched back until she brushed against the door. 'You thought I was coming on to you. It proves we don't know each other anymore.'

Chris scuffed the toe of his boot into a crack in the vinyl flooring. 'Yeah. About that.' He looked at Victoria. 'I'm sorry I blew up. I was caught off guard and I said the first thing that came into my head.' He tapped his skull. 'It's no excuse, but the present sometimes escapes me.' He came to a halt, and focused on the damaged flooring.

He was still there in body, Victoria could see that, but his spirit had vanished, sucked down through his feet, and jammed between the fractures of the ripped vinyl.

'I'm trying to hold onto memories of Lacey and Todd. If I forget how they smelled or how they spoke, I'm frightened I'll lose them forever.' Chris closed his eyes. 'It was hard leaving them behind.'

As he opened his eyes again and looked at Victoria, he inclined his head. The intensity of his stare sent a shiver to her stomach. He was back in the room.

'It was hard leaving you behind, too,' he said.

'Then why did you?' Victoria couldn't help herself. It was a chemical reaction, the elements – years of conjecture and self-loathing – were carried in her bloodstream. They were an integral part of her, and it was impossible to stay calm.

The air around her stirred as Chris moved closer.

'I didn't want to.' He raised a hand as if to place it on Victoria's shoulder, but then let it drop. 'I had no choice.'

Victoria looked up, undecided as to whether or not she believed him. It was a convenient get-out, blaming someone else. She'd perfected the art. 'There are always choices,' she heard herself say. Her dad had pointed that out.

Chris acknowledged the remark with a wry smile. 'But sometimes they're taken out of our hands.'

So he was blaming someone else. 'You chose to have sex with me that night. You chose the time, the place ... the way.'

The memory stole the strength from Victoria's legs, and she leaned against the door. It rattled. It shook. It gave in the same way as the metal surround of the sea defences when they'd stumbled and lurched onto them, caught on a tide of desire. She'd never been so completely immersed, nor had she felt so unconfined than when she was entwined with Chris's body. But that moment was her undoing. That moment had brought her to this.

She locked her knees in position, testing their stability before putting her weight on them, and then, with a less than confident stride, carried herself across the room to the old, ceramic basin. The metal tap, resisting Victoria's attempt to twist it into life, creaked and groaned, delivering nothing but frustration; a sensation with which Victoria was all too familiar. Of course there was no water, but she needed something to reduce the heat building inside. She clamped her hands around the rim of the washbowl, gratified by the instant chill to her palms. If only she could lay her cheeks there too.

Chris was right. Coming to the cottage was a bad idea. She hadn't considered how confined the kitchen was, or the fact there was nowhere to run other than the beach, and that raised more issues than it solved.

Gee, what she'd do for a drink. Something to moisten her throat. She whacked the cold tap.

'I want us to be okay.'

The inadequacy of Chris's statement cycloned its way into Victoria's conscience, and she reeled round. 'I can never be okay. You saw to that. And just so we're clear, I would never give myself to you a second time after what you did to me.'

A crusty silence, and a moment of mutual glaring followed. Chris took a defensive stance. He rested against the stove, with his ankles crossed and his arms folded. Victoria mirrored him, using the Belfast sink as her support. The worn flooring Chris had scuffed at provided a natural battle line in the war zone that was the cottage kitchen.

Victoria's supply of ammunition, latent for seventeen years, rallied for position; explosive words, damaging thoughts, and delicate sensibilities were all landmines waiting to be trampled on. All her triggers were primed.

The minute he attacked, she would unleash her arsenal.

Chris raised both hands level with his face.

An act of surrender, so soon?

'And just so I am *clear*, tell me what I did to you.' He threw his arms down and slammed his palms against the metal hob. The bang was deadened by the surrounding debris.

'You used me,' Victoria hissed. She pushed away from the basin. 'I gave you the one thing that was mine. The one thing no one else had or would ever have again. Innocence, virginity, call it what you will, I gave it to you because I thought you loved me. I believed we had a future, but I was a cheap parting gift before you left for America, wasn't I? You fucked me, and then you fucked off.'

'No, no, no.' Chris dragged his fingers through his hair. 'It wasn't like that.' He strode across the kitchen, stretching for the door, but halted and switched back.

Now he was in Victoria's face, close, tight, his personal heat merging with hers, creating an intense pressure between them. A tornado of wild emotions whipped and swirled around her.

It would be easy to get carried away.

Victoria planted her feet firmly to the floor, and once more anchored herself to the sink. She ordered her oldest memories to the frontline. *Remember, he screwed with your life, and he hurt you.*

Saint-like in his innocence, with his fingers steepled at his mouth in silent prayer, Chris retreated behind the vinyl line. 'That's how you remember it?'

Loaded with self-doubt and apprehension, his question defeated Victoria, and the water welling in his brown eyes diluted her anger. His tears extinguished the fuse he'd lit in her youth. Her bullets of reprisal had backfired. What Victoria believed would bring resolution, brought crushing, crippling pain.

As with her resentment, Chris's colour drained, leaving him as grey as the rubble strewn around the cottage.

After a moment of uneasy ceasefire, Victoria tested the boundary. 'See? A trail of destruction.'

Chris pressed his fingers into his eyes, sniffed, and then cuffed his nose. The silvery snail-trail streak on the leather caught Victoria's attention. She dug into her coat pocket and retrieved a tissue, waving it like a white flag. 'It's clean.'

'Thanks.' Chris lent forward, accepted the peace offering, and wiped his jacket.

'It was for your nose.' Victoria forced a flat-line smile; it was all she could manage. The potency of Chris's sadness overpowered the room. 'I think it's time we got out of here,' she said.

Firing off a text to Olivia, who was delighted to have Seth to herself for another hour, Victoria closed the rear door to the cottage. As she inhaled, the salty air raced through her, cleansing the grime of the last few minutes. She decided to overlook the nasty stain left behind.

She strode towards the main road, leading Chris away from the beach. They couldn't lay the past to rest if they were stomping all over it.

Walking was good though. Walking provided both purpose and personal space. The old quarry at the top of the hill wasn't far – they could be there and back in an hour, and the stone sculptures would fill the awkward silences. 'Come on,' she said. 'Follow me. We can walk and talk, and admire some culture.'

Halting before reaching the top, Chris listened to Victoria's footsteps, each heavier than the last. Her breathing was rapid, with a short rasp at every intake. He turned as she drew level. 'I'm meant to be following you,' he said.

'I'd forgotten how steep it is,' she replied, in between gasps. 'And how breezy. My ears ache.' She scraped her hair away from her face, but the disobedient copper spirals resumed their position the moment she removed her hands. She squealed into the wind.

Chris smiled. 'It's still rebelling then?' He'd combed his fingers through those tresses.

'Bloody hair.' Victoria continued the climb, passing Chris, and leaving him standing.

He was lost in a memory – he and Victoria skinny-dipping, making love in the dark, and then using his T-shirt to rub her dry. She'd attempted to wrap it around her head, to hide her wilful, wet mess of tangles, but it wasn't large enough. She'd let out a despairing scream then.

'Are you coming?'

Victoria's voice, strengthened by the wind, blew Chris's thoughts out to sea. It took a moment for him to remember where he was. It took another to send an apologetic prayer to Lacey. The past had a lot to answer for.

As they touched the flat ground of the plateau, the breeze dropped, and the late afternoon sun gave one last valiant burst of winter warmth. Chris removed his jacket, slung it over his shoulder, and surveyed the surrounding area. Some joker had wrapped red and gold tinsel around the neck of a stone bear rearing up on his hind legs. Chris patted its hard, cold nose, and tugged at the decoration. 'All right, boy?'

He settled on a wooden bench that overlooked the sweep of the bay, and watched the gulls swooping in and out of the waves.

Lacey would have loved the sense of freedom here. She'd have been happy. Safe. He should have brought her home when he had the chance. Introduced her to his father.

177

Ha. His father. The man who thought no woman was good enough for Chris. The man who'd promised to smooth things over with Victoria. Chris let his jacket drop to the floor. Only now did it occur to him that his father's statements conflicted. What did that mean?

'Are you okay?' Victoria approached the bench and sat down. 'I recognise that look.'

Aware he was scowling, Chris lifted his eyebrows, and tried to make light of his dark mood. 'Yeah. I was thinking how much easier life would be if there were no misunderstandings, you know? People should say what they mean, and not imply or infer, or whatever the damn word is. There's no doubt then, is there?'

Victoria agreed. 'Computers don't misconstrue. They process the information fed to them. If we issue ambiguous instructions, it's our fault. User error.' She shrugged and then occupied herself tracing the circles of a knot in the seat.

Chris turned his knees in Victoria's direction, and clasped together his hands. Time to say what he meant. 'I'm sorry you felt I'd used you. That was never my intention.'

Victoria shuffled to the end of the bench, and cast a look of deliberation across the white ground of the quarry. 'I don't suppose it was,' she said, picking up a shard of shale. 'But that's what happened.' She skimmed the stone along the powdery floor, and it landed with a plop in a small puddle. 'Perhaps you'd like to feed me the right information so I can process it correctly?'

That didn't sound like the Vicky Paveley Chris remembered. He checked to see if she was smiling, but her expression was as serious and straight as the blackening horizon. This was Victoria Noble. Controlled. Ordered. Efficient. Her lust for life had gone. If it had vanished along with her virtue, it wasn't any wonder she felt resentment and anger towards him.

In one swift move, Chris grabbed his jacket, leapt from the seat, and put two metres between him and Victoria. 'Do you blame me for how you've lived your life?' He looked over his shoulder. She was staring right at him, her lips pursed. 'Am I responsible?'

'I thought you loved me.'

'That's not an answer.' He swivelled in the gravel to face her. 'What did I do that was so wrong?' He whipped his hand into the air. 'You led the way, Vicky, with your whispers and touches and kisses. I held back. I wasn't sure we were ready, but because it was what you wanted, because you told me it would make you the happiest you've ever been, we made love. And it was the best feeling in the world. I was totally into you.' He rubbed the back of his head. 'Leaving you made me sick. I mean, I actually threw up when I realised what was happening. I loved you.'

He saw Victoria's eyes narrow as she tried to comprehend. The heat of her gaze made his neck prickle, and his confession made his forehead throb. He ran his fingers around his collar, and then massaged his temples. The word *love* stirred his stomach, and left his tongue with nowhere to go. He passed it over his lips, tasting the salt the air had deposited there.

Victoria's mouth tasted of the sea last time they kissed. His tongue had found its way then. They were young, but it hadn't made the experience less intense.

Snapshots of their last night together flashed through his head, provocative and exciting. 'I need to walk,' he said.

He headed for the next set of sculptures, searching for distraction, allowing himself time to calm down. The depth of his emotions shocked him. Scared him. He was thinking of Victoria in a way he reserved for Lacey. *She* deserved prime position, not his old lover.

But Victoria was a woman now, and it was not only

in attitude she'd changed. Where youth had granted her attractiveness, maturity had graced her with timeless beauty. Her body was different too. He imagined her skin beneath his fingers, softer and fleshier than before. And her kiss … Would their mouths still mould to one another, airtight and seamless?

He stopped in front of the first carving, concentrating on admiring the handiwork – anything to take his mind off Victoria. The sculpture was a vertical half of a naked woman. He spread his fingers over the granite. It was cool and smooth and unforgiving. Was that how Victoria would be? Or would she liquefy at his touch, plead for his breath to glide over her breasts? Fall at his request?

Retracting his hand, he scoured it down the side of his leg, and shoved it in his pocket. He jiggled his head, attempting to dislodge the pictures, as the shifting shingle behind him alerted him to Victoria's presence.

She spoke. 'If you loved me, why did you leave?'

Chapter Sixteen

Victoria positioned herself between Chris and the stonework. 'Was it something I did? Am I a poor lover?'

It hurt Chris to know his actions had left Victoria unfulfilled and insecure. That wasn't who he was. He was not a user, and he hadn't set out to damage her. He loved her.

There was that word again. He had loved her, but that was a long time ago, and it was Victoria who'd called a halt to their relationship. That fact didn't help him understand her current distress, or why she was asking questions to which she knew the answers. He needed to start from the beginning, pick through the story and find out at which point it unravelled.

'I had no choice,' he said. 'I had to go.' He took a deep breath. 'Before I met you, I'd applied for a summer job in the States. A small film studio offered me six months' work and the chance of some acting lessons. I was looking to build that into something more, maybe get into an American uni—'

'University?' Victoria's shock was evident. 'You never said …'

'My father didn't explain?'

'Your father?' The news further perplexed Victoria. She retreated into the cold statue.

'Perhaps he was sparing your feelings, the same reason

I never mentioned it.' That was the probable explanation. 'The thing is, I'd fallen in love, and decided LA could wait. But Dad thought differently. Without me knowing, he'd posted my acceptance and arranged everything, my flight, my apartment, my acting classes. He said he was proud of what I'd achieved, but I had the ability to do more, and this was a once-in-a-lifetime opportunity. He told me not to let him down.' Chris hesitated, still confused by Victoria's response. 'I really thought he'd explained this to you.'

'So, your father sent you away?'

In a spontaneous move, Chris grabbed Victoria's hand and pulled it to his chest. 'It could look like that to outsiders, but I didn't see it that way. Wheels were in motion. Money had changed hands. And this is my father we're talking about. I'd not seen him with hope in his eyes since Mum died. He'd had eleven years of misery, but that night … *that night*, a spark appeared. I couldn't snuff that out.'

Victoria slipped from his grasp, and the cool air rushed to take her place. The loss was tangible. Chris braced himself, as he realised he'd held another woman's hand, and he'd done it without a second thought for Lacey. Guilt was bound to feast on his insides. But before he had time to indulge his conscience, Victoria sidled away.

'Why didn't you call me?' she said, scuffing a path over to the edge of the cliff. 'Why cut me out of your life like I was a malignant cell?'

'I … didn't.' Chris faltered over his words as he mentally replayed the telephone conversation he'd had with his father seventeen years ago. His dad had been very clear about Victoria's take on the whole *true love* thing. He'd told Chris she was glad to be shot of him.

He glanced at Victoria. She was wiping her palms across her eyes. Her tears revealed a different story to the one he'd been led to believe.

His head pounded as he tried to take in the enormity of the situation.

He took the spot beside Victoria and looked to the English Channel for assistance. The light was fading fast, and the grey water was reflecting the cloudy sky. It offered only one solution: his father had lied.

With both hands in his pockets and his back hunched, Chris opened his mouth. At first, nothing came, but as he straightened up and breathed in, like a fresh mountain spring, a stream of clarity poured out. 'I didn't want to go. I didn't want to leave you, but when I got home that night, Dad was so happy. He smiled as he told me he'd sold his shares to pay for my expenses in America. All of his shares, even the ones he'd put by for his old age. He'd sold his car too, and I knew how much he loved that. It was a classic. But he wanted me to have the chance to live my dream, and he was prepared to go without for my sake. How could I not go?'

Chris stopped to catch his breath, not daring to look at Victoria. 'He told me the flight was at six the next morning, and he took me to my room and pointed to my rucksack. He'd packed it. He said we were leaving in ten minutes. Ten minutes! That's all I had. I spent eight of them throwing up.'

Now Chris was ready to face Victoria. He turned in her direction. 'I asked him for some time to come and tell you, convince you six months wasn't forever, that I'd be back, but he said I'd come home so late, we were already way behind schedule. I only just made it onto the plane.' He paused. His father's crumpled, red face appeared in his mind's eye. 'He promised he'd tell you himself, first thing, and I was going to call you as soon as I'd arrived.'

Victoria was shaking her head. 'Your father never spoke to me. If he had—'

'I've just worked that out.' Chris was shaking his head now. 'He lied to me. He told me you were relieved I'd gone, that I'd saved you the trouble of ditching me, that we'd run our course.'

'And you believed him?' The incredulity registered in Victoria's pitch. 'After everything we'd done?'

'He had no reason to lie.'

With his father no longer alive to justify his actions, the only way Chris could handle the deception was to accept it was done with his best interests at heart. It didn't help shake the shame and embarrassment crawling over him.

'I don't think he set out to hurt us, Vicky. He just wanted me to reach my full potential. Have a shot at the big time. And I think he considered you a distraction.' He quickly adjusted the statement. 'Not you. Any woman.' This was going to take some working out. The ramifications of what his father had done were enormous. The *what ifs* colossal.

'And then you met Lacey.'

'And then I met Lacey.' One of the ramifications.

'And you fell in love.'

'Yes.'

Victoria nodded. 'How did your father feel about your marriage?'

'He was angry, shocked, told me I needed my head seeing to, but he was five thousand miles away, what could he do? He didn't come to the wedding. He said he'd spent all of his money on me, and had nothing left. Lacey and I couldn't afford to cover his costs. I didn't speak to him for years, not even when the boys were born, then I received a call from the hospital and was told he was in the last stages of liver failure. I managed to get home and see him before ... His wish was to be cremated and scattered out to sea, like Mum.'

The conversation drew to a natural close, Chris wearied

by his past. He assumed Victoria's quiet was brought about by her taking on board all he'd said. He hoped she would understand, but above all, he wanted his explanation to take away her pain. He wished for his words to heal, as they had helped Lacey.

He backed away and watched. At least Victoria hadn't walked off, or thrown herself over the edge. That had to count for something. 'I'm sorry,' he said. 'I honestly thought I was doing the right thing.'

She teetered, startling Chris into action. He lurched towards her, grabbed her waist and tugged her to safety. 'What the hell are you doing?'

'Seeing what it's like on the other side.' She wriggled free from his grasp. 'It must be nice to have all the answers.'

Chris dropped his arms, snorted, and shook his head. 'I have questions more than answers. What if I'd stayed with you? What if I'd ridden horses instead of motorbikes? What if my dad had left me to live my own life? Huh? Well, then I'd not have met Lacey, not had my sons, not lost half my family to the goddamn, *bloody*, awful accident.'

He pummelled his head with his fists, and collapsed to his knees, white dust pluming out in front of him. 'This whole thing is one horrific tragedy from start to finish.' He looked at Victoria. 'You asked me what happened, and I told you. I even apologised. What more do you want?'

After a moment's quiet, and with her eyes scrunched tight, Victoria said, 'I want it to stop hurting.'

When Victoria relaxed her eyes, she saw Chris standing in front of her, his head to one side and his brow furrowed. She noticed a scar running across his forehead. It was white in comparison with his bronzed skin. An old injury. The temptation to touch it was compelling, but she couldn't allow her fingers to go there; they might wander.

She couldn't think like that. She had to be single-minded. She had to achieve closure, because that would bring her peace. And help Seth.

But it was impossible to focus with Chris breathing on her neck. She couldn't think straight when he angered her, frustrated her, excited and thrilled her. She wanted to kick him and caress him, repel and embrace him. Hate and love him.

She'd heard his explanation, and she believed him. She remembered his father. He was a self-absorbed, balding gorilla, who pointed and grunted as his means of communication, and beat his chest whenever he was challenged. At the time, Victoria determined he must have suffered a loveless childhood, but now conceded it was more likely his way of coping with losing his wife. The sad fact was, his behaviour directly impacted on Chris's life, ensuring his upbringing was centred on making his father happy. Chris discarded everything else dear to him, including Victoria, who, in turn, disconnected from the real world. And from her son.

Seth's angelic face floated through her mind. He was born perfect, with no marks, no scars, and no preconceptions, and yet, he could behave like a beast. He was the result of her input. He was her creation.

Now, more than ever, Victoria knew she had to break the chain, and offer Seth unconditional love; the love she saw between Chris and Rick.

And now, more than ever, she should put the past behind her. Forgive, then forget Chris.

But a cloud of yearning didn't evaporate into the mist; it hovered, it followed and it rained down, cycle after cycle, each downpour as heavy as the last, never washing her clean.

What a mess. 'We need to get back.' She balanced her weight on her front foot, and took five quick steps in succession, on the decline of a slope. It was all downhill from there.

Her hand was given a gentle nudge. Chris had fallen in beside her.

'Tell me what it'll take to stop the pain,' he said. 'And if I can help, I will.' He brushed her fingers again.

That was three times he'd touched her hand. What he was doing and what he was saying was inconsistent, and the illogical nature of his words and actions threw Victoria into a dizzy confusion.

Then it struck her. He was in chaos. His thoughts and emotions were in conflict. It was down to Chris to decide whether to follow his head or follow his heart.

Earlier, when he explained his extreme reaction at Victoria's attempt to comfort him, it resonated with her. She understood the desire to keep precious memories close – she had too few to throw away. She'd held onto her and Chris's time together for her entire adult life. She'd lost hours, possibly nights to intense fantasies, imagining and reliving the mood, recapturing the sensuality and sexuality of the evening on the beach. She lived in her dreams. She connected. And she fought a very private battle to preserve the sensations and passion Chris left behind, because that was all she had.

She lost her footing and skidded down the hill, landing on her backside, winded.

'Vicky!' Chris covered the distance between them with one leap. 'Okay?'

'I would be if my hair wasn't debuting its *Lord of the Dance* routine.' She directed her cast into a chorus line, and tutted.

Chris, with one leg raised on a boulder, and his hands on his hips, smiled. 'If you're still bothering with that, I'll assume there are no broken bones.'

'I don't think so.' Victoria flexed her ankles. 'At least I missed the rabbit ... sorry, *bunny* droppings.' Portland habits. Portland myths. No one said rabbit around the quarries. The creatures, albeit indirectly, were held responsible for quarry collapses and the deaths of workers.

Chris covered his mouth with the back of his hand and shook his head. 'They're meant to signify a rock fall, not Victoria falls.' He pointed to something behind Victoria.

She followed the line of his finger. What once would have been a smattering of little black pellets now resembled a miniature cow pat, where, Victoria presumed, her bottom had squashed them together; a *rabbit*-dropping patty.

She could still *think* the word.

'Another trail of devastation?' Chris failed to stifle his laugh.

Victoria raised an eyebrow and produced her steeliest of stares, so much so her sockets and cheekbones ached.

Resting on his elevated leg, Chris was chuckling. 'Come on, Vicky. It's funny.' He offered his hands. She refused. 'The old Vicky would have found it hilarious.'

'Well, she got left behind years ago.' Victoria flipped onto her knees, pushed herself up, and brushed herself down. 'Life got serious.'

She proceeded to the bottom of the hill, abandoning the old quarry to the distance and Chris to his rock.

'Life got very serious, didn't it?' he said, as he caught up. 'And me leaving was part of the reason.'

'Until a few moments ago, it was all of the reason.' What was the point in saying anything other than the truth? Victoria was responsible for opening this particular can of worms, so she might as well pick at its contents. 'I blamed you for everything, my mistrust of men, my divorce, my diabolical attempt at being a mother. I traced it back to the night you left me.'

'Okay. So tell me about your husband.'

That was his response to her statement of blame? Astonishing. 'My ex-husband,' she muttered. 'Ben. We met at a New Year's Eve party. He was a friend of a friend of Juliette's. I'd shut myself away, but she nagged me to go to this wretched do, promising it would make me feel better. Even Dad pestered me, saying it was unhealthy for a girl my age to be shut away.'

'So you went, and there you met Ben. What happened next?'

'I fell for his charm. He was easy to talk to, laid-back, good-looking. I thought he was the one to fix me.'

'Did you love him?'

Victoria squirmed. This baring your soul lark was uncomfortable, and she knew her answer was a little contentious. 'Not how I expected, but I was happy to marry him. Life was steady. Everything was as it should be, but there was no magnificent spark.' Her laugh was wistful. 'No fireworks.' She slowed her pace as they neared the fishermen's cottages. 'It was like my house; a perfect front, but a mess inside.' She stopped, leaned against the wall of the first terrace, and sighed. 'And then we had Seth.'

She related the story of how Ben had reneged on his word, and how she'd chosen work over Seth. Chris, his attentive brown eyes scanning her every word, responded with nods and quiet replies and promises of help, if indeed, that was what Victoria wanted.

'It's my fault,' she concluded. 'I should have taken responsibility for my actions years ago, but admitting I was failing as a mother was tough. *Is* tough.' She lowered her head. 'Life has changed me, and I don't like who I've become. I'd love to have some of that old Vicky back.'

'I've seen flashes,' Chris said. 'She's still there. Time and experiences do change us. It's inevitable. But the core, the very soul of who we are must remain, don't you think?'

He stepped into the road and sat on the kerb, reclining on his outstretched arms. 'You say we've both changed, but I bet our goals aren't that far apart.' He sprang up from the verge, reached inside his jacket, and produced a pen and a scrap of creased paper. He examined it, accepted it was fit for purpose, and then scribbled on its reverse.

Victoria waited, enjoying his energy.

'Tell me your greatest wish. The one thing you'd sell your soul to achieve. Then we'll see if we match.' He cocked a brow. 'Be honest.'

'To find my son,' she said, surprised by the speed with which she'd answered, and with the reply itself. Seth was to the forefront of her mind, a place he rarely occupied. It was a peculiar feeling – a fusion of guilt and elation. 'He's lost, trapped in the ruins of my mistakes.' She paused as visions of her crumbling cottage reminded her how easily he could have gone from her life. 'I need to find a way through.'

'I've had an idea.' Chris checked his note, screwed it into a small ball, and thrust it in his trouser pocket. 'It's a bit radical, so don't feel pressured to answer today.' He pointed to Victoria's cottage. 'You can't live there, because it's a deathtrap, and you've said yourself, your dad's bungalow isn't big enough for three of you, so that leaves you with two quick-fix options – renting or moving back to London. Right?'

Victoria gave a hesitant nod, unsure as to where Chris's words were leading. 'I don't want to go back to London,' she said. 'I'll be sucked deep into the corporate world I'm trying to escape.'

'So, that leaves renting.' Chris turned to her. 'I've plenty of space at the castle. You and Seth could live there. Just until you're sorted.'

'What?' She choked with surprise. 'No. *No.* I don't think that would be a good idea. What will the boys think?'

'The boys get on great. They'll love it.' Chris swooped on Victoria. 'Honestly, the place is big enough for us all. There's an annexe to the side you can have. Our paths don't need to cross unless you want them to.' He backed away. 'Like I said, it's a bit radical. If it helps, I'll charge rent.'

Rent wasn't the issue. Living in the same house was the issue. 'I don't know, Chris. It's …'

'Mad?' His shoulders dipped. 'You know what I'm like. Act first, think later.'

Victoria deserted the wall and stepped over to Chris. 'It's very kind of you to think of us.'

He spun round. 'Confession time. While I hope it would help you, I have an ulterior motive.'

Victoria's heart skipped to the left; her head knocked it back on course. There was no way Chris was about to declare his undying love for her. *No way.* 'Go on,' she said, daring herself to listen.

Chris retrieved the screwed up paper from his pocket, unravelled, it and showed it to Victoria.

It read: *To save my boy.*

'You see? Our goals aren't that far apart. You want to find Seth and I want Rick to live again. And I saw how he connected with you. He told me himself, you *get him*. He said he was talking about his mum with you. No one, and I mean no one, has managed to get him to talk about Lacey.'

'I'm not following. What's your point?'

'I've spent thousands of dollars on experts trying to help my son, but you, in one lunchtime, brought the old Rick back. It wasn't for long, but it happened.'

With the note returned to his pocket, Chris seized Victoria's hands. 'I don't know what it is you have, but I'd give anything to see my son light up again. Stay with us. Until your cottage is fixed. Come on. For the boys.'

Chapter Seventeen

Her hands were still enclosed in his; secure, warm, protected from the sea breeze beginning to whip around the buildings. He made no effort to release them. Victoria couldn't tell if it was a pleading tactic, or habit. His sense of horror about touching another woman had vanished. He was doing the very thing that led to this conversation.

Victoria withdrew from his clasp. 'It's a lovely gesture, but I can't accept.'

'It's not a gesture, Vicky.' Chris lurched to grab her hands again, but she stepped back.

'I'm not comfortable. I'd be walking in someone else's footsteps.'

Chris blinked. 'What does that mean?'

There was no tactful way of articulating her anxiety, besides, Chris was the one who expressed the wish people spoke with clarity. 'All you and Rick know is Lacey. Wouldn't it be hard for you both to have a different woman in the house?'

Chris frowned. The furrows created were deep enough to plant seeds in. 'Lacey never lived here. You know that.'

Victoria fiddled with her bare ring finger. 'I'm worried that having a woman in the house, any house, will distress you, in the same way putting my arm around you did.'

The rutted forehead transformed from a ploughed field

into a flat plain, as comprehension flooded Chris's eyes. 'That's for me to deal with.'

'What about Rick?'

Chris's lips thinned. 'I'm doing it for him. I'd do anything to have him back. I thought I'd made that clear. God, Victoria, you're infuriating. Say yes, and let me do all the bloody worrying. It's not your concern.'

'But we have a history.'

'Yes! A history.' He took to pacing the pavement, from the end of the terraced cottages to Olivia's shop. 'It's in the past.' He came to a standstill next to Victoria. 'I promise you, my only motive is to help the boys.'

She knew that. She wasn't suggesting he'd try a move on her, but their past had to be taken into account. Her past. It was apparent it meant more to her than Chris. It wasn't holding him back in the slightest. 'I still don't know. I need to think about it.'

Chris nodded. 'And so you don't feel under any pressure, there's no time limit. As and when you're ready.' He smiled. It wasn't a full smile. 'Maybe in the New Year?'

After a few awkward moments of stilted thanks, Victoria made her excuses, wished Chris goodnight, and knocked on Olivia's door. While she waited for it to open, she watched Chris amble along the street, in the direction of the castle. It was madness to even consider staying there.

'Here she is.'

Victoria turned to find Olivia and Seth in the doorway, both wearing coats, both expecting to leave the shop.

'You go with your mum, and I'll lock up and see you by the other door.' Olivia transferred Seth's hand from hers to Victoria's. 'I won't be a minute.'

The door closed, the bolt clunked, and the shop was plunged into darkness.

Victoria looked at Seth. He was staring into the distance.

'Is that Chris?' he asked, pointing to a dark, hunched shadow. 'I like Chris.' Silence. 'And Rick. When can I see Rick?'

'I thought you were coming round the side?' Olivia teetered towards them. 'Don't make me walk in these things.' She pointed to the pair of skyscrapers posing as shoes. 'If I fall, I could break my hip.'

'That would never happen,' Victoria said. 'You're indestructible.' She noticed Olivia's hair was tied into a neat ballerina's bun, and although the light wasn't brilliant, it looked as if she was wearing make-up. 'Are you and Dad out tonight?'

Olivia laughed. 'Hasn't he told you? Typical Frank. Yes. We're heading off to Bournemouth to see *The Nutcracker Suite*. It's a Russian production. We booked it weeks ago. You don't mind taking me back to your dad's, do you?'

'It's his car,' Victoria said, smiling. 'It's the least I can do. And thank you for looking after Seth. I'm sorry I was so long.'

'He was a joy. Can we get in now?'

'Of course. You look lovely, by the way.' It was as Victoria reached for the car keys, she realised Seth was still holding her hand. It felt so natural, so easy, she didn't want to let go. She didn't want to lose the amazing swell of love that was inflating her heart to twice its size. Handholding was the order of the day. She peeked at Olivia, then at the car, and then at Seth.

'I'd like to get in the car now.' And with that, Seth tugged his hand away, and pulled at the rear door.

Victoria obliged and settled him into his car seat, while Olivia performed nothing short of a contortionist's act, to get in without toppling over. Victoria kept half an eye on her, ready to leap to her assistance should she lose her balance. Or tie herself in knots.

'You and Chris had a lengthy chat, then?' Olivia pulled her skirt over her knees, as Victoria climbed in the driver's side.

'Oh, yes.' Victoria turned the key.

The air bed was being difficult. A challenge. More of a challenge than Seth. He'd had his bath and gone to bed hours ago, without any arguments. Victoria assumed Olivia must have worn him out.

Asleep for a short while, Victoria had been disturbed by her father returning from his evening out. He wasn't noisy, but in the small bungalow, sound carried, and she wasn't certain, but at one point, she thought she heard Olivia's voice. She hoped he, or possibly they, wouldn't hear her slapping the air bed. Eventually, she abandoned it for the sofa, and lay staring into the semi-darkness. Her thoughts weaved in and out of the twinkling Christmas tree lights.

Chris had made an exceptional offer, inviting her and Seth to stay at the castle. She was satisfied he was doing it for Rick's sake, and could see the benefit in Seth having a male role model younger than his granddad, but she questioned if it was the right thing to do. For it to work, she had to be strong enough to let the past go.

She curled onto her side, and cuddled into the duvet. Chris had asked for her help. She and Rick had connected in the same way Seth and his nanny had. If Chris felt the same about his son's relationship with Victoria, as she did about Cerys and Seth, she couldn't refuse to help. And if Chris didn't have a problem with their past, then neither should she. Of course, chances were, he'd set it aside in order to help Rick.

She buried her face into her pillow, letting it soak up a stray teardrop. The wretchedness of Chris's plight moved her. Since losing his wife and son, he'd devoted his energy and time into resurrecting Rick. Every minute of every day, when Chris wasn't picturing Lacey, or remembering Todd's voice, he was consumed with thoughts and ideas of how to help his surviving son live again. In a strange, sad way, he was mourning the loss of both boys. And all the time he was looking after Rick, no one was taking care of Chris. There was Tommy, but it seemed he'd grown tired of his friend and taken off.

Victoria kicked off the duvet and sat up. *She* cared for Chris, and now she understood why he left for America, she was in a position to exorcise her demons. If she could do that, she could move into the castle, help Rick, and remind Chris how to let go. Like he'd shown her in their teens.

She snuggled back down on the sofa, dragged the pillow from the arm to under her head, and closed her eyes. Sleep wasn't far away.

'Frank!' Olivia's voice.

'Shh!' Stifled laughter. 'You'll wake the others.'

'Then stop doing that.' A giggle.

Olivia *was* in the house and seemingly staying the night. Frank must have settled his differences with Iris's ghost, and put his past to rest.

Victoria cushioned her ears with the pillow. One way or another she and Seth had to move out. It wasn't fair on her father, or Olivia. They deserved privacy. And Victoria had no wish to learn how their sex life panned out.

She made a mental note to check the Internet in the morning to research *exorcising demons*.

Chapter Eighteen

Christmas was a squeeze in the small bungalow with Juliette's family visiting for three days, but somehow they'd managed to fit, without extending into a tent in the back garden. Olivia had been invited to stay, but she declined, opting to join in with festivities during the daytime, with Victoria running her home at night.

Frank was in his element with five grandchildren, two daughters, one son-in-law and Olivia seated around the small kitchen table, admiring the crisp, golden turkey. Vegetarianism went out the window as he wielded his knife with the skill of a samurai. Everyone tucked into the one o'clock lunch, including Seth, who despite a major outburst on Christmas Eve, had responded well to the boundaries Victoria had put in place.

On Boxing Day, when all the toys had batteries in, occupying Alex and Seth, and Juliette's three youngest were playing ships with a large cardboard carton, Victoria, sitting back and quietly observing, promised herself she would never miss another family Christmas.

With Juliette and her brood back in London, a peaceful New Year's Eve was followed with New Year's Day at Chiswell Craft Centre. Seth was at the desk, using chalks and pastels, Frank was posing for a pencil sketch for Olivia, and Victoria was looking on.

'You're quiet, love.' Frank glanced across the room, instantly reprimanded by Olivia with a wave of her pencil.

Victoria smiled. 'I'm enjoying the tranquillity. It's been hectic. The turkey had more resting time than me.'

Frank chuckled. 'It's been good, though.'

'Francis!' Olivia folded her arms and tapped her foot. 'How am I expected to draw those gorgeous lips of yours if you keep moving them?'

Frank welded shut his mouth and fought to keep a straight face. Victoria broke eye contact to give him the best chance of survival.

'Livia? Are you cross with Pops?' Seth lifted his head from his work and studied both his granddad and Olivia. His face contracted with the effort of understanding.

Olivia addressed him. 'I'm a little bit cross with him, yes.' She abandoned her pad and sat on the chair next to Seth. 'Do you think people can be a little bit cross?'

Seth put his chalk on the wooden lip of the drawing board, and folded his hands together.

Victoria noticed he was mirroring Olivia's pose.

'Yes. And I think people can be a lot cross,' he said.

Victoria held her breath, waiting for him to accuse her of being one of those people.

'But if you're only a little cross at Pops, he's only been a little bit naughty.' Seth returned to his picture, and the discussion was over.

Olivia patted him on his back, and then smiled at Victoria. 'Happy New Year,' she whispered as she passed by.

Victoria acknowledged Olivia with a fleeting grin, before turning her attention on Seth. The research on child attachment disorder suggested Victoria should attend therapy to help increase her bond with Seth, but since progress was already being made, she wasn't convinced an outside influence would help. Olivia was a great source of encouragement, and her years as a teacher gave her an invaluable insight as to how to relate to Seth, so Victoria took the opportunity to watch, listen and learn.

She discovered time was a major factor, and having handed responsibility of EweSpeak to Juliette, and with the insurance company taking care of the cottage repairs, it was something Victoria now had. And she was using it wisely.

Spending time with Seth was having a positive effect on both parties.

There was still a long way to go, but they had a foundation on which to lay the path, and with her father and Olivia guiding the way, Victoria believed she and Seth would one day travel life's walkways together. Maybe even hand-in-hand.

She flicked a rampant curl from her eyes, and rubbed her nose. In reality, her fantasy family, which included Chris, was the equivalent of a tiny island on the horizon, and there was plenty of swimming and gasping for air ahead of her, before she reached dry land.

Chris had given her plenty to think about over the holidays. He'd invited her into his home, no strings attached, other than to be there for his son. In return he'd provide support for Seth. He'd mentioned something about an annexe, so they weren't going to be on top of one another, unlike in Victoria's dreams, where they tumbled and rolled with each other, kissing and laughing.

With thoughts like that, it was stupid to consider staying at the castle.

She refocused on the room. Her father was fidgeting, Olivia was casting spells with her pencil, and Seth was observing.

'Livia's a little bit cross, again,' he said. 'Pops keeps being silly. I think he's going to be told off.'

Seth was becoming quite the conversationalist. Victoria nodded, appreciating the moment. 'I think he is, too. Naughty step for Pops?'

'Don't know. Livia's laughing. I'm making a picture for Rick.'

Victoria's eyes darted from her father, to Olivia, to Seth's artwork, managing to keep up with the change of topic. Seth could flit with great ease, yet leave the impression he'd given serious thought to each subject. If Victoria applied his technique of moving on, there was a chance they could stay at the castle. All she had to do was acknowledge her feelings for Chris, and then set them aside. 'Easy,' she muttered.

'Right then,' said Frank, dismounting his stool and inspecting his portrait. 'Shall we go back to the bungalow? Seth? Will you help me make turkey curry this evening?'

Victoria groaned. 'We still have turkey?'

Frank grinned as he held his sketch up to the light. 'It's the last batch. I took it out of the freezer this morning. We could do a stroganoff instead. This is very good, Olivia.' He ducked as Olivia's hand brushed the top of his head.

Seth packed away his things, collected his coat, and waited by the door. 'I like curry.'

'You do?' Victoria slipped on her jacket, and wrapped a scarf around Seth. 'I didn't know that.'

'Cerys makes it.' He waited as Victoria pushed his mittens over his hands. 'I like Cerys.'

Ah. Cerys. A name Victoria had avoided mentioning in front of Seth in case it upset him.

She'd phoned the nanny agency at the beginning of December, explaining her situation, and they said they understood. As a gesture of goodwill and with the chance she and Seth could return to London at short notice, Victoria agreed to pay Cerys a three-month retaining fee. It was money well spent, as no price could be put on peace of mind, but had it become an unnecessary expense?

Now was the perfect opportunity to determine Seth's feelings about his nanny. 'Do you miss Cerys?' Victoria straightened his scarf.

'No. But I like her.'

Victoria crouched in front of Seth and fussed about with his coat buttons. 'If we live here, we won't see Cerys. How does that make you feel?' She'd phrased the question so Seth had control of his reply. It was important for his self-esteem.

'Okay.' He turned to Frank. 'May I pour the rice into the pan, please?'

And that was that. Decision made. Victoria would cancel the contract with the agency.

A second chance had been granted.

The next week passed without incident. No one ventured out apart from Frank, who braved the cold, biting January weather to visit Olivia. He kept an eye on Victoria's cottage, too, but had nothing to report. The damp, freezing air was prolonging the drying out process, even with two dehumidifiers working night and day.

On a quiet Saturday afternoon, sitting at the kitchen table in her father's bungalow, Victoria searched through the information she'd collected on the local playgroups and schools. At some point, she and Seth would be living on Portland in the cottage, and she needed to sort out his education. Ideally before she had to investigate senior schools.

She wondered where Rick would attend. It was possible he'd started this term – schools had been back two weeks already, according to Juliette, who was missing her holiday breakfasts with her tribe.

Victoria let out a great breath of air as she pictured Rick trying to find his way in the world, and questioned whether or not the connection they'd formed would still be there. She'd not seen him or Chris in almost a month. She'd sent a card, but she'd deliberately not called them, aware how difficult Christmas was having lost someone close. As an adult, she experienced the pain with her own mother, even a few years on. How awful it must be for a thirteen-year-old, not having his mum or brother around when the whole world insisted on universal happiness.

She shuffled her papers together and pushed them aside.

New Year would have meant nothing to the Framptons. It wasn't an opportunity for rebirth. It was a time of intense reflection, regrets and sorrow. It must have been horrible at the castle.

Victoria bit her bottom lip. She should have shown them that someone cared.

It was time to step up to the plate; come out of hiding; be fearless. Chris trusted her enough to ask for her help. All that other stuff in her head would have to go. This wasn't about her unresolved feelings, or whatever it was Olivia had suggested. This was about Rick. And it was about Seth. Somehow, they went hand-in-hand. She hadn't worked out how yet – Juliette would say the boys were destined to meet – that their fate was mapped out years ago, and last November, Victoria would have scoffed at the idea. Now, in a totally illogical, inexplicable way, it made sense.

Some things simply happened.

Having dropped Olivia at Chiswell Craft Centre for a ten o'clock Sunday opening, Victoria continued on to Hope Cove Castle. Wriggling with excitement in the back of the car was Seth.

'Do they know we're coming?'

'No. Which means they might not be in.'

'So why are we going?'

'We're being spontaneous. We're doing something without planning it first.'

Surprised by the castle's lack of security, Victoria drove the car onto the gravel drive and switched off the engine. 'If they're not here, we'll do something else.' She smiled into her rear-view mirror. 'Okay?' Please be in, she thought. I need you to be in, before I change my mind. 'Come on. You can get the bell.'

Much to Seth's obvious pleasure, Rick opened the door.

'Hi. Great to see you. Come in. Dad's in the conservatory. It's that door on the right.' Rick pointed inside, to where a shaft of light stretched across the floor. Then he focused on Seth. 'All right, Seth? What do you want to do?'

So natural, like they'd been there yesterday.

'May I see your bedroom?'

'Sure. That's okay, Mrs Noble, isn't it?'

'Of course.' Victoria looked at Seth. 'Please behave.'

Rick bounded up the stairs, waiting at the top for Seth to catch up, and then they both disappeared round the corner.

Victoria surveyed the entrance hall. *Grand* came to mind.

'Hey, Vicky. Come on through.' Dressed head-to-toe in black, Chris waved her in. 'Boys gone already? Sorry. Rick should have shown you through. Happy New Year. It's good to see you.'

He looked tired, dark skin defining his eyes. It matched his clothing.

'I'm not interrupting anything, am I? It's okay to drop by?' Victoria made her way into the conservatory, squinting at the brightness.

'Well, that depends,' Chris said, inviting her to sit in the porter's chair.

'It does?' She perched on the end of the seat, wondering what Chris's conditions were.

'No.' He released a gentle laugh. 'You and Seth are

welcome any time.' He pulled out a chair from under the dining table and straddled it, supporting his chin on its high back. 'It's a great view, isn't it?'

With her eyes now adjusted to the strong light, Victoria could see the horizon. A small fishing boat, surrounded by gulls, caused the only break in an otherwise perfect horizontal line.

'He's out there every day, but he's usually back in the harbour by now. I assume that's where he goes. I should think he's got a good catch on board with all those scavengers hassling him.' Chris turned to Victoria. 'Have you had breakfast? Can I get you a coffee or tea?' He stood as if he was about to leave the room.

'No. I'm fine, thanks. Can you sit down? I've come to talk about your offer.'

'I hadn't forgotten.' He slumped onto the chair, returning his chin to the back, but placing his hands either side. He reminded Victoria of a cartoon character Juliette used to draw on the back of her exercise books. What was it called? A Chad. Yes. That's what he looked like. A Chad. A very, handsome, fit, sexy Chad.

'Well?' he prompted, his manner that of a crushed man. 'Get it over with. My idea of you staying here ranks as the craziest, most idiotic thing you've ever heard.'

Victoria smiled. 'Yes, it's made my top five.'

Chris's head disappeared behind the rungs of the chair. 'Is there nothing I can say that will change your mind?'

'There's plenty.' Victoria rose from the porter's chair and crossed to the panoramic windows. 'But I don't want it changed.'

'Right.' Chris's voice was becoming more muffled by the minute.

His chin must be on his chest, Victoria thought. He's talking into his jumper. 'I've given it considerable thinking time.' She coughed, aware of her understatement. 'And I've weighed up the pros and cons. If Seth and Rick are agreeable, and the accommodation is suitable, I'd like to accept your offer. If it's not too late.'

She turned round to find Chris bolt upright, with his mouth and eyes open to the same degree. 'Catching flies, Chris.' She grinned.

He reduced the gaping aperture. 'Is that a yes?'

'Yes, it's a yes. But the boys have to be happy with the decision, and I haven't said anything to Seth yet.'

Chris dived off his chair and bounded to Victoria's side. 'That's brilliant. I'm so relieved. And pleased. Does that mean you've forgiven me?' His level of energy, and his eyes dropped at the asking of the question.

'I think it should be me asking for your forgiveness. I misjudged you, and I should have known better.'

'I have a suggestion,' Chris said, his tone and head lifting. 'How about we get to know one another as the tortured adults we are, and we leave the past behind?'

'Tortured adults?' Victoria choked on the words.

'Yep.' Chris smacked his lips together. 'I was going easy on us. Come on. Let me show you the annexe.'

His smile, his buoyancy, and his eagerness to show her around, demonstrated his happiness with the situation. And it was contagious. 'Lead on,' Victoria said, excited to see what lay in store.

She followed Chris into the hallway, past the dining room, through the kitchen and down three steps to a closed fire door. It opened inward to a narrow corridor.

'There's a bedroom either side, the living room there, the bathroom opposite, and at the end, the kitchen-diner. It's not very big, but you can always eat with us. The last door on the left is the annexe's private entrance.' Chris invited Victoria to investigate.

'In a minute,' she said. From her initial assessment, it definitely fell within her description of 'going back to basics'.

'Well? What do you think?' Chris bobbed in front of her. 'It's probably smaller than you're used to, but at least you'll both have your own bedrooms.'

Victoria agreed. 'I imagine it's bigger than Dad's bungalow.' She rapped her knuckles against the wall and approved of the dull thud. 'Solid, too.'

'Yeah. Thankfully, you won't hear a thing from down here.' He laughed. 'Rick likes his music loud.' He stopped and looked at Victoria, a question hovering in the air. 'It's not too remote for you, is it?'

'Remote? No. I'll be glad of the peace.' She ventured down the corridor and looked in on the first bedroom. It was carpeted in blue, with matching curtains, spotlights in the ceiling, and white furniture, including a bed. Fresh, adequate. Suitable for Seth. She crossed the hall to the bedroom opposite. This was a little larger, with beige flooring, pink walls and rose-coloured blinds. The furniture matched that of the smaller room. 'Both single beds?' she queried.

'That's not a problem, is it?' Chris peered into the room. 'The realtor was kind enough to organise a few fundamentals before we arrived. I say kind. He still sent me the bill.' He paused, dwelling on something. 'Did I say realtor? I meant estate agent.'

Victoria exited the bedroom and wandered down to the kitchen. 'You're bilingual,' she teased. 'I am too. I speak English and Binary.'

'Computers feature a lot in your life.' Chris pulled shut the bedroom door and joined Victoria in the kitchen. 'I haven't a clue about them. Rick's had to show me how to watch Genesis videos through the TV Internet. So, that's what you do for a living? Work with computers?'

This wasn't the moment to mention EweSpeak, just as

it wasn't the moment last month, or the time before. It appeared Rick hadn't discussed it, either. What were the chances Victoria could keep her involvement from Chris? She feigned fascination with the contents of a wall cupboard she'd opened; one box of powdered soups, three small candles, and a pair of rubber gloves. To be fair, it was an interesting if odd assortment. She could answer Chris and then move on. 'Yes. And you're still into Genesis?' Smooth. She gave a miniscule shake of her head.

'Oh, yes. Greatest band on this planet. Can't get Rick on board though. His mum wasn't a huge fan either, but at least she tried. She'd get the words wrong in *Follow You, Follow Me,* mind you.'

His pause drew Victoria's attention to him.

'She'd get the *you* and *me* muddled.' He shrugged and waved a dismissive hand. 'You don't know what I'm on about, do you?'

He turned his back, but Victoria had already seen his sad, wistful smile. It didn't hide the obvious pain his memories had evoked. She closed the cupboard, and changed subjects once more. 'May I see the bathroom?' She brushed past him on her way through, and poked her head around the side of the door. 'No bath?'

'No. I guess technically I should have called it the shower room. We have a bath upstairs. You're very welcome to use that.'

Good grief, no. That would never happen. Far too exposed. The thought of Chris seeing her naked, accidentally or otherwise, filled her with dread. She had the body of a thirty-five-year-old, not an eighteen-year-old, as Chris had last witnessed. The shock would kill them both. Or render them insensible. Or render them insensible and then kill them. Whatever, it would be a bad move. A very bad move, and it wasn't worth the risk.

'I'm fine with the shower, but Seth might like a bath,' Victoria said, allowing her hot face to cool before showing it in the corridor. She heard Chris move in behind her.

'While we're on the subject of other rooms, I know I said our paths don't have to cross, but the downstairs of the castle is open to you both. If you're comfortable with us occupying the same space, so am I. To be honest, it would be nice to have the company.'

Victoria returned to the hallway. 'Tommy's still away? Rick mentioned it,' she quickly added.

'Yeah. He went away for the holidays.' Chris smiled. 'Shall I call the boys down?' He stepped into the main body of the castle, gestured for Victoria to exit, and then shut the fire door.

Her conscience was troubled by his enthusiasm and look of expectation, and she blocked his path. 'Wait. There's something I need to tell you. It might make you change your mind about having us here.'

'I doubt it. I'm so convinced you're the one, it would take a juggernaut of an issue for me to go back on my offer.'

'The one?' He hadn't spoken in desirous tones, but it was best to clarify. Like it was best she confessed her part in EweSpeak, before any agreements were made.

'For Rick. Don't you see, Vicky? I need you here. For my boy. I'd do anything to get him back.'

'Of course.' EweSpeak could wait. She'd have to quash the guilt for a few more weeks. Or as the insurance assessor had estimated, six months.

'What's this thing you need to tell me?'

Thinking quickly, she said,' We'll be here over Easter. The cottage won't be dry until late spring, early summer.'

'Is that all?' Chris laughed, as he danced passed Victoria into the hall. 'Then we'll have plenty of time to get reacquainted. Boys. Come down.'

As Victoria approached the conservatory, Chris held out a hand. 'I have a confession, too.' He lowered his voice. 'I've already run my crazy idea past Rick, and he loves it.'

'He does?' It must have been a difficult decision to make. 'He's okay with a woman being in the place? He doesn't feel I'm—'

'Walking in his mother's footsteps? That's how you put it. No. He accepts you for who you are. He understands we're friends, and he gets that you're not a replacement for Lacey. In any sense of the word. As far as he sees it, we're helping you out until your home is habitable.'

'Oh.' So, he hadn't told Rick the whole reason for inviting the Nobles there. She was about to ask why, but the boys charged down the stairs and careered into the conservatory. Rick claimed the porter's chair, before offering it to Seth.

Victoria took the seat Chris had lodged upon earlier, and sat side-saddle. 'Seth, I have something to ask, but I'd like you to listen until I've finished.' She raised a finger to her lips, then returned her hands to her lap. 'We can't move into our cottage until the builders have fixed it, and Pops' home is too small for us to live there for a long time. Chris and Rick have very kindly invited us to stay here for a while. Is it something you'd like to do?'

She held her breath, waiting for his response; the child who wrestled with change.

Chapter Nineteen

> *Juliette Higham @EweTwo*
> I love what we do at EweSpeak, but I do enjoy
> weekends with my tribe. Family time is so important.
> Catch you all soon.

Seth remained silent. His eyes flitted from one person to the next, and he kicked his heels against the solid base of the chair.

'I want to stay with Pops.'

Here we go, thought Victoria, steadying herself for the verbal melee. 'His bungalow is too small.'

'I want to stay with Pops.' Seth's feet whacked the chair with every word.

Victoria assessed the situation, deciding whether to slug it out in front of spectators, or continue the fight in the car on the journey home.

This could be the point Chris withdraws his offer, she thought. Although, by the growing anger behind Seth's eyes, it was more likely to be her reneging on the deal. Time to test whose mettle was the strongest. 'We'd have our own rooms here.'

Seth's hands compressed into tight fists. 'I have a room at Pops'. I want to stay there.'

From the corner of her eye, Victoria saw Chris cast a look at Rick, at which point Rick crouched in front of Seth, tapped his knee and got his attention.

'I think it's really cool you want to stay with your pops. That's your grandpa, right?'

Seth nodded, and his legs stilled.

'Grandpas are great. I bet he loves having you stay with him.'

Victoria watched in astonishment at the speed with which Seth unfurled his fingers and engaged in conversation.

'He says I keep him busy and being busy makes him happy.'

'You keep everyone busy, man.' Rick rumpled Seth's hair. He received a passing smile.

'Being busy makes me tired.' Seth rubbed his eyes and yawned.

'Yep. Me too.'

There was a silence, while everyone digested the contents of the exchange. Then Seth spoke.

'I can't leave Pops because he won't be busy, and then he'll be sad.'

Victoria brought a hand to her mouth to stifle a mounting sob. Seth wasn't fighting change; he was trying to fulfil what he understood to be an expectation. She chewed on her tongue and concentrated on the pain there. It hurt, but it was nothing like the agony crushing her heart. In a peculiar way, Seth's logic was flawless.

Rick kneeled on the floor. 'He's a lucky grandpa. Do you think I could meet him one day? Maybe when you're not keeping him busy?'

'Yes. Do you think he's sad when I'm here?'

Rick looked to Victoria for assistance.

She composed herself before replying. 'May I tell you what I think?'

Seth wriggled to the front of the seat, and fastened his fingers together. 'Yes.'

His direct answer elicited a mewl from Victoria. Without a trace of anger or hatred, Seth was centred on her and nothing else. It was the most significant moment yet, but it was imperative Victoria gave him a response. She reined in her emotions. 'No. I don't think he's sad when you're here, because he knows you're happy being busy.' It was a risky strategy, but one she felt Seth would comprehend.

'That's true, man,' Rick said. 'Grandpas, and moms and dads are like that. If you're happy, they're happy.'

Victoria watched with interest as Seth accepted the statement, and settled into the chair. Rick, on the other hand, with a puckered brow, was studying his father. She could sense Chris willing him to speak. The funny thing was, Rick didn't need to; his expression said it all. Victoria found him as easy to read as Seth's bedtime story. He was working through the consequences of what he'd just said.

It was turning into quite a day. A breakthrough moment for both families, and the Nobles hadn't even moved in.

'Okay,' said Seth, hopping off the chair. 'Will you show me my room, please?' He held out his hand for Rick to take.

Once the young American had obtained Victoria's agreement, he was on his feet, leading Seth out of the conservatory.

'It's the blue room,' Victoria said. 'But check over the whole place.'

Chris relocated to the large chair, nestled in, and gazed out across the gardens.

Victoria could guess where his thoughts were. She was learning to read him too. 'I saw it,' she said. 'Rick's leap of understanding.'

'Yeah.' The leather creaked as Chris adjusted his position. 'But I want him to be happy for his own sake, not mine. Been there, done that. Didn't work out. Why didn't he say anything?'

'Give him time. He's processing it.' Victoria stretched out her legs, rubbed her thighs, and stood. 'You've got yourself a thinker.' She ran her hand along the smooth surface of the oak table. She could be seated there tomorrow, eating lunch. 'And two lodgers.'

Victoria starfished on her single bed. Her jeans ruffled and creased the duvet and her arms and feet hung over the sides, but she didn't care. It wasn't an inflatable mattress, it wasn't a sofa, and it wasn't situated in her dad's living room. It was a proper, bona fide, wooden bed, with linen sheets, a headboard and springs that didn't eject her at every breath.

The move had gone well. Not that there was much to move; it was the explaining to her father that took the time. He wasn't against the idea per se, but he was concerned for Seth, worried he would confuse Victoria's friendship with Chris for something more.

'He's four, Dad. He doesn't think like that,' Victoria had said.

'I don't know. I remember you at that age. You had some peculiar ideas about the world.'

'I still do. That's nature, not nurture.' She wrapped her arms around her father and gave him a squeeze. 'You'll get your bungalow back, Seth gets a bigger room, and I'll get a decent night's sleep. It's been great here, but it wasn't meant to be long term.'

'It hasn't even been short term,' Frank grumbled.

'It's been two months. That's long enough on an air bed.'

Olivia was the one who pointed out the *up*side to an empty living room. Pun intended, she'd said.

Victoria grinned. Life was full of surprises.

She was startled by ringing coming from under the bed. She flipped onto her stomach, lifted the edge of the duvet, and located the phone. She grabbed it, hauled it onto the pillow, and picked up the handset. It had to be her father, he was the only one she'd passed Chris's number to. 'Hi, Dad.'

'Victoria, it's me.'

'Joo!' Victoria scrambled up the bed, made herself comfortable, and rested against the headboard. 'Dad didn't hang about getting my details to you. I was going to call you later.'

'Rewind, Victoria. The last I heard, you were *staying* at Dad's.'

'Chris and I are helping each other out, that's all. There's nothing going on. We're not even sharing the same living space.' She browsed around the room. 'Not technically. Seth and I are in an annexe.' She'd had this discussion the night before with her dad. 'Why am I justifying it to you?'

She heard Juliette laugh. 'I have no idea, but good on you. How is Seth?'

'He's doing all right. I'm still making mistakes, but I'm beginning to understand him.'

'Have you read that info I printed off?'

'Most of it. I need to go through it again, though. I've had to cross-reference a million medical terms to gain a decent understanding. I did read something the other day that made sense. If your child has the disorder, telling him you love him isn't enough. It's an alien concept. He needs something tangible. Seth needs to know I'm here for him, and that he always has a home.' She paused. 'Okay, that second one's been a little less tangible of late, but once we've been here a while, he'll grasp the idea.'

'That's excellent. You sound so relaxed. And optimistic. It's brilliant. The Dorset air suits you.'

Victoria could hear the genuine joy in her sister's voice, which at once pleased and troubled her. 'I'm sorry I left you in the lurch. How's it going? Any comeback from the Tiresome Trio?'

'Nothing. And the board is so much better for their departure.'

'Thank goodness for Annabel.' Victoria owed her friend

a huge debt of gratitude. 'She pulled out all the stops. What a business brain.'

Juliette concurred. 'She did amazingly well. She's still helping me out. I hope you don't mind.'

'Why would I mind?' If it took the pressure off Juliette, it was a great idea. 'I should think Anna's agent has a few things to say about it, though.'

'Oh, she's dealt with him.' Juliette laughed. 'She's been a godsend.'

A splinter of a thought embedded itself in Victoria's brain. 'Is she enjoying it?'

'She's in her element. She said if she never saw an arena again it would be too soon. I think she's here for the coffee.' Juliette's chuckle travelled down the line. 'She's got her tour in less than two months and she's dreading it. She's threatened to cancel. Her agent's on the phone five times a day about it. Or he was, until she told him if he bothered her again this week, she'd sue him for harassment.'

Victoria belly-laughed. 'That sounds like Annabel.'

'Of course, she couldn't sue him,' Juliette continued, 'but he got the gist of her message.'

'Juliette?'

'Yes,' she replied, with an obvious air of suspicion. 'I know that tone. What are you thinking?'

'I'm thinking the solution to our problems is right under our nose.'

'I don't have a problem.' Juliette seemed insulted by the suggestion.

'Yes you do,' Victoria said. 'With me stepping back from EweSpeak, you're overworked.'

'Not now Anna's here.'

'But she's off to – how did she put it? – sing songs that should be consigned to the bargain bins? She said it herself, she's ready for a change; a new challenge. She'd make a great business partner.' Victoria hesitated, trying to find a gentle method of dropping a bombshell. Apart from raiding a cotton wool factory and stuffing the swag under Juliette, there wasn't one. 'And I'm ready to step down.'

There was a pensive silence, as Juliette's breath ebbed and flowed in and out of Victoria's earpiece. 'I think it's the right decision,' Juliette eventually said.

'You do?' With the relief of hearing her sister's words, Victoria sunk into the bed. Until that moment, she had no idea if leaving EweSpeak was a good or bad move. The company was in her blood; it defined her. It made her who she was, but destroyed who she should have been. It was her means of escape, yet it imprisoned her. It provided comfort, but delivered pain.

It had given plenty, but taken so much more.

'Victoria?'

'Yes?'

'I'll let you know what Annabel says. Victoria?'

'Yes?'

'Annabel says what took you so effing long?'

An hour later, standing in the kitchen waiting for the kettle to boil, Victoria reflected on the telephone conversation. Things couldn't have worked out better had she planned them. She'd spent so long closed off in her logical, well-ordered universe, it was hard to believe in ethereal forces, but Annabel's timely appearance caused Victoria to re-evaluate her ideas on fate. People made their own luck – it was a well-known adage, and one she promoted at EweSpeak – but recent experience suggested coincidences had their place.

It was agreed between the three women that before retiring from the world of high heels and microphones, to enter the corporate domain of suits, boots and dictaphones,

Annabel should honour her commitment to her fans in Japan.

'That way you have a few weeks' trial period, and time to reconsider,' Victoria said.

'I won't change my mind,' Annabel replied. 'This is the new start I've been crying out for. I just need somewhere in London to call my own. How about I rent your apartment until I find something? It gets me out of the hotel *and* I can send your stuff on.'

'Saves the place from being empty,' Victoria said. It was a good plan. 'Okay. Be selective in what you send, though. My mobile, a suitcase of clothes, a few of Seth's books and toys.'

'That's all you want?'

'Yes. I'm sticking to my back to basics philosophy.'

Annabel had laughed, unconvinced residing in a castle fell within the definition.

Victoria opened the cupboard and pulled out the powdered soups. The box was squashed, the colours faded, and the packets inside were solid. If Annabel could see me now, she thought. *I'm traumatised by the use-by date.* The candles were more appealing. Thank goodness she'd placed a grocery order online.

She'd sorted Chris's computer and established an Internet connection first thing, much to Rick's pleasure. The setting up had taken a little longer than anticipated as Chris had asked Victoria to install remote access software, and give the PC a once-over.

'Please, Victoria,' he'd said. 'I'm hopeless with technology. It doesn't stand a chance in my hands. I swear, if the bloody thing goes wrong again, it'll end up in the sea. Rick says with the right software you can fix it, even if you were on the other side of the world.'

It was true. She could.

She threw the soup box in the bin, closed the cupboard, and glanced through the window. Despite Rick's face illuminating the living room at the prospect of accessing the World Wide Web, he was outside with Seth, cleaning a bicycle. Seth was listening and taking instruction with the utmost diligence, which was remarkable following his weekend of significant change. Whatever magic Rick was casting, Victoria hoped the spell appeared in her research. Time to trawl though it again.

Without further ado, she grabbed Juliette's printouts from the bedroom and bustled into the castle's kitchen.

'Whoa!' Chris lurched back in surprise. 'Steady on. Where's the fire?'

Victoria hugged the paperwork to her body. 'No fire, but lots of reading to do.'

Chris tapped the documents. 'Is this for work?'

Hmm. That thorny subject. 'No. This is information on how I can help Seth.'

'With what?' Chris helped himself to a biscuit, and held the jar for Victoria. They ate without speaking, until each had finished.

'With his temper, mainly,' Victoria said, flopping the heavy bundle of sheets onto the worktop. She reached into the jar for another biscuit. 'Olivia thinks he may have child attachment disorder.'

Chris raised an index finger. 'Is this to do with him lashing out?'

'Yes. And I need to find a way to fix it.'

Having brushed his hands together, Chris reached for two mugs. 'Coffee? I have instant at the moment.'

'Instant's fine, thanks.'

'So, is this a health issue?'

'Drinking instant? Should be, but my body's adapted.'

Victoria smiled. In the time she'd spent at her dad's she'd acquired a taste for caffeine-filled granules. 'It's amazing how quickly one becomes used to something.'

Chris shoved the kettle under the tap, and turned the water on. It ran at full force. He muttered under his breath as the splashback caught his face. 'Stupid faucet. It either drizzles or it cascades. There's no bloody in between.' He knocked the tap to off.

'Like Seth,' Victoria said, handing Chris a towel. 'He's either charming and compliant, or stubborn and hurling abuse.'

'He's such a little thing.' Chris's voice was muffled by the towel, as he dried his face. 'It's hard to imagine.'

Victoria stiffened. 'You don't believe me?'

The towel was whipped away and thrown onto the draining board. 'You jumped in before I'd finished. I was about to say, it's hard to imagine, but I saw him yesterday, when you were asking him about moving in here.'

'Staying here,' she corrected.

'Staying here.' Chris closed his eyes for a second. 'It's the same thing. Anyway, Seth was like an unexploded bomb.'

'It's not the same thing.' At first, Victoria hadn't been sure what to call it – staying, holidaying, living – but they hadn't moved in. Seth needed to feel secure but she didn't want him misunderstanding their relationship with the Framptons. 'This is a temporary solution, for which I am very grateful, but we have not moved in. I need this to be explicit. Seth needs to understand we are staying. As if we were on holiday.' She picked up the towel, folded it in half, and returned it to its rail. 'This coffee isn't very instant.'

'I'm getting there.' Chris pulled a face, his molasses eyes spreading to their widest point. 'Milk's in the refrigerator, Mrs Noble.'

Fair enough. Unlike her kitchen in London, where all

the white goods were camouflaged as matching cupboards, Chris's fridge stood tall and proud. And silver. 'Nice feature.' Her sarcasm was obvious. 'And yes. Seth is like an unexploded bomb,' she said, attempting to get back to the point. 'Anything can trigger him.' She passed the milk to Chris, and he added a drop to each of the mugs. 'Usually it's a change to his routine.'

Victoria took a teaspoon from the counter and mixed the milk into her coffee. 'All things considered, he's coped admirably this week. I think Rick's had a hand in that.' She checked to see if Chris was listening, but he appeared to be hypnotised by the swirls in his drink. Wherever he was, he wasn't in that kitchen.

She watched him, curious, wondering what had taken him so deep inside his own head. His pallor suggested the impact of having a woman and a child in his house had finally hit him. 'I'm sorry. I should have told you this before. I'll understand if you'd rather not have us here.'

Chris snapped out of his reverie and rubbed his eyes. 'What did you say?'

Victoria could see he was in desperate need of comfort, but she didn't understand why, and knew better than to make the approach. She clasped her hands around her mug, deciding they were safer there. The shame of it was, she was used to not providing solace. Years of living in a virtual world had that effect. 'I said I'm sorry.' A pause. 'Are you all right?'

Chris sipped his coffee. 'Yeah. I'm fine. I was thinking.' He turned round, leaned against the cupboard and closed his eyes. 'And it's given me a headache.' He pressed his fingers into his forehead and massaged his temple with his thumbs. 'Seth's not a problem,' he said, easing open his eyes. 'And I'll help in any way I can. Will you excuse me?' He stood upright, took his mug, and left the room.

Chapter Twenty

With her coffee in one hand, the wad of printouts in the other, and Chris seeking peace in the conservatory, Victoria settled in the living room. The blood-red leather sofa, while a little gauche for her taste, was sinfully comfortable. She understood money didn't buy everything, but there was no denying indulgence had a price.

She set her coffee on the oak side table, and studied the top sheet of paper. Between the search she did at her father's place and Juliette's findings on child attachment disorder, the World Wide Web had plenty of information caught in its threads.

As Victoria thumbed through the thick pile, a page decorated with diagrams caught her eye. She'd not noticed it before. She pulled the sheet free and examined the pictures. It was hard to see how it related to the disorder, but if Juliette had included it, there would be a reason. Victoria read the caption under the pictures. *'By following a simple set of exercises, your body and mind will be free from stress. My new regime will help you achieve deep relaxation, muscle tone, and pain relief.'* She flipped over the page, and on the reverse was a link to a step-by-step YouTube video.

She put the papers on the couch, and scanned the room for the remote control. It was half buried in an armchair.

Victoria extricated herself from the sofa, retrieved the handset, and switched on the enormous wall TV. She found the Internet connection, clicked on the YouTube application, and searched for the link. It advised it was a thirty minute video on the origins and purpose of the exercises, with a *How To* guide at the end. Returning to the sofa, Victoria reclaimed her coffee, swung her legs round onto the seat, and watched.

Everything its presenter said made sense. Victoria had experienced enough anxiety and stress in her lifetime to know her core suffered from its effects, and if she felt it, Seth must too. His anger and resentment, tightly balled in his stomach, grew larger by the day, as layer after layer of bitterness wrapped around it. A release was necessary, and according to the testimonies on the video, these exercises were the way forward.

After twenty minutes of total absorption in the theory, Victoria placed her cold mug of coffee on the table, and stood up. It was time to try the drills for herself. She scanned the room to ensure she was alone, brushed her hair from her eyes, and then spread her feet apart. The calming voice on the TV assured her there was nothing to fear and she should 'relax into the exercises and go with it'. On the previous two occasions when she'd done just that, Chris moved away, and Ben made her pregnant. Well, neither man was present now, and she was fully clothed. No harm could come of a simple workout.

She stuck to the instructions, bending, rolling and stretching in turn, and took a deep breath each time the video prompted. She was concentrating so hard, relaxing was proving difficult, but the conscious part of her brain told her she was doing something worthwhile. She hoped the unconscious part agreed, and that she wouldn't suffer too many aches and pains the next day.

'*Next, you're going to stretch your legs apart, touch the floor with your hands and send them across to one foot. Like this.*' The model on the video demonstrated. '*Breathe, then move your hands to the other foot.*'

'This could be the part of the programme that fails,' Victoria said, as she stared in amazement at the model's flexibility. She took a deep breath, threw out her arms, and reached for the floor. To her surprise, her fingertips touched the quarry tiles. She tiptoed them to her left foot, breathed, finding this action more difficult than touching the ground, and then tiptoed her fingers across to her other foot. 'Bloody hell,' she murmured. 'That's a killer.'

'*Once you've done that,*' the model continued, '*return your hands to the middle, and walk them underneath your body.*'

Bent over, straining to inhale, but giving the manoeuvre everything she had, Victoria's fingers lost touch with the floor. 'That's awful,' she groaned, allowing herself a moment to hang.

'It looks pretty cool from where I'm standing.'

Like a rag doll possessed by a spirit, Victoria sprung up, and swivelled in the direction of the voice. A man, almost as broad as he was long, was leaning against the door frame, grinning.

'Who the hell are you?' she said. Thank God the blood had already rushed to her face from being upside down. Any other redness could be blamed on that.

'Tommy Stone. Chris's ... well, I never know what to call myself ... manager, cook, dogsbody. All of the above.'

'You're Tommy?' He looked nothing like he did on TV. 'Chris said you'd taken leave.'

'Of my senses?' Tommy laughed. 'Yeah. Well, I came back. He needs me more than he knows.' He strolled into the living room and gawped at the TV. 'What on earth is this? Aerobics?' He turned to Victoria. 'Is this how you keep so trim?'

She wasn't practised in the art of flirting, but Tommy's attempt didn't bypass her. What was it Juliette said about compliments? Accept them graciously. 'Thank you, but that's not what this is about.' She grabbed the remote and shut down the TV. 'I was trying something out for my son.' She saw Tommy's eyes widen.

'Your son? Why isn't he trying it?'

'He's four. I thought I'd see how I got on with it first.'

Tommy's face screwed up, like a foam puppet, squashed by its owner's hand. 'Is he overweight, or something?'

Taking a seat on the sofa, and collecting together her papers, Victoria said, 'No. There's not much to him at all.' She placed the remote on top of her research.

'Then what?' Tommy, uninvited, sat next to her. 'Is he an adrenalin junkie?' He raised his palm. 'No! Wait! I've got it! You're a double act. You're a ventriloquist and he's your dummy.' He flashed a set of brilliant white teeth.

Victoria frowned. 'How did you reach that conclusion?'

'It's a reasonable explanation based on how I found you a moment ago, all bent over, waiting for life to be pumped into you.' He stopped talking and grimaced. 'That didn't come out how it was meant. Sorry.' He shied away from Victoria, and pulled a sad puppy face, which, within seconds was replaced with a beam so wide, Victoria was tempted to count precisely how many teeth made a set.

They sat for a moment in silence, neither party moving, until Tommy cocked a leg up onto the sofa and twisted round to face Victoria. 'So, you know who I am, but who are you?'

She extended a hand. 'Victoria Noble. I'm an old friend of Chris. He's invited my son and me to stay here while my cottage is repaired.'

'Right. Chris to the rescue. Always the hero.'

'He was. He saved my son from a collapsed ceiling. If Chris hadn't been there, I doubt Seth would be now.' Victoria refused to think about that possibility.

'I meant giving you a roof over your head, but it must have been awful. Seth is your son?' Tommy drew his fingers together and leaned in.

'Yes.'

'And he wasn't hurt in the accident?'

'No.'

Tommy reclined. 'So, these exercises aren't physiotherapy then?'

Victoria smiled. 'No.'

'Good grief.' Tommy ran his hands through his hair. 'I'm going to rip up one of these tiles in a minute, and squeeze the blood out of it. It's got to be easier than getting information from you.' He liberated the remote from Victoria's research and aimed it at the TV. 'Don't make me do the splits.'

Victoria couldn't help but laugh. 'I'm of a mind to make you,' she said. 'Fair's fair, after all.'

Tommy dropped the controller and leapt to his feet. 'Oh. It's like that, is it? You've shown me yours, so I must show you mine?' He flung his arms above his head and swung them down towards the floor. 'Impressed?' he asked, craning his neck to look at Victoria. 'No? How about this then?' He attempted to flatten his palms to the ground. 'Closer? What … about … now?' He squeezed out the words, struggling for breath. 'Fit … as … a … butcher's … Oh. Sod it.' He walked his hands to his knees, rested for a moment, and then pushed himself upright. 'That really hurt.'

'I know. I don't think it's for Seth.'

Tommy rubbed the back of his legs before resuming his seat. 'Wise decision. He'd beat us hands down, for want of a better phrase.' He laid his arm out along the back of the sofa. 'Right. A deal's a deal. What's all this in aid of?'

Victoria adjusted the sheets on her lap while considering what harm could come from sharing her concerns with Tommy. 'Okay,' she said, sighing. 'Seth has trouble controlling his temper.' She paused and reconsidered her words. 'No. That makes it sounds as if it's his fault, and it's not. I have trouble relating to him. I've been researching probable causes and possible solutions.' She put the sheets on the floor. 'I've not learned enough to make an informed decision yet.'

Tommy whistled. 'Wow. You've got your work cut out. We've been trying for two years to get through to Rick. I imagine his circumstances are completely different, but still, working out how a child's mind ticks is a tricky business.'

Victoria agreed. 'The thing is, I'm the problem where Seth's concerned.'

A firm hand landed on her shoulder. If she had room to move away, she would.

'I feel for you.' Tommy gave Victoria a couple of friendly pats, and removed his hand. 'I mean, I'm not a parent, but I'm godfather to Rick, and I was to Todd too, and I've known them all their lives. Todd and Lacey's deaths hit me hard, but Rick, well, he's lost his twin, and he's lost his mother. He was lucky not to lose his father.'

'Lose his father? Was Chris contemplating … ' The unsaid word hung in the air between them.

Tommy plucked it down. 'Suicide? No. He went off the rails for a while. Withdrew from society, didn't eat, well, nothing of any substance, didn't talk except to me, and couldn't face Rick. I guess he was a reminder of everything he'd lost.' Tommy fell silent.

That wasn't the story Chris had shared with her. 'It must have been awful,' Victoria said, trying to work out

Tommy's angle. 'I saw all the footage at the time. They've been showing it again.'

'I know. He looks a right state.'

'But he's found his way.'

'I guess. He was determined to move here. Thinks a fresh start is what Rick needs.'

There was doubt in his voice. Victoria questioned him. 'But you don't?'

Tommy pulled a face. 'It's not my place to think. I do what I'm told. Go where I'm directed. Straighten out the mess.'

'What mess?' What did Tommy know? Was he party to the information Victoria had paid to keep buried?

'Every mess. I've taken the blame for most of them, too.' Tommy retreated into the corner of the sofa. 'Chris would have lost his licence twice over if I'd not said it was me at the wheel.'

That didn't sound right. Chris was a responsible driver. Victoria looked at Tommy. 'What happened?'

Tommy shook his head. 'No. I shouldn't be telling you this. I've learned how to keep quiet over the years.' He became interested in the buttonholes along the arm of the sofa, and then shot a glance at Victoria. 'Look. I don't know the story between you and him, but by the way you said you were an old friend, I'm guessing you were a girlfriend.'

The turn in the conversation made Victoria's hackles rise, and she hesitated before replying. 'Yes. He knew me as Vicky Paveley. It was before he went to America.'

Tommy sat bolt upright. 'Vicky Paveley? You're Vicky Paveley?' He tapped his fingernail on a hard button, his face full of contemplation.

'You say that like you know me.' Victoria eyed him with suspicion.

'I do. Sort of.' He cast his eyes to the floor. 'I met Chris within days of him arriving in LA. We were both working as odd-jobbers at Harley Film Studios. That's where he met Lacey.' He looked up, his eyes round. Bulbous. 'Don't Google Harley Film Studios.'

Victoria knew why he'd said that. She'd been aware of the studio's reputation for some time, even before it was exposed as a company producing blue movies. They'd concealed the more lucrative side of their business behind the acceptable front of making adventure films.

'I know about Lacey's career, Tommy. What surprises me was how it never made headline news when she and Chris got married.' She watched for a glimmer of recognition. 'Or when Harleys were found out.' Nothing. 'Go on.'

Tommy inhaled slowly and deeply, covering her hand with his. 'I'm telling you this so you know what you're getting involved with. He bragged about you. He said he'd had a girl the night before he left England. He said he had sex in the sea and on the beach, and had grazes on his knees as proof. There was more, but you don't need to hear it. Eventually, your name found its way into the boast.' He clutched her hand. 'I'm sorry. Chris Frampton is not the man you see on the big screen. He's no hero.'

Chapter Twenty-One

With tears budding and growing, Victoria whipped away her hand, grabbed her papers, and ran out of the room. She passed Rick in the kitchen, as she made her way to the annexe.

'Mrs Noble? Are you okay?'

As she scrambled to open the heavy fire door, he appeared beside her, holding a tissue. He pressed it into her hand.

'Did you fight with Dad?'

She tried to lift her eyes; tried to thank him for his kindness, but she couldn't risk it. She was on the verge of losing control, and if she opened her mouth, her words could ruin Rick's life.

'Hey, Rick. Let her be, man.'

Victoria froze. Tommy had followed her in. She continued to face her door, not wanting to see concerned eyes or sympathetic smiles.

'Tommy. You're back.'

She heard the scuffling of footsteps and the slapping of backs. Reconciliatory hugs?

'Where'd you go? I missed you. Well, I missed your cooking.' Ricky's undulating timbre.

'Listen to you. When did you get so chatty?' Tommy had a gruff element to his voice Victoria hadn't noticed in the lounge. It made her skin crawl. Trusting her instinct was a new sensation, but it was screaming out for her to avoid this man.

She'd heard enough. She closed her door, locked it, and forced herself to take slow, deep breaths. 'In through the nose. Out through the mouth.' That's what the model on YouTube had said.

She dumped her papers in her bedroom, unhooked her coat from the back of the door and went in search of Seth. She needed reassurance he was safe. Last she'd seen, he was outside. Using the external door, she peered out and called for him. No answer. She stepped onto the slabbed patio and marched round the corner. Rick's bike was there, as was a bucket and two cleaning cloths, but no Seth.

'Come on,' she muttered. 'Where are you?' She was desperate to stop Tommy getting to him first. As she looked across to the woods, she saw Seth running out of them and towards the front of the castle. He was waving, but not at her. Something or somebody on the driveway had his attention.

Despite her swift turn of speed, Victoria reached the gravel last. There, standing with his hands on his hips, a crash hat at his feet, and two boys looking on, was Tommy.

'Hey, Vicky. Is this your boy? He's a lot like you with those curls.' He extended a hand. 'Nice to meet you, Seth. I'm Tommy.'

Seth backed away, as Victoria drew level. She positioned herself in front of him. 'It's Victoria, and I was hoping to talk to Seth about you, before you met him.'

Tommy looked up. 'Oh. Is this to do with that thing you told me? Sorry. I should have thought it through, but I wanted the boys to see my new motorbike.' He stepped aside. 'Isn't she a beauty?'

As Victoria appraised the great lump of metal, a small hand slipped into hers. She squeezed it, and held it securely. There was something about Tommy that Seth didn't care for either. Rick also shifted nearer; close enough for Victoria to put her arm round, which at that moment, felt like the thing to do. She didn't understand the subtleties of what was going down, but it was plain to see Tommy was the only one happy with his recent purchase.

'Rick, go and get your dad. Tell him Tommy's home,' she said.

'I can't.'

'It's okay. He'll be glad he's back. Go on.'

Rick's reluctance to leave her side was evident, but after an encouraging, guiding hand on his back, he skirted round the motorbike and ran into the house.

'What do you think, Seth? Would you like to hear it purr?' Tommy straddled the wide, black leather seat, turned the ignition and poked his finger at a button. The roar reverberated around the courtyard scaring the birds from the trees, and Seth further behind Victoria.

'Switch it off. Now!' Chris stormed onto the gravel, the force spitting stones in every direction. They were as mad as hell, too. He made a grab for the key, but Tommy got there first.

'Settle down, mate.' Tommy deadened the engine. 'I got a second helmet in case you fancied a spin. I don't mind sharing.'

Victoria watched as the men squared up to each other, neither willing to look away – a Mexican stand-off at Hope Cove Castle. She saw Rick monitoring the situation from the entrance hall. He shook his head, disbelief smeared across his face.

'No motorbikes,' Victoria heard Chris say. 'I don't want it here. Get it off my land.'

Now she understood. And now she knew for certain that Tommy was there to cause trouble. Why remained a mystery. She shielded Seth from the rowing men, took him through the main entrance, and signalled for Rick to follow. Once she had them both safe inside the annexe, she closed the door, and ushered them into the living room.

'Right, boys. Why don't you choose something to watch on TV, and I'll see if I have anything more appetising than candles in the kitchen.' She smiled, hoping her levity would distract them from what they'd witnessed. 'I think I've said before, Rick, I'm a terrible cook. I'm not sure how this candle cuisine will work out. Of course, there's a chance I could set the cooking world alight with my latent brilliance.'

Rick slumped onto the sofa, still shaking his head, and Seth sat beside him. Solidarity.

'I don't like candles,' Seth said.

'Can't say I'm keen.' Victoria stooped to see Rick's expression, but he stuck his chin to his chest, and covered his face with his hands.

'What's wrong with Rick?' Seth picked up the remote control and pressed the on button.

Victoria eased herself onto the small, tiled coffee table. Her notes had mentioned how children with attachment disorder struggled with empathy. She gave herself a moment to recall the advice. *Explain emotions to your child. Help him to identify each feeling.* 'Rick's sad,' she said. Seth understood sadness. He'd not wanted to move to the castle because his Pops would be sad. It wasn't the example she wanted to use, but it was all she had. She was about to speak, when Seth beat her to it.

'You get sad.'

For a heartbeat, his eyes broke away from the TV and connected with Victoria's. She caught her breath. 'We all get sad sometimes.'

'Did I make Rick sad?' He was back to watching the screen.

Rick lifted his head and looked from Victoria to Seth.

'No,' Victoria said, quickly. 'I think it was hearing the motorbike. It scared him a little. That's right, isn't it, Rick?' She raised her brow. It wasn't an accurate description of why Rick was suffering, but it was enough for Seth to handle.

'Yeah. It's not you, bud,' said Rick, wiping his nose with his hand.

'Your dad does that.' Victoria reached for the tissue box behind her, and passed it to Rick. 'Repaying your favour from earlier.'

He took a tissue and blew his nose. 'Thanks. What you watching, Seth?'

'*Tom and Jerry.*'

'Cool.'

'I don't like Jerry.'

With the boys more settled, Victoria left them discussing the intricacies of good versus evil, and as she entered the kitchen, someone tapped on the door. She prepared herself for confrontation, expecting Tommy to be the other side, but stood easy when she saw the delivery man with three boxes of groceries. 'Excellent timing,' she said, signing his electronic receipt pad. 'You've saved us from candle stew.'

'That's good. I find the wick gets stuck in my teeth.' The man smiled and then carried the crates one-by-one into the kitchen. 'Everything all right out the front? With the two blokes, I mean.'

Victoria was touched by his concern. 'Yes, thank you. They're old friends.'

'Fighting over a motorbike.' He tutted. 'I reckon you should serve them candle stew.' With a nod and a smile, he hopped over the threshold and went on his way.

Victoria poked her head into the courtyard and listened. Chris and Tommy were still arguing. She slammed shut the door and concentrated on finding something less waxy for lunch.

Chris swung for the keys. It was the second time he'd

missed. 'I'll swing for you in a minute, if you don't get this out of my sight.' He stabbed a finger into Tommy's sternum. 'What the fuck are you playing at?'

'Shit. Talk about over the top.'

That was a second time in a week Chris had been accused of theatricals. He accepted it from Vicky, but this? This was Tommy at his calculated best. This was Tommy doing the one thing he knew would cause Chris excruciating pain – disrespecting Lacey and Todd's death by bringing, and unashamedly flaunting, a killing machine on his land. 'Why are you doing this?'

'It's a motorbike, Chris. That's all.' He knocked his arm. 'Don't know about you, but it reminds me of Lacey; expensive, with bodywork to die for. Great ride, too.' He pulled out a helmet from the under seat hook. 'Come on. Vicky's got the boys. We could go now, there and back to Weymouth in thirty minutes.' He thrust the crash hat into Chris's hands. 'And then you can tell me why there's a small child and a woman living in our house. I'm guessing it's so you can screw her senseless. Or have you done that already? Was she as good as the first time? Have you taken her to the beach yet?' A nasty, slimy slug of a smile slithered across his mouth. 'Is she as good as Lacey?'

Chris slammed the helmet into Tommy's gut and rammed him into the castle wall. 'You filthy piece of shit. Why have you come back?'

'To make your life hell, Frampton.' Tommy wrestled Chris to the ground, and loomed over him. 'I've had a long, hard think about you and me. I never liked you. We aren't mates, and I'm nothing more than your lackey. Your errand boy.' He yanked Chris up by the front of his shirt, and then pushed him away. 'You know what? I can't be bothered.' He pulled his jacket square, gathered the helmets from the floor, and spat in Chris's direction. 'I came back for Rick.'

That statement winded Chris more than any punch Tommy landed. It sounded like a threat, not an act of love. 'What does that mean?' he asked, willing his legs to stop trembling.

'It means he needs to know the truth about his mother, and if you don't tell him, I will.'

Tommy's threats were never just that. He always followed through.

'You leave me no choice, then,' Chris said, heading for the castle.

Footsteps crunched behind him, and a substantial hand landed on his shoulder. Once, that had been a gesture of reassurance. Now it added weight to Tommy's threat.

'Not so fast, cowboy. You think you can charge in there and blurt it out? Pay the boy some respect. This is going to shake his world.'

Chris swiped Tommy's hand away. 'You've left me no option.' He marched into the hallway, and was stopped again.

'Man, I'm not a tyrant. I love Rick. I'm not doing this to hurt him. I'm doing it because he has a right to know.'

Chris spun round. 'What do you want, Tommy? Spit it out.'

'I want everyone to be in full possession of the facts. But don't do it in a fit of rage. Do it with tenderness, and love, and understanding. The poor kid's been through enough. Sleep on it. I give you my word, I'll not say anything tonight.'

Chris sneered. The currency of Tommy was at an all-time low. His word held no value.

'We can tell Rick together, if you like. Would that make it easier for you? And then Rick can decide whether he wants to stay with you, or come with me.' Tommy swaggered into the kitchen and opened the fridge. 'Back to America.'

'The hell he will!' Chris thundered in after him and kicked the fridge door shut. 'He's *my* son. You have no rights.'

Tommy extended to his full frame, folded his arms and scoffed. 'It's not about rights. It's about right and wrong. It's about a boy of thirteen, lied to and plucked from his home, forced to live thousands of miles away from his mother and brother's last resting place. Do you think he wanted to come here? He cried in my arms like a baby. He pleaded with me to talk some sense into you. He begged not to be taken away from everything he knew.' Tommy leaned in and lowered his voice. 'Heard of a Petition for Emancipation? It's where a child divorces his parent. The legal age in LA when this can happen? Fourteen. It's only a matter of time.'

The words hit Chris with the force of a hurricane, and he reeled back, catching his thighs on the table.

Tommy continued. 'You came here for you, and no one else, you selfish bastard. And look who you found. Little Vicky Paveley, eager and keen to please you.' He was in his face now, his teeth clenched and his breathing hard. 'And does she please you?' he hissed. 'I bet she does. She's got fire in her eyes. And you know what? I'm going to have her. I get such a kick from having a woman I know you want.'

Another reference to Lacey? The fury travelled from Chris's head to his fist at breakneck speed, catching Tommy on the chin. He recoiled, momentarily stunned, but stood back the second the fire door opened.

'I think it's time I took control of the kitchen again,' Tommy said, his voice light and airy. 'What on earth have you been doing in here?' He turned towards the door. 'Rick. *That's* where you went.' He placed his hands together, and held them to his mouth. 'Let me apologise. I'm sorry for upsetting you with the motorbike. It was thoughtless.' He lowered his arms. 'But I'm going to be honest with you, because you're old enough to understand, and you deserve the truth.'

He directed a hostile glare at Chris, before continuing his conversation. 'The thing is, as much as I loved your mom and brother, I need to live my own life. If there's one thing I've learned it's that you don't know what's round the corner. If you want something, you should go for it, and if something or someone is making you unhappy, cut it and them out of your day. Life's too short. Now, I'm going to think about dinner so I can prepare something you can actually eat.'

Once Rick was out of earshot, Chris struck back. 'You're full of shit. I can't believe I trusted you all these years. You're nothing but a miserable and lonely little man. And I want you out of my house.'

'I'll go when Rick wants me to go.'

'You'll go or I'll call the police and have you done for trespassing.'

Tommy smirked and his entire face changed shape.

For the first time since he'd known him, Chris saw the true Tommy – vulpine, sly, opportunistic. He'd arrived there today with no reason other than to cause as much chaos as possible. 'You're full of shit, Tommy.'

'Hey, Rick?' Tommy shouted, leering at Chris. 'I've something to tell you.'

Rick, with his hands in his pockets, and his hair hiding his features, plodded back into the kitchen. 'Yeah?' He'd resorted to monosyllabic replies, and he wasn't making eye contact. His entire body drooped, like a discarded marionette; his spirit and energy, in the hands of the puppeteer, granted only if he wanted him to dance. And Chris would make sure his son never danced to Tommy's tune.

'Is lasagne okay?' Chris said, allowing Tommy to take round one.

'Yeah. All right.' Rick headed for the stairs.

'I can do lasagne,' Tommy said, another smirk forming at his mouth. 'Good choice, Chris.'

That was no choice. 'The minute I tell him, you're out of here.' Chris scowled at Tommy, and then left the kitchen.

'Can I come in?' Chris dragged his arm off the wall as Victoria opened her external door.

'Of course. Why didn't you knock on the fire door?' She gestured for him to enter.

'Tommy's in the kitchen. Didn't want him seeing.' Chris checked the lie of the land before proceeding. 'He's not come through, has he?'

'No. He's somebody I wish to keep at arm's length. I know he's your friend, but what he did was cruel.'

'Can we talk?' Chris proceeded to the living room, but was stopped by Victoria's hand on his arm.

'Sorry,' she said, taking it away, as if a sudden movement would cause an explosion. 'Seth's in there. We can sit at the table in my kitchen.'

Chris froze. Lacey was there, right in front of him, her eyes as desolate as the dunes of Death Valley. He wanted to say something; speak with her, reassure her things would be fine, but with his throat desert dry, he couldn't even swallow.

'Chris? You're sweating. Are you okay?'

Victoria's concern coaxed him from his trance, and Lacey vanished. 'I'm feeling a bit—' Before he could finish his sentence, his knees buckled, and he collapsed against the wall.

Victoria was with him in an instant, wedging one shoulder under his nearest armpit and her hand under the other. Between them, they shuffled into her room, where Chris slumped onto the bed. He managed to twist onto his side and catch sight of Victoria, before giving in to the hammering in his head. He closed his eyes. 'Don't look so worried. I'm all right,' he said. 'Headache. Would you fetch me some water, please.'

He heard Victoria leave the room, say something indistinct to Seth, and then run the kitchen tap; it gave him a moment to collect his thoughts. He'd seen Lacey in the hallway, standing there, as lifelike as Victoria. He knew she wasn't real. He knew it was his mind playing tricks, but what troubled him was that it wasn't a typical flashback. He'd taken Lacey out of a familiar situation and transposed her into a place she'd never been. And she was so solemn.

Chris groaned, curled into a tighter ball, and clutched his head between his hands.

'I've brought painkillers, and a cold cloth,' Victoria said.

'Thanks,' he mumbled, unfurling a little. 'I'll take them in a moment.' He flinched as a gentle hand brushed his fringe to the side, but he didn't open his eyes. At the second pass of Victoria's fingertips, he relaxed, and by the third, he was aware his breathing was heavy, and he was on the brink of sleep, ready to fall. A cool, damp towel was laid across his forehead, and held in place.

'What's going on, Chris? These headaches in such quick succession. Are they normal?'

He placed a hand over Victoria's to increase the pressure above his eyes.

Her fingers twitched.

'Sorry.' He slid his hand away. 'Press harder.'

She obliged.

'I didn't mean to make you uncomfortable.' He opened his eyes to find Victoria kneeling on the floor beside him.

'I wasn't uncomfortable,' she said.

Her enquiring expression led Chris to think there was more on her mind. 'Still the thinker.'

She nodded. 'And you're still the wild one.' She lifted the cloth, and ran the soft pad of her thumb over Chris's scar.

He tensed.

'You keep this covered.'

'Yes.' This was dangerous ground, and he wasn't yet sure enough of his footing to walk there. He pushed himself up, fingered his hair into place, and rested against the cushioned headboard.

Victoria dropped her hands onto her knees, the cold compress tucked in her palm.

They both jumped as the internal door was knocked.

'Stay here,' she said, leaving the room.

Chris strained to hear the conversation. If it was Tommy, he needed to be out there, not cowering in the bedroom. He tried to rise, but his head and vision, working in tandem like professional tag-wrestlers, took him down. Before he had chance try again, Victoria returned. She tipped her head to the side as she looked at him.

'It was Rick. He's taken Seth to show him the smugglers' graves. Said they'd be back for tea. Are there smugglers' graves on this land?'

Chris held his forehead as he gave a tentative nod. 'Smugglers or pirates. Have you got those headache pills?'

Victoria gathered the items from the bedside table, passed them to him, and then resumed her seat on the carpet. 'Have you seen a doctor?'

Chris swallowed the tablets. 'Yeah. It's stress.' He could tell from the way her eyes widened she wasn't convinced. It was time for honesty. He pinched the bridge of his nose. 'Okay. I sometimes have flashbacks.'

'Of the accident?'

He nodded. 'And things that happened before and after.

They're very real. They're not like memories. They're living, breathing re-enactments of what happened, but in my head. It's called re-experiencing. All it takes is a trigger.'

'Like what?'

'Situations. Smells. Circumstances.'

'Like Tommy and his motorbike?'

'Yeah.' There was nothing more to say about that one. Chris had expressed his thoughts in an exact and succinct manner already. He released a great sigh and rolled his head from side to side. Every muscle in his body was as tense as a highwire; even his jaws ached.

'What about me?'

He straightened his neck. 'What about you?'

'Am I a trigger?'

In one unsteady motion, Chris lumbered off the bed and crouched next to Victoria. 'No. Nothing you've said or done has provoked a flashback.' He made a split-second decision not to mention the one in the cottage, when he was searching for Seth. 'You're the one person I'm safe with.'

'So what happened in the hall?'

He scratched his head, messed with his hair, and then rubbed his nose. He didn't talk about his visions; not about the detail. That meant verbalising, and verbalising meant acknowledging them. He'd spent two years keeping them to himself. If he'd wanted to talk about them, he'd have accepted therapy back in the States. 'I can't tell you. I'm not even sure it was a flashback.' He raised himself back onto the bed. 'So it wouldn't help.'

Victoria slid her legs out from under her, flexed her feet, and then joined Chris. 'Do you know that from experience?'

Caught out, he snorted. 'No. But it didn't help Rick, did it?'

'That's because he needs time to work things out for himself. He's like me.'

'And I'm not?' His strength returning, Chris took to his feet and paced the floor. By his own admission, he was a doer, not a thinker. His reaction drew a smile from Victoria. 'What?' He rubbed at his palms. They were sticky and itchy.

'You were always the talker, Chris. You used to tell me every thought that crossed your mind, and moan at me for keeping quiet. And good grief, you did go on.' She was laughing now. 'To this day I can dismantle, service, *and* restore a BMX.'

Chris ceased his marching. 'I thought you loved all the detail.' The unexpected recollection sent a dart of desire through him. He remembered how attentive she was, moulding his hands with hers, as he worked on the bike; how she hung on to his every word, watching his lips until she had to kiss him. And he remembered how much it turned him on.

'I did,' Victoria said. 'I still do. So, tell me what you saw in the hall.'

The rapid change of conversation forced Chris back to the present, and he floundered as he tried to stop the erotic visions flooding his body. He couldn't talk about Lacey and his love for her, when at that very second he was betraying her. It was as if his subconscious had summoned her to remind him where his loyalties lay.

Victoria caught his eye and simply said, 'Tell me.'

He studied her for a moment, considering all the things that could happen to him – or her – if he opened the door to his very personal, very frightening world. He could run head first into another flashback, if that was what it was; Victoria could leave and never come back, or God forbid, he could cry.

'It might help,' said Victoria, as if she was picking up on his thoughts. 'Call me a hypocrite, but at least I accept I store stuff here.' She tapped her head. 'That's not who you are. You never were, and I doubt you ever will be.' She lifted her legs onto the bed, settled back and closed her eyes. 'I'm not looking at you. Talk.'

Well, at least if he cried, she wouldn't see. He swallowed, finding little relief from the action. 'Okay,' he said, gearing himself up. 'I saw Lacey. And she was staring at me. And she was sad. I wanted to ask her why, but I couldn't speak. I think she was upset with me.'

He waited for a reaction. Nothing. No flashback, no tears, no screaming woman yelling at him to never go near her again. Nothing. And then another thought occurred to him, churning his stomach and making the back of his throat rise. 'What if she wasn't upset with me? What if she was sorry for something she'd done?' The final time she'd made love with him, she'd arrived with a sense of urgency. He'd accepted it as one of her shaky days, nothing more, but with hindsight her actions could be viewed as desperate. Guilty, even.

Victoria looked at him in astonishment. 'Are you saying she came to apologise? What for?'

Chris dropped onto the bed. Tommy was threatening to take Rick away, but it was possible he'd already managed to steal Lacey. 'What if she'd had an affair?'

'Who with?'

'That bastard next door.'

Chapter Twenty-Two

Victoria was stunned, and struggled to find the right words. 'I don't understand. I thought you and Lacey were devoted to one another.' *And what about the HIV issue?* Letting that slip would be an almighty mistake. She clamped her mouth closed.

'I thought so too, until Tommy said something the other week. At first I thought he was lashing out.'

Victoria swivelled round so that she was adjacent to Chris. 'Why would he do that?'

Chris flattened the duvet next to his leg, and then flattened it again. Victoria waited. When Chris had finished levelling the non-existent lumps, he leaned in to her, causing the bed to dip. She put her hand out to steady herself, and Chris caught it.

'I need to tell you something,' he said, his voice urgent and husky, his fingers hot and restless. 'It's about Lacey.' He abandoned Victoria's hand and turned away. 'I can't say it.' He climbed off the bed, crossed the room, and opened a window. He gulped in three deep breaths of air, before returning to the centre of the room, a sense of determination on his face. 'Lacey had a secret. One she didn't want the world to know. Or Tommy. Or the boys. And we paid a lot of money to keep it quiet.'

The pulse of Victoria's heart was so strong it was beating in her neck. Confessions were either going to spill from her like rice from a split packet, or she was going to vow to herself never to tell Chris what she knew.

'The thing is,' Chris continued, 'Tommy found out, and because of the nature of the secret, he demanded to know why he wasn't informed. It's why he went away, and I imagine it's why he returned with that stupid machine. But he told me ... No, he never actually said, but he intimated that he and Lacey had something more than friendship. He said he loved her, and that he took infinite pleasure in having something he knew I wanted. I let it go, but with seeing Lacey, I'm wondering if I knew all along. Maybe I'd seen something between them, a glance, a knowing look, a smile, something, but hid from the truth. Now he's saying that when Rick knows everything, he'll want to go back to America with him, and—'

It was too much for Victoria to take in, and she waved a hand in the air. 'Slow down. You're talking too fast.' Still undecided as to whether or not to come clean, she fidgeted, finally settling with one leg tucked beneath her. 'What is it Rick should know?'

Chris bowed his head, the stance of a defeated man. 'Lacey was HIV-positive.' He looked at Victoria, and frowned. 'You don't seem shocked.'

'No?'

Chris's glare was so intense, so demanding, it would have been easy to cave. Victoria could get her secret out in the open, and absolve her conscience. She'd be free from the guilt. Free to tell him about EweSpeak, how she'd followed his career, and how she'd dreamed of him every night. She'd have nothing to hide. She would be exposed. And Chris? He'd be mortified, outraged, and humiliated. He considered her safe. That's what he'd said. She'd thought it an interesting word at the time. A telling word. And she was all he had right now. She was the one person he trusted, and in order to keep his trust, she had to keep her secret. She had to lie to him. There was nothing logical in her argument, but it made complete sense.

'I'm sorry,' she said, 'I'm trying to grasp everything. Go on.'

He nodded, placated by her reply. 'When I first met Lacey she worked in the adult film business. She'd put a stop to her acting career at that point, and was trying her hand at casting. She told me later it was because she was waiting for her test results to come back, although she'd led the studio to believe she was keen to diversify. When the test came back positive, she broke down in the middle of a shoot she was overseeing. She was terrified she was going to die. Guilty for not telling me before we slept together. Petrified she'd already passed it to me. She hadn't,' he added, quickly. 'We were careful, you know? Right from day one. But I still got checked out. To be certain. We didn't really understand. We weren't so well informed in those days, and people were ignorant. Cruel.' He paused and rubbed his eyes. 'She insisted we hid it from everyone, apart from the owner of the studio. She said he needed to know, and he needed to take responsibility for allowing an infected actor through the screening process. He offered an insulting amount to pay her off, which she refused, but she chose not to sue. Instead she asked him to destroy her files and never link her name to the industry. She relied on the studio never going public on the basis it would have destroyed their reputation.'

'You must have been sick with worry.' Victoria gave a gentle shake of her head. What a horrendous way to start a life together.

Chris agreed. 'We were young, frightened, and had no one to turn to. We thought we were doing the best thing. If she'd sued it would've hit the newsstands big time, and she didn't want that. She wanted anonymity. Distance. Time.' He returned to the window, yanked it shut, and remained facing away. 'And she wanted me to leave her.'

Victoria was lost for words. She'd never thought about the impact Lacey's condition had on Chris's emotional life. It was hitting home now, though.

'I didn't want to leave.' Chris's voice was deadened by the glass. 'I loved her, and I knew she loved me. She didn't want her mistakes to be my undoing. She wanted me to pursue my career without fear of reprisals. I was in a dangerous business, where accidents happened. Blood got spilt. She said if people were aware I lived with a HIV victim, they wouldn't touch me with a bargepole. She said my career would be over before it had begun, and with whatever life she had left, she didn't want to live it knowing she'd ended mine.'

'But you loved her and you chose to stay.' It wasn't meant as a criticism, or a reflection of what happened between Victoria and Chris; Chris had learned from experience, and was deciding his own fate.

'Yeah. I grew up,' he said. 'I made a few enquiries, adopted a pseudonym for Lacey, and found a great doctor, who was paid well for his discretion.'

He wasn't that discreet, Victoria thought. His error of judgement had left her pockets empty for some time.

'We married, and learned to manage the condition. And after a lot of soul-searching, we decided it was too risky to have children of our own. But Lacey found this article in a magazine. It proved that with the right treatment it was possible to have a healthy baby. We got lucky with the IVF and had two.' A transient smile passed across his mouth. 'She never wanted the boys to know, certainly not about her movie career. And now Tommy, for God knows what reason, has threatened to tell Rick everything. You can bet your bottom dollar he'll put a filthy spin on it. He'll make it dirty and lewd, and suggest I didn't protect Lacey. He'll paint me as a demon.'

Victoria shunted to the other side of the bed so she too was facing the outside world. Chris was leaning on the windowsill, his shoulders curved, his head pressed against the pane.

'He already has.' Victoria saw Chris's back rise and fall.

'What's he said?'

'That you bragged about having sex with me on the beach.'

There was more of a kick to his breath this time, but he continued to stare in the direction of the gardens.

'You know I wouldn't do that, don't you?'

'I'm surprised he knew,' Victoria said. 'It upset me that you'd spoken about it, whatever the reason.'

'Okay. I told him,' Chris said, turning round. 'But it wasn't a brag.' He spread his arms along the sill, in the same manner as when he'd sat on the kerb outside the cottages.

It was an open gesture. Inviting. Victoria watched his mouth, mesmerised by the way he formed his words, wondering if his lips were as soft and warm as they used to be, when a kiss from him carried her to nirvana. She admonished herself for the inappropriate thought and lifted her eyes to his; the trouble was, they were telling a different story to his words.

What she heard was, 'We were two, young British lads in a foreign country. We spent a lot of time together and we talked. I had to get you out of my system.'

What she saw was his molten eyes pouring over her, and if she was reading him correctly, she was responsible for the magma flowing through his blood. The revelation set her insides alight; her nerve endings detonated, and fire blazed along every fibre.

Chris stepped away from the sill, guided Victoria up by her elbow, and drew her to him. 'Have you any idea what you did to me?'

'Have you any idea what you're doing to me now?' Victoria averted her eyes and concentrated on freezing the lava scorching her body. How did they get to this point? Two minutes ago they were talking about how much Chris loved Lacey.

It was those red-hot lips of his, drawing confessions from her.

'You feel it too?' He let out a long, deep breath.

She hadn't misinterpreted his look. She stood rigid, not daring to move, thinking that if she retreated, he'd let go, and she wasn't ready for that. If she moved closer, she was in danger of fanning flames she couldn't extinguish.

'I thought it was me, clinging on to the past.' Chris murmured the words into Victoria's hair, the vibration sending a tremor through her core.

This was the moment she'd imagined a thousand times. More. But in her fantasies, they were young lovers, freethinkers, unscathed by life's battles. Now they sported scars of the flesh and mind; would they withstand the ravages of an inferno?

'I keep remembering how we were,' he said, easing her into him and enveloping her in his arms.

The power of his hold shocked Victoria. He was nothing like the slight, bony teenager she remembered. As an adult, he was firm, broad, and muscular. A flurry of anticipation fluttered through her. If his kisses sent her to delirium back then, where would they take her now?

She held her breath and listened to his. On the surface, he was in control, maintaining a rhythmic rise and fall of his chest. The only clue she had to what was going on inside his head came from the transmission of tiny trembles through his fingertips. She raised her hands to his solid pecs and pushed back far enough to risk a look. 'Are you okay with this?'

He had his eyes closed, but he nodded. Then he pulled Victoria's head into the crook of his neck. 'I know why I overreacted when you put your arm around me.'

She brushed her fingers along his cheekbone. Exposure to sun, sweat and shaving had given his skin a rougher quality. 'You told me. It was because I ruined Lacey's imprint.'

Opening his eyes, Chris reached up, took her hand and entwined it in his. 'I was wrong. I thought that was the reason, but it wasn't. It reminded me how much I miss touch. Giving and receiving. To hold and be held. I don't even get to hug Rick, he's so insular.' He paused, removed his arm from around her, and tipped her chin up. 'Yes. I'm okay with this.'

Their mouths were inches apart. Was it too much to hope he would go further than an embrace? Her question was answered, as her hand was released and he cupped her face in his palms.

'Everything about you is familiar,' he said, skimming his thumbs over her lips. 'Yet it's as if I'm holding you for the first time.'

She understood. It was the same for her. The way he studied her face, his lightness of touch, and his impulse to act first were how she remembered him, but his body was that of a man's, and his eyes were those of an old soul.

Breathless with expectation and heady in the haze of his heat, Victoria pushed up on her toes, leaned into him, and brushed his mouth with hers; not quite a kiss, but a collision of colossal proportions.

It was the coming together of the past and present.

The aftershock hit her in waves, and shame and embarrassment flooded her body. 'I'm so sorry,' she said, pulling away. 'I shouldn't have done that. Bad idea.'

'Do it again,' Chris said, seizing her waist and boosting her height with a lift. 'And then tell me why you think it's a bad idea.'

'Again?' Surprised by the request, she checked his eyes. The skin around them was more giving than in his youth, but what lay behind them was instantly recognisable; excitement, discovery, danger and a glimmer of something he'd been missing for two years; hope. She couldn't follow through on a promise of hope. 'It's wrong,' she said.

Chris lowered her so her feet were flat on the floor, and then he let his arms fall to his side. 'Explain.'

'Here and now, it's the wrong place and definitely the wrong time.' She couldn't define why, the original reason for them being in her bedroom lost in the sexual fog. 'I don't want either of us to do something we'll regret. I was caught in the moment.' It was no wonder. She'd been celibate for years, she was in the arms of the man she'd never stopped loving, and her dreams of them together had become more explicit by the night. She tensed her stomach muscles, praying it would choke the scarlet assault threatening to invade her face.

Chris closed in. 'You were caught in the moment?' A warm, compassionate smile creased the corners of his eyes. 'Then that makes this the perfect time.'

It was a compelling argument and one Victoria failed to refute. He talked such sense. She breathed out. 'I don't want you to get hurt.'

'I don't want you to get hurt, either.' He slipped off his shoes, kicked them under the bed, and stepped behind Victoria. 'So, we're agreed? No one's getting hurt.'

He lifted her hair, exposing her neck to the cool air, and traced a finger along her collarbone. As she tingled from his touch, his breath created tiny ripples of pleasure over her nape. A few of them extended to her hips, which responded with an involuntary sway.

'Your skin's so soft,' Chris said, his voice losing volume, but gaining depth. 'Womanhood suits you.'

He walked his fingers up her neck, and ran his hand through her ringlets, teasing them straight, before letting them rebound. The gentle tugging and combing motion sent cluster bombs of desire around Victoria's body, and they exploded at her centre.

'Victoria?'

She didn't want the sensations to stop, but when he loosened his fingers from her hair and withdrew his touch, she turned round.

He was as aroused as her.

'Victoria.' The gruffness emanating from Chris's throat surprised him; it was carnal. Hungry. It was the voice he'd muted and locked away two years ago, thinking he'd never hear it again. It was the voice convincing him it was time to embrace the future. Trust Victoria to hold the key. 'Safe,' he murmured, pressing his body to her. For a second, she tensed, then her shoulders relaxed, and he felt her weight lean into him. 'What I told you, that I keep remembering,' he said, his lips finding the line of her ear, 'I do. I keep seeing you on the beach, and in the water, your eyes closed and your head back, giving yourself to the ocean. Do you remember?' She whispered *yes*. 'The way you let go amazed me.' He nuzzled her lobe, and then caught it in his teeth, giving it a gentle bite.

He heard a moan of pleasure.

'I keep seeing how you were then, and the thought stops me sleeping at night.' He kissed the soft skin of her neck, arching his back so he could reach the hollow. It was as he recalled. It tasted of the sea. He passed over it with the tip of his tongue, and continued down until his progress was impeded by Victoria's collar. He raised his head, and locked eyes with her. 'I want to see how you are now.' A pause, to give Victoria time to breathe. 'Let me see.'

She bowed her head, and looked at him from under her brow. 'Okay.'

He slid his palms from her ribs to her hips, scoring his fingers along the bottom edge of her sweater, which he slipped over her head and dropped on the floor. He was shaking – not enough for Victoria to notice, but enough for him to stop, step back, and allow himself to settle. He couldn't risk transmitting his nerves to her; she could misread them as anxiety, which was as far from the truth as heaven was from hell. It was obvious from everything she'd said that she had demons of her own to battle, but right now she was responsive and at ease, and he wanted to go with that.

He regarded her. Her black bra was in stark contrast to her pale skin, and with no jumper, her concave figure was accentuated where her jeans met her waist. He hooked his thumbs in the belt loops at the front, and rested his fingers along the ridge of the waistband. 'You're more beautiful than I remember,' he said. 'Let me see all of you.'

He swallowed as she unfastened her top button, undid her zip, and directed his hands down, driving her jeans over her thighs. He knelt, removed her shoes, and released each foot from the denim. Even her toes were exquisite. He bent lower and kissed both insteps.

'That tickles,' Victoria protested, but there was no weight to the complaint.

Chris kissed them again, and then rose to his full height. He took Victoria's hands, and drew her to him. 'You are gorgeous.' He reached around her, unclasped her bra, and guided the straps over her arms. She closed her eyes and nodded for him to proceed. He removed it, and then smoothed his fingers along her back, round to her breasts, and down to her hips, where her final defence lay – a flimsy piece of black material, protecting their past, and preventing their future. 'I won't be able to stop,' he said, enjoying the texture of the cool cotton against his hot skin.

'Nor will I.' Victoria opened her eyes. Her hips strained under his fingers. 'Everything will change, though.'

Things had already changed. Until he ran into Victoria again, Chris's fantasies concentrated on Lacey, the woman beyond compare. Now Victoria took centre stage. The only comparison occurring in Chris's head was between Victoria's eighteen-year-old virginal self and her thirty-five-year-old equivalent.

And something else was different; his fear of losing Lacey's essence had diminished, alleviated by the realisation that touching Victoria's breasts had not erased or blemished his memory. 'I'm not big on the word change,' he said, curling the top of her briefs down. 'This is us, evolving.' He rolled them a little further, but kept his eyes level with Victoria's. He saw the longing there he felt sure he was displaying. It made him want her more.

His hands were replaced by hers, and she stripped herself of her last vestment. With all her barriers gone, she stepped away.

He allowed himself one last comparison, before setting Lacey aside. Unlike her, Victoria hadn't sought him out for sex, didn't need his permission to let go, and she wasn't making it about her. There was no apology, and no wishing the situation was different.

'Man.' He slumped onto the bed, slouched forward, and put his head in his hands. Some things were the same.

Victoria padded across to him. 'What is it?'

He raised his head. His mouth was level with Victoria's navel. His gaze fell lower. No scar. He sighed. 'At the risk of killing the mood, but in the name of common sense, do we have protection?' He looked up. Victoria was smiling.

'Unless you mean anti-virus software, I can't help.' She sat next to him, and took his hand. 'I am, however, on the pill.'

'Really?'

'Why are you surprised?'

'I thought you'd shut yourself away after Ben left.' That was awkward. 'Sorry.' His hand was squeezed.

'I did, and while I was shut away, being nun-like and celibate, I researched reasons why I should come off the pill. There weren't any.' Her sentence came to an end, as she ducked to see him. 'You do remember I'm naked?'

'I hadn't forgotten.'

'You don't look like a man on the point of no return.' She let his hand slip from her grasp, as she rose from the bed. 'Is there something you're trying to tell me? Do we need a condom?'

'I'm no risk,' Chris said. 'If that's what you're asking. No more than you.' *Damn it!* He shook his head at his own idiocy. That was not the thing to say to the woman he so desperately wanted to make love with. 'I'm sorry. I didn't mean anything by it.'

'No,' Victoria said, gently. 'I'm sorry. This was a mistake.' She retrieved her clothes from the floor, separated out her underwear and began dressing. 'This isn't the right time.' Her tone had a sense of 'I knew it'.

'You've too much going on, and to be honest, I'm feeling more than a little self-conscious right now.' She concealed her front with her jumper.

Chris looked on, not altogether surprised by the change of mood. Talk of condoms had that effect, but he had to ask; his years with Lacey taught him to never be complacent. And it was good Victoria cared enough to check. Sensible. Ironically, the only time he'd not used one was the night he slept with her. It had been incredibly stupid of them, but it was a spur of the moment act, and they were young and indestructible. Life had taught them both some harsh lessons.

'Don't cover up,' he said. 'You've nothing to be embarrassed about. You have a fantastic figure.'

'No, I haven't. You're confusing me with Lacey.'

An uncomfortable silence filled the room.

Victoria sighed, and pulled on her jumper. 'I've tried not to think about her, but she must be on your mind. She was the love of your life and the mother to your boys. Who am I? A girlfriend from a different time. How can you want me?' She stepped into her jeans and wriggled them into place, pausing before fastening the button. 'But this isn't about me. My issues are nothing next to what must be going through your head.' She batted her curls behind her ears. 'And it must be serious, because you're not talking it out.'

Chris gave a small shake of disagreement. She'd got that wrong. He wasn't talking because words wouldn't pay justice to what he was thinking. 'Let me show you what's going on.' He clambered off the bed, took her face in his hands and kissed her. A proper, full-on, man-on-the-edge kiss.

Her mouth was receptive and giving, and she returned his passion with equal measure. If his kiss was soft, so was hers. If he explored beyond her lips, she teased his tongue, and a caress to her neck was rewarded with a stroke to his. Every reply sent a pulse of pleasure round his body.

And she made no demands, presenting him with the gift of pure acceptance.

For a fleeting moment, the spectre of love floated before him; was it a ghost from the past or a portent of the future? His skin erupted in goosebumps, and he shivered. Whatever it was, life was too short to ignore what was happening in the present.

He kissed Victoria off her feet and carried her to bed.

Chapter Twenty-Three

The only reason Victoria broke away was to reclaim the breath Chris had stolen. Twice. He was everything and more than she'd imagined, and she was in no doubt he could have and would have indulged and satisfied her a third time, had she not stopped.

She peeled back the duvet to be greeted by a pair of dark, mischievous eyes; cognac, ready to warm her on the way down.

'You have an amazing body,' he said, kissing both breasts, as if to endorse his statement.

'Lie here.' Victoria patted the narrow space beside her. 'Nice to know I'm not the wrinkled old prune you were expecting.' She kissed his nose as his head landed on the pillow.

'I'll keep saying it until you believe me. You have an amazing body. It's so feminine.' He laughed. 'That's a compliment. Everything about you is real. Nothing is fake. There's no pretence.'

'I'm a hundred per cent natural, is that what you mean?' She gave him a gentle nudge with her elbow. Receiving no reply, she glanced at him. 'Have I said something wrong?' She rolled onto her side, tugged at the duvet, and tucked it under her chin. He'd disappeared again, like before. His eyes were glazed. Had their lovemaking triggered a flashback? Was he in bed with Lacey? Victoria counted the seconds. One, two, three. With a deep breath and a palm to his forehead, he was back. She smiled when he focused on her. 'Okay?' With her hand wrapped in the cover, she wiped away a trickle of sweat from Chris's temple.

'Yeah. I'm with you. I'm safe.'

Victoria freed her arms and hugged him to her. 'Talk to me.' She felt his body press further into hers, so she strengthened her hold. 'Tell me where you go.'

His entire body expanded within her arms as he breathed in.

'My ranch. Sometimes I'm running to the stunt arena, mostly I'm knee-deep in detritus, trying to find Lacey, or searching for Todd. I never see the whole story. It's fragmented, but it feels as if each episode lasts for five, ten minutes. In reality they're seconds, but it's enough. And I have the fear and panic every time.' He turned away from Victoria, but their bodies remained in touch. 'They come, and I deal with them. And I thank God Rick was spared the trauma. The poor lad carries guilt around in a bucket. He thinks he should have got Todd off the bike.' He paused, and cuddled Victoria's hand to his cheek. 'Do you know what happened?'

'Yes.' She wished she didn't, but the digital jungle drums, including those beaten by EweSpeak, pounded the incident out in explicit detail. 'I cried for you.'

His eyelashes flickered on her fingers, and a tear coursed its way through.

'It was horrific, and for you to keep seeing it is heartbreaking.' She blinked away her own gathering swell. 'I've learned a lot recently, lessons that bypassed me or I'd failed to heed, which I've now listened to. I have good people around me who will do whatever it takes to set things right. Let me do that for you.'

'I can't be fixed, Victoria.'

'Then I'll help Rick. Get him to a good place before he has to face all the stuff about his mother.'

'Yes,' Chris said, nodding into her palm. 'I'd like that.'

With Chris returned to his side of the castle, and Seth and Rick safely installed in the annexe's lounge, Victoria sat in her bedroom and set her mind to Tommy.

It was difficult to believe his anger stemmed purely from his exclusion of Lacey's secret. The degree of devastation he was threatening indicated there was far more at stake, but Victoria knew so little about him, it was impossible to determine what.

She rumbled her fingers on the dressing table. Her contacts at EweSpeak would have no trouble obtaining background information, but that would mean a trip to London, and there was no time. Tommy's threats came with an execution date. If she could negotiate a stay ...

'Mrs Noble?' Rick's voice echoed through the closed door. 'Are you coming to dinner? Seth said he loves lasagne.'

Dinner. An informal setting, with social chatter, and Tommy at the table. If Victoria asked the right questions, she could learn a thing or two. Every little nugget of information would help. 'We'd love to come to dinner,' she said, as she entered the hallway. 'Thank you.'

She pointed the boys towards the internal door, opened it, and strolled into the kitchen.

Tommy was at the counter dishing up. He cast a look in their direction. 'You've brought company, Rick. Just as well I made a trough full. Sit down.' He waved the serving slice in the air, before returning to his task.

Victoria examined the table, trying to determine the seating plan; she wanted to sit next to Tommy. Scrutinise him. Ask him as many awkward questions as she could. *Pile on the pressure.* 'Where are you sitting, Tommy?'

'At the end.' He brought two plates across and put them in front of the boys. 'They're hot. Don't touch. And Vicky, there's garlic bread in the oven.'

It was an instruction rather than a statement, but Victoria pulled out her chair, and made herself comfortable. 'I love garlic bread.' She gave a playful shrug, making Rick produce one of his typical teenage lazy smiles. 'This smells delicious, Tommy. Where did you learn to cook?'

She watched him drag two more plates from the cupboard. 'Rick's mom.' He slopped a portion onto each of the cold plates, and carried them to the table. He put one down at the spare place next to Seth, and handed Victoria hers. 'She taught me a lot of stuff.' He collected his, and took the seat at the head. 'Where's your dad, Rick? Doesn't he know it's rude to keep us waiting?'

Victoria watched for Rick's response. He shoved a forkful of pasta into his mouth. Seth copied. 'I think the bread's burning,' she said.

Tommy cursed, scraped back his chair, and swiped the oven gloves from the side. 'That was your job.'

'We're guests,' Seth said in his pragmatic way. 'It's your job.'

Victoria thought she heard a growl resonate from within the cooker. As Tommy backed away, and stood up, Chris walked past and sat at the end of the table. It amused Victoria, although now she wasn't sitting next to Tommy. Opposite was good, though. She could keep an eye on him there.

Tommy banged the tray of bread into the middle. 'Help yourselves,' he said, the sarcasm aimed at Chris. 'You usually do. I'm going to check on my bike.' He left the kitchen.

'You took Tommy's seat,' said Seth. 'I think he's gone to cry.'

'He's all right, buddy.' Rick patted Seth's wrist, and they both carried on eating.

Turning her attention from the boys, Victoria spoke to Chris. 'He's not happy we've joined you.'

'I suspect he was planning a little chat with Rick and me.' Chris kept his voice low.

Victoria replied in a similar hushed way. 'I'm planning on a chat with him.'

'You are?' Chris's nose rumpled.

Their conversation was brought to a close by Tommy striding in, taking his plate of lasagne and settling next to Seth. 'What are you grown-ups whispering about?' He threw his ignition key onto the table. 'You looked mighty cosy there.' He turned to Rick. 'What do you think, son? A bit too cosy?'

Victoria jumped into action. 'You have an interesting accent, Tommy. How long were you in the States before you picked it up?'

Tommy pushed back in his chair. 'Not long. I'm a fast worker.' He clicked his tongue and winked.

'I can't decide if it's West Country or West Coast. Where were you born?' Victoria bit into her bread, attempting to give the impression she was making small talk.

'Ha!' Tommy ran his tongue around his gums, making wet, sucking noises. 'I'm from Bristol. You've a good ear.'

Victoria forced a smile and hoped it appeared natural. 'It's my party trick. What made you go abroad?' As she asked, it dawned on her that Tommy had no idea she knew about his threat to Chris. The last time they'd spoken, he'd told her Chris was no hero, and she'd run off crying. If she played this correctly, and conveyed to him the suggestion that her enemy was his enemy, she stood a chance of extracting the information she needed to speed up her inquiry. Not exactly moral, but then neither was blackmail, which was Tommy's game.

'There was nothing keeping me in this country,' he said, breaking into her thoughts. 'I'd been there a few months before I met Chris. Isn't that right, mate?'

Chris mumbled into his glass of water.

'Yeah. I was working at the studio as a carpenter's mate, constructing sets, that sort of thing. I wasn't qualified, but like I said, it doesn't take me long to pick things up.'

He bared his teeth in what Victoria assumed was a smile. It was more of a leer, and there was a spot of parsley from the garlic bread stuck to his incisor. Victoria gestured for him to remove it and he picked it off with his nail, wiping it on his trouser leg.

'I'm very good with my hands.' He rubbed his palms together and laughed. 'Lacey was impressed with my work. She often asked me to patch things up.' He grabbed his glass and slugged its contents down. 'I often wonder what would have happened had Chris not turned up. What d'you reckon, *mate*?'

The emphasis on the word mate was so pointed, Victoria flinched. She was aware Rick had finished eating, and he was listening to Tommy with great intent. This was not a conversation to have in front of the boys. A change of direction was called for.

'Did you come home for visits?'

Tommy scoffed. 'Why would I? I told you, there was nothing here for me.'

'What about family?'

'They washed their hands of me before I left. I was on my own until I met Lacey.'

Back to her again. The ability to make every comment relevant to Lacey was a trait Victoria recognised. She possessed the same skill when it came to Chris, but she'd mastered the art of keeping her thoughts to herself.

It was possible Tommy was bringing her name up purely

as a dig, but there was something in the way he spoke her name that led Victoria to think there was more. The bells of obsession were ringing. Time to increase the pressure.

She pushed her plate aside, finished her water, and excused herself from the table. 'You're a good cook. I could get used to that standard.' From the corner of her eye she saw Chris slant his head at her and glare. 'You did all the hard work, Tommy. Let these three clear up. Come and talk to me.' It was the most staged, most flirtatious moment in her entire life. She fought the urge to shake off the maggots crawling all over her. She pushed her chair in, gave a warning nod to Seth to behave, and then left the kitchen.

It was a short distance to the living room, but she had more than enough time to think about what she was doing. Tommy was responding well to her; he was relaxed in her company, and enjoyed having his ego massaged.

That was all she would massage.

She let the double shudder out before he entered the room.

'I thought it would be strange having another woman about the place,' he said, as he sat beside her.

'But you're okay with it?'

He stretched his arm out along the back of the sofa, reminiscent of their meeting that morning. 'I'd be okay with several if they were like you.'

She forced out a laugh. 'You're only saying that because I approved of your lasagne.'

'There is that. And the fact you've kept yourself in pretty good nick.' He edged closer. 'What's the story with you and Chris, then? I don't mean your history. I know all that. I mean now. Why are you here?'

'His offer was too good to refuse.'

'Don't be fooled by his charm. I thought I warned you about that side of him.'

'You did. And I'm sorry I took off.' She paused, realising this was a perfect opportunity to feign further dislike of Chris. 'It's upsetting to discover my private life isn't private. It'll be the last time I trust Chris with anything.' She knocked off her shoes and curled her legs onto the seat. 'Right, enough about me. I want to know about Tommy Stone. You've a high profile job. How do you manage to keep out of the spotlight?'

'I keep my head down. Anyway, it's not about me, is it? It's about Chris. It always has been. Lacey gave everything up for him. She went into exile so he could follow his dream.'

Lacey again. 'Can I ask you something?' Victoria copied his move, resting her forearm on the sofa back. She knew mirroring was a powerful way to build rapport. It was another business technique she could use to her personal advantage. 'Were you and Lacey an item, before Chris spoiled the party?'

Tommy pursed his lips, and rubbed his mouth and chin. 'Nothing serious, but it could have been. I liked her.'

It was hard to know if this was sheer bravado or the truth.

Tommy closed the gap between him and Victoria, clasped his hands together, and shook his head. 'Lacey and I slept together a fair few times, but after Frampton arrived, she and I were nothing more than friends. I wasn't happy. I was very fond of her.'

Victoria maintained a straight-face despite the shock of Tommy's admission. Her stomach was dealing with the fallout. She took a slow, deep breath and refocused. 'I thought you and Chris were like brothers.'

'He thought so, too.'

Victoria unfurled her legs and assumed the new identical position to Tommy. 'So ...?'

'So, at the beginning, I pretended for Lacey's sake, and when Chris hit the big time, she asked me to help out. I wasn't going to say no, was I?'

'But how did you settle all of that in your mind?'

'I got a great place to live, Lacey close by, and a job that eventually paid well. What's not to like?' He reclined and crossed his ankle onto his thigh. 'Money can buy anything.'

'You sold out on your friendship?'

'It wasn't a friendship. Everything I did was for Lacey. And when she asked me to be the boys' godfather, I knew I had to stay. What if something was to happen to Chris? They were family to me. Rick still is.'

Victoria resumed her relaxed stance, nestling into the corner of the sofa, and swinging her legs up. 'You must feel Lacey and Todd's loss deeply.'

Tommy gave a sharp, dismissive shake of his head. 'I've told you. It wasn't about me. Like the night on the beach wasn't about you.'

A few days ago, Victoria would have believed that. Now, she had to pretend. 'I won't be making that mistake again.' She leaned in, and lowered her voice. 'And after what you told me, I don't feel the least bit guilty for taking advantage of Chris.' She tapped the side of her nose, hoping she was convincing enough to draw Tommy in. His sly smile gave her the confirmation she required.

He put his leg down, turned to Victoria, and rested his hand on her foot. 'You and me both.'

If he didn't remove his sweaty fingers from her ankle in two seconds … She forced a smile.

'Mrs Noble?' Rick, in his lanky, self-conscious, teenage way, entered the room and addressed Victoria without looking in her direction.

Grateful for the interruption, she took her feet off the sofa, and stood. 'Rick, please call me Victoria.' She excused herself from Tommy's company, hooked her arm through Rick's, and marched him out of the room. Once in the safety of the conservatory, she set him free and apologised for their rapid exit.

Rick smiled. 'It's okay. Dad sent me to tell you we've finished the dishes. I think he wanted to know what you were doing.'

Victoria attempted to return the smile. 'Well, thank you. Where is he?'

'In the kitchen showing Seth his cell phone.' He paused, as a thoughtful expression worked its way from his eyes to his mouth. 'Actually, I think Seth is showing Dad.'

'Really? At four?'

'Hey. Todd and I knew how to access games on the Internet by that age. Anyway, Seth's like his mom.' The sloppy grin Tommy had stolen was back. 'Come on.'

Victoria accepted the arm he offered, and they walked together into the kitchen. Seth was sitting on Chris's lap, huddled into him. Their heads were locked together over a mobile phone.

'Not again.' Chris peered over his shoulder. 'Your son's a master at noughts and crosses.' He tickled Seth's ribs.

Seth giggled. *Seth giggled.* Its beauty floored Victoria, temporarily knocking the last few minutes from her mind. Thank goodness she was holding onto Rick.

'I won.' Seth picked up the phone, clambered off Chris, and showed the screen to Victoria. 'Look.'

Letting go of Rick, Victoria knelt, cradled Seth's willing hand in hers, and admired his win. It was hard concentrating on the game, when what she wanted was to hug Seth and thank him for making her feel special. 'Wow! Well done,' she said, enlarging her eyes so her delight was visible. 'Did you enjoy playing?' He nodded. 'Perhaps we can do it tomorrow?'

'Okay.' Seth returned to the table, waited for Chris to lift him up, and engaged him in another round.

With her insides fluttering, Victoria took a steadying breath and occupied herself by boiling the kettle. 'Cup of tea?' She pitched the offer into the air.

'No thanks, Mrs Noble,' Rick said. 'I'm off to bed. Gonna watch a movie.'

'You can watch one down here.' Chris broke away from his game and linked his fingers across Seth's stomach. 'Don't hide yourself in your room.'

'I'm not hiding. See you in the morning. Night, Seth. Mrs Noble.'

'Sleep well, Rick.' Victoria waved her good night as Rick left the kitchen.

'Oh, no. Again?'

She swivelled round at Chris's exclamation to find Seth beaming and holding his hands aloft.

'Is this going to happen when I play you?' Victoria said.

'Yes.' Seth lowered his arms and attempted to stifle a yawn. 'Show me another game, please.' His words were stilted by the broken intakes of breath.

Chris looked to Victoria, and she gave a subtle shake of her head.

'No more tonight, thanks, Seth. My pride won't stand another beating.' Chris palmed his phone and slid it into his top pocket. 'Are you ready for your first night in your new bed?'

Seth hopped down. 'Yes. Rick gave me Spider to cuddle.'

'Spider?' Victoria threw an inquisitive glance at Chris, who looked confused by her son's comment.

'Spider? Black, fluffy, a leg for each eye. About this big?'

Victoria estimated the distance between Chris's hands to be eight inches. 'He's not real, is he?' Seth had an unsettling fondness for spiders, but he'd not yet got round to requesting one for a pet. Victoria recoiled at the thought.

'Don't panic. He's a soft toy. The boys had one each. Rick's been guardian of them since …' Chris swept his arm across the table, but then said nothing further.

'Since Todd died.' Seth's direct statement smacked both adults off balance. It took Victoria seconds to regain her equilibrium, but Chris appeared to be rocking in the wind for several heartbeats. 'Rick told me,' Seth continued. 'I don't mind Spider has seven legs.'

Victoria kept watch on Chris. His eyes hadn't glazed, so she didn't think he was experiencing a flashback. She laid a cautious hand on him.

It revived him and he looked at Seth. 'Seven legs? You have Todd's Spider?'

'Yes. Rick said Todd would be pleased.'

'Is that okay?' The situation was uncomfortable for Victoria. She admired and loved Rick for having the courage to part with his brother's treasured possession, but she didn't want it upsetting Chris. And then there was Seth's fallout should Spider be taken away.

Chris reached up and patted her fingers. 'It's fine. I couldn't think of a better keeper. It's Rick's decision, and I think it's the right one.' He smiled at Seth. 'Todd cut the leg off with a penknife. He did it so he knew which spider was his. Brutal.'

Seth reached into his trouser pocket and pulled out a spindly, fuzzy, black worm. 'Rick gave me the leg. Look.'

'Huh. He kept it. I thought that went years ago.' Chris held out his hand, requesting permission to inspect the limb. Seth passed it across. 'Would you look at that? I had no idea.' He returned it to Seth's waiting palm. 'We could sew it back on, if you like.'

'No, thank you. I like seven. I have seven favourite colours, and seven crisps I like, and seven friends.'

'Seven legs it is, then.' Chris gave a nod of acceptance to Victoria. 'Funny boys.'

She removed her hand and opened the annexe door. 'It's gone seven now, Seth, so it's time for bed. Bring the leg.'

'Things you never thought you'd say,' Chris murmured, pushing back his seat. 'Hey bud, are you too big for a night time hug?' He opened out his arms, and with no hesitation, Seth hurled himself into them. 'You are such an excellent hugger. Have you been practising?' Chris ducked to see Seth's face. 'He's smiling,' he said, glancing up at Victoria. 'And so are you.'

She was. She couldn't stop herself. The sight of the man she loved embracing her son sent a million sensations flitting round her body.

'Time for bed.' Chris patted Seth's back and presented him to Victoria. 'I'll finish making your drink. It'll be ready when you get back.'

She thanked him as she marshalled Seth down the steps and into the annexe. Assuming she'd be gone for a mere few minutes, she pushed the door to, not bothering to close it. She sighed with relief as Seth entered the bathroom with no resistance.

'Is Spider snuggling in with you tonight?' She squeezed toothpaste onto Seth's brush and showed him her teeth, hoping he'd do the same. He nodded, but his mouth remained closed. Victoria didn't want to fight. 'Would you like to brush your teeth?'

'Yes, please.'

Victoria sat on the lid of the toilet, as Seth viewed himself in the mirror, diligently cleaning each tooth. At the point he had more paste on his mouth than in, Victoria rinsed out his flannel and passed it to him. 'Excellent job. Show me how well you can wash your face.'

He responded to the instruction, putting his brush on

the basin, spreading the cloth over his hand, and scrubbing his cheeks and chin. He was good. Thorough. Victoria approved and applauded his effort, not understanding what had urged her to hand him the responsibility. She hadn't given it any thought; it had simply happened. Maternal instinct.

She caught her reflection, peeking from behind Seth's golden curls. She was smiling. Again.

After the necessary toileting and hand washing, they moved to the bedroom, and Seth climbed under his duvet. With Spider tucked under his arm, and the leg clutched in his hand, he blinked several times, each longer than the one before, until finally, his eyes closed.

'Night, Seth,' Victoria whispered. 'Love you.'

'Night,' he whispered back.

She stared in wonder at her son. Christmas was over, but Seth wishing her a goodnight was the perfect gift.

'I've decided to stay another week.' Tommy's voice echoed from the castle kitchen through to the annexe.

Victoria cursed under her breath. For a few minutes, she had nothing else on her mind but Seth. Now it was flooded with thoughts of Tommy with Lacey, and questions as to how Victoria was going to break the news to Chris. She revelled in one last glimpse of Seth, and then exited his room.

If Tommy was true to his word, another week would give her the chance to get to London and dig around in his past. There had to be something he was hiding. She crept closer to the internal door, and waited.

'I had a long chat with Vicky, and it's worth my while hanging around. I know she wants me, and I reckon she's one hot shag. What do you think, Chris?'

'I think you're a disgrace and the sooner you leave the better. I'm telling Rick everything tomorrow, so why don't you just piss off?'

Tommy's caustic laugh corroded Victoria's insides. Vile, repulsive, repellent man.

'She won't sleep with you,' Tommy said. 'I'm going to tell her about Lacey's HIV. She'll want nothing to do with you then. In fact, when this whole story explodes, no one will want anything to do with you. Not even your own son. So. We're good for another week, yeah? Mate?'

Victoria, not daring to breathe, strained to hear what was happening. Footsteps were shambling away from her. Hopefully Tommy's.

She jumped back when her door was knocked.

'Did you catch that?' A mug of tea appeared, followed by Chris. 'I'll carry it through to the lounge.'

'Let's go to my kitchen,' Victoria said, aware she had a tricky conversation ahead. 'It's further away from Seth.'

Closing the door, Chris obliged and followed Victoria the length of the hallway. 'Why does Tommy think he's got a chance with you?' He placed the mug on the small table, sat opposite Victoria, and narrowed his eyes.

'He was winding you up.' She sipped her tea, waiting for a reaction, but Chris sealed his lips and said nothing. 'Looks like it worked.' She could see he was agitated, but that was understandable with someone as nasty as Tommy skulking around the place.

'What did you talk about in the living room?' Chris reclined, crossed his ankles, and linked his fingers behind his neck.

If it was an attempt to appear unbothered, it had failed. The rhythmic bouncing of his foot gave him away.

Victoria tapped the side of her mug, while she decided how best to answer. 'I wondered what took him to Hollywood.' Her reply was deliberately vague. She ran the risk of alienating Chris by keeping her plan to herself, but by revealing it, she suspected he would vehemently object, and insist she dropped the whole idea. She'd have to disclose her part in EweSpeak, too. She was convinced he wasn't ready to hear that yet. There was also the matter of Tommy's fling with Lacey. She had no idea how to broach that subject.

'Why?' Chris's relaxed posture transformed into a defensive one, as he pulled in tight to the table, and folded his arms. 'What's the sudden interest?'

'Why the sudden interrogation?'

Chris was brooding now. His dark brow was low, and his usually pliable lips were thin and hard. Victoria held herself together, so his razor-sharp look didn't dissect her.

'Because you're the reason he's staying,' he said.

'As I understand it, I'm also the reason he's given you a few extra days grace.'

Chris shoved back his chair, scrambled to his feet, and jabbed at the table. 'That's prolonged my agony, not reduced it.'

Victoria winced. Of course it had. 'I'm sorry,' she said, concentrating on a bubble floating in her tea. 'I didn't mean to encourage him.' She looped her thumb through her mug, approached the sink and chided herself. Although her intentions were honourable, she'd managed to cause Chris more pain and anguish. Worse still, she had no guarantee her actions would provide a positive outcome. She could make his and Rick's situation a hundred times worse.

She rinsed out the cup and placed it on the draining board. It glinted under the fluorescent strip-light. I'll have to come clean, she thought, blinking at the white mug imprint behind her eyes. Drawing strength from a deep breath, she turned and found Chris staring at her. She pulled at her collar. 'I have to tell you something.'

The fire of suspicion blazed in his eyes. 'Go on.'

Scalded by his glare, Victoria retreated, and gave herself

a moment to recover. If she told him everything now, their bright, new beginning could burst into flames, burn out, and leave nothing but ashes. Ashes she'd have to bury. Next to her past.

She opened her mouth not knowing what was going to come out. 'I have to go to London tomorrow.'

Her words dowsed the fire, and Chris frowned. 'Is that it?'

Victoria nodded. That was it. 'I need to sort out my flat, collect a few things, and pay the bills.' She'd tell him the truth once she'd investigated Tommy. If she found damning evidence – information that would send Tommy running, then everything would be okay.

'It's a bit sudden.'

'I'd like Seth to see his cousins.'

'He saw them at Christmas.'

'Am I missing something?' Victoria reclined against the counter.

Chris shrugged. 'I thought with this afternoon …' He trailed off. 'I thought wrong.' He pulled a face, shoved his chair under the table, and slunk into the hallway. 'See you when you get back, then.'

The door clicked shut.

Chapter Twenty-Four

'This office could do with some colour.' Sitting at her EweSpeak desk, Victoria cast a critical eye over the room. 'How long since it was decorated?'

Juliette laughed. 'We had it done last year, but you insisted on keeping it white.'

'Must have been a phase I was going through. Anyway, where's Annabel?'

'She's having lunch with her agent. It could go on a bit. Did you need to see her about something specific?'

'I wanted to thank her for stepping in.' Victoria looked at Juliette, who was perched on the corner of her desk. 'Do you think it's going to work?'

Without missing a beat, Juliette said, 'Oh, yes. She's amazing. Such a quick learner. And she doesn't take prisoners. I'll miss her when she goes to Japan.'

Ah. Japan. 'Would you like me to cover those months?' Victoria offered because Juliette was her sister, and no other reason. EweSpeak wasn't the driving force behind her decisions as it once was. 'I could work remotely from the castle. I don't mind.'

'Yes, you do.' Juliette patted Victoria's hand. 'Besides, I think you've enough going on without worrying about this place.'

'It's you I'm worried about.'

'No need. I'm having a ball.'

There was a definite glow to Juliette.

'You're not pregnant, are you?'

'Goodness, no.' Juliette fanned herself with her hand. 'Four's enough.'

'So, you're just enjoying life?'

Juliette eased off the desk, and faced Victoria. 'Getting rid of those board members has made such a difference to this place. Everyone's happy. And Annabel's made a huge impact on the staff.' She stopped and backed away, as Victoria raised an eyebrow.

'So what you're saying is Annabel's more fun than stuffy, intense Victoria?'

Juliette fiddled with her wedding ring, and then produced a hesitant nod.

Victoria couldn't maintain her stern expression any longer, and she released the smile and the emotions she'd held back. 'It is such a relief to hear you say that.' She watched as her sister gave quiet thanks. 'You're the human element of this company, Joo. You made it the success it is, and I'm glad things are working out.' She left her seat and invited a surprised Juliette in for a hug.

'We made it a success, Victoria, and I'll miss working with you. We've been partners a long time.'

'We've been sisters longer.'

They broke away from the embrace, and smiled at one another.

'You're doing the right thing, you know that?'

Victoria nodded. 'I feel it.'

With Juliette out for a late lunch, Victoria made good progress on researching Tommy Stone. The trouble was, the more she learned, the more there was to uncover. He had a trail as long as the Cotswolds Way. The most interesting fact that one of her British contacts unearthed was Tommy's real name.

As the door to the office opened, Victoria switched off her monitor. There was no need to involve Juliette.

'Found what you're looking for?' Juliette hung her coat on the stand.

Victoria acted distracted. 'Hmm? Oh. Yes. Tidying my files. Housekeeping. I'll transfer my personal stuff. There's no need to keep it here anymore.' She reached for her bag and pulled out a USB stick. She needed to copy across Tommy's information anyway.

Juliette hovered by the corner of the desk. Her downturned mouth matched her wilted posture. 'You're wiping out any trace of you being here.'

It wasn't something Victoria had thought of before then, but having used it as her excuse, she realised she was now committed to doing it. It was another job to add to the never-ending list. 'Not every trace,' she said, trying to bolster Juliette. 'There's plenty of evidence I've interfered.' She smiled and pushed back her chair. 'I had no idea so much of me existed in binary. It's going to take hours, and I was hoping to head back tonight.'

'Stay, then. Your apartment's still empty. Let Seth sleepover with his cousins, you can finish becoming the invisible woman, and tomorrow, you can see Anna.' Juliette leaned in. 'We could have breakfast together, and you could tell me about Chris Frampton.' She smiled.

Victoria rested on her elbows. 'I could. And I could also sort out the stuff to take to Weymouth. It would save Annabel the job.' Her initial reluctance to stay derived from her concern Tommy would act up while she was away, but she needed to follow through with the information she'd received. And delete her personal files. 'Okay. We'll have breakfast together.'

Both women smiled.

At the point Rick was excused and left the kitchen table, Chris scowled at Tommy. The bastard had been making snide remarks from the moment they'd sat down to dinner. Thankfully, Rick appeared unaware of the underlying threats.

'Did I tell you Vicky asked me to go with her today?' Tommy folded his hands together and rested them on his stomach. 'Yeah. She'd booked a room. I wonder what she had in mind.' He kicked Chris's foot. 'I told you she was hot for me.'

Chris tried not to take the bait, but Tommy was a proficient angler. 'Why didn't you go then?'

'I like playing the waiting game. The pay-off's sweeter. I bet Vicky's sweet. I bet she tastes of honey.' Tommy fidgeted in his seat. 'Shit. I'm getting hard thinking about her.' His shoulders jerked up and down as he laughed. 'I'm building tension, mate. Great sex stems from anticipation, and when I give it to her, she's gonna come like a train.' He pulled at the denim stretching over the top of his thigh. 'Man. I gotta go.' He slid back his chair, shook himself down, and disappeared into the hallway. 'Don't wait up,' he called. 'I'll be gone some time.' His snigger carried all the way up the stairs, vanishing once the door slammed shut.

Chris slumped forward, cushioning his head with his arms. 'Bastard.' It had to be lies. All of it. Victoria wouldn't have invited him to London.

He held up his head and gazed at the door leading to the annexe. Her departure was swift, and the excuse of sorting her London apartment didn't warrant such speed.

If she was regretting sleeping with him, and she and Seth had gone home, he rather she'd have told him, than left him wondering.

There was an easy way to find out.

He rubbed his chin, as he chewed over the right and wrong of entering the annexe. He had a key. He could nip in, and be out in moments, and no one would be the wiser. He wouldn't touch anything. Well, maybe a drawer or two. That was all.

He scolded himself, and looked away, hoping the temptation would dissolve. Victoria had the right to privacy. Going in there was a bad idea. Crazy. It was the action of a dishonest and desperate man. He wouldn't put it past Tommy to do such a shameful thing.

As he cleared away the dishes, and tidied around the quiet kitchen, his mind led him through the fire door and down the hall of the annexe, stopping outside Victoria's room. It was there he'd seen Lacey. He hadn't thought about her since … since he'd been in Victoria's bed. He collapsed against the fridge as the realisation and the guilt belted him around his head.

Dazed, he stumbled into the conservatory and fell into the porter's chair. Its high sides, deep back and domed roof provided a cavernous refuge, but it did nothing to protect Chris from his wild thoughts.

He'd slept with another woman. He'd initiated it, he'd enjoyed it, and he'd have kept doing it had Victoria not brought it to an end.

As the consequences of his actions hit home, and the enormity of the situation rose from his stomach, he slapped his hand over his mouth.

The last time he and Lacey made love, she'd said she'd never want another man.

He sat upright, his thought distracting him from his original course. She wouldn't betray him – not in life and not in death. Tommy, with all his ridiculous inferences and digs was talking crap. Stirring. Goading and saying the things he knew would hurt Chris the most.

He thrust his head into his hands and pushed back into the chair. He'd allowed Tommy to burrow beneath his skin like a deathwatch beetle, and infect him with thoughts of duplicity and infidelity. If Tommy had slept with Lacey, he'd have known about her HIV. She would have told him.

Chris punched the leather on the inside of the chair. If he'd not been such a hothead, he'd have worked it out sooner. There was never anything between Tommy and Lacey, and he was a fool for thinking otherwise.

His conscience developed the spikes of a cactus, and it pricked him into believing he'd used the idea of an affair as an excuse to sleep with Victoria.

Having tucked Seth and his cousins in for the night, Victoria left Juliette's house and returned to the office. Her promise to her sister that she wouldn't work throughout the night was in danger of being broken. As the hours rattled by, Victoria was sinking in the mud that accompanied Tommy Stone's name. His real name.

Max Cooper was born in Bristol, worked in finance, and was imprisoned in London. Victoria's contact had provided links to the court case, including a pastel image of the defendant as portrayed on news reports.

Working as a financial advisor, Cooper got away with twenty months of embezzlement before being discovered. He was given a custodial sentence of two years.

Victoria scrolled down the screen. The information suggested he was released after a year, at which point he changed his name. She knew he would have lost his professional licence and his reputation, so there would have been little point in returning to the finance sector, but his change of name struck her as odd. It implied he was prepared to try his luck again.

She tipped back her chair, yawned, and stretched out her arms. Based on what Tommy told her and what she now knew, she made several assumptions; one – ashamed and embarrassed by their son's crime, his family disowned him; two – he struggled to find work in the UK; three – he knew of only one way to make a quick buck, and four – he left for America to start again. He had two jobs during his stay. The first was with the film studio and the second was with the Framptons.

Victoria threw the chair onto all four wheels, as part of her conversation with Tommy volleyed into her thoughts. 'I got a great place to live, Lacey close by, and a job that *eventually* paid well.'

Choosing that moment to return to sleep mode, the monitor presented her with the face of Chris Frampton. Dark, gorgeous, sexy. And probably a few thousand dollars poorer than he imagined.

Victoria sighed, nudged the mouse and brought the monitor to life. What she was about to do was immoral, and possibly unforgivable, but as long as she was doing it for the right reasons, she would continue. It helped that she had administrative privileges to Chris's computer. It also helped that she'd installed the remote access software he'd requested. It was a bonus he'd left his PC switched on, and a godsend he had no technological expertise whatsoever.

Unless she told him, he'd have no clue she'd entered his personal files.

Another hour on and she'd found inconsistencies within Chris's accounts. Every so often there was an expenses entry twice the cost of the regular, more reasonable claims. Then there were cash withdrawals, referenced with 'Lunch with producer', or 'Surprise for boys', and for the most recent purchase, the Ducati Panigale, listed as 'Motorbike – Work Tool', Tommy hadn't even bothered to cover his tracks. He either relied on Chris not verifying the paperwork, or he simply didn't care.

Victoria chose the latter. Tommy had got away with stealing for so long, he'd become complacent. He considered himself untouchable. Immune.

His arrogance would be his downfall.

Satisfied she had enough evidence to get him off their backs, she copied the data to her USB stick, slipped it into the inside pocket of her bag, and shut down the computer. She resigned herself to the fact she'd have to tell Chris what she'd done, so she could present him with the information. It was up to him to decide how to proceed.

As she left the building, she glanced over her shoulder for one final look. 'Bye, EweSpeak,' she said. 'Be good.'

Chris rolled onto his side and checked the clock. Two-thirty, and still nothing from Victoria. That was it then. She'd taken fright and returned to London. Well, that was fine, because she wasn't the only one to think sleeping together was a mistake. At least this way they didn't have to confront one another, and Rick would be spared a long goodbye.

He pushed the duvet away and kicked it onto the empty side of the bed. Without Victoria around to hold Tommy's interest, there was a chance he'd bugger off, too. He wouldn't go without carrying out his threat, that went without saying, but maybe it was time Rick knew the truth. It was the way the news was conveyed that concerned Chris. He'd have to explain everything to him first thing – Lacey, her film career, the HIV, Victoria leaving. The shit was going to hit the fan, but Chris would deal with the fallout. He'd have to. And no one knew what the future held. Maybe, in time, Rick would learn to live again and Chris would learn to love again.

Whatever happened, they'd be in it together. Father and son.

Perhaps this was what both of them needed.

Chapter Twenty-Five

With less than four hours sleep, Victoria was grateful for the extra-strong black coffee Juliette passed her. The smell was having the desired effect, and Victoria's thoughts fell into line. 'What time is it?'

'Just gone seven. Did you get everything sorted?'

'As much as I could. I've loaded the car with our personal belongings, and managed to pile the stuff to send to storage into one room.' Victoria sipped at her drink. 'I have my mobile now.' She held it up. 'Not sure I want it.'

Juliette sat down at the table. 'Didn't you miss it at all?'

'Not really. But it has its uses.'

'And there is a limit to going back to basics,' Juliette said, nodding.

Victoria agreed. 'Do you know how difficult it is to find a payphone?'

'So, what's your plan?' Juliette opened the jar of Marmite, stuck her knife in, and spread the dark substance on her piece of seeded toast.

'As soon as Seth's dressed and breakfasted, we'll head off.'

'Will you be coming back?'

Victoria looked at her sister. 'Not for EweSpeak. It's in good hands.'

Juliette put her toast on her plate, and wiped her mouth with her napkin. 'What will you do with your shares?'

'I hadn't given it much thought. I'm reluctant to keep them. I've come to realise money's held me back.' She swilled the dregs of coffee around the bottom of her cup. 'But EweSpeak could be Seth's future. According to Rick, my son has a natural talent for technology.' She sighed. 'Any suggestions?'

'I have a few, yes. And it's wrong to judge Seth based on your mistakes.'

Victoria accepted the sisterly scolding. 'You think I should set the shares aside?'

'I think you'd regret selling them.'

'Even to you?'

Juliette nudged her knife further onto her plate. 'I don't want them, Victoria. Keep them, put the dividends into trust for Seth, and when he's eighteen, transfer the shares to him.'

Victoria leaned her elbows on the table. 'How do I know he won't make the same mistakes as me?'

'You don't. That's life. Sometimes we get by on a wing and a prayer.' Juliette smiled, and resumed eating her breakfast.

'Winging it? That's always your answer.'

'It's working for you, isn't it?'

She had a point. 'Well, I guess that's decided then. I'll set up a new account when I get home.'

'Home?' Juliette looked over the top of her toast. 'You mean Portland, right?' She grinned.

A warm, heady, brandy-like sensation spread throughout Victoria's toes, rose up through her body, and settled on her lips. As her eyes and mouth responded, she said, 'Yes. I mean Portland.'

It was news to her, too.

By the time Victoria and Seth reached the castle, they'd driven through three weather fronts, stopped for two comfort breaks, and argued once. On the whole, the journey had gone well.

Seth ran straight through the hall, into the conservatory and out onto the patio. Victoria followed, expecting to see Chris nestled in his porter's chair. She was disappointed to find the room empty.

'Can you see anyone, Seth?' she called, stepping through the open doors.

'I can see you,' he replied, running into the woods.

'Don't' go far.' Victoria shivered. Something was wrong. 'Chris? Rick?' She wandered down to the waist-high boundary wall and scanned the area below. No one. Not even the fishing vessel was out at sea. It was all a bit *Mary Celeste*. Her stomach played Twister as her mind conjured with the possibilities. She screamed as large hands landed on her hips.

'Vicky. I thought you'd left me.'

She was forced round so the base of her spine was resting against the wall.

'Did I get your heart pounding?' Tommy laughed, edging closer.

Victoria grabbed his wrists and pushed them away. 'I was looking for Chris.'

'What do you want with that loser?' Tommy hitched himself onto the wall, and propped himself up by his hands. 'I was thinking of you last night. You're very sexy. A mother I'd like to—'

'Dream on, Tommy.' Victoria resisted the temptation to add *or whatever your name is*.

'I'll do that all right.'

In one smirk he conveyed all the things he'd like to do to Victoria. It sickened her, sending her insides on another rollercoaster ride. She pressed her hand into her stomach, and focused her mind on relaxing. *Picture the ocean.*

Breathe with the ebb and flow. As the tension drifted out to sea, an image of Olivia floated into Victoria's head. Wise old woman, she thought.

She walked away, refusing to respond to Tommy's call of 'You don't know what you're missing'.

Hopeful that Seth had found Rick and not strayed onto the beach, she headed for the woods. As she found the great oak, she saw both boys sitting on its prominent roots, drawing circles in the earth with dead twigs. 'Everything okay?'

Rick jumped to his feet. 'Mrs Noble. Victoria. We missed you. Good time in London?' He gave her a brief, awkward hug, and invited her to sit with him and Seth.

'I'd have loved to have been a tourist for the day, but it was all business, I'm afraid.' She crouched, deciding the ground was more lunar-landscape than sofa.

'It'd be cool to go. Perhaps ...' Rick hesitated, first looking at Seth, and then Victoria. 'Perhaps I could go with you next time?'

Victoria nodded. 'That's a great idea. We'll take your dad, too. Any idea where he is?'

'On the beach. I'm meant to be joining him, but I stopped here for a while. Can I show you something?' He stood, took Victoria's hand and helped her up. He led her round the back of the great oak and pointed to the base of its trunk. 'Dad crashed his bike. There.'

Victoria watched as Rick ran his finger over the rough gouges. She'd seen the marks before. 'Both your dad and the tree suffered wounds that day.'

'You knew about this?'

'He couldn't wait to show me.' *Or kiss me. Or lie with me on the leafy ground and ask if I loved him.* Victoria tutted with mock disapproval. 'Typical man, flaunting his battle scars.'

Rick put his hands behind his back and leaned on them, against the oak. 'Trees don't repair injured wood. They sort of seal it off. Make out like it doesn't exist. I think people can do that, too.'

His insight didn't surprise Victoria – he was one of life's philosophers – but his approach was a matter of concern. There was more to looking at the damaged tree than he was letting on.

'So Dad brought you here?' he asked her.

'Yes. When we were dating.'

Rick's expression brightened, as if a shaft of sun had broken through the forest canopy and kindled his face. 'This was his special place. He said he wanted to share it with me because he loved me and knew I'd respect its history.' He paused. 'He didn't tell me he'd brought you here.'

Victoria bit down on her bottom lip. Rick was making connections as fast as super fibre broadband. 'It was a long time ago.'

'But if he trusted you with this place, he must have loved you.'

It wasn't Victoria's story to tell. 'You should ask your dad that.'

'Did you love him?'

Seth hopped from one root to the next until he too was looking at the scar. 'Beetles live in there.' He continued hopping. 'I know a song about beetles. And a woodpecker who says knock knock.'

The funny, random, little comment broke the tension, and Victoria laughed. 'You do?'

'Cerys taught me. We sing it together.'

Victoria's smile vanished as swiftly as it had appeared. She'd never sung a song with Seth. She couldn't even recall reciting a nursery rhyme. She'd have to YouTube a few to jog her memory. 'Will you teach me the words tomorrow?'

Seth nodded. 'I know *Dingle Dangle Scarecrow* too. We can do the dance.'

'The dance?' Victoria looked to Rick, hoping he'd clue her in as to what was required, but his expression was as vacant as her apartment.

'Sure,' she said, smiling at Seth. 'We'll do the dance.' That was going to be one hell of a moment, and one she wouldn't miss for the world. Another step forward, she thought. A *Dingle Dangle Scarecrow* kind of step.

She returned to Rick's question. He'd asked about her feelings. This part was hers to tell. 'I loved your dad very much. He was daring and incredibly handsome.'

The colour swamped Rick's cheeks, and he scratched at his neck. 'How old were you?'

'Eighteen.'

He gave her answer serious consideration. 'Seth tells me you're thirty-five.'

'Seth! You should never give a woman's age away.' She beamed at him, hoping he'd understand she was teasing. He skipped across to the next tree and carried on with his game, repeating knock knock each time he stepped on a different root.

'So seventeen years ago, you and my dad were together?'

Victoria nodded, wondering where the line of questioning was leading.

'Three … four years before I was born.' Rick frowned. 'So how come you didn't marry?'

Victoria moved away from the tree, eager to project an air of calm. She was the proverbial swan at that moment. 'We were young, Rick. Even in our day.' She laughed, inwardly cringing at its terse delivery. 'Who marries at eighteen?'

Rick emerged from behind the great oak. 'People who love each other. Age doesn't matter. As long as it's legal.' He raised his shoulders in a prolonged shrug. 'Can I tell you something?'

Ensuring Seth was in sight, but out of earshot, Victoria said, 'Anything. You know that.'

Rick bowed his head and shuffled his feet, kicking a stone into the ferns opposite. 'You're a pretty cool mom. I know you and Seth sometimes fight, but I used to fight with my mom. It didn't mean I didn't love her.' He sniffed. 'Todd and I had terrible ... what's that thing Dad says? Ding dongs.' He smiled. 'Yeah. Mom would put us in separate rooms and tell us not to talk to each other. Sometimes Mom and Dad didn't talk to each other.'

Victoria paid close attention, keeping still and remaining silent. Rick needed her to listen, even if what she was hearing was difficult to take.

'I don't want to argue with Dad. I don't want to upset him, and I don't want him to go back to how he was before he found you, but I know secrets about Mom, and I think Tommy knows too, and ...' Overcome with emotion, tears trickled down his cheeks, and stemmed the flow of his words.

Victoria grabbed him and held him as securely as he allowed. 'What do you know?' she whispered.

'Everything,' he sobbed. 'She was in adult movies. And she had HIV. Todd knew too. He was the one who found out. He showed me a file from Dad's desk. He'd been in his office trying to sneak a look at Dad's new stunt, and that's when he found the stuff. We didn't know what it meant, so we Googled it on the Internet. We couldn't understand it, so we were going to ask Dad, but then ... then the accident happened.' He buried his head into Victoria's neck, his lanky frame heaving up and down. 'I couldn't tell Dad I knew. Not then. And I didn't want to tell all those therapists and doctors, so I didn't talk. They can get stuff out of you. I've seen it on TV.' He stopped and took a great, rasping breath. 'I don't want him to leave me, Victoria.'

If Victoria could have suffered Rick's pain instead, she would have. 'It will be all right,' she murmured, surprising herself with the gentle tone. 'Your dad loves you. He wants you to be happy. I promise he won't leave you.'

Rick pulled back, his red-rimmed eyes searching Victoria's. 'He left you.'

Chapter Twenty-Six

Victoria brushed Rick's hair away from his face. 'I never said that.'

'But he loved you, then he married Mom.'

'You're confusing two kinds of love. Romantic love is rarely unconditional, and it's totally different to what we feel for our children.' She took him by the shoulders, set him back a few inches, and adopted a stern expression. 'I know how much Chris loves you. All he's done for the last two years is try to make life better for you. It will never be the same, you've both lost those dearest to you, and from what I've learned, you both feel responsible for what happened.'

Rick nodded.

'You're not,' Victoria continued. 'Your mum did what every mother would in that situation. She protected you, and tried to save your brother.'

'But I should have stopped him.'

Victoria stooped to make direct eye contact again. 'How?' She wanted him to keep talking, get it out of his head and into the world. Shout it into the wind. 'Convince me, and I'll agree with you.' She felt his shoulders give.

'I should have tried harder.'

'So you did try and stop him?'

'He waved me away. Told me not to be such a baby, that he was going to look at Dad's bike to see if anything needed fixing. Mom and Dad were in the office by then. I don't remember where Tommy was.' He paused and settled his breathing. 'When Todd took Dad's spare keys out of his pocket, I knew he meant business. I shouted at him to not be so stupid, but he laughed, and kick-started the bike. I ran back to the office and Mom came out. She had bare feet.' He frowned, wrinkling his young forehead. 'We ran to the arena, but she told me to stay outside. She was mad. She shouted. Then the whole place lit up and there was an explosion. The next thing I know I'm surrounded by police and firefighters and sirens. It was like one of Dad's film sets, only I knew it was real.' He fell quiet. 'Dad says it was his fault. He didn't lock the gates to the arena. But it would have made no difference. Todd had the keys. Nothing Dad could have done would have stopped him.'

'And there was nothing you could have done either.' Victoria released Rick from her hold and tipped up his chin. 'Todd was determined to ride that bike. What happened was awful. Tragic. And it will stay with you forever, but he and your mum would want you and your dad to live life remembering the good times. The spats you had. Sitting in separate rooms. Eating broccoli. And they'd want you to remember them with love in your heart, not guilt. Not blame. And your dad wants to see you smile, hear you laugh. He doesn't want to lose you, and he will not leave you.'

As Victoria looked up, she saw Chris ten feet away, drawn, pale, and clasping Seth to his chest. She hadn't noticed him until then, but his pallor suggested he'd heard most, if not all of the conversation. Rick was still unaware of his father's presence. 'Your dad's here.' Victoria pulled away and nodded to Chris.

Seth wriggled free and ran to her.

'Everyone's sad,' he said, holding up his hand for Victoria

to take. 'Chris has tears. I gave him my tissue. He hugged me. Should I hug Rick?'

Victoria, her head thumping and her heart contracting with sorrow, shook her head, and led Seth towards the castle. She stopped beside Chris and brushed his sallow cheek with the back of her fingers. 'He knows about Lacey,' she said, softly. 'He's known for two years.'

Chris blinked.

'That's not all.' She gave him a second to breathe. 'He's worried that if he tells you, you'll leave.'

'I don't understand.'

Urging Seth to go on, Victoria took Chris by the elbows and guided him away from the stony path. 'Rick needs your assurance you're here for him, and he needs to understand the truth about his mother.' She held onto him until he nodded. 'He's aware Tommy knows too. I imagine he overheard the arguments.' Chris's arms tensed, his skin firm to Victoria's touch. 'Be strong. Your son needs you.' As she let go, Chris lifted his head, straightened his posture, and filled his lungs with oxygen. 'I'll keep Tommy occupied,' Victoria said. 'For as long as it takes.'

'Okay.'

Although Chris's voice was dry and husky, it was unwavering, filling Victoria with admiration and confidence. Left to their own devices, father and son would work things out.

Once she was on the path to the castle, Victoria didn't look back.

Seth was waiting for her on the patio. 'Tommy's in Chris's chair. Will Chris be angry?'

'Not for that,' she said, taking Seth through the conservatory and into the kitchen. 'Wash your hands and I'll make us a drink.'

So much had happened in the last twenty-four hours, it

was difficult to know how to process the information. For the time being, all Victoria had was questions, and they led to further questions.

She made strawberry milk for Seth, opened the fire door and sent him into the annexe. 'I'll be through in a minute,' she said. 'Switch on the TV.' As she turned to pick up the kettle, Tommy strolled in.

'Coffee for me,' he said. 'Or is that in my dreams, too?'

'I'll do it,' Victoria said. 'But no complaining it's bitter.' She took two mugs from the cupboard, the jar of instant from the side, and a teaspoon from the draw. 'You'd think a man with Chris's money would have a decent coffee machine.' She checked Tommy's expression; he was sporting his usual sneer. She tried again. 'I wonder what else a man with Chris's money would buy.'

'Anything he wants.'

The sneer transformed into a self-satisfied grin. He'd taken the bait; all Victoria had to do was keep her nerve.

'Clothes? Technology? Sex?' She made the drinks and passed one to Tommy. He leaned against the counter, folded his arms and crossed his ankles – a stance she'd seen Chris take. 'Cars?'

'Yeah. Like I said. Anything.'

'A Ducati Panigale?'

Tommy's lips pressed together, and his glare intensified. 'A what?'

'A Ducati. The motorbike. The one parked on the drive.' She dug deep into her reserves of boardroom bravado. 'The one you bought with Chris's money.'

Tommy's mouth twitched.

'The one you're passing off as yours?'

He still didn't reply.

'I'm right, aren't I?' Victoria relaxed her stance, smiled and chinked her mug against Tommy's. 'Good job.' Would he see through her performance, or had she done enough to lull him into a false sense of security?

'Thanks. Call it a bonus for long service.' He stretched to his full height, and transferred his mug, and himself to the table. 'How did you know?'

Victoria followed him, and settled in the master chair. 'It was a hunch, nothing more.' She softened her tone, hoping to draw him in further. 'How much?'

'Twenty-six thousand. Thereabouts.'

'That's restrained for a man of your capability.' She saw his lips curl as he snorted.

'You don't think that's all I had, do you?' His arms landed on the table with a thud as he flung himself back and laughed. 'You have to take it little by little, like that Johnny Cash song, you know? One piece at a time.'

She didn't know the song, but she wasn't going to allow that to cut across their conversation. She leaned in. 'So you've supplemented your income. I thought you said you were paid well.'

'Well enough, but it's not about that.' He slurped down his coffee, swung the chair onto its rear legs and put the mug on the counter. 'It's about seeing what you can get away with.' He slammed the chair back into position. 'It's about outsmarting the guy who has everything.'

'And everyone?'

'Yeah. If you like.' Tommy shoved his hand inside his shirt, and scratched his chest.

'But in the end you didn't get Lacey.'

'I had her, but I didn't win her. Loving her made no difference.' The tendons in his neck tensed. 'Did you know she had HIV?'

Victoria remained quiet, leaving Tommy to fill the silence.

'I've been given the all-clear, by the way. As soon as I found out I went to a clinic. They told me by text within two days of the test. I can show you, if you like.' He raised a brow at Victoria. 'No? God knows how I got away with it. Lacey and I got down and dirty *so* many times.' He made a sweeping motion with his hand as if he was brushing his comment aside. 'She fell in love with Chris, so what could I do? I promised to be there for her should something bad happen to him.'

The ambiguity of Tommy's statement left Victoria cold and clammy. She locked her hands together to stop them shaking, and hid them in her lap. 'That's what mates do.'

'Chris was not my mate. I thought we'd established that. I tolerated him for Lacey's sake, and later, for the boys'. Frampton's not the only actor.' He reached into his back pocket, removed his wallet, and flapped it open. 'This is all I have of her.' He flipped it round, revealing an old, dog-eared photograph of Lacey, holding a baby in each arm. 'It was taken at the boys' christening. I swore to God I'd take care of them.' He dropped the wallet onto the table. 'If I'd had what Chris had, there's no way I'd have carried on with the stunt work. I told him so many times it would be the death of him.'

Another dubious remark. The ends of Victoria's fingers were numb from where she clutched her hands together.

'Trouble was, my warnings made him vigilant,' Tommy said. 'I guess that's the nature of a stuntman. He triple-checked his equipment, his calculations, distances and heights, fuel consumption. If his ramps were a millimetre out, it would throw the whole stunt and put him at risk. A fuel leak would too. But a shoddy pipe would never have got past his inspection. Unless he was distracted. The fact of the matter is he was careless the night of the accident, too caught up in screwing Lacey. And mistakes happen when people don't pay attention. I knew he wasn't focused. Anyone with a mind to could have rigged the ramp that night, and Chris wouldn't have noticed.'

Victoria bowed her head, held her breath, and concentrated on not reacting. She was hearing veiled threats, and a possible confession, and as much as it disgusted her, she needed Tommy to follow through.

Slowly, she withdrew her mobile phone, kept it below the level of the tabletop, and switched on the voice application. If Tommy was about to admit causing the deaths of Lacey and Todd, she wanted it recorded.

Mercifully, he wasn't watching her. He was gawking at the wall.

'It was Lacey and the boys I was meant to care for, not Chris.' He snapped out of his reverie and looked around the room, before scowling at Victoria. 'Why are you staring at me?'

'I'm listening to you. Carry on.' She willed him to continue, but he kicked back, and put his hands behind his head.

'Nothing more to say. It was a terrible day. Lacey and Todd shouldn't have been anywhere near the arena. It was Chris's fault. He was meant to go straight back there.' He jogged his chair closer to Victoria, bent low to the table, and thrust his head towards her. 'And if he'd not been such a bloody smart-arse *hero*, his kid wouldn't have tried to emulate him. Kaboom!' He jerked upright, smashed his hands together, and then rubbed his forehead. 'I saw Rick and Chris lying in the dirt, both stunned and covered in blood. When the paramedics arrived, I made sure they dealt with the boy first. Chris was okay, he was muttering, and coming round. I left him to it and tried to find a way into the arena through the debris, but I couldn't. The heat held me back. I was frantic. When Chris finally came to, we ran to the back and got in through the mechanic's pit.' He gulped, audibly.

'I was sick to my stomach. I had to play the supportive

friend, when what I really wanted was for Chris to see what he'd done. But it didn't matter what I wanted. That never mattered to him. He only cared about himself.'

Tommy rose from the table, grabbed his mug, and filled it with cold water. He swigged it down in one go, and then wiped his sleeve across his mouth. 'I wasn't allowed to grieve. I wasn't allowed to miss them like Frampton. God forbid I should show any emotion.'

He seized the upright of Victoria's chair and lent over her, his mouth brushing her ear. His unpleasant odour of sweat and grease, and the heat from his breath made her skin pull and her throat burn. She was one swallow away from gagging when she remembered the phone in her lap. She concealed it under her hands.

'I don't regret what happened,' he hissed. 'But I regret who it happened to.' He pushed away from Victoria's chair. 'I found out Lacey had HIV.' He pulled his own seat round, and straddled it, facing Victoria. '*Found out*. They didn't tell me. How's that for trust? Even Rick doesn't know.'

'Yes he does.'

Both Victoria and Tommy turned to see Chris striding down the hall.

Tommy laughed. 'Calling my bluff? Pathetic.' He addressed Victoria again. 'I want to take Rick away from these lies, take him back to America where I can look after him. Properly. I'll put him back in his old school. Give him the American life I know Lacey wanted for him.'

Victoria was watching the kitchen entrance, where Rick was now standing level with Chris.

'Why would I go anywhere with you?'

Tommy reeled round and held his palms out. 'Rick. You don't understand.'

Aware of Tommy's increasing frustration, and anxious for Seth's safety, Victoria slipped unnoticed from the kitchen into the annexe. She poked her head into the living room to find her son fast asleep on the sofa. The TV was showing a black and white film.

From inside the room, she pushed the door to, switched off the recording app on her phone, and dialled the police. She had no idea if Tommy had orchestrated the terrible accident, but he had confessed to theft, and Victoria had documentary evidence to support that.

After a few moments of speaking to the local station, she closed Seth in the living room, and returned to the kitchen. Chris acknowledged her, but Tommy was too involved with Rick to pay her any attention. She crossed the floor and fell in next to Chris. 'Are you okay?' she whispered, reaching for his hand. His fingers recoiled at her touch. She questioned him with a frown.

'Not now,' he said, folding his arms.

She respected his wishes, and withdrew into the grand hall, giving herself space to consider her predicament. The police had requested she visited the station in the morning, with the evidence to support her claim. They explained the case would be assigned to the Fraud Team, to whom she would hand over all the information, including a statement and authorisation to access the bank accounts. She was expected to explain how the books worked and why and how Tommy had been stealing. They also required a statement from the employer – Chris. Once the investigator had collected all the information, they would arrest Tommy and interview him. It could take months.

It was the correct path to follow, Victoria knew that, but it didn't solve their current problem. She re-entered the kitchen, and swooped to the annexe end.

Chris loosened his collar, stood erect and raised his hands. 'I've heard enough,' he boomed. 'Rick, you don't have to take this crap from Tommy.'

Victoria opened the fire door and waved for Rick to go through. 'Seth's asleep in the living room. He'll be glad of your company when he wakes.'

'I'm not asleep.'

Victoria whirled round at the sound of Seth's voice. He stood, small, vulnerable and wide-eyed, taking in the scene before him. 'Go back to the living room,' she said. 'Please.' She turned as she heard a chair scrape along the floor.

Tommy was on his feet, large and menacing. 'Do as your mummy says, you stupid little boy, before I knock you there myself.'

Before Victoria moved, Rick was in the kitchen, squaring up to Tommy, a man twice his size, three times as powerful. Immediately, Chris was backing Rick up.

'Don't talk to my brother like that.' Rick pressed his fingers into Tommy's chest. 'He's not stupid.' He jerked forward, scoring a flinch from the big man. 'And don't you ever threaten him or go near him again. Got it?' He held eye contact until he removed his hands. 'You're the stupid one, you filthy piece of shit.'

The contempt on Rick's face told them all he wanted nothing further to do with Tommy. Without another word, he entered the annexe, put an arm across Seth's shoulders, and marched him down the hall.

'You said shit.'

Victoria closed the door. *Brother?* The simple word with its intricate implications, choked her.

Chapter Twenty-Seven

Rick Frampton @SonoStar
Shit.

Chris moved in on Tommy. 'If Rick hasn't made it clear, I will. There's nothing here for you.'

Tommy pushed him away and leered at Victoria. 'Oh, I don't know.' He looked at Chris. 'Did you think telling Rick would shift me? No chance. I like it here. The money's easy, and from what you've told me, so's Vicky. What more could I want? Besides, aren't you forgetting something? The world doesn't know about Lacey, yet. One bleat and you're history. The media will be over you like gonorrhoea.' His malicious laugh rebounded off the walls. 'What an apt word.' He returned to his chair, linked his fingers, and stretched his arms along the table.

Chris stepped back and rested against the counter. 'Do it.' He fished his mobile from his top pocket and offered it to Tommy. 'Use my account.' From the corner of his eye, he saw Victoria start. 'It's okay,' he said. 'I've no career left to destroy. They all go on about my best film, my most amazing stunt, their favourite character. It's like I'm dead already.'

'You'd let Rick suffer the humiliation?' Tommy knocked back the phone.

'Rick's told me everything. He wanted to move to England.'

'Of course he's going to say that to you.'

'And he's not ashamed of who his mother was.'

'He's thirteen! What does he know?' Tommy swung round.

'He understands compassion, and loyalty.' Chris pointed at Tommy. 'Something you haven't mastered.'

'Oh, that's rich coming from you, you thieving bastard. Until you walked into the studio, Lacey and I were having a great time.'

'You were never an item.' Chris raised his palms to the ceiling.

'Oh, we so were.' Tommy left his chair and approached Victoria. 'You know, don't you?'

'Are you and he … Is that what you meant when you said you'd keep him occupied?' Chris swiped his hand through the air and turned away. 'Unbelievable.'

'Of course we're not together,' Victoria said. 'He's a repulsive, vile, dishonest man. Why would I be with him?'

'Vicky. You've hurt my feelings.'

Chris shot round to find Tommy laughing in Victoria's face, but she was holding her ground. He needed an explanation before paranoia set in. 'Tell me what's going on,' he said.

Tommy shifted his attention to Chris. 'Me and Lacey had something before you showed up. She kept it casual, but once you were on the scene, the sex stopped altogether.' He paused, and smoothed his finger over his chin. 'But on the day she died, she came to me. In the ranch. She was … anxious. She led me into my room and asked me to hold her. It was easy to think we were together again.

'I thought she must have rowed with you, but it turned out she was scared your latest stunt would kill you. She didn't know how much more she could take. The stress was making her ill. What if something happened to you? Who'd take care of the boys? Protect her?' Tommy broke off and spent a few seconds in silence, as if he was taking stock. 'I comforted her. Told her I'd never leave, no matter what. She thanked me, and said I should change my name from Stone to Rock, because that's what I was for her. When I told her she made me as hard as a rock, she kissed me. I thought I'd see how far I could take it.' His tongue passed over his lips. 'It was far enough to make her come. I kissed her *everywhere*.' He smirked. 'And then I did the same with my hands. I'd not lost my touch.' He inspected his fingers. 'She returned the favour. The heat of her mouth sent me right over the edge. I thought we were back on. I thought she was going to let me in, properly, but she panicked, pulled her dress on and went running to you.' He poked at Chris. 'You received the full benefit of my warm-up, you bastard. Lacey's guilty conscience, I expect. She left her shoes in my room.' He laughed. 'And her bra. I've still got it.'

With his muscles tensed and his heart pounding, Chris roared and charged at Tommy, sending him hurtling backwards. 'Feel the full benefit of this, you lying shit.' He balled his fist, drew back his arm and unleashed two years of fury on the man to whom he'd entrusted his family. He connected with Tommy's jaw. There was a satisfying thwack.

Tommy responded with a hard shove to Chris's gut, knocking the breath from him. 'Deal with it, Frampton. Like I've dealt with sleeping with an infected woman.'

'You call this dealt with?' Victoria stepped between the men.

Chris reacted by pulling her away. He cringed with the pain in his stomach. 'Stay out of this, Victoria.' The whole time, he remained focused on Tommy, waiting for his next move.

'But I'm involved,' Victoria said. 'More than you know.'

For a fleeting moment Chris took his eyes off Tommy and looked at Victoria. 'Do I want to hear this?' He switched back to Tommy, whose low brow was compressing his face into a solid block of suspicion. For now, the fight appeared to have left him. Chris stood down and retreated to the table. 'Go on,' he said to Victoria.

'I have information on Tommy that could see him locked up for a very long time.'

Tommy took a threatening stride towards her.

'You want to add assault to your list of crimes?' Victoria folded her arms in a display of defiance, and after a few seconds of posturing, Tommy withdrew.

'You've got nothing on me,' he said. 'I was bigging myself up with all that stuff. Impress you into bed. Like I did with Lacey.'

Chris jammed his jaws together, refusing to be provoked by the comment. He indicated for Victoria to continue.

'He's been in jail,' she said.

'What are you on about, you stupid woman?' Tommy waved his hand and shook his head, switching his concentration to the contents of the fridge. 'You've got no beer.'

'Before he went to Hollywood, Tommy was a financial adviser.'

'You've got that wrong.' Tommy continued searching for a drink.

'I have, haven't I? It was Max Cooper wasn't it?'

Chris watched the interaction. Tommy was statue-still, with one hand on the open fridge door, and the other gripping onto the kitchen counter. 'Max Cooper?' Chris repeated.

Tommy's knuckles blanched.

'That's his original name. He changed it when he left prison. He was in for embezzlement. He stole thousands of pounds from his clients.' Victoria's eyes widened, as Chris looked at her.

Tommy slammed the door shut and spun on his heels. 'I never told you that.'

'No, but you admitted you'd stolen from Chris. You bragged about the Ducati.'

'We covered this. I was talking you into sleeping with me. You and I had something.'

Chris heard the derision in Victoria's laugh. The mock smile on her face displayed the repulsion she was feeling. She detested Tommy. Chris had misread the earlier signs and jumped to conclusions that were so far off the mark, he'd miss if he kicked himself. Victoria was a clever woman. Everything she did had a purpose. A reason. He'd been too consumed with guilt and jealousy to realise she was working to a plan. 'Dream on, Stone, or Cooper, or whoever the hell you are.'

'I have no idea who Max Cooper is.' Tommy wiped his thumb across his forehead, and looked at Victoria. 'She's a nutcase. Good God, Frampton. You know how to pick them.' He turned to leave. 'You're welcome to her.'

Victoria took a pace towards Chris and held out her hand. 'He's been stealing from you for years. I've informed the police.'

Chris studied her expression. It relayed apprehension, as if there was more to what she was saying. At some point she must have accessed his accounts, that much was obvious, but if that was all she was concerned about, she needed to know it was okay. He took her fingers and drew her to his side. 'How much?'

'Rough estimate? Two hundred thousand.'

He dropped Victoria's hand. 'How much?' He gawped at Tommy. 'Why? I'd have given it to you if you'd asked.'

Tommy crossed into the hallway. 'Would you have given me Lacey?' His hostile eyes were trained on Chris, who held his stare.

'I shared my home, my boys, my money ... hell, Tommy, I shared my life with you. Why weren't you content? Why did you steal?'

'You stole Lacey.' Tommy returned to the kitchen and stood toe-to-toe with Chris. 'A couple of hundred thousand makes us equal, I'd say.'

'You're putting a price on her?' Chris sidestepped, placing himself in front of Victoria. She was standing by the fire door to the annexe. Aware the situation could flare at any moment, Chris's priority was to keep the others safe. Tommy was a hulk of a man. The more distance Chris could put between the parties, the better. He headed for the hall.

'Running away?' Tommy scoffed.

'Nope. Going to check on my new motorbike.' Chris marched to the front door. He knew the sight of the Ducati would fill him with horror – there was a chance it would trigger a flashback, but threatening Tommy's pride and joy was the only way he could think of to entice him from the castle. He hoped that once he was out, Victoria would shut the door and bolt it from the inside. *Please let Tommy follow me.*

Chris steeled himself and advanced towards the bike. Fighting the breathlessness, he reached out a hand and touched the leather seat. His fingers were trembling. He pressed them into the black padding, locking his arm, hoping it was enough to stop the shaking. As he forced himself to view the machine, he saw the key. Tommy had left it in the ignition. Stirring into action, Chris whipped it out and shoved it into his pocket. A second later, Tommy ran across the gravel.

'Get your hands off.' He shoved Chris away, grabbed the helmet from the handlebars and took a possessive stance. 'This is mine.'

Chris shrugged. 'You're welcome to it if it means you'll piss off.'

As the men exchanged scowls, there was a long silence, broken only by the sound of the front door closing.

Thank goodness, Chris thought, waiting to hear the bolt slam into place. *It's me and him now.* The stones shifting under light footsteps took him by surprise. 'Go back inside,' he said to Victoria. 'And lock the door.'

Victoria shook her head. 'He's not getting away with what he's done. The police have the evidence and the Fraud Team's already investigating him.'

There was a delicate tremor to her voice. Her words weren't delivered in her usual confident manner. Thankfully, there was nothing in Tommy's expression to suggest he'd picked up on Victoria's diffidence. She needed backup. 'Go on,' Chris said. 'Tell him how much shit he's in.'

'You were careless, Tommy. Your trail was easy to follow.'

'I could have programmed a bloody satnav and Frampton wouldn't have found it.' Tommy searched and patted his jacket, then glowered at Chris. 'Key.'

Chris reached into his pocket and clenched his fist around the cold metal. His instinct was to hurl it at Tommy and tell him to eff off out of it, but Victoria stopped him.

'Think for a minute,' she whispered. 'Make sure you have everything you want from him.'

Victoria had made it clear she was as keen as Chris to rid the place of Tommy, so she wouldn't stop the process without good reason. After a moment of silent reflection, Chris nodded.

There was only one thing he wanted from Tommy. Closure.

He relaxed his fist and let the key fall back into his pocket. First he had to reclaim his home. 'I want my house back,' he said.

Tommy rooted around the inside of his jacket, produced a bunch of multi-coloured keys, and chucked them at Chris's feet. 'You can have them. I'm not coming back here.' He held out his hand.

Chris picked up Tommy's set, turned to Victoria, and in a low voice asked, 'How long until the police get here?'

Victoria shielded her face from Tommy. 'They're not coming. I have to take the documents to them. But *he* doesn't know that.' She returned to her original position.

'Give me the sodding key.' Tommy thrust his hand further forward, his irritation and desperation noticeably building. He was blinking in quick succession, licking his lips, and looking around, as if expecting to be ambushed. Or arrested.

Something to play upon, Chris thought. 'So. Jail? Was it good for you?'

'Fuck off and give me the key.' Tommy was as white as the Portland stone of the castle. 'I'll be gone in sixty seconds.' He *whooshed* his arm through the air. 'I've got enough of your money to start again, and I'll make more. Might screw a rich widow this time.'

'The police are onto you,' Victoria said. 'They'll be here any minute.' She raised a questioning brow at Chris. 'Do you have everything?'

It had been over two years since he'd acted, but he had to pull this scene off if he was going to settle his mind and put his worst fear to bed.

Not the best choice of words.

He plucked out the bike key from his pocket, and dangled it between his thumb and finger. 'I'll give you the advantage.'

'Don't bother. I'll be out of the country in seconds anyway.' Tommy caressed the red bodywork of the Ducati. 'It's the fastest, sexiest ride I know. I doubt even a quickie from Vicky would get me as stiff as this does.' He rubbed his crotch and sniggered. 'Now give me the fucking key, Frampton, before I tell the world your sordid little secret.'

He'd used that threat once too often. It held no sway with Chris. The news would break sooner or later. The only person it appeared to bother was Tommy, which led Chris to his final question.

He sucked in his lips and took a deep breath. He needed to know. Once and for all.

'Did you have sex with my wife?'

Tommy banged his hands together. 'Which bit about kissing her *everywhere* don't you get? So, I didn't fuck her, but there was plenty of sweating, and moaning and coming. I'd say that was sex.' He stressed each word, as if he was talking to an idiot. 'But if oral doesn't count, I can tell you we had a shitload of full-on fun when I first met her.'

Before Chris had time to react, Victoria grabbed his hand and encased it firmly in both of hers. It brought him back from the edge of his darkest place.

'That's why he's not broken the story,' Victoria said. 'His wounded ego won't let him.' She dropped Chris's hand, wheeled round on the gravel, and confronted Tommy. 'You won't risk having your name linked with Lacey's, will you? Nobody would want you then, would they?' She'd used his own words against him.

A resounding 'Ha!' echoed around the courtyard, as Tommy closed in on Victoria.

'I've got no worries in that department, Vicky. I know how much you wanted me.' He dragged his heavy-booted feet through the stones on his way back to the bike and leaned against the machine, his arms folded and his ankles crossed. 'First off, if you remember, I was giving Chris a chance to come clean. Rick was owed the truth.' Tommy paused and his eyes flicked to the castle housing the boy. 'And then you came along, Little Miss Easy.' He winked at Victoria, and scanned her from head-to-toe.

Chris lunged forward, but Victoria pulled him back.

Tommy laughed. 'I had to stick around. It was only a matter of time before I got into your knickers.' He held his gaze with Victoria.

'You're full of yourself,' she said.

'Play your cards right and you could be full of me too.'

The sleazy grin accompanying the lewd suggestion was the final red rag to Chris. He broke free from Victoria, dived towards Tommy, and cast a wild, flailing punch. Tommy fielded it, catching Chris's fist in his palm. He pushed him away.

'Seriously? You think you can take me out?' Tommy seemed genuinely astounded. He tutted and returned his attention to Victoria. 'I realised there was money to be made. An exclusive. An insider's view of the Framptons. But *The Starburst* offered peanuts. I was holding out, making them sweat. Making them *want* me. I thought I'd play the paper off against View TV, but Garcia's scruples are shockingly high.' He shrugged and flashed his palms to the sky. 'They never came up with the goods. Anyway, watching Chris squirm was all the pay-off I needed.' He bared his teeth. 'It hurts, doesn't it, Frampton? Having the sword above your head, not knowing when it'll fall. That's how I felt when I found out about Lacey. I could've been carrying the virus for years. You should have told me.'

Chris narrowed his eyes. 'And you shouldn't have messed with my wife. You deserve everything coming to you.' He tossed the key at Tommy, who caught it in one hand and slotted it into place.

'And you can have this, too.'

Chris reeled at hearing Rick. His son was standing in the

main entrance, with Tommy's loaded rucksack cradled in his arms.

'I've packed everything of yours I could find. No need for you to come back.' Rick marched across to an astonished Tommy, and thrust the fat bag at him. 'You thieving bastard.' Rick shook his head, scuffed some gravel at the bike, and pushed Tommy's shoulder. 'Go on, then. Piss off.'

Chris looked on, stunned at Rick's eloquence and conviction.

Tommy wrangled himself into the rucksack, thumped life into the Ducati, and raised his middle finger. 'I used this one.'

Within seconds, the stones had settled, the birds had returned to the trees, and Tommy was an insignificant speck on the causeway.

Chris put his arm around his son. 'You learned some new words.'

'No. I knew them already. Thought Tommy needed to hear them.'

Desperate to release the tension, Chris rolled his head back and discharged a long, hard breath. He pressed a hand to his heart. 'Seth okay?'

'Yeah. I left him watching TV.'

'And are you okay?' Chris rubbed his neck, then clutched Rick to him. It was so incredibly healing holding his son.

'I'm good,' Rick said. 'I bet Tommy will head straight for the airport.'

'Yep.'

'Oh, man.' Rick twisted to reach for his back pocket.

Chris loosened his hold. 'What is it?'

'I forgot to pack his passport.' Rick grinned.

Chapter Twenty-Eight

Having satisfied themselves the boys were safe, Victoria and Chris, each clasping a hot drink, repaired to the warm, bright conservatory.

'I've got some brandy if you fancy something stronger.' Chris set his mug on the oak table, and pulled out a chair for Victoria.

'This is fine, thanks,' she said, taking the seat. 'You go ahead, though. It'll settle your nerves.'

Chris declined. 'Later. I want to keep a clear head. Got plenty of thinking to do.' He collapsed into the porter's chair. 'I'm guessing you hacked into my accounts.'

This was the moment Victoria had put off for months. She sipped at the scalding coffee and winced. A burnt tongue was no reason to further delay her admission. 'Not hacked. I have admin rights, but I should've sought your permission. We need to go through the paperwork together and take the evidence to the police.'

She put her cup next to Chris's and leaned forward, resting her elbows on her thighs. 'My gut screamed at me not to trust Tommy. He had no history. Every time I asked him about his past or family, he gave a vague reply. I'd come across his type in the business world. And I'd dealt with them.' She hesitated, wondering how to continue without sounding like a crazed stalker. She fixed her hands together, and rested her chin on her upturned thumbs. Her mouth was partially covered by her fingers. 'I lied about why I went to London.' There. She'd warned Chris of her dishonesty.

He shifted in his chair, then crossed his legs. 'I knew you had.'

'You did?' That was a shock.

'Your decision to go was so sudden. At first, I thought you were going away with Tommy.'

'Good God, no.' The thought of spending a night with that creep was more sickening than admitting to Chris she owned EweSpeak. 'I was playing him. Gaining his confidence. The biggest thing about Tommy Stone is his ego. It was easy to get him to brag about his transgressions when he thought you were our mutual enemy. I allowed him to think I was upset with you for telling him about our night on the beach.'

'You were.' Chris gazed out at the panoramic view of the sea.

'I got over it. Anyway, I was telling you why I went to London.'

'Because sleeping with me was a mistake.'

'No.' Victoria crossed her heart with her hands. 'I haven't thought that for a second.'

Chris rose from the chair and drifted towards the patio doors. He invited Victoria to stand with him. 'So what was the cause?'

She took the space to his left. The horizon ahead was stunning: an eternal line of perfection. 'My work gives me access to a lot of people. People who know how to obtain information.' She saw Chris's head shift in her direction.

'What the hell do you do? Work for the Government?'

'No. Nothing like that.' She turned to him and saw the muscle at the side of his jaw pulsating. 'I've a few things I need to tell you.' There was no going back. She reached for her mug and relieved her dry throat with the coffee. 'Until recently, I was head of EweSpeak.' She held her finger up to prevent Chris from butting in. 'Juliette and I set it up to help Annabel's popularity when she was in UK Starz. When she won, EweSpeak took off.'

Chris's mouth had fallen open.

'I didn't sign clients, my sales team handled that, so when your name appeared on the list, I was really shaken. I'd tried so hard to leave you behind, but you were everywhere – TV, radio, online. It was difficult to escape. It was impossible to avoid finding out about your life.'

'You've followed me all these years?'

Victoria hummed her response and quickly continued. 'I watched you marry Lacey, I saw your career go from strength-to-strength, and I witnessed the devastation of the motorbike crash. You weren't allowed to grieve in private, and the only way I could help was to put an end to EweSpeak's perpetual bleats. But the board wouldn't let me. The board insisted we covered the story. I hate what it did to you, and I'm appalled I was part of it.'

Chris retreated to the porter's chair. The red leather contrasted with his pale complexion. He was breathing in short, sharp spurts. 'You were part of that relentless media circus? And what? You forgot to tell me?' He glared at Victoria. Rage was now colouring his cheeks. 'Your company put me through hell. And let's not even *think* about what it did to Rick.'

Victoria's heart hit ground zero. She knelt in front of Chris, lowered her gaze, and prayed for his forgiveness. She didn't know what else to do. 'I am truly sorry.' She risked touching his fingers, expecting him to yank them away, but he didn't move. 'There's something else.' She braced herself, and increased her hold of his hands. 'I knew about Lacey's condition. I've known for years. One of my contacts came to me with the news. I traced the leak to your doctor. He and I … reached an agreement, and I made sure the details never saw the light of day.'

She released Chris's hands and dared to look at him. His hunched body was filling the chair, but his beautiful brown eyes were vacant. He'd retreated within himself – gone to some other time, some other place – somewhere she wasn't, and somewhere he didn't want to be.

Her confession had triggered a flashback, and there was nothing she could do.

She moved to his side, and waited. His rapid blinking alerted her to his return. His anger had gone. He looked exhausted. 'Where were you?'

He closed his eyes and kneaded his temples. 'In my office, at the ranch. With Lacey.'

'The day of the accident?'

He nodded. 'She had no shoes. No bra.' He tipped back his head and looked to the ceiling. 'Tommy was telling the truth. Lacey had been with him before she—' He came to an abrupt halt.

'Oh, Chris.' Victoria wanted to pull him to her and hold him, but he'd closed off.

'She came to me that day making promises, saying she'd never love another man, that I was enough for this life and the next. That was guilt talking. That was her trying to make herself feel better for what she did with Stone.'

Victoria couldn't answer. Her knowledge of Chris and Lacey's relationship was based on media speculation and magazine images. They appeared to be very much involved, but Victoria knew it was possible to simultaneously love two people. In the same way she'd never expelled Chris from her system, Tommy spent years holding out for Lacey. And, in the same way Victoria loved Ben, while fantasising about Chris, Lacey was with Chris, while never quite letting go of Tommy.

Love was complicated.

Love was hard.

It wasn't news to Victoria.

News. She had one last piece to deliver. She opened the doors and stepped onto the patio, shivering as the sea breeze licked around her ribs. 'Join me,' she said.

Chris wandered into the garden and stopped by the low-level wall. 'It's cold out here.'

'It's freezing. Could use that brandy right now.' Victoria gave a half-smile. At least, it felt as if her lips had moved. 'Walk with me.' She waited for Chris before heading to the left of the castle, away from the wood, and away from the beach. The garden opened up into a lush, green lawn, and beyond the border, steps descended to a large, dry, rectangular pond. There was a statue of Cupid at its centre.

'I've never come this far,' Chris mumbled, shoving his hands into his pockets.

'New ground?'

'I guess.'

'There's a path,' Victoria said, pointing to a line of slabs leading away from the pond. 'Shall we walk it together?'

They followed the course, neither person talking, until they reached the furthest perimeter of the grounds. It wasn't an uncomfortable silence. It was a necessary silence, to absorb all that had happened.

As they looked out over the Jurassic coastline, Chris spoke, 'Rick told me everything. How he felt responsible for Todd and Lacey's deaths, how he knew about Lacey's condition, how he was frightened to talk in case it all slipped out.' He sighed and shook his head. 'The poor boy's been carrying it around for two years.'

'He's strong.'

'He was the quiet one. Todd was the daredevil. The doer. It didn't surprise me to hear he'd stolen my keys, nor that he was on the bike, but to crash it …' Chris cuffed his nose. 'I've never understood how. Okay, he was eleven, but he'd been brought up around bikes. He was a skilled rider for his age.' He clasped his hand around the back of his neck. 'There was nothing wrong with the bike. I'd checked it over before … before I was distracted by Lacey.'

Another silence.

'What did the investigation reveal?'

Chris frowned. 'You must have seen the TV reports.'

'I couldn't take it in. Didn't want to.'

'Yeah.' He moved away from the boundary and nodded for Victoria to follow. 'There was too much of a mess for any conclusion to be drawn. There was a suggestion Todd had tried to make the ramp, but I don't know. I've gone over the possibilities, but whatever happened, the responsibility for my boy's safety was down to me. My carelessness killed him and Lacey.' He stopped, closed his eyes, and chewed down on his lip.

It was very restrained for a man whose heart was breaking for what must have been the millionth time.

Victoria watched, tears forming in her eyes. She wasn't ashamed to let them fall. She'd learned to let go, and she was sure that was what Chris needed to do. Like Rick, he'd carried the tragedy inside for too long.

She had to relay her suspicions about Tommy and pray to a God she almost believed existed, that her words would bring release and comfort.

She traced a finger down Chris's cheek and along his chin. He opened his eyes.

'It's possible Tommy rigged your bike and moved the ramp,' she said.

Chris lurched forward. 'He what?'

Victoria grabbed Chris by the arms and steadied him. 'He didn't admit it, but he made very strong insinuations.

If there's a chance he was behind it, then you and Rick will know you're not to blame.'

'It doesn't work like that, Victoria. I will always be responsible.' Chris yanked himself free and stormed towards the castle. 'Why have you told me this?'

She chased after him. 'But what if he did something?'

Chris swung round, his eyes ablaze with anger. 'What if he did? It doesn't change a thing.'

'I'll tell the police what he said. They'll question him.'

'And he'll deny everything.' Chris looked away, and then turned his back on Victoria. 'Don't talk to Rick about this. You've done enough damage.'

He stomped away, leaving Victoria alone, upset and wondering how she'd got it so wrong.

The great oak provided all the company Chris required. It was strong, silent and reliable. It didn't expect conversation, it made no apologies, and sprung no surprises.

Chris had spent the last two hours working through the momentous events of the day, trying to slot all the pieces together. It hadn't been easy, but the picture was taking shape.

Victoria's involvement in EweSpeak had shocked him, although he now realised why her married name had seemed so familiar, and his predictable reaction to the news was very likely the cause of her delay in telling him. He accepted that. But he had every right to be angry. Victoria was part of the reason the Framptons couldn't escape the media spotlight. For a year after the tragedy, he and Rick were under constant scrutiny. That alone was enough to break some families apart. Thankfully his bond with Rick was strong.

Stronger since Victoria's reappearance. A fact Chris couldn't deny.

He really couldn't care less about her hacking into his accounts. Sure, it was pushing the boundaries of their friendship, but if Chris had been more vigilant, Tommy wouldn't have stolen the money. Not so much of it, anyway. And Victoria had put together a case which would see the man locked up.

However, the intimation Tommy had engineered the motorbike accident infuriated Chris. There was no proof, so there was no point in raising the matter, unless guilt or regret wrangled a confession from Tommy. The only chance of that happening was if he truly loved Lacey. And Chris couldn't deal with that idea right now.

'What of Lacey?' Chris said to the sympathetic oak, rubbing his palm over the coarse bark. 'Vicky's known for years and yet she never told a soul. She paid my surgeon off and has asked for nothing back. Selfless. And do you know what's funny, old man?' He glanced at the top of the tree. 'Had Vicky not been part of EweSpeak, Lacey's secret would have been exposed a long time ago. I can't imagine what that would have done to us.'

With the picture now fully formed in his head, Chris patted the trunk of the oak and thanked it for listening. Then he went in search of Victoria, acknowledging she'd put herself and her company at risk, just for him. Her remorse was genuine. As was his love for her.

He didn't go far before he spotted her in the ornamental garden. He approached with caution. 'I'm sorry. I took my frustrations out on you. It was unnecessary and unkind.'

Victoria raised her head, her red-rimmed, puffy eyes the give-away she'd been crying.

Chris dug into his pocket and retrieved half a tissue. 'It's the clean half,' he said, wiping the damp stains from her cheeks. 'I gave the other half to Rick. I try to carry one on me these days.'

'You still use your sleeve.' Victoria relieved Chris of the half-tissue and blew her nose. 'For what it's worth, I'm sorry too.'

'Accepted,' Chris said. 'It shook me up. I didn't want to believe Tommy would go that far. That he wanted me dead.' Saying it out loud didn't help. It was still a bizarre concept.

'He was obsessed with Lacey.' Victoria paused, and twisted the tissue round her fingers. 'He was obsessed with your boys, too. And your money.'

'And you.' Chris shuddered. This was frightening stuff. 'He wanted my life.'

'It looks that way,' Victoria said. 'The sooner we get the evidence to the police the better.'

'We'll go through it tonight.' Chris cast an eye around his land. 'I didn't realise betrayal hurt so much.'

'Lacey?'

He nodded. 'I knew she wasn't perfect, but I never thought she'd have an affair.'

'It wasn't an affair, Chris. It was a moment. A mistake.'

'You think there are degrees to sex? Is what Lacey did with Tommy more acceptable than what we did? Does it only count if you go all the way?'

Victoria pulled at the scraggy piece of tissue, then screwed it up and tucked it in her trouser pocket. 'It doesn't matter what I think. You have to find your own resolution.'

'She could have said no.'

'Ultimately, she did.'

'She still let him … do stuff.' He gave his chin a hard rub, and then closed his eyes.

Victoria sighed. 'Okay. Perhaps you *should* hear what I think. Lacey used Tommy. She was so scared of losing you to a stunt, she held onto him by whatever means necessary. He was her safety net. Someone who'd look after her and the boys if you died.' She paused. 'I actually think it proves how much she loved you.'

With his eyes still shut, Chris tried to see Victoria's point, but there was just a jumble of words tumbling around in the dark. He shook his head. 'I'm going to struggle with that.'

'I don't know what else you expect me to say,' Victoria continued. 'We're all guilty of making bad choices. We put right what we can and learn to live with the rest.'

In less time than it took to inhale, Todd's entire life raced through Chris's mind. No parent was prepared for the death of their child. 'I live with a lot,' he said.

'I know.'

He felt a disturbance in the air around, and when he looked, Victoria was beside him, offering to take his hand. He accepted, and was stilled by her touch. It was as if she'd soothed his forehead with a kiss.

'But you have to give yourself permission to grieve,' she said. 'It's your time now.'

Chapter Twenty-Nine

The number of people Frank could accommodate in the bungalow kitchen never ceased to amaze Victoria. Today wasn't as much of a squeeze as Christmas, although that had been fun, but six was still a tight fit around the old table.

Her father's permanent smile and the glint in his eye led Victoria to suspect there was more to the invitation than an Easter Day lunch.

She watched him from her seat. 'Are you sure I can't help?'

'No, thanks. Nearly ready. Will Chris be here soon?'

Victoria pushed back the sleeve of her red jumper, to reveal her watch. 'Another ten minutes. He's organising an Easter egg hunt for the boys for when we get back.'

'He said to start without him.' Rick hovered in the doorway.

'Hands washed?' Olivia's voice drifted in from the hall, her frame hidden by Rick's. He nodded. 'Then stop being a teenager and go and sit down. I'm hungry.'

Rick obeyed, grinning as he pulled out a chair for Olivia. 'So how's school?' She nodded her thanks.

'It's good, thank you, ma'am. I'm on the basketball team.' Rick took a seat next to Seth, who was concentrating on colouring a page of complex patterns. 'And I scored top marks in media studies on the last day of term.'

Victoria smiled. Rick had settled into secondary school life far better than she or Chris imagined. He was still a thinker, and still quiet on occasions, but his confidence was growing, as was the light in his eyes.

She switched her attention to her father. He was skipping from left to right as he took the plates from the oven, checked the pot on the hob, and stirred the veg. He had the energy of a man half his age. And the love of a good woman. She nudged Olivia. 'How's business?'

'Hectic. I don't know my arse from my elbow most days.'

Seth broke away from his work. 'You said arse.'

'I did, and I shouldn't have, but you're so quiet, I forgot you were here. What's your excuse?' Olivia pulled a face at Seth, and he responded with a giggle. She returned to Victoria. 'I've got so many orders for driftwood craft, I'm having to work on several projects at once.'

Adorning oven gloves, Frank swung round with a large, orange, ceramic pot, and placed it in the middle of the table. 'Olivia's turned her living room into a second studio to accommodate the materials.' He collected the plates, stacked them in the centre, and removed his mitts, hanging them over the back of his chair. He took his place beside Olivia. 'She's a very popular lady.'

'I think you'll find it's my prices that are popular. I enjoy art for art's sake. That's why I became a teacher. Speaking of which … How is Seth getting on at pre-school?'

'He's doing very well.' Victoria gazed at her son. 'He's come so far in five months.'

'I think you both have,' Olivia whispered, giving Victoria's hand a congratulatory pat. 'And the counsellor the school suggested? Worth the effort?'

'Despite my initial resistance? Worth every second. Which is also what she said about you and Dad, and the support you provide. We wouldn't have got here without you.' Victoria smiled. 'Thank you.'

'That's what families are for. Remember, boundaries,

patience, and a sense of humour. It's a parent's mantra.' Picking up the oven mitts, Olivia removed the lid from the casserole dish.

'Along with consistency and realistic expectations.' Victoria peered through the steam at her dad. 'I had my very own expert to show me that.'

Frank grinned and picked up a serving spoon. 'I'm proud of you,' he said. 'For everything you've achieved. Personally and professionally. Both you and Juliette.'

'Where is Aunty Joo?' Seth, collecting his paper and pencils together, looked expectantly at Frank.

'They've gone to see Uncle Dan's mum. Your great aunty Gwendolyn.'

Seth sat back, ready to receive his dinner. 'I like Great Aunty Gwendolyn. She's funny.'

'Eccentric,' Frank mumbled. 'Anyway, I'll phone them after lunch to see how they all are.'

'Exhausted, I should think, after all the fuss.' Victoria set Seth's plate before him and he thanked her. 'Did you catch the news?'

'I've just read last week's *Echo*,' Olivia said, reaching behind for the recycling box. She grabbed the topmost paper. 'I saw EweSpeak made the headlines.' She pointed to the photograph of Annabel, and ran her finger under the caption, *Lamb to the Slaughter?* 'It's a tad harsh.'

Victoria laughed. 'Annabel can handle it. She's like Juliette. They're so much better at publicity than me. Neither of them gets stuck for something to say.'

'I think you're more than capable of holding your own,' Olivia said.

'I am now. I can even stand on the beach and scream into the wind with minimal embarrassment.'

'We can do that.' Seth turned to Rick. 'You're better than me, aren't you?'

'I'm louder.' Rick's wonderful sloppy smile received an equally adorable response.

'Tommy Stone's story broke this week. I expect you saw.' Frank retrieved the paper from Olivia, folded it in half and returned it to the recycling box. 'That's one less crook on the streets.'

'Dad.' Victoria frowned, hoping her father would say no more.

'What? He deserves a custodial sentence.'

'Can we practise a little diplomacy? He's Rick's godfather.'

Rick cleared his throat. 'Mr Paveley's right. Tommy stole from my family, and I'm glad the police caught up with him. I'll sleep better knowing he can't hurt us anymore.'

'I didn't like him,' Seth said, shaking his head. 'I'm glad he went away.'

'Me too, bud. Would you like my broccoli?' Rick speared a floret with his fork and offered it to Seth, who accepted with an enthusiastic nod. Rick grinned. 'Cool. Dad will be pleased.'

Victoria looked on, her heart light with contentment. Six months ago she had no idea life could be so fulfilling.

It hadn't been the easiest of journeys, but every step advanced her, even the baby steps she'd taken with Chris. They travelled together, slow and steady, and when the wounds inflicted by Tommy healed, and Victoria and Chris had got to know one another as adults, they'd made love. Proper no holds barred, man-and-woman-on-the-edge love.

Victoria's thoughts were brought to a close by the ringing of the doorbell. 'That'll be your dad,' she said to Rick, rising from her chair.

'Sit down,' said Frank. 'You're looking a bit flushed. I'll go.'

The gentle clattering of cutlery took the place of

conversation, as the party waited for Frank and Chris to appear.

'Here he is,' Frank said, bundling Chris into the kitchen. 'Sit down, lad.' He guided him to his seat.

Beaming at Victoria, Chris tapped Seth on his shoulder, and quickly hid his hands under the table so as to cover up his mischief. It was a game he played with the boys from time-to-time, which usually induced a fit of giggles in Seth.

Victoria smiled as Seth stared at Rick.

'Wasn't me, bud. I'm too busy eating.' Rick nodded towards Chris. 'There's your culprit.'

Turning to his right, Seth eyed Chris with suspicion. Without a word, he pushed his fork into a tree of broccoli and replanted it on Chris's plate. Then he raised his hand for a high five with Rick.

'Nice one, man,' Rick said, rewarding Seth with a gentle clap.

'I hate broccoli,' Chris said, laughing.

'Eat your greens,' Frank said, directing his order at Chris. 'And then open this.' He passed over a bottle of champagne, and then filled the boys' glasses with lemonade. 'Bubbles for everyone.'

Chris wiggled the champagne cork free and poured each of the adults a glassful. 'Special occasion?'

Frank, still standing, glanced at Olivia, and then gave a small cough. 'I am pleased to report that even at my great age, one *can* fall in love again, which I didn't think possible until I met Olivia. Now, we've been seeing each other for some time, and a few days ago I asked Olivia to move in with me.'

Victoria grinned. That explained the glint in her father's eye. 'That is wonderful news.' She hugged Olivia.

'Wait. Olivia DeVere said no.'

'Frank, don't tease.' Olivia tutted. 'I said no to moving

325

in here because I know Frank's heart lies on Portland, as does Victoria's.' She gave Victoria a knowing wink. 'So I suggested Frank move in with me. Above the craft centre.'

'And I said yes.' Frank raised his glass. 'Of course, this was before the living room was turned into a studio, but I'm game.'

'If I may?' Chris pushed back his chair, and picked up his champagne. 'That's the best news I've heard in ages. Welcome home. To Olivia and Frank.'

Victoria repeated the toast, gave Olivia another squeeze, and skipped around the table to her dad. 'Good decision,' she said, hugging his neck. 'Local babysitters.'

Chapter Thirty

'Follow me.' Chris hooked his index finger and beckoned Victoria out of the annexe.

She did as he requested – she'd been following him for years – she wasn't going to stop now, not when there was a twinkle behind his every look. He was as bright and sunny as the early summer weather. Something was going on. 'You do know I'm not a stalker, right?'

The corners of Chris's mouth twitched as the warmth of his brandy eyes spread across his face. 'I never had you down for one. I should think it's tricky keeping tabs from behind that fire door.'

'Almost impossible.' Victoria smiled.

Every night the free access between the castle and the annexe was closed, with the Nobles one side and the Framptons the other. It didn't stop Victoria and Chris enjoying each other's company, but she was yet to spend a whole night in his bed. She longed to wake up beside him, and for them to make love in the light of the rising sun.

It wasn't her call to make.

'Come on, slowcoach. Pick up the pace.'

'Is it time to collect the boys already?' As Victoria left the confines of the castle walls, Chris curled an arm around her waist.

'No. Frank said he'd give them lunch, so I've arranged to meet them on the beach at two.'

Victoria flicked her wrist over and squinted at her watch. 'It's almost one.' The boys had been gone for three hours. 'Where did that time go?'

'We spent most of it in the conservatory.' Chris turned his head from side-to-side, and rubbed his neck. 'One day, I *will* replace that porter's chair.'

Victoria grinned. 'The high sides are a challenge.'

'You're surprisingly flexible for a woman your age.' Chris squeezed her to him.

'Don't start that mature woman stuff again,' she said, as she nudged her elbow into his ribs. She kissed him as he stooped. 'It's a glorious day.' She breathed in the summer air, taking the salty essence deep into her lungs. 'So, what are we doing?'

'First we're going to the cottage, then before we collect the boys, I'd like to take a stroll along the beach.'

'Can we manage that in an hour?'

'As long as we don't get distracted.'

She knew what he meant. It was easy to get caught up with one another when it was just the two of them. She sighed. 'I expect the cottage is ready.' She hadn't visited it for a fortnight, putting off the inevitable. The moment the decorating was finished, she'd have no reason to stay at Hope Cove. A grey cloud darkened her thoughts, and the sun. Victoria shivered. 'Why is June so unpredictable?' She huddled closer to Chris.

'I like impulsiveness.' He spun Victoria from his arm, caught her by her fingertips, and reeled her back in. He clasped her to his hard body, threaded a hand through her wayward hair, and eased her head to his.

As she snatched a breath, he pressed his lips to hers, and claimed it for his own. Her insides contracted with instant desire, and she thrust her hands down the back of his jeans. The blast of a car horn brought her back to the roadside.

Hot and flustered, she pulled away, whistled and shook her head. 'You're a dangerous man, Chris Frampton.'

'Me? I'm a pussy cat. Hear me purr.'

Her skin lifted into bumps of pleasure as he produced a full-throated, low-level rumble close to her ear. From her breasts to her pelvis, her body responded to the continuous vibration, and she closed her eyes, allowing her mind to send Chris's mouth further down.

When all she could hear was the cawing of a gull, she opened her eyes. 'I'm so alive when I'm with you.'

Chris stroked a finger along her collarbone. 'As much as my ego is desperate to accept that, I can't take the credit. Everything you feel comes from within. That sense of freedom was already there.'

'Not with Ben.' Victoria pinched at her T-shirt to loosen it from her skin. 'I couldn't let go with him.' She broke away from the embrace, bounced on her toes, and set off at a steady pace. Love made light work of walking, even with legs aching from a morning of inspired sexual positions. 'I'm not questioning it. I'm enjoying it.' She swung her arm back and Chris took her hand.

'I'm glad,' he said. 'I am, too. Now, no more distractions. We need to get on.'

Victoria stood in the front room of the cottage inspecting the crisp, white décor. There was still an odour of fresh paint, but another day or two would see to that.

Another day or two. That was all the time she had left at Hope Cove. After years of missing breakfast, she'd grown accustomed to sharing tea and toast in the morning, with Chris and the boys. And Seth was going to feel Rick's absence in the same way he missed his front tooth. He'd developed an ulcer from where he kept poking his tongue through. Not seeing the Framptons every day was going to hurt.

Victoria tried to view it through rose-tinted spectacles – Seth would be settled, Frank and Olivia would be next door, and the castle was literally only a ten-minute walk away.

It didn't help. The bright side remained shady.

And she didn't know how it would affect her relationship with Chris. Her main concern was that the physical separation would cause an emotional detachment, and she'd had enough of that in her life. Over the last few months she'd learned that spending time with the people she loved was the best way to maintain a bond. The old dictum about families playing together was true.

She exited the front room and wandered down to the kitchen. While it hadn't been destroyed by the collapsed ceiling, or damaged by the water, Victoria opted to have it updated at the same time as the repair work. Choosing kitchen units and wall tiles was fun, and she'd stayed within her budget, sticking to her philosophy that the best things in life were free. She'd allowed a little movement on that maxim. Some of the best things in life cost, but as long as she didn't go overboard, her conscience maintained its integrity.

She'd saved the large Belfast sink and the Aga, and spent two days giving them both a thorough clean. Rick had pitched in. There was something James Herriot about him, dressed in green overalls, with his hand shoved into the depths of the ovens. Victoria joked he'd have to wash the floor if he pulled out a calf. He didn't understand, which made Victoria laugh more.

She hitched herself up onto a worktop and wondered what was to become of him. They'd grown extremely fond of one another, and often spent a few quiet moments each day talking about Lacey and Todd. He found it hard to hold a conversation about them with Chris, anxious the memories would trigger flashbacks. No amount of reassurance convinced him it would be okay, but while

Victoria was living in the annexe and pottering around the castle, it wasn't an issue.

Things were going to change for everyone.

'What do you think?' Chris's voice reached her before he did. His footsteps echoed on the wooden floor of the hall. 'Upstairs is great. You know, that first bedroom is big enough to split into two. This could be made into a three bedroom property.'

'I don't need three bedrooms.'

'What about when Seth's cousins come to stay?'

Victoria gave a half-hearted shrug. 'They could stay in Dad's bungalow. He's keeping it on for the time being.'

Chris lifted her chin. 'Don't you like the cottage?'

'I do, but I'm tired. Can't muster the enthusiasm.' Victoria slouched against the wall. 'I'll look upstairs later, when I show Seth. My legs are cramping at the moment.' She rubbed her thighs to reinforce her point.

'You should drink more. It's good for the muscles.' Chris opened the under sink cupboard, rooted around inside, and pulled out a plastic bottle. 'Rick's,' he said, with an air of triumph. 'From when he was here cleaning.' He smiled, ran the cold tap and filled the container, handing it to Victoria. 'So, are you up for a walk? It might help?' He offered to lift her down from the counter, but she declined, choosing to slide off instead.

'I'm going to miss you,' she said, throwing her arms around his middle. The bottle, hanging loosely between her fingers, banged on his bottom.

'I promise you won't.' Chris opened the rear door of the cottage, and hustled Victoria into the garden and onto the stones of Chesil Beach. 'We'll still see each other every day.'

Victoria relaxed her hold, and they walked side-by-side. It didn't escape her notice they were heading towards the gabion baskets.

'I keep thinking back to the day when Rick called Seth his brother,' Chris said.

'Brothers,' Victoria murmured, more to herself than Chris.

'Yeah.' Chris smiled. 'It's stayed with me.'

Victoria often thought about it too. It had been a significant moment in her son's life. A touching one in hers. 'Seth asked me if that made you his dad.'

'Do you think that's how he sees me?' Chris tugged at Victoria's waist.

'I don't know what good can come of answering that. In two days we'll be out of the annexe and living in the cottage. His perception will change again.'

Chris halted, bringing Victoria to an abrupt stop. 'So it is how he sees me.'

'Yes.' Victoria swiped a mutinous coil out of her eyes. 'And I see Rick as a son.'

Chris twirled her on the spot, so she was now facing him. 'You do?'

'Yes. I'm going to miss his company. And Seth will too. But we knew it wasn't forever.'

As swiftly as he'd turned her to him, Chris rolled her into his arm again, and they continued walking.

'Are we going to the defences?'

He nodded, and his fringe fell forward. 'We need to put our past to rest and since this is where I got it so wrong, it seems like the place to put things right.' He brushed his hair to the side. He no longer hid his scar.

Whisked along at speed, Victoria was going to the wire cages, whether or not she thought it a good idea. She gave a nervous giggle. 'We're not recreating that night, are we? I don't object in theory, but it's ten to two on a Saturday afternoon, and our boys will be here soon. The sight of me naked would damage them for life.'

As soon as they were within touching distance of the defences, Chris stopped, kissed Victoria, and cradled her hands in his. 'I would love for you to get naked. You're incredibly hot. But it's not what I had in mind.'

A blend of relief and disappointment filled Victoria's veins, leaving her heart drunk on oxygen, and her muscles devoid of strength. She held her breath, counted to five, and then expelled it forcefully through her mouth. Her nerves responded well. Her legs not so much. She leaned against the pebble-filled cage, a gentle *chink* ringing in her ears as her back connected with the metal. It unlocked more memories than she recalled storing. Good memories. Happy memories. Ones she'd failed to attach to her life with Ben. Now she understood why. They were times she'd shared with Chris. Times that hurt and pain had buried so deep in the caverns of her mind, she'd forgotten they existed.

The summer sun bleached her dark thoughts, and she felt a lightness she'd not experienced in a long time.

She couldn't stop the smile from taking control of her mouth.

She didn't want to.

'You were right to bring me here,' she said. 'Thank you.'

'You're welcome.' Chris frowned, his brown eyes tracking hers. 'I don't know what just happened, but it's made you smile, and it was worth it for that. I could do without the Herculean grip on my hands, though.' His voice increased in pitch, ending the sentence a tone on from its original note.

'You're a Hollywood action hero.' Victoria laughed. 'Don't be such a wimp.' Before she had time to say anything else, she was gathered in his arms, swept into the air, and carried to the warm beach wall. She dropped the bottle as her smile relinquished control of her mouth to Chris.

After a moment of glorious, sexy, erotic kisses, Chris

placed a finger on Victoria's lips, and spoke, 'I don't want you to stay at Hope Cove anymore.'

She felt him apply a gentle pressure to her mouth, which prevented her from speaking, but it wouldn't stop her from throwing up, which she was certain was about to happen. His words, acting like chemical agitators, stirred the bile in her gut. She pushed his hand away, jumped down from the wall and leaned over.

Nothing came.

Refusing his help, she stood upright, took a gulp of air, and concentrated on preserving her dignity.

'Victoria. Listen to me. I hadn't finished.'

There was more? She grabbed the bottle and swigged down the water. How could he do this to her again?

'Victoria. Look at me. Please.'

'What?'

'First of all, I love you. Secondly, I don't want you to stay at Hope Cove because I want you to live there. I want you and Seth to move into the castle. Properly.'

'You love me?' Victoria couldn't disguise the tremor in her voice. She'd been to hell and back in sixty seconds and her insides were alight.

As she was enveloped in Chris's embrace, she rested her head on his chest. Her breathing soon synchronised with the comforting beat of his heart.

'I've always loved you,' he said. 'And I know I denied it, but I've had time to think this through. I did come back for you, because I knew you'd heal me. And look what else you did. You brought my son back to life.'

Victoria shook her head, her face grazing on Chris's shirt. The noise reminded her of the waves washing over the stones. 'I didn't do that. We did.' She wiped her eyes, lifted her chin, and parted her lips, longing to reconnect with Chris.

They shared the deepest, slowest and most honest kiss of their relationship.

When they broke apart, Victoria said, 'My declarations of love come with an addendum.'

'Oh, yes?' Amusement danced in Chris's eyes. He moved behind Victoria, draped his arms over her front and nuzzled into her neck. 'And what's that?'

'I love you. And you're stuck with me.'

'I'll take that.'

His laugh, like his purr, resonated through her body. 'Do you think we'll get it right this time?' she said.

'We've already got it right.' He kissed her cheek, as if proving his point. 'Remember I once mentioned *Follow You, Follow Me*?' He hummed a verse.

'Genesis? I remember.'

'YouTube a version with the lyrics.'

'Why?' Victoria laughed. 'You're not expecting me to learn it, are you?' She would, of course, given time. Chris's love of the band was legendary.

And she'd make sure she got the words right.

'YouTube it. It sums up how I feel about you.' He gave a playful bite to Victoria's lobe. 'Uh-oh. Here comes trouble.'

Victoria turned to see Rick and Seth running along the beach, with Frank and Olivia close behind.

'You've gone quiet,' Chris said. 'What are you thinking?'

'That there's a newly refurbished fisherman's cottage going begging.'

'And there's a small flat above the craft centre that's rapidly turning into a piece of living art?'

'That too.' Victoria smiled. 'Perhaps Dad and Olivia would like to live in the cottage. The whole flat could become a studio then.' She waved at the older couple, delighted they had found one another. 'I owe them a lot. Especially Olivia.'

Privately praying to a God she now believed existed, Victoria gave thanks for the people in her life.

'Hey, Dad!' Rick shouted his greeting, kicked off his Crocs and headed for the sea. 'I'm going in. You coming? Last one in's a gorilla.'

'Gotta go.' Chris planted a noisy kiss on Victoria's ear, and darted across the shingle, discarding his T-shirt before diving into the water.

Victoria, standing very near to where she used to think her soul was buried, watched as the man she loved splashed and kicked and horsed around with his son. Their laughter and pleasure invaded the beach, and captured her heart.

A small, hot hand slipped into hers.

'Rick says we might be living inside the castle with him and Chris. He says it would be very cool if we did.' Seth's grasp tightened around Victoria's fingers.

Her son initiating any type of contact thrilled Victoria, and filled her with wonderment, but in respecting his comfort zone, she had to maintain a calm exterior. It was a hell of a challenge, when inside, a thousand butterflies were emerging from their cocoons. 'Do you think it'd be cool?'

'Yes. Rick said I'd have a big bedroom next to his, and he said you would live in Chris's bedroom because you loved each other, but it's a different love to how mums and dads love their children, and we must knock on the door and wait to be told we can come in.' He stopped, and tugged Victoria's hand.

Still taking in everything he'd said, she looked down to see his large, enquiring eyes staring back.

'Are you and Chris girlfriend and boyfriend? Like Livia and Pops?' A hint of a smile worked its way across Seth's lips.

Victoria would have missed it if she'd blinked. 'We are.'

'Is that why you kiss a lot?'

Digging a heel into the golden pebbles, Victoria created a well large enough for both her and Seth. As she wriggled to get comfortable, she noticed her feet were the same sandy hue as Chesil beach. This time last year, she was as pale as the walls in the EweSpeak office. It was one more reminder that life was good. She patted the space next to her, encouraging Seth to sit down. 'Do Chris and I kiss a lot?'

Seth nodded. 'But it's cool, because it makes you smile.' He knelt beside Victoria, and put his free hand on top of hers. 'I like it when you smile. It means you're happy. I know what happy is.'

Her chest heaved with emotion at her son's unprecedented and intimate gesture, and she marvelled at his burgeoning understanding of the world.

Her perception too had changed. Real life wasn't white and sterile. It didn't come with plans, or rigorously defined algorithms, and chaos often reigned, but disconnecting from it had been a mistake. Even with all its problems, all its risks, and every emotion known to man assaulting heads and hearts, real life was for living.

'Will Rick call you mom?' Seth snuggled into Victoria's side.

Having yet to reflect on the intricacies of family statuses, the question caught her off-guard. She considered Rick's position. He was fourteen now, and a fourteen-year-old was unlikely to call anyone other than his mother, mum. Particularly a boy with his circumstances. 'I think he's happy calling me Victoria.'

Seth made no comment, and his silence concerned Victoria. Huge changes were taking place, and the situation needed addressing. 'Living together will feel a bit funny for all of us at first,' she said. 'Some things will be different. We'll have to take turns at choosing which programme to

Epilogue

LA Starburst @MackTheHack
Exclusive: In addition to his charge of embezzlement to
the tune of $321,000, @TommyStone aka Max Cooper
confessed & charged with the murders of Lacey &
Todd Frampton.

Echo @NewsdeskDel
What do you think to the speculation the huge mystery
donation to the charity, 'South West Sibling Survivors',
came from Victoria Noble. Message me your thoughts.

LA View TV @GainerGarcia
Lots of bleats about @ChrisFramptonActor on yesterday's
show. Details for his new internet forum and charity
'Hope for Families' can be found on his website *here*.

Francis Paveley @HeadShepherd
@CraftyLady Today's the day I carried you over the
threshold of Crab Cottage. *#movingday*

Olivia DeVere @CraftyLady
@HeadShepherd I'm sitting behind you. You didn't need to bleat. Talking is one of the joys of living together. ☺

Rick Frampton @SonoStar
@ChrisFramptonActor's still trying to teach me Genesis songs. ☺ *#Coldplayalltheway*

Rick Frampton @SonoStar
Little Lamb's too young to bleat but he wants to share his new word with you: Mom. *#coolbrother*

Chris Frampton @ChrisFramptonActor
America was great, but glad to be back with my boys and @EweOne. Victoria said yes. ☺

Victoria Boss @EweOne
Know what's in your heart. Follow it and true love will follow you. *#followmefollowyou*

About the Author

Laura is married and has two children. She lives in Dorset, but spent her formative years in Watford, a brief train ride away from the bright lights of London. Here she indulged her love of live music, and, following a spectacular Stevie Nicks gig, decided to take up singing, a passion that scored her second place in a national competition.

Laura is a graduate of the Romantic Novelists' Association's New Writers' Scheme, a member of her local writing group, Off The Cuff, and an editor of the popular Romaniacs blog.

Laura was runner-up twice in the Choc Lit Short Story competitions. Her story *Bitter Sweet* appears in the Romantic Novelists' Association's Anthology. *Truth or Dare?*, Laura's debut novel, was shortlisted for the 2014 Joan Hessayon New Writers' Award. *Follow me, follow you* is Laura's first Choc Lit novel published in paperback.

www.lauraejames.co.uk
www.twitter.com/Laura_E_James
www.facebook.com/LauraE.JamesWriter

More Choc Lit

From Laura E. James

Truth or Dare?

The path to love …

Kate Blair's sick of unrequited love. She's quietly waited for Mickey for the past six years and finding a compass-carved heart, with their initials scratched through the middle, only strengthens her resolve: no more Mickey and no more playing it safe.

It's time to take a chance on real love and Declan O'Brien's the perfect risk. He's handsome, kind and crazy about her so it's not long before all thoughts of Mickey come few and far between.

But old habits die-hard. Kate may have started to forget … but has Mickey?

Visit www.choc-lit.com for more details, or simply scan barcode using your mobile phone QR reader.

More from Choc Lit

If you enjoyed Laura's story, you'll enjoy the
rest of our selection. Here's a sample:

Follow a Star
Christine Stovell

**Sometimes your heart's the
only navigator you need**

May Starling's had enough
of her demanding career and
even more demanding ex.
Responding to a 'crew-wanted'
ad, she follows her dreams of
escape only to find herself at
sea with red-haired Bill Blythe.

Bill warns May that close-
quartered living can create a boiling pot of emotions, but
even May is surprised by the heat building up inside the
vintage wooden boat. And when May and Bill tie up at
Watling's Boatyard in Little Spitmarsh, May's determined to
test her new-found feelings on dry land.

But May's dream of escaping her former life is in danger of
being swept away when several unwelcome blasts from the
past follow her ashore, all seemingly hell-bent on reminding
her that it's never that easy to clear the decks.

Visit www.choc-lit.com for more details
including the first two chapters and
reviews, or simply scan barcode using
your mobile phone QR reader.

Is this Love?
Sue Moorcroft

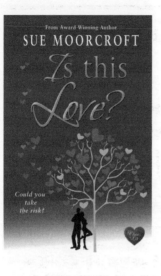

How many ways can one woman love?

When Tamara Rix's sister Lyddie is involved in a hit-and-run accident that leaves her in need of constant care, Tamara resolves to remain in the village she grew up in. Tamara would do anything for her sister, even sacrifice a long-term relationship.

But when Lyddie's teenage sweetheart Jed Cassius returns to Middledip, he brings news that shakes the Rix family to their core. Jed's life is shrouded in mystery, particularly his job, but despite his strange background, Tamara can't help being intrigued by him.

Can Tamara find a balance between her love for Lyddie and growing feelings for Jed, or will she discover that some kinds of love just don't mix?

CLAIM YOUR FREE EBOOK

of

*follow
me
follow
you*

You may wish to have a choice of how you read
Follow me follow you. Perhaps you'd like a digital
version for when you're out and about, so that
you can read it on your ereader, iPad or even a
Smartphone. For a limited period, we're including
a **FREE** ebook version along with this paperback.

To claim, simply visit ebooks.choc-lit.com
or scan the QR Code.

You'll need to enter the following code:

Q1501407

Introducing Choc Lit

We're an independent publisher creating
a delicious selection of fiction.
Where heroes are like chocolate – irresistible!
Quality stories with a romance at the heart.

Choc Lit novels are selected by genuine readers like yourself.
We only publish stories our Choc Lit Tasting Panel want to
see in print. Our reviews and awards speak for themselves.

We'd love to hear how you enjoyed *Follow me follow you*.
Just visit www.choc-lit.com and give your feedback.
Describe Chris in terms of chocolate
and you could win a Choc Lit novel in our
Flavour of the Month competition.

Available in paperback and as ebooks from most stores.

Visit: www.choc-lit.com for more details.

Keep in touch:
Sign up for our monthly newsletter Choc Lit Spread for
all the latest news and offers: www.spread.choc-lit.com.
Follow us on Twitter: @ChocLituk and Facebook: Choc Lit.

Or simply scan barcode using your mobile phone QR reader:

Choc Lit
Spread

Twitter

Facebook